MEMOIRS OF A COUNTERSPY

THROUGH THE EYES OF A STREET-LEVEL COUNTER-ESPIONAGE OPERATIVE

DONALD BRADSHAW

authorHOUSE®

AuthorHouse™
1663 Liberty Drive
Bloomington, IN 47403
www.authorhouse.com
Phone: 1-800-839-8640

First published by AuthorHouse 9/2/2010

ISBN: 978-1-4520-6470-3 (hc)
ISBN: 978-1-4520-6471-0 (sc)
ISBN: 978-1-4520-6472-7 (e)

Library of Congress Control Number: 2010911739

Printed in the United States of America

This is a historical novel. Incidents described herein are based on actual events. Some names and specific locations have been changed to protect the innocent. Many characters in this book are fictitious and any resemblances to persons, living or dead are purely coincidental.

To the reader:

As the major characters within this set of novels are identified and begin to unfold during the first few chapters of this book, you the reader will develop your own intimate, personal acquaintance with each individual personality along with a significant insight into what makes them tick.

Hopefully, by the time you reach the culmination of this first story, you will realize not only the differences between, but will even begin to recognize the subtle similarities among the counterspy nemeses.

Some of the characters I feel are significant or essential to the story of my life will continue through memoirs to come.

For Elizabeth,

Thank you, thank you, my darling daughter Elizabeth, for your unending encouragement and support, and for the amazingly talented editing abilities you applied to the final draft of this book.
So now you know... L, D. "Muh!"

For Betty

For you, the woman; the dedicated and devoted wife and mother of our child. You were always there through the good and hard times. You kept me going from the beginning. This book, in its entirety is dedicated to you, for without you-my bright spot, it would never and could never have been completed. L, D.

INTRODUCTION

To the disappointment of moviegoers, and spy-catcher wannabes, Counterintelligence activities consist 100 percent of security programs and operations. Various levels and types of security activities are employed commensurate with that which is required to protect United States' interests and secrets. Maintenance of our security systems, from security fences and barriers, to security guards and pedestrian traffic or transportation control at border-crossings, air and seaports; to the management of security clearances, are Counterintelligence responsibilities.

However, to our reader's delight, certain intriguing forms of aggressive activities such as counter-espionage and other offensive techniques which are categorized within the parameters of counterintelligence also exist.

Federal "Agency" schools in Virginia and Georgia, DOD schools at selected Army, Navy, Air Force and Marine installations, all teach counterintelligence; and include within their curricula such subjects matter as basic security, surveillance/counter-surveillance, special operations (such as aggressive counterespionage and Offensive CI Operations), tradecraft, the conduct of background investigations, various security inspections to include the almost-exciting penetration inspections. Of course the curricula must also include counterinsurgency training and other counterintelligence support activities requiring a degree of expertise in such as fields as documentation fabrication, technical support services, and the existence and utilization of confidential contingency funds. In the end, each and every phase of counterintelligence activities must be documented in writing, and of course that would involve the arduous and occasional boring art of report writing, which in no case should be de-emphasized.

You may find my book short on grammatical perfection, but one thing you will learn for certain is my unending dedication and keen enthusiasm for the true value and importance of various aspects of the world of Intelligence. Ignore if you can, any stated preferences I may have made in favor of or against any political party; or any snide reference to other agencies or their personnel. I served with pride during my career for every US President from the time of Eisenhower; and proudly with the men and women of all the Intelligence collection agencies of the US as well as with foreign counterpart agencies.

Also, due to limitations placed on the publication of certain aspects of the intelligence field, I have been forced to edit and substitute throughout this writing. My sincere hope is that in doing so I have not reduced or cheapened its value or quality.

I am not being vain when I say that the bulk of my 40 odd-year career was dedicated to aggressive, human intelligence (HUMINT), offensive counterintelligence, collection activities and spy-catching. But there exists a little vanity in all of us. Without a measure of vanity there can be no pride. I am extremely proud of the career in which I became involved, and in which I achieved a more than adequate degree of success.

I believe that for every phase of HUMINT (and particularly within the collection and counterintelligence operations arenas); there are required qualities in which an operative must maintain the maximum degree of proficiency.

It is a common joke among those of us who have been pleasured both to serve and to teach in the intelligence field, that the operative must first and foremost possess an unlimited and vivid imagination. The operative must be handsome (or pretty), dashing, daring and debonair, almost flamboyant, and be gifted with a photographic memory, and a natural capacity for the art of love-making. They must be able to drive fast cars, or fly small jet planes and jet packs; be able to respond to physical attack with the trained attributes of Jackie Chen; able to drink all night, make love to a beautiful counterspy, and then wake up alert and totally aware of their new and strange surroundings. While these qualities do exist (rarely) among the operatives, it is the non-descript, the average-looking, the quiet, the conservative, the sedate and calculating, slow-talking Joe, and usually the lower ranking, dedicated field Case Officer who initiates, manages and then succeeds in the accomplishments of HUMINT intelligence-collection tasks. He will go on with his business, accepting little or no recognition for his accomplishments. When things go wrong, likewise, it is he who sits at the bottom of the totem pole, and who will ultimately absorb most of the blame. Gravity rules and shit flows downward in his or her direction. This is not to diminish in any way the levels of importance and responsibility born by team leaders, operations officers, commanders and senior management, section and station chiefs, to mention just a few of the red-tape levels of communication through which the operative must continually coordinate and request guidance and support. Methods do exist for an operative to occasionally be able to orchestrate an expeditious response to his requests for support, but it is not wise to move ahead on an operation without the tacit or at least oral "go-ahead!" approval of his superiors. More often than not, taking the initiative would put the operative in line for punitive action, and he/she would be referred to as a renegade, a rogue or a cowboy.

Everything by the book. Patience is a virtue. Timing is an art. Luck is often just an opinion of success, as bad luck is an opinion of failure. The operative will, at all times, maintain a high-level sense of humor, and strive to "do it right – the first time".

On the other hand, there are times when an Intelligence operative has no choice but to act on his own during the conduct of his operations, and he is expected to make the appropriate decisions without hesitation and without direction from superiors. Those are decisions based on the unexpected actions of the enemy counterspy, which cannot be completely anticipated.

For example, if the CI operative detects surveillance, he is expected to immediately decide how to react. Generally, and unlike James Bond, he will continue on the route he has chosen to take, but participate in no operational activity at all. He will have no operational contact, make no operational telephone calls, leave no obvious signals or signs, and lead the opposition surveillance on an extremely boring trip, hoping to discourage any further activity on their part. Also unlike character Bond, there would be no confrontation, no high-speed automobile, bicycle or Pedi-cab chase through Moscow or Hong Kong, and likewise, evasive activity is rarely employed.

Also, it is a rare occasion indeed in which he/she is required to carry firearms. Those times are limited to combat assignments, VIP Protection duties and the like. His actions must be logical and non-provocative. To act otherwise would only alert surveillance that one is aware of their presence.

The importance of surveillance:

To me, a most important facet contributing to the successful accomplishment of counterintelligence activities is surveillance. It matters not whether the subjects or targets be followed on foot, in a vehicle, on a train or plane, to or from his home or place of business/ activity, across international borders, electronically traced through credit card purchases, with concealed transmitters, by satellite reconnaissance, by tape recording, photographing or by any other means. It is the precision of the surveillance, and the timeliness, completeness, accuracy and clarity/simplicity of the surveillance report that counts. The difficulty in conducting this type surveillance is that it should be conducted discreetly, to prevent detection at all cost. At first indication of detection, a surveillant should abort as quickly as possible and fade into the crowd or environment.

When a series of surveillance reports are compiled and submitted regarding the movements or activities of a foreign agent, target or activity, they must stand alone as a final report. In most cases the surveillance cannot be recreated. By the same token, when a surveillance report is submitted in a timely manner, is pertinent, accurate, clear, complete and concise, it can be a most invaluable tool. It is most important to learn and understand the activities and capabilities of your target, whether it be an installation, a foreign method or technology, or an individual. And the ability to discreetly learn the customs and habits of your human subject, the identification of his contacts, his signals, his routes to and from, the identification of his modes of transportation, his quirks, strengths and weaknesses, along with every aspect of his activities during the course of the specified surveillance period, is vital.

While Counterintelligence (CI) Special Operations do include certain aggressive or offensive (HUMINT) activities involving the skill of well-trained agents, the majority of CI activities are all encompassing under the umbrella of security. As you read my book, you will come to realize I was fortunate to have served primarily in the "positive" HUMINT field during my overseas assignments, limiting the fundamental security duties to the first few months, and to the stateside assignments of my career.

Noteworthy is the fact that HUMINT is all-encompassing, and reaches far beyond the realm of the Counterintelligence field. While the importance of "positive" Collection, activities relating to such disciplines as Signals Intelligence (SIGINT) involving the National Security Agency (NSA), and Photo Intelligence (PHOTINT), involving such technological advancement as satellite reconnaissance and high/low resolution photography of missile systems, enemy troop movements and capabilities, cannot be over emphasized, it is the actual collection activities of human sources, directed by human beings ON THE GROUND, that I believe cannot be replaced. It is true that technological collection is precisely superior to HUMINT, in that it's timeliness and accuracy is almost 90 to 95 percent pure and complete; but it is the well-trained agent on the ground who can methodically locate, evaluate, identify, verify, and to some degree analyze the situation, the personalities, the technology, the systems; and then report that information in a timely manner. It is he/she who will undoubtedly provide the missing 10 percent. And it is he or she in my opinion who is the true hero of the intelligence field.

Before going any further, please allow me to explain the following points which are requisite to the operative's frame of mind

"Patience", it is said, "is a virtue." This holds true in all facets of life, but is particularly important during the implementation and conduct of intelligence operations. One must first develop a concept. It may be a broad-spectrum, umbrella concept relating to an entire group of operations, or may be specific to any one operation. The next step is the writing of an Operational Plan (Oplan), and outlines the step-by-step expectations of one specific operation. The processing of the Oplan is generally not expeditious. Before an operative's Oplan is approved it must go through various stages of discussion, approval, rejection/resubmission, coordination (often with "other agencies" who will be involved periodically in the approval processes and in providing technical support); and each level of headquarters. Each echelon, both operational and administrative, will then submit or prepare formal suggestions for the implementation, which will of course be incorporated. From the time the Oplan leaves the operative's headquarters, he will hear very little of the results of his request, other than an occasional 'it is still pending' or 'still under consideration' memo. Generally, by the time the Oplan is approved and returned, the operative has at least one or maybe two more Oplans on the way. Yes, patience is a virtue.

A true regard for accuracy and detail is especially important, and again, it applies to each facet of an operation, as well as to each phase of the operative's life. Unlike James Bond, an operative must be versatile and thorough within each of his covers. He must have a broad knowledge of the field in which he is supposedly employed, and a vivid and current picture of any place his cover could have taken him. For each assignment, there is an organizational cover, for every operational group there is generally a different cover, and for each operation there is a separate cover name and background; and therefore at each level, a separate set of backstopping is required.

Counterpart situations differ. Most counterpart situations involve direct, daily contact with host country personnel, who are as aware of the CI operative's basic identity as he is of theirs. Generally, a mutual exchange of biographic data is provided on a regular basis. The operative must however be on guard not to reveal his past experiences and operations which hold the never ending caveat of "NOFORN". This is particularly important if the operative has served in unnamed special operations assignments. To their detriment, some operatives have an uncontrollable tendency to brag about operations which have yet to be declassified. A no-no.

For the most part, non-counterpart, counterintelligence operatives avoid over-exposure to his host country security and intelligence services.

Now, having said all that, please relax, select your favorite beverage, sit (or lie) back and enjoy my first book, as I draw from my memory banks the excerpts, chapters and tales of a dedicated 'street man', and introduce you to some of the family, friends, nemeses and personalities that have had a profound effect on my life and career.

BACKGROUND -
AN EARLY CURIOSITY.

I was born Donald Wayne Bradshaw in the small coastal town of Petoskey Michigan, located at the northwest tip of Michigan's Lower Peninsula on Little Traverse Bay. My brother Bob and I were virtually raised by our mother, as our father had passed near the end of WWII. Our single mom was a devout Christian, and we were obliged to attend Sunday school and Church every Sunday morning as well as two prayer meetings weekly on Tuesday and Thursday evenings - just as regularly as the mailman delivers mail. Young boys who attended our Sunday School and turned eight years old before the first day of June, were randomly selected to go to Summer Camp for two weeks during the summer, school vacation period. In the summer of 1949, I was still seven, but my brother Bob was selected to attend the coveted Camp Daggett summer camp. I was the unfortunate one to play alone during the long, long two weeks of his absence. I recall clearly how difficult that period was. It is my earliest recollection of being without my brother. Bob, a year and a half older than I, was always the slow-talking, slow-walking older brother, who possessed what appeared to be unending patience and common sense. Since our father was no longer with us, Bob automatically took the role of the senior male in our remaining family of three. I was completely lost without his knowledge, his supervision, and most of all, his companionship. Although, like most siblings, there were times when I thought he was a little too serious as he seemed to enjoy bossing me around a little too much. He was noticeably heavier and a head taller than I, and to argue with him meant only I would be the one to pay

9

the consequences of combat. I had learned early on - sometimes it's just better to be non-confrontational.

We resided at 915 Kalamazoo Street, in an area dotted with small, 10-20 acre farms. It appeared most of the homes in our area were built by the same builder, in the same period, around the turn of the century. They all looked alike. As long as I could remember, the farm across Kalamazoo Street from our place had been empty. The home had been torn down for an extended period, leaving the foundation, and the sub-floor of the first level of a large colonial home. That sub-flooring had been covered with a heavy canvas tarp to prevent water seepage and rodent infestation. Scattered around the property were about 5 acres of apple trees.

Our own place was also an old colonial. The estate included a large garage-barn with two full floors and a full basement. The basement was made with stalls for a few cows and stanchions for two horses. The first floor – ground floor from the front – housed the garage and a tack room; and the second floor consisted of one-half living quarters which were never used, and a separate hay loft. A hay chute passed downward, through the garage area into the basement, and was probably used at one time for passing hay to animals in the basement. Our home and the garage-barn were perched twenty yards apart on the edge of the hill that sloped away toward our orchard. I recall two, large and very climbable Oak trees standing tall within a circular driveway that entered along the south side of the house. We kept a cow, and generally two sows, and a few chickens. Bob and I played with the animals, wild birds, worms, and anything else we could put our hands on. We seemed not to need toys.

But with Bob away for this two-week eternity, nothing seemed to capture or even deserve my interest. I sat on a bench in front of the garage-barn, gazing across the street toward the vacant farm. As my mind wandered, I recalled when Bob and I would make our annual early autumn trip into that old orchard, where we would fill our stomachs on green apples – and then we would suffer the penalty of 'the green-apple stomach'. Mom always knew what we'd been up to, but let us do it every year – I suppose as a harmless lesson. Soon now, Bob would be home, and again this autumn we would venture into Robin Hood's Sherwood Forest and steal apples from the rich.

Today was different though, as somehow without my knowledge - or permission - large truckloads of lumber had been delivered to the farm, and stacked neatly near the old foundation. Automobiles had arrived and carpenters were cleaning the foundation, measuring, checking brackets and mountings, in preparation, I assumed, for reconstruction. As I watched, my curiosity seemed to magically draw me in the direction of the unknown, and I found myself sitting on a stack of lumber, watching the carpenters going about their inspection duties, and the plumbers checking lead-ins and sealed water line joints. Yup, they're going to rebuild the old house. I knew it, and surprisingly enough, I didn't need Bob to tell me what was going on.

Unable to pay attention to anything else around me, I sat, transfixed at the well-organized group, trying to listen to their conversations, pretending that I was fully cognizant of what was happening, and of course that I was among the members of the supervisory board, making decisions.

Suddenly, without warning, I came out of my trance, to notice an old man sitting by my side. I mean, he was really old. My guess was that he was around a 65, or maybe a hundred. Just as I was beginning to wonder if he was too old to talk, he looked at me, smiled, and said "Hi Wayne".

That he knew my name was not at all a surprise. Mom had worked as a practical nurse since our father had passed, and there were many older folks in our church, and in the neighborhood who knew my brother Bob and myself. In those younger years, I had always been addressed by my middle name "Wayne".

When I asked him his name, he replied only "When you're my age, you'll know who I am".

I asked myself 'is this old guy OK? Is he speaking in riddles?'

Then I thought I'd take my elicitation another step, and brazenly asked "How old <u>are</u> you?"

He simply stated "When you know who I am, you'll know my age." He smiled again, and now I was beginning to think that perhaps he was just a little touched.

But, I smiled anyway, and we sat there together watching the construction workers decide that the foundation was sound. I looked at the old man from time to time, smiled, and he would smile back at me. Like I said, he was really old. The breeze gently tossed his white, thinning hair around his forehead and over his face, which seemed to have less wrinkles than it should. His smile revealed deeper wrinkles around his eyes, but they were not repulsive. His eyes were clear and grayish-blue. His bushy white eyebrows turned up in the middle. I knew he was kind.

After what seemed an eternity, he turned to me and asked "Wayne, do you like riddles?"

It was as though he had heard my mind! "Of course I do." I replied anxiously, "Do you have one for me?"

"I'll give you one, if you promise you'll never forget it; and when you solve it, you will think of me, - OK?" he asked.

"Okay!" I agreed readily. That wasn't much to ask for.

"Here goes", he started. "This is the riddle. *I am young, and I am old, and I am your brother's brother.*"

"Wow!" I said, "That's a hard one. But, I'll keep my promise." I then turned and called my brother's name, "Hey, Bob. Come here and listen to……" Suddenly, I remembered my companion brother was far away at Summer Camp. I stared momentarily at the men working in the construction area, and then turned back to speak to the old man again.

He was gone.

The writing of this book has taken several decades, as putting together a piece here and there, adding an article, or a description of a friend or acquaintance; and occasionally, the act of adding a memory from my past had to be placed on the back burner long enough for another episode or chapter of my life to unfold.

Near the end of the writing however, long after retirement, on a warm autumn afternoon, I stretched out in a canvas lawn chair on the second-level back deck of my home in Spokane, Washington. My feet were perched on the top rail, and I had just finished a cold beer - a rare but refreshing habit after spending an hour or so in the garden below. At this age, I no longer toil for hours in the garden, nor do I spend an inordinate amount of time on the continuing task of restoring my 1972 MG Midget in the garage. And, occasionally I may spend a complete day just contemplating doing those things that need to be done.

On this particular day, I was concentrating on a mass of white rabbit, poodle and polar bear-shaped cumulous clouds, contrasting with a clear, sky-blue backdrop. My lovely little wife, Chang-ping (Betty) was busying herself around the house. She had just finished watching a Chinese language TV mini-series involving some of the historical characters of the Ming Dynasty. The faint echo of Chinese flute music passed through the windows and across the deck to caress my ears. In the distance far across the view from my back deck and into the Rockies, I could clearly see the peak of Silver Mountain about 70 miles due east as the crow goes. The aroma of sweet-soy flavored sizzling pork with bitter melon provided a hint of the gourmet dinner of which I would partake in a few hours. I closed my eyes.

The dream took me to familiar surroundings – familiar to the extent that I seemed to have drifted into the zone well-known to my childhood. Looking around, across the street, I saw the old farm on which I had lived as child. The old Colonial stood proudly; almost majestically about 40 meters from the street along the south end of the front court, and a driveway entered and encircled two large, well-climbed oak trees.

But instead of walking toward home, I chose to move in the opposite direction and into the lot across Kalamazoo Street, where some reconstruction had begun. I watched the crew preparing their project, consulting blueprints and charts of the water lines and the original foundation plans.

I then recognized the young boy sitting on a stack of lumber near the construction.

At his young age of seven, he has no idea what is in store for his future. No idea what his life will entail or what adventures or misadventures he may encounter. He will have a wonderful life, full of joy, happiness, international intrigue, war, peace, and love. Occasionally, he may even feel the pangs of hate and sorrow. But most important of all - he will have fulfillment.

During his 12th year of school, he will compose a list of 50 items, entitled *"Things to be Accomplished Before I Die"*. Some of the items on the list, such as: #6) 'learn at least two foreign languages', #7) 'travel to exotic, foreign lands', #19) 'fight in a foreign war', and #24) 'ride an elephant', will be easily accomplished during the routine achievement of his life's tasks; while others such as #34) 'be alone, in a cage with a lion' and #35) 'go over Victoria Falls', will be postponed to a more convenient time. Sadly, some of those items will likely never come to pass.

The young boy was so engrossed in every facet of the construction workers' duties that he was unaware when I first sat casually at his side. Finally, he turned and noticed me.

I smiled and spoke to him, "Hi, Wayne." ... I awoke.

EXCERPT.
THE BEGINNING OF THE END.

At 1127 Ivan glanced at his watch and then looked out the window in time to see Strübel pull into the parking lot. Habitually, Ivan glanced around the lot, searching for possible surveillance. He made note of a pair of businessmen entering the Motel office. Since they were driving a sub-compact, with luggage in the roof-rack, he dismissed them temporarily. He picked up the briefcase containing his well-prepared résumé and writing samples, and met Strübel at the door.

They shook hands enthusiastically, and walked to Strübel's car talking casually of the weather. Exiting to the right out of the motel, George Strübel drove toward Van Ness Avenue, and then turned left, away from downtown San Francisco and the location of his 'office'. Observing Ivan's sudden alertness, Strübel announced "I've got to make a stop along the way at a friend's place. I hope you don't mind."

"Of course not," Ivan relaxed.

The radio was playing *"I left my heart..."*, and Ivan was habitually humming along with the tune as they started across the Bridge. Then, without signaling, George turned off the exit to Treasure Island and made his way toward the safe site. As they approached, George noted a step-van parked adjacent to the garage, bearing the sign *Ace Landscaping and Maintenance Services.* Several green-coverall uniformed 'gardeners' were working in the immediate area. Security was in place. The garage door was open.

George pulled directly inside the garage and parked. He switched off the engine, and pulled the keys from the ignition.

This action was also to Ivan's surprise, but still allowing George some benefit of doubt, he asked. "So your friend allows you to use his garage?"

George Strübel did not answer directly, but instead said "You might as well come inside, Ivan. It's time to talk."

From out of nowhere two unidentified 'gardeners' appeared behind George's car. Ivan looked around.

"What's going on here?" he asked. "I demand you tell me what's happening!"

"Take it easy, Ivan." George suggested calmly. "We're only going to have a short discussion. Everything's under control now."

A gardener resembling *The Incredible Hulk* opened Ivan's door. His tight-fitting coverall uniform seemed to exaggerate his size and appearance. It was obvious to Ivan he had no choice. Walking from the garage to the house, Ivan looked around. In addition to the 'gardeners' on either side of him, he counted another eight. His heart was now pounding in his ears. "*They are all over the place,*" he thought. "*To cut and run would be futile.*" His mind was racing, trying to put everything in perspective; Ivan decided he wouldn't struggle at this point. He had already reached the conclusion that this was part of some conspiracy. His plans seemed to be coming apart – "*What about Mom,*" he thought.

They entered the back door as one of the 'gardeners' went back to trimming hedges and raking the freshly mowed lawn around the safe site. *'Incredible'* entered the safe-site with Ivan.

16

Ivan obeyed when asked to remove his shoes, and on request gave his jacket to Gaylord who hung it in the closet near the secured front door. Rad spoke to him in Russian, introducing himself only as "Richard". The fact that Rad spoke fluent Russian did not seem to relax Ivan in any way. He was introduced to Gaylord and then to me by our first names only. Looking directly into Ivan's eyes, I saw not the slightest indication that Ivan recognized me from our few near encounters in Bangkok. As I shook hands with Ivan, I noticed perspiration beading on his forehead, nose and upper lip. His hands were cold and damp. He was totally unprepared for confrontation.

Rad, Ivan and I walked into the sun room, where a small rectangular dining table had been arranged with four chairs. At one end of the table, several photo albums and a small *Kodak Super-8* movie projector with a built-in, 12-inch viewing screen had been set up. Note pads and short pencils were placed at each setting. Three more chairs were placed in the outside corners of the room. The blinds had been opened and tilted slightly upward to allow ample lighting. I counted two miniature movie cameras partially obscured from view by the drapes that had been opened to the corners of the room. Through reflective plastic curtains I could clearly see the 'gardeners' outside doing their job. I knew they could not see us, but since they all wore ear phones resembling hearing aids, I assumed they were listening.

Gaylord entered the room with a coffee pot, a tray carrying 4 mugs and a heap of varied, fresh donuts, which he placed in the center of the table. When Gaylord left, Rad came back in and offered Ivan a chair at the end of the table, near the projector. Ivan was slightly taken aback at the apparent level of hospitality. When Rad offered donuts, Ivan raised his hand in polite refusal; but as Rad poured coffee, Ivan accepted. He waited until I had taken a sip from my cup, then took a quick drink and sat quietly. Gaylord came back in to take his seat at the opposite end of the table, facing Ivan. Rad and I sat on opposite sides. Rad, sitting at Ivan's right started the conversation.

"I'm sure that by now you've figured out why you are here."

Before replying, Ivan turned to me and asked "What's your connection here anyway?"

What's my connection?

CHAPTER 1.
THE FIRST DECISION

It was the December 1959 - Riding in my stepfather's 1948 Blue Chevrolet *Fleetmaster*, along State Highway route 395 north from the ranch in Springdale, through the town of Valley, to my step-grandparent's home in the town of Chewelah in Washington State, my heart was sinking. I had made an unbelievably brave and perhaps foolish decision over the past few months – to join the military service. I had decided that I would rather volunteer than be drafted at 'Uncle Sam's' will. I wanted just to get the military commitment over with.

Family good-byes are always difficult. On this, my first farewell, I recall the episode at the home of my step-grandparents. My favorite Uncle Everett, older brother of my stepfather and Aunt Josephine (Jo) had timed their visit to coincide with my stopping by. From next door, Cecil Upp – a life-long friend and neighbor of the grandparents - was also in attendance. After Supper we all sat in the living room. Mom played the piano and anyone who could, sang. Then we sat around, talking about everything – except my joining the army. All in attendance knew that I was there to say my goodbyes, but no-one wanted to start the conversation. It was as though I was going off to war – or prison.

Everett and Jo had as usual brought their children, Larry and Loretta along. At one point, during a lull in the conversation, Loretta piped up with "Are you really going away to fight in a war?"

The peace had been shattered, and when I responded that I didn't think I'd have to fight, her little brother Larry came up with his own quip. "If you don't fight, you'll get killed." I thought that was a logical follow-up for a ten-year old, so I took Larry onto my lap and said, "I'll only fight if there's a war, and if I have to." Larry and Loretta's respective hugs provided an opportunity for me to announce my departure. Granddad Andrew went into the kitchen, and retrieved his faithful brandy bottle from under the sink. He returned with a few glasses and poured an equal amount into each, passing one to Everett, one to my stepfather, and one each to Cecil and me. He then poured a generous amount into his own glass. Lifting his drink, he proposed a toast.

"May this man, this soldier, go peacefully into the army, and return peacefully into our arms." The men drank as the women looked on with religious disapproval.

It was difficult to bid farewell to them. Grandma Edna's lips trembled as she spoke, and on this one, solemn occasion, my Step-grandfather hugged me for what seemed a little too long. He asked me to come back soon and often. When he let go of me, he turned away momentarily complaining of his "damned allergies!" He pulled out his red handkerchief and blew his nose. As the rest of us said our goodbyes, I noticed Larry pick up my glass to whiff the single remaining droplet of content. When he began to put it to his lips however, Aunt Jo spoke to him very clearly with the single word warning: "Larry!" He put the glass down quickly, and then looked at me. I couldn't help but smile.

As we departed, I looked back into the living room at "the family". All had been said. I also prayed that I would return home safely and that they would all be there to greet me.

The world was at peace. There was no reason to believe I would be away for more than my three-year enlistment.

Two weeks later, winter had really set in. The *Greyhound* bus, generating puffs of diesel exhaust, slowly made its way south, along the snow-banked, two lane state highway in sub freezing temperature, occasionally turning east toward the sun, and then back south toward Spokane. Fog was too thick to see past the road, and the bus crept along passing through what I knew to be farmland and forest. Leaning my head against the window I half-dozed, watching silhouettes of trees emerge against a bright, sunlit, fog-silver background as the fog was beginning to lift with the warming of the sun. It was almost surreal.

I closed my eyes. I could hear the distant voice of my Army recruiter.

"This is the army, boy; you gotta act like a man!"

"Had I made a mistake? Why did I ever believe him?! Why am I here? Why am I leaving the security of home?"

Half asleep, my mind meandered. *"Let's see now, I'm supposed to meet up with Harley Gilmore from Colville who will be going to the same basic training company as I – Company B, 8th Battle Group, 3rd Brigade, at Fort Ord. Well, maybe the weather won't be so bad down there."*

I missed the family – especially my favorite adoptees – Andrew, Edna and of course Loretta and Larry, already. But this is an important move in my life. I need to get on with it.

Overseas!?! That's for me! I'll get away and start my own life; that's it; I'll never have to come back here; ...not really - not if I don't want to..."

I had no idea how soon I would long to just go home.

Suddenly, it was August 1961

Twenty months later, and on the Greyhound bus again - a little *De-ja-vu.*

I was proudly wearing my US Army uniform. In those days, we traveled in uniform. – All pride and no shame.

This time, we were crossing the Golden Gate Bridge, coming into San Francisco. In 10 minutes I'll be downtown. I think I'll close my eyes…

Enter - my Clown

It was that haunting, confused, recurring dream. - *The clown was sitting on the rail laughing. Was he laughing <u>at</u> me, or <u>with</u> me? He began to fade – to slip away; but I could still hear the sound of his Goofy-style laugh. Now I hear music. It was San Francisco, and I was at 'the wharf'. I could see the fish market, the Italian Restaurant - but I couldn't make out its name. As I walked closer, trying to read the sign I could hear the clown laugh again. He was way over there, standig next to... I still can't read the name of the restaurant from this distance. Who is that with him? It's her, and she's crying.. No, please...don't cry.*

"Alioto's"! That's the restaurant's name, and I can see it clearly now... The strange dream is releasing me back into reality.

…and I'm awakening.

The bus rocked back and forth, gliding across uneven pavement in the parking lot of the San Francisco Greyhound Bus Station. Here, I would catch the army shuttle to the Presidio, and then take a second shuttle across the Bay to Fort Barry.

I had spent two weeks back on the farm with Mom and my stepfather, explaining that I was planning a career in Criminal Investigations. I had told them of a new investigative technique I had read about involving 'forensics'. I wanted to be a Medical Examiner…. Mom was proud. I could see it in her smile. She had always envisioned me as "Doctor Bradshaw"; while my stepfather's only real concern was if I was ever going to return home and work on the farm. I didn't have the heart to say that after twenty months in the army, I had already decided that I would probably never live on 'the farm' again.

Twenty months ago, My Army life had begun with two months of Basic Training at Fort Ord, California. I was already in excellent physical condition, having bucked hay bales all summer and worked hard on the farm through the fall, leading up to my enlistment. The rigorous, 8-week physical routine was not a challenge. But, throughout those eight weeks, I was barely able to tolerate our platoon senior drill instructor Sergeant Ortega. He was part gorilla, part man and totally without conscience. Ortega was built like a chopping block, with short legs, no neck, and shoulders that seemed as wide as he was tall. His pointed, pig-like ears were affixed too low, and he often used them as hooks on which to drape his dog-tag chain. Passing around the back of his neck, Ortega's dog-tag chain disappeared in a fold of skin and flesh where his neck should have been. With all due respect however, Ortega was able to take four squads of raw recruits and turn us into running, screaming, shooting, fighting machines; but he seemed to want to do everything the hard way. I never quite figured out how we got back to the barracks every night, when it seemed we had spent every minute of every day running only uphill.

I clearly recall that Ortega never allowed the heels of his boots to touch the ground. Ortega chose to walk, run, stand, strut and exercise only on his toes. He even stood on his toes in the chow line at the mess hall. He spit-shined the bottoms of his heels, and constantly bragged that he never had to buy new heels. Apparently he achieved that for which he had been striving, because by spending every wakened hour of every day on the balls of his feet, he had developed calves that were as large as my thighs. And, with heels lifted off the ground, he appeared at least 1 inch taller than his stated height of 5 feet 6 inches. Ortega however was not to be disrespected or challenged in any way. None among us wanted to bear the burden (or the mortification) of his punishment.

Ortega spoke with a slight accent or speech impediment – I never could decide which. He could not pronounce the word "sheet"; as it always came out "shit".

On the first day of Basic, when Ortega was introduced to the troops, he gathered us around a bunk and showed us how to "dress" our bunks in a military manner.

Speaking constantly through pursed lips, Ortega spoke: "Now, you take da shit and fold eet like dees….." He glanced around to see if anyone noticed.

"Den," he went on, "you fold da blankeet, and put eet on top of da shit like dees." …. Glancing again "..And den you fold da last shit like dees." Looking around one last time, "and put eet …"

Someone was snickering, and Ortega's pointed little ears heard it.

For the next 5 days, the private carried his M-1 rifle everywhere he went. It was an embarrassing and difficult task to take the weapon into the mess; prop it near the shower when bathing, and even take it to bed. No-one ever laughed at Ortega again, and for some strange reason, now, 50 years later, when I'm introduced to someone named Ortega, I automatically call him 'Sir!'; and I can still feel the cold barrel of the M-1 rifle in my bunk.

After Basic Training the next two months of training occurred at the Military Police School, at Fort Gordon Georgia. MP school consisted twenty percent of introductions to the conduct of law enforcement activities with an emphasis on riot control, and directing traffic. The remaining eighty percent was spit and shine. Polishing brass, ladder-lacing our boots, spit-shining the heels and toes to a mirror reflection, pressing and repressing uniforms that had just returned (pressed) from the cleaners. The emphasis was on image, including three parades a week on the 'tarmac', which began with a rigid, in-ranks inspection that could last for hours in preparation for a 5-minute pass-by for the School Commandant.

Graduation was a gimme if you could tolerate the harassment. I of course, had set my high goals early on, and was looking forward to the ten-hour class listed on our schedule as "The Introduction to Criminal Investigations Training", and wondered if there was as much harassment during that phase as well. To my disappointment, that introduction class was only four-hours long. We learned only that the Criminal Investigations Division was, in fact, part of the Military Police Corp. The remaining six hours of the class were wasted on 'spit and shine'.

After graduation, we received our orders, and the next move for me was back to California for assignment to Fort Barry, a Nike Hercules missile sight, located in Marin County, across the Golden Gate Bridge from San Francisco. Some of the students had gone on to advanced individual training in the Military Police Corp to such coveted schools as 'Dog Handling', 'Airborne School', and to various overseas assignments. At Ft Barry, I would perform the duties of an MP Security Guard, with training and occasional duties at the MP Battalion Headquarters on the Presidio of San Francisco "as required".

Fort Barry, missile Battery A of the Second missile Battalion, 51st Artillery, was commanded by Army Captain Glen D. Spradling. Spradling impressed me. He impressed me because his leadership demeanor was outstanding in that he had a way of convincing you that you *wanted* to do well for him, and I had always felt that such a talent was the identification mark of a good leader. I have to admit though that he also impressed me because he could click his heals by quickly sliding them together with one loud, quick pivoting 'CLACK', and it made him appear… well… so West Pointish. He loved inspecting the MPs each morning, because we were spit and shine all the way - as was he.

Battery A was designated a 'show battery', and was used by the army to show off the missile defense capabilities of the army Air Defense Command. We MPs were required to spit-shine our boots, and spin shine our brass. Ladder-lacing our boots was mandatory. All medals were on display for each uniform, to include our rifle, pistol and even sawed-off 12-gauge shotgun qualification medals which were shined to a brilliant mirror finish; chrome-plated helmets and Battalion crests were not only required for our class "A" uniforms, but for the OG wool fatigues as well. It was good, and it was fun; but not always good fun.

Exciting? Yes, but MP duties were not for me. I had believed the army recruiter when I enlisted, who had convinced me that if I really wanted to get into the Criminal Investigative field, I first had to enlist for military police duties, and then, after a year or two it would be a 'foregone conclusion' – All I would have to do is keep my nose clean, do my job, and apply for the CID, and I would get it automatically…..
Not necessarily so…

CHAPTER 2.
A LESSON LEARNED.

Enter Special Agent Smedly.

After a full year and a half of fulfilling my commitment as an MP, I visited the Criminal Investigations Division (CID) detachment at the Presidio of San Francisco. Per instructions, I announced my arrival through a microphone mounted on the front door entrance to the CID office. Almost immediately a uniformed MP answered, and ushered me inside. He even gave me a quick 'pat-down' - for weapons, I presumed - and then ushered me further inside to the office marked "RECEPTION". I was impressed with the security, passing through a long corridor with cameras mounted high on the walls; showing proper identification and after signing in, stating the purpose of the visit: "Application and interview for CID, of course". I thought *They should already know."*

With his military haircut, freshly cleaned dark grey suit, heel-clicking, *(he must be a West Pointer like Spradling)*, and more than a little courteous attitude, the CID agent in the reception office looked like the typical John Edgar Hoover-type FBI agent. He wore a nametag on his jacket, mounted directly over the left, vest pocket, identifying him simply as 'S/A Jones'. Yeah, right, *"Jones". He couldn't fool me, I already knew that these guys were under cover, and used aliases to conduct their investigative operations..." I knew that much!*

He glanced at the schedule, located my appointment, and ushered me even deeper, into the bowels of the building, to an "Interview Room" with no windows, saying "Agent Smedley will be right with you."

As I sat, I noticed two more cameras mounted on the walls – one was directed at my chair, and the other toward the Special Agent's desk. I realized that this was probably an interview room where suspects were interviewed, or maybe interrogated; and found myself daydreaming to the time when someone would say to a suspect: *"Agent Bradshaw will be right with you." Then, from a remote location, I would first watch the suspects' actions while he sat alone in the interview room; and because of my superior training in the techniques of observation, and in the conduct of interviews and interrogation, I would be able to ascertain his demeanor and level of guilt immediately - even before the actual interrogation had begun......"*

Oops, someone was approaching the door.

A near clone of the reception room agent entered the room, introducing himself as 'Agent Smedley' (confirming my suspicion), as he sat behind the desk. I was getting the hang of this already!

Agent Smedley however did not impress me as much as did S/A Jones. For one thing, he didn't even believe I was already in the army.

The very first words from his mouth were: "So, just how old are you – fourteen?.... fifteen?"

I was only slightly insulted. "I'm nineteen, almost twenty," I replied indignantly. "I've already served in the army for nearly two years."

He stifled the urge to laugh, and ignoring my reply, responded that before I could submit a formal application for CID, I would first have to join the army, and when I reached the age of 21, I could apply for CID. I would have to take the exams and of course, pass them before going to school. All this, he indicated could take several years. Agent Smedley then said I would also need a degree or degree equivalent..... And then, as though he wanted to add insult to my injury, he added,

"It would be good if you had a year or two of training and experience in law enforcement before even considering the application...." His smile was almost sardonic.

Even more insulted, and trying not to show it, I quietly handed him my military identification. He examined both sides closely, as though he thought it to be counterfeit. I told him that I was already an MP, assigned to the Presidio and attached to Fort Barry. He again insisted that I looked 14 or 15 years old, but he excused himself and left the room with my ID card. I presumed he was going to verify my existence.

About two minutes later, he returned to the room carrying a very thin folder and a large manila envelope. As he sat and placed the folder on the desk, I noticed my name handwritten on the label. Apparently someone else had made arrangements for this interview. In a less than apologetic manner Smedley said only "Sorry."

Round one goes to Bradshaw.

We sat for a few minutes and I answered questions while glancing through the 2-pages in the folder, and he then handed me the envelope containing a stack of documents, explaining that these were the forms I would "eventually" need for the application. By stressing the word "eventually", he was reminding me that I had plenty of time to work on the application. When we shook hands, he smiled (sardonically), and as I departed the office with a handful of regulations and forms to fill out for the appropriate security clearances, I recall hearing laughter........

The interview was over - brief and impersonal. I was shattered. The dream I had of becoming a Criminal Investigator now seemed a world and a lifetime away. An application for forensic training would be even more insulting.

"A foregone conclusion," my recruiter had said. Right! *"The Impossible Dream"* was more like it.

Little did I know that Special Agent Smedly's indirect advice would eventually put me in line for training and assignment at Fort Holabird Maryland and the Counter Intelligence Corps. Still, rounds two and three went to Special Agent Smedley.

The Enlightenment.

Within a few days after my encounter with Smedley, an incident occurred at Fort Barry that I can now describe as a 'Godsend' or 'Enlightenment'.

I had been on guard duty when my partner's dog alerted. Almost simultaneously, the ADT Alarm system signaled an intruder near the northwest corner of the exclusion area. The dog was released under voice control of Private First Class Howell, and our investigation resulted in pursuing an individual who had already breached the restricted area fence, and was attempting the exclusion area fence at Fort Barry which housed the missile control center. Our entire platoon was alerted and they responded immediately apprehending the culprit who was now trying to leave Fort Barry, the Security lights, the sirens and the guard dogs altogether.

The ensuing interview and mild interrogation revealed that the perpetrator, a 16-year old High School Sophomore from Mt Tamalpias High School had become intoxicated and disoriented following a beach party at Baker Beach, about 300 meters to the north of the Ft Barry Complex. He had thought he was taking a shortcut out of the area. An early morning search of the surroundings turned up a single beer can in the area of the fences, and negated any suspicion that he may have been carrying explosives or incendiary devices of any kind into the missile complex.

In accordance with standard procedures, the Counterintelligence Corp (CIC - about to be a new term in my lifetime vocabulary), was called and notified of the incident. They instructed that he be held until later that morning. They further instructed that witnesses and guards involved in the incident be made available for interview as well. That meant me!

The young man's parents were called and notified that their intoxicated son had been apprehended, and that we planned to deliver him to his home at their convenience the following day. His angry father, an Army Lieutenant Colonel requested that we keep him under lock and key at Fort Barry as long as possible. To the father's dismay, we did not have a 'brig' where we could 'lock up' his son; but we agreed to make him as uncomfortable as possible.

CHAPTER 3.
INTRODUCTION TO THE CIC.

At 0930 the next morning, Mr. Charles Philips, Special Agent, Counterintelligence Corps, drove into the parking lot of Battery A. He was driving a new, unmarked military Plymouth, 4-door sedan. MP Howell and I were at the 'Ready Room', awaiting Philips arrival. When he entered, Captain Spradling made the introductions, and was immediately dismissed by Philips who said, "I'm sure you have other things to do Captain; I can take it from here." He added "I assume you have the perpetrator in custody." Spradling confirmed the assumption, and asked Philips to let him know when he wanted to talk to the "perp". Spradling then 'clicked' his heels and walked into the adjacent Orderly Room (Commander's Office).

Frankly, I was surprised that Spradling was so quick to relegate the responsibility of an investigation in his own operational area to this virtually unknown individual.

Philips, turned to Private Howell, and asked him to relate his story from the night before. He listened to Howell, took a few notes, and then turned his attention to me, saying "Corporal Bradshaw, you were the NCO in charge last night, why don't you give me the story as you saw it, sir." He then turned to Howell and said "Mister Howell, I'm sure you have better things to do as well." My buddy Howell reluctantly left the ready room and walked in the direction of the MP barracks.

I hoped my shock was not obvious. This Special Agent was not even 10 years my senior. He had just excused my Captain and now he was calling me 'Sir'. I felt my face heat as I blushed. I handed him the CIC-marked copy of my report from the previous evening. He took the report and excused himself while he began reading it. Moments later, he turned to me and said "Did you write this yourself, sir?" I'm sure I blushed again, and responded that I had written it as soon as the incident was over. When I added that the report also identified the actions taken by the other MPs from headquarters who were involved in the actual arrest, Philips responded that he had read their reports, but found my first-hand account much more complete. Still feeling the heat of blush, I stammered something to the effect that I do the best I can.

While he continued to read my report, I volunteered to call SSG Bryant - our Senior MP, if he needed to speak with him.

"Was he there when you guys picked up the suspect?" He asked.

"No, Sir," I found myself saying. "But he's our senior NCO, and he was there right after we brought him into the Ready Room."

"In that case, I won't need to talk to him right now", Philips stated frankly. I provided him with Bryant's contact information in case he would want to talk to him later.

As he finished reading my report, Philips asked if I had also typed the report myself. I bragged that I could type over 60 correct words per minute, and sometimes as high as 75. He whistled, and just as I was about to believe that he was a little overboard with his compliments, he asked if I had ever considered 'joining up' with the CIC. I told him I knew nothing about CIC, but would be more than willing to learn about it. There was a good possibility I might be interested.

Philips glanced around, noticing the pool table near the back of the Ready Room and asked if I played pool, and if I had time for a game or two. I responded that it was my day off and indicated that

I would be happy to oblige with a game. He challenged me, and we immediately racked the balls and played pool for the next hour while he 'enlightened' me as to the varied training and assignment opportunities of the army Counterintelligence Corps. Spradling entered the Ready Room twice during the time we were playing pool, and as a joke, even challenged the winner. Both Philips and I tried to lose the next game, and it was I who eventually won the right to play against the Captain.

Philips looked at his watch, and commented that it was time to talk with the "perp", adding that he was expected back at his office for other business at 1430. He asked that I sit in on the interview. Overwhelmed with pride, I thanked him and stammered again, saying something like "myeeplesshr", which meant "my pleasure. "

Captain Spradling announced that he had business elsewhere and left the area, promising to have that game of pool at a later, unspecified time. The interview lasted an even shorter time than the discussion with Private Howell, and consisted mostly of obtaining driver's license and dependent ID information from the student. His quick story was no change from the report I had given to Philips. We called his parents to notify them that we were prepared to bring their son home; and the father insisted we put him on the military shuttle bus back to the Presidio. Per his father's request the "suspect" was released, and without hesitation, ran hurriedly from the Ready Room, down the main road in the direction of the shuttle bus stop. Before leaving, Philips wrote a quick "Thank You" on the back of his business card, walked to Spradling's office and placed the card on the Captain's desk. Philips then turned to me, saying "Sir, I'll send you some information on the CIC. After you read it, and if you're interested, call and I'll personally set up an interview with one of our **'Special Agents'**". He also handed me his 'Special Agent' Business card. He departed on schedule.

He had surfaced the magic words.

Spradling returned as I was straightening out the ready room. I told

35

him that Philips had departed, and had left a note for him. Spradling looked at me and observed "That guy Philips took quite a shine to you, Bradshaw. What was that all about?"

I responded, truthfully saying "Philips was trying to convince me to apply for the CIC."

Captain S. then further encouraged me, saying "It's a really good deal, you know; civilian clothes, free car to drive around, espionage, women, intrigue, foreign contacts, women, embassy parties, briefings, debriefings, women, shoot'em-up, bang, stab." He smiled and patted me on the shoulder, saying "All joking aside, you'll get a good recommendation from me."

I was rapidly becoming hooked.

Army Regulation 614-46 pertaining to Intelligence Field Operations training and assignments was my bible for the next few months, while I prepared and re-prepared my application. I also discussed my intentions with several friends in the San Francisco area, one of whom was Miss Helen Chen. In addition to her regular duties in the army, as a second job, Helen taught Report Writing at the army Education Center at the Presidio. An extremely attractive lady in her late forties, she proudly displayed a flowing abundance of premature silver-white hair.

I had met Helen a year earlier, when I enrolled in her 'English Composition and Report-writing' class. I knew nothing of her position at the Presidio, and didn't even know that her duties were that of an Intelligence Analyst. I knew only that I had secretly held a crush for her from the moment we met, and constantly looked forward to our Saturday morning classes. But, due to our age difference, I didn't even have the nerve to ask her to lunch following my Saturday classes. Then, one day when I was the only student present for class, during casual conversation she confided in me that she was an active duty, Army CIC Warrant Officer and had spent most of her career in Asia as an intelligence operative.

Wow! Whooda thunk?!

It was through her advice and encouragement as well as her excellent proof-reading that my application was finally completed and submitted through S/A Philips. Philips conducted the initial interview – the one designed to weed out undesirables, and forwarded my official application packet, along with his and Miss Chen's recommendations to CIC headquarters at Fort Holabird, Maryland. Within two weeks, Philips called me to let me know that I had been tentatively accepted for the CIC. He explained that there would be a short wait while my clearance was upgraded to "Top Secret" and a follow-up appointment for conduct of a battery of tests. Within a week, Philips called again with an appointment at Oakland Army Terminal CIC Detachment. He asked me to meet with him at the Presidio Snack-bar following my next report-writing class, saying he would provide me with a few pointers and a list of subject matter to read in preparation for the exams.

The following Saturday I attended my Report-Writing class, and afterward, walked to the snack bar. During that short walk, I heard Miss Chen calling my name. I turned and was pleased to see her walking in my direction. I waited while she caught up with me.

"Are we going to lunch?" She asked.

"Actually," I started. "I have an appointment."

"And, so do I," she replied, smiling knowingly. "Same time, same place and with the same person."

I wasn't at all surprised to find that Miss Chen had already learned of my pending application, so we walked together to the snack bar. *"Finally,"* I thought, *"we'll have lunch together..."*

I know I blushed when she took my arm.

We met with Philips at the snack-bar overlooking San Francisco

Bay. From our table, we could watch yachts, ferries, and passenger and container traffic as it drifted in and out of the bay, beneath the Golden Gate Bridge. From 1130 until nearly 1430 in the afternoon, we lunched and talked. They coached me through the exam procedures, explaining the outline and purpose for each of the examinations I would be taking. When we parted, they both spoke with confidence, saying that I would do fine, would find the exams to be challenging, but quite logical and would need only to rely on common sense to get through them. I was flattered again that they had so much confidence in me.

After lunch we shook hands and said good bye - for the last time.

(Staff Sergeant Chuck Philips would be killed in 1964, while assigned as an advisor in a civilian-directed operation near Cu-chi, Vietnam.)

(In 1968, Miss Helen Chen died in a car accident, colliding with a train at a railroad crossing, near Portland Oregon. The autopsy revealed that she had been suffering from brain cancer, and the Medical Examiner opined that Miss Chen likely had not seen the train coming.)

While awaiting the results of my background investigation for a Top Secret clearance, I was removed from "sensitive duties" at Ft Barry, and temporarily attached to the Artillery Battalion Headquarters at the Presidio as a Finance Clerk.

Time dragged on and I began wondering if somehow the army had forgotten me, as week after week passed and I heard nothing. My new boss, Chief Warrant Officer McMullen continued to encourage me saying – "It takes awhile". He was right.

After a short indoctrination at Battalion Headquarters, I was tasked with the duties of maintaining finance records for C Battery, located in Pacifica California. My duties required me to maintain and manage all the Finance and Accounting Office records for each member of that unit.

Enter, Frank V. Liles

One morning, during my first mid-month review of the finance records of Charlie Battery, I noticed a compounded mistake in a deduction from a Sergeant's pay for his contribution to his off-base housing allowance. He was receiving the allowance, but his personal contribution for the payment was not being deducted from his pay. This had been going on for over a year, and I assumed that was the reason I'd not noticed it during my two-month tenure. At $77.10 per month for the past 13 months, it now amounted to over $1000. No Army sergeant could afford to pay it back in one lump sum.

I called SGT Frank Liles, and informed him of the error, and invited him to the office to straighten out the mistake.

Frank showed up that afternoon. A few years my senior, he was a stocky young fella from McAllen, Texas. My estimate was that he weighed in at about 195 pounds, but he was in great shape, and could easily have touched a deceptive 225. I began by telling him that Finance was not my regular job, and that I was only a temp, awaiting my BI.

Frank stated that he had known the compound error had been accumulating for over 10 months. When I asked what he may have done with the extra money, he admitted "Ah spent it!" He was staring at the floor like a little boy who had just admitted to eating green apples.

"Well, you know you'll have to pay Uncle Sam back, even though it was a Finance Office oversight."

"Yeah, Ah know", he grinned sheepishly; "I was just hopin' nobody'd ketch it so soon."

"A new broom sweeps clean." I complimented myself.

We filled out the forms for a debt liquidation schedule, allowing Frank to pay off the debt over the next 12 months. After taking care of that small problem, we had coffee in the lounge area, and Frank asked about the Security Clearance. I told him I had applied for CIC, and when the BI is finished, would be reassigned to Ft Holabird for training.

"How'd y'all wind up applyin' for that – what do Ah have to do?" Frank asked.

I gave him the regulation number and a basic outline of the events leading up to my acceptance. I also gave him the information from Philips card, and suggested he give him a call.

I had categorized Frank as a 'good ol' boy'; and the kind of friend one can always use. How could I have known that our paths would cross numerous times over the decades, through an established friendship that would last a lifetime? Or two.

CHAPTER 4.
FORT HOLABIRD - THE COLLEGE ON THE COLGATE CREEK.

Fort Holabird Maryland was the US Army Intelligence Center and School, located on the outskirts of Dundalk, a suburb of Baltimore, Maryland. The Colgate Creek was a small, year-round brook which ran through Ft Holabird from the Northeast to the Southwest corners – thus the nickname. "The College on the Colgate Creek".

I had applied for the Counterintelligence School in early-1962, and following the routine background investigations, was accepted for The Special Agent Course. I traveled to Ft Holabird, and learned that my class was overbooked. The four of us who had been placed in 'standby' were then detailed around the base, performing clerical and other menial but important tasks, such as gardening and painting rocks. Since our security clearances had been granted, we were allowed to sit in on other ongoing courses, provided they were completed in time to attend the S/A course. Then eventually, in late summer, we were notified that we would begin class during the first week of September.

Enter: Ed Neiman

Since I was not assigned to regular duties, I had ample time to learn my way around base, and once I discovered the library and the museum, I spent most of my spare time at those two locations. At the library, I spent hours reading tales of espionage and intrigue that I fantasized were examples of my own destiny; and at the museum, I befriended Mr. Edwin P. Nieman, the curator, who himself had served in Europe during the so-called "Cold War" years immediately following WWII. Nieman had been involved with the recruitment of agents with the appropriate degree of motivation, intelligence and access, to assist in US espionage activities. He had also served in Korea, where he met and married his wife, Sue.

I was especially attracted to the technical division of the museum, where such items as clandestine listening and concealment devices, miniature cameras, and microdot equipment were on display. Occasionally, Mr. Nieman would remove an article from one of the shelves to educate me on the significance of that particular piece of history to the art of espionage, and after showing me how it functioned he would dust it off and place it back on the shelf from which it came.

One day, I noticed a 'new' camera on one of the shelves. He immediately retrieved it and handed it to me, explaining that it was one of the actual cameras used by legendary Russian spy Oleg Penkovsky; and he proceeded to intrigue me with the story behind Penkovsky. That was the day I also noticed a numerical tattoo about 2 inches above Mr. Nieman's left wrist. When he first saw that I had noticed it, he tried to cover it; but then after thinking only a few seconds, he rolled up his sleeve and showed the tattoo to me. He told me of the holocaust and of his incarceration and experiences in the camp, and of Schindler. From that point on I respected him even more.

Once the first day of class began, I learned that I was the youngest in my class by more than two years, and during the fourth week of training, when we had our credential photographs taken, mine, not surprisingly looked like a 14 year-old high school freshman, rather than a CIC Special Agent. The rest of the class finally settled on the nickname 'kiddo', and although it would not have been my choice, within a few days I found myself responding to that term of endearment.

The students in our class ranged from our class leader, 41 year-old Master Sergeant Fournier, to me, and surprisingly enough I still fell a full month short of the ripe old age of 21. Fournier and I shared our birthday, and on the day I turned 21, he turned 42. He was exactly twice my age.

During the sixth week of class, we students took an excursion to the Holabird museum. Ed took care to explain the various sections of the museum, and when we reached the technical division, asked me - yup, me - to show and explain the significance of the Praktika, 35 mm camera that had been used by Russian Spy Penkovsky over the past few years. I was able to remember every word and every point made by Ed during his personal presentation to me; and my fellow students were surprised that I had such a clear grasp of the specific importance and application of that particular item. Nieman proceeded with his tour. I made it a point to visit with him several times during the course of instruction. Ed had always liked me.

I believe also that most of the instructors liked me well enough; but to my disappointment, most of them agreed that I still looked too young to be 'on the streets'. On one occasion, Joe Fandiera, an actor from the training division, advised me to grow a beard. I tried, and grew my light, fine, blond beard for a full week before Fournier even noticed. He then ordered me to shave before the next duty day.

Enter, JK Jong.

During our 9th week, the students were informed that we would have a special guest speaker who happened to be in the Washington DC area preparing to go to Viet Nam. He would be going on a temporary duty assignment first, and would serve a full tour at a later date. The Speaker, Mr. J. K. Jong, was a well-known Counterintelligence Operative who had served in the Far East for most of his impressive career. When invited, Mr. Jong had readily volunteered to speak to our class.

He arrived on Thursday Morning, and the two-hour lecture on his career was interjected into our morning schedule.

JK Jong was introduced to our class as "Asia's #1 American Spy". He had been described as an individual who had dedicated his professional lifetime to espionage and counterintelligence, spending the majority of his career in Taiwan. According to our instructor, JK Jong had single-handedly run operations directed against the Communist Chinese, while also conducting sensitive CI, counterpart operations on the island of Taiwan. Without going into specifics, the instructor stated that JK Jong's fluency in the Chinese language dialects, allowed him to operate under an official cover and to realize exemplary success in the accomplishment of the clandestine duties of his assignment. JK was an Army Sergeant First Class.

The instructor complimented Mr. Jong, saying that he had sought neither fame nor fortune, and had simply followed orders in accomplishing his duties. JK had recently been selected to go to Vietnam to help set up an office for his Chinese counterparts. He would later return to the area and serve as a military advisor, assigned to "another agency", but working with the Chinese Counterpart agency, collocated with the Military Security Service (MSS). In describing JK's assignment in Taiwan, the instructor simply described the extended assignment simply as a cover assignment. Mr. Jong's TW counterparts regularly provided advisors to the MSS detachment in Saigon.

After his temporary duty and full, one-year term were completed, JK was to be reassigned back to Taiwan, where he would continue his career.

I found it inspiring that one of our own Army guys could realize such a degree of success.

I had expected a little, round-faced Chinese guy, speaking with a heavy *Charlie Chan* accent; but then this Chinese business-man walked out on stage. Wearing a light-gray three-piece suit, he approached the podium and introduced himself. His youthful appearance led me to think that he too may once have been the youngest student in his CI class. His perpetual trademark smile was deceptive. No-one would ever guess his true purpose in life.

JK Jong Spoke with the eloquence of a statesman; and totally without accent. As he described his counterintelligence duties, our entire class was spellbound. They found his exciting and optimistic vision both welcoming and informative. JK further encouraged our class, saying that we were just now entering the beginning of a stimulating and exotic new career.

In Taiwan, JK had been involved in 'black' infil-exfil operations involving Chinese, mainland-born citizens whom he had trained and dispatched back to the mainland. He had been involved in supervising their initial debriefing and training when they came to Taiwan, and on several occasions was personally involved in the extrication of these sources from their 'fishing boats' in the waters of the Taiwan straight when they returned.

After his lecture, while on break, I managed to work my way past the front of the crowd and speak momentarily with JK, telling him how impressed I was with his lecture, and convey my hopes that we would be able to work together sometime in the not to distant future. He smiled broadly, and said merely "Yes, it would be nice. Too bad, you are Caucasian."

At that time, neither of us could have known that we were destined to meet and to work together many times during the course of our careers.

As the course continued, I tried my utmost to emulate James Bond, but it was to no avail, and only made me appear even younger and more immature. Graduation day was an honor. While I was not in the top three at graduation, I was the youngest graduate in my class, and I did receive an honorable mention for my intuitive and inventive surveillance techniques. At the graduation ceremony, our host speaker joked, saying that I was an excellent surveillant who could disappear in a crowd during surveillance, but surely not so much because of my expertise, as because of my size and apparent age. He taunted that without much effort, I "could probably go through life virtually unnoticed." I'd always hoped that was a joke.

On that graduation day, I received my orders, and was being assigned to duties with the Counterintelligence Records Facility at Fort Holabird. It was a 'desk job', and not what I had expected. The day after graduation, I went directly to work as a member of the "Activity and Biographical Coding Branch". Our duties were to categorize (biographically and by activity) every name in every file in the facility. This was an unending job for our small, 3-man office. We would provide lists to the keypunch operators who would then prepare the cards for inputting reference information into the humongous computers in use during those days. With that information on file one could locate any active or 'cold' file by name, activity, or by providing limited biographical information, within minutes.

The job may sound extremely boring, but for me, it was an excellent opportunity to read, read, and read. The operational reports I read were much more exciting than the novels that had led me down the road to this location. The reports contained actual photographs and maps; they outlined descriptions of tradecraft and methods of operation, techniques and often detailed synopses of entire operations - the successes as well as the failures. The reports were not just from the army CIC archives, but all the investigative and intelligence services within the government. How exciting this was to me, and what an excellent training experience it became. This treasure, this accumulation of information, along with the stories related to me by Miss Chen and Ed Nieman, will forever be imbedded in my mind, and until this day, I consider those accounts, their advice and their coaching as invaluable tools in the honing of my own career. How fortunate I was.

One of my deepest developed interests during this period was the precise "art" of surveillance. I was convinced that if surveillance activities were conducted as trained, there was not an agency or adversary in the world that could evade or detect the activity; and without detection there could be no successful counter-surveillance activity directed against the well-trained, well-disciplined and coordinated American operative. All one had to do was make no mistakes. I became obsessed with that theory to the extent that I talked about it daily with anyone I thought was interested enough to listen, and eventually I became a member - the youngest member, of course - of the coveted CAST (the Capital Area Surveillance Team). While this was a special activity and not my primary duty, I could only be involved when the "Team" was short-handed. Nonetheless, surveillance, counter-surveillance and surveillance detection became my *forte'*. Even older members of the team would often come to me for 'new ideas', and while I will always consider them my mentors, I also believe I earned the respect of them all, and gained the reputation as a *'surveillant' extraordinaire'*. Somewhere along the line I lost the beloved nickname of 'Kiddo'.

The day would come however, when I would have to leave the protection, the security of Fort Holabird. And, although my duties, particularly those involving surveillance - which occasionally took me as far as Miami, Albuquerque or San Francisco - were becoming more exciting and intriguing, I accepted this fact, and began to make plans for my future endeavors.

Enter Major Fletcher and the army Language Aptitude Test

With Fort Holabird training, and experience with the CRF and CAST, I felt as though I was ready for that long-awaited 'overseas' assignment. But, how could I orchestrate; how could I choose the assignment, to a location of my choice, where I would really get into the espionage game – where would it be?

I knew that without an acceptable level of fluency in a foreign language, I would be relegated to the conduct of support duties. The prospect of being lodged behind a desk, processing someone else's expenditures of classified funds, proofreading someone else's operational reports, or some other menial task, was no longer acceptable. I wanted to be the 'someone' who was doing the real thing. *After all, I'd completed the training hadn't I?*

The language billets to be filled at Army Language School were varied. *Should I attempt an exotic or erotic language like Greek, Swahili, or Serbo-Croatian? Or should I stick to something like Spanish, German, or French? High School Spanish might even give me a head start.*

The Army Language Aptitude Test was designed to make that decision for me. Through use of the Lingali examination, I would be able to determine what language would suit my capability, and would therefore excel.... Right! I was daydreaming again, *of the day when I could pass as a local civilian, incognito, under-cover, drive fast cars, unlimited expense account, YES! James B (for Bradshaw) Bond!* But, common sense dictated, and it was beginning to look more and more like I'd have to choose blond-haired, blue-eyed countries as my operational destination. It just wasn't fair. Why wasn't I born with a dark complexion and dark hair, so I could blend in - so that I could literally 'disappear into the crowd' - so to speak?!

But the first step was to take the exam. After thinking it over, and making the appointment I went to the testing facility at Fort Holabird, where I met Major Fletcher. He was a thin man in his fifties who sat at the military position of attention behind his desk. It seemed he was able to move only his hands and arms, and turn his head slightly. (*My initial impression, and what I really wanted to believe, was that he had been wounded during bare, hand-to-hand conflict during operational activities in the Sudan, but was too valuable to retire, so he had been retained in "the business" and provided with this rather unimportant task of administering the army Language Aptitude Tests.*)

His voice squeaked - *probably a knife wound to the throat* - as he asked me a few questions in order to ascertain my linguistic background. I answered, explaining that my Swedish-background mother had spoken Swedish from time to time during my formative years, and that I had studied Spanish for one year during High School. I claimed no fluency in either. Obviously not impressed, he then handed me the exam. Surprisingly, I was the only person being tested that day.

The exam began with a brief, written explanation of Lingali and its grammar, along with a four-page dictionary to be used as a guideline for selecting the proper formats, vocabulary and construction of these 114 strange sentences. The language was based on Latin, and to me, the idea of conjugating verbs, constructing sentences and utilizing the proper vocabulary of any foreign language was completely intimidating. The exam lasted only 120 quick minutes. While Fletcher remained rigidly glued to his seat, I was able to answer only 76 of the 114, or about 65 percent of the problems, in that allotted time. Knowing that 70 percent correct answers was the minimum requirement, there was no doubt that I had blown the exam. Major Fletcher accepted my answer sheet with a squeaky "humph!", and asked me to return to my seat while he graded it. I watched intently as he marked and made columnar notes on my answer sheet, and the longer it took, the more I decided that I should probably start thinking of becoming a funds custodian, rather than a Counterintelligence Agent, Agent Handler or Case Officer. On the other hand, there was always the possibility of an assignment to London, where hopefully I would not be linguistically challenged.

When he had completed the grading, Fletcher stood and walked to my table. I was surprised he could actually walk. He casually propped himself on the table and told me that I had muffed the test; but he was quick to add that there was still a chance I would be able to attend ALS. I was all ears.

Major Fletcher then acknowledged that the Lingali test had absolutely no bearing on many of the languages of the world. We had a few comparative exchanges regarding 'Germanic' and 'Latin-based' as opposed to 'tonal' languages. Out of nowhere, Fletcher then asked if I could sing. I bragged that I not only could sing, but our church choirmaster had once told me I had perfect pitch. Fletcher quickly placed my exam on the table, carefully aligned the hole-punched correction sheet on top and proceeded to mark about a dozen more answers - - - correctly.

"Congratulations, he said. "You just got a 75!"

The good Major then spent the better part of an hour guiding me through the application procedure, wherein I was instructed to list my three choices of language as 1) Chinese Mandarin, 2) Spanish, and 3) Vietnamese. Before I left his office, Fletcher stated "I guarantee you'll get your first choice."

He was right, and a few days later when the application was returned, it was noted: 'Approved for Chinese Mandarin, 47 weeks language training.' And was signed: John B Fletcher, Major, Chief, Language Testing and Evaluation Center. It was Major Fletcher all along who was responsible for helping me continue on my selected career tract. I remained forever grateful to Major Fletcher, and at that time, had no way of knowing our professional paths would cross again during our careers. I did learn however from Corporal Kim Smith, a fellow student at ALS, that John B Fletcher, the son of Hong-Kong missionaries, was fluent in three Chinese dialects, as well as in Japanese, Korean and Russian. *Well, there goes my Sudan incident theory.*

Prior to departing Fort Holabird, I was privileged to be allowed to attend the CIC Army Field Operations course. An 'abbreviated course' had been cut from 16 weeks to an accelerated 10 weeks, in order to fulfill Army requirements for intelligence "collectors". Rumor had it that if the army were to fulfill the projected "collection" position vacancies for Viet Nam alone, that particular occupation specialty would be drained from the rest of the world.

Based on that statistic, I was happy that Major Fletcher had selected me for Chinese language training. At least for 47 more weeks, I would not be going directly to Viet Nam.

I drove across country from Baltimore to Monterey, via Chewelah Washington. The side trip home was to inform my mother and stepfather of the changes in my career tract. I did not have to worry about disappointing my mother, as she had proudly told everyone she knew that I was going to work for the Secret Service, and that was okay with her.

"At least', she told her friends "my son won't be in the army any more, and I won't have to worry about his going to war……."

She had explained to me that during the course of my background investigation for a Top Secret security clearance, some of our friends and acquaintances had been visited by the 'Secret Service' to discuss my loyalty, integrity, and moral character.

"Don't worry, Son" she said, "I'll not tell anyone what you're really going to do. Your secrets are safe with me." She said that as though she actually knew what I'd be doing, and I didn't even try to explain.

Until Mom passed away in 1987, I had no reason to believe she ever revealed my "secrets".

CHAPTER 5.
ARMY LANGUAGE SCHOOL

When I arrived at Army Language School, I was somewhat concerned about my abilities to study a tonal language. I had always heard the rumors about the 'sing-song' languages, but had never in my mind been able to envision what I was up against. The first day of class was spent meeting our instructors. Conversations, questions and answers were in English. One of my fellow students, Marine Captain Flinn, already had a degree in Chinese from the University of Michigan, and the rest of our 7-man class found this somewhat intimidating. It seemed unfair that someone who already spoke the language was going to be in class with the rest of us who had never been immersed in such an endeavor. As a result of his rank and background, Captain Flinn was designated the class leader.

Two of my classmates were FBI agents, and by virtue of the Roman alphabet, I was seated between them. As it turned out, they both had also studied the Chinese Cantonese dialect, and although their spoken dialect is somewhat dissimilar to Mandarin, the written languages are virtually the same. They too had a head start. As civilians however, their attitudes were not like Captain Flinn, who made sure that the rest of us were fully aware at all times that he was "in command" and that we should have to answer to him for any disciplinary action we deserved. Being the only enlisted member of the class, I made up my mind early on that I was on equal ground with the rest of the class, and refused to be intimidated. Besides, I had FBI agents sitting at either side, and I made sure we three became friends early on. After all, we also had something in common. The three of us were *Special Agents*.

In the beginning, our entire class, including Captain Flinn struggled through the language training, fighting the tones and grammar of this strange and different language. Suddenly, somewhere along the 5th week of training, something snapped inside my brain. As the grammar became clear and simple, the only challenge was to learn new vocabulary and apply it clearly and fluently. The instructors all seemed to sense this sudden enlightenment, and began to focus more than my allocated 14 percent of the class's attention on me. I found it both challenging and rewarding to take on the fastest talking instructors who would pellet me with questions and try to confuse me with fast-talking, tongue-twisting phrases. I even amazed myself from time to time. It was as though I had already learned this language somewhere during one of my previous lives. Although Captain Flinn was far in advance of the rest of us in writing and reading newspaper articles, Corporal Bradshaw had passed him up when it came to speaking and responding to the instructors. And, I was rapidly gaining on his reading and writing skills. Flinn made several attempts to learn my secret, and would often corner me during class breaks to ask me how I was doing it. Finally I told him that I was doing my best to stay a week ahead of the schedule in vocabulary, and in learning new grammar and sentence structures. Studying ahead, I informed him was the secret to success in the language classroom. As we were nearing the end of the 47 weeks of training, I had managed to maintain my vocabulary lead on Captain Flinn, and while he attained the title of Distinguished Graduate, I earned the second-place title of Honor Graduate, and earned the coveted Admiral's award for my speaking ability. As a result I was privileged to give the graduating class speech. To my dismay however, I was also the student selected by the staff and faculty to continue another six hair-pulling months of advanced Chinese Mandarin training. This honor of course required approval from my Branch – the CIC.

From the date of the initial request to CIC, the reply was received from Fort Holabird in one short week. When Dr Lee called me in to inform of the approval, he stated that his old friend "John Fletcher sends his congratulations." For the next few months I realized that if I had only refrained from taking on Captain Flinn, and elected to remain in the middle of the class, Flinn would probably be sitting in this advanced class, working his buttocks off and struggling to reach the end of the advanced course.

For this privilege however, I became personal friends with the staff and faculty in the China Section of the Far East Division of ALS. Far East Division director, Dr. P.C. Lee, was a graduate of Yale University with a Doctorate in music. And, he was my favorite of all instructors. My new class was considered a 'single, one-on-one class', wherein I spent 7 hours daily in the classroom. I spent one hour every day with one of the following instructors:

(White Horse) Harry Lee, Drs. Wu or Mrs. Wu, Dr. Chang (of Beijing Opera fame), Col (machine-gun) Wang, the elegant Mrs. Liang, beautiful Mrs. Chen, and Victor Wen were among my professors. By the time the course ended, I had become personal friends with all the instructors, and they all became my favorites.

Dr. Ting Su was the rare substitute instructor in case one of the others couldn't teach. I recall that he was the oldest of all the instructors. He and his wife ran a grocery store in Pacific Grove, and gave me ridiculously cheap prices on my frequent visits to their place of business. I clearly recall that Dr. Su disliked being challenged during class, and his favorite response to those who questioned the grammatical basis for any specific sentence was: "Always remember Mr. Bai (or whoever asked), six-hundred million Chinese cannot be wrong!"

It was Dr. Pao Chen LEE, who would alternately administer an aural or written examination at the end of each week during the final phases of the advanced class.

I had learned that if I continued studying ahead, I could also take the exams ahead of schedule; and was eventually able to cut a few days off my total study time. By the end of 5 months I was prepared to graduate. When I finally completed the course and received my second diploma (which was issued by both ALS and Yale University), I stood alone in Dr Lee's office, in a nice quiet ceremony, conducted in the Chinese language.

When I left Monterey, the Su family invited me to their home for a mouth-watering, catered Peking duck dinner. My instructors were all in attendance.

My follow-on assignment would be to the CI Detachment on Okinawa.

CHAPTER 6:
OKINAWA

Enroute to Okinawa, I stopped one more time to visit my Mom and stepfather. When I mentioned 'Okinawa', she frowned and said "I thought you weren't going to go to war." Although I explained that Okinawa was not part of Southeast Asia where things were now beginning to stir, Mom stubbornly refused to understand. As far as she was concerned, it was all Asia, and that's all that mattered.

"Besides," she said, "Your Father died during that horrible battle when you were but a child. I just don't have good feelings about it."

I then recalled how she had told the story of Father being recalled during WW II, and how, during the Battle of Okinawa, he had been declared missing in action for such a long time. It was not until the early 50's that she had received a final letter from the Department of the Navy declaring him deceased. She had spoken little about the death of our father and how the turmoil of raising two children alone had burdened her; and I had nearly forgotten about it.

Now, here I was – on my way – back to 'war'.

Miss Okinawa and 'Kinpatsu'

It was 1965, and was beyond doubt the hottest and most humid July afternoon I had experienced in my entire life when I disembarked on Okinawa. According to the weather reports over the past few days, a typhoon had passed over this semitropical island, on its way north toward the Japanese mainland. Stepping off the air-conditioned plane was like entering a sauna. The steaming humidity caused clothing to cling to my body like wet chamois and although the temperature was not all that high - perhaps 95 degrees, the humidity matched that count in percentage, raising the "feels-like" temperature factor another 15 degrees.

In the first few days on the island, I learned that fine cotton clothing was an answer to the weather conditions, at least to a degree; and adhering to the saying that less is more - wearing less is much, much more comfortable.

Within weeks, I found myself venturing out and around the city of Naha. My duties allowed me the freedom of learning my way around the city, and my curiosity, combined with the desire to plant my staff firmly in fresh new Asian soil, was encouraging to my adventurous side. Having Saturday and Sunday to do just about anything I wanted was also to my liking, and I took full advantage of the opportunity to visit the Nakagusuku Castle, Shuri temple, Suicide Cliff, Nokandakari Falls and other sights around the island. Although Okinawa is only 42 miles long, and ranges from 1.5 to 15 miles wide at the respective narrowest and widest points, I did not feel confined. In my opinion the outdoor, SCUBA-diving and other water sports activities of Okinawa can rival those of such locations as Australia if one has the desire to search just a little.

I clearly recall the Sunday I met the lady I will call "Miss Okinawa", for lack of a better or bona fide name. I had been walking through a district of Naha city, Okinawa, which was commonly referred to as "Black Market Alley". BMA was then located in mid Naha, near the intersection of *Kokusai Doori* (International Street) and Naha Road 3. It consisted of hundreds of small stalls constructed of wood and canvas, and was situated over the cover of what Americans called "The Big Benjo". I shall separately address the Benjo later in the memoirs. After going through fifteen minutes of ritualistic bargaining, I had purchased a "London Smog" rain jacket (an article of clothing much needed during the monsoon season), when I noticed a small alley leading up the hill, away from BMA. My curiosity tugged at my young body, and I began walking up the hill – with the simple goal of reaching the top.

I made good progress, and within a few minutes, found myself cresting near the top of the hill. Then, a movement caught my eye, and the essence of food caressed my nose. I stopped to determine direction, and again curiosity moved me into an even narrower path, where, squatted on an earthen floor in a small wooden lean-to was Miss Okinawa.

I thought 'she must be a hundred years old', as she appeared older than anyone I'd ever known, and the mere sight of her caused me to stare, transfixed at her image. Her face was wrinkled and leather-like, her eyes a light gray, and her body appeared as frail and delicate as the withering petals of a rose. Her broad smile revealed a near toothless grin. I came out of my trance to see her beckon to me. She was talking away in a language I'd not heard before. I later learned that she spoke Okinawa *Hoogen*, a tonal language and although considered to be a dialect of Japanese, it is the language of the Ryukyu Islands, dating back to the days when Okinawa and the Ryukyu Islands comprised *Lyou Chou*, the main island and the archipelago province of historical Chinese occupancy.

She motioned for me to sit, as she ceased separating dark from white rice. She pushed her tray of rice aside, and picked up what appeared to be a piece of wood. She tapped on the wood with her fore knuckle and said "*sakana*", and allowed me to smell the piece of wood. It was as she had said - fish. She used a small plane-like tool to shave off a few flakes of the fish, and dropped the shavings into some water, which was conveniently boiling over a charcoal hibachi. Using a large kitchen knife, in her hand she cut fresh tofu into cubes, and dropped them into the soup. She added a scoop of *Miso* paste, and after chopping some leaks, she also placed them into the boiling water. She then covered the boiling water for a minute; then removed the soup from the hibachi and poured the contents into rice bowls from the small kitchen shelf. She brought one to me, and we sat and partook of the broth. It was quite tasty. I tried to communicate with my extremely limited Japanese, saying *"arigato gozaimasu"*, but she would only laugh, and after repeating my phrase several times over, she would lapse back into her Okinawan dialect. She talked continuously to me for almost an hour, laughing and apparently joking. Occasionally she would reach over and touch my hair, and say *"Kinpatsu, Kinpatsu"*, which I also learned later was the equivalent of "Goldilocks".

As I finished the broth and stood to leave, Ms Okinawa gestured to prepare more broth, indicating perhaps that I was large and needed more. I politely raised my hand in refusal, and patted my stomach to indicate that I had partaken sufficiently. She then approached me and hugged me, saying *"Kinpatsu, kinpatsu"* again. I didn't know exactly how to tell her I would be back – but I tried to communicate that meaning with makeshift sign language, which seemed to make her happy. I vowed to myself that I would. And I did.

Two to three weeks later, I found myself thinking of Ms Okinawa constantly. So on a Friday, I visited the local US commissary and stocked up on bread, canned dice, *Campbell's* tomato and mushroom soups, a can opener, and as a last thought, picked up a package of cocktail crackers and two small flat glass containers of *Osetra* caviar.

I anxiously waited for Saturday morning and at the first break of dawn, took a local cab to Black Market Alley, and walked to my destination. As I neared her small wooden shack, I saw her sweeping dust from inside. I couldn't imagine sweeping dust from an earthen floor. It must be an unending task; and as I approached, she looked up and her toothless smile lit up the sky. *"Kinpatsu, oh watakushi-no kinpatsu"* – and then back to the Okinawa hoogen. As I presented her with my very humble gifts, she examined each and every item, exclaiming "oh, oh", and *"arigato gozaimashita"*. I wanted to think I had taught her that Japanese phrase.

As she would allow, I assisted in preparing our broth, and opened the crackers and caviar. As she poured the mushroom soup, with her own added fish shavings and tofu, I spread caviar on the crackers. We sat and she talked for another hour, and when the broth was nearly gone, I passed the caviar crackers to her. I suppose I was not surprised when she gagged and spat the caviar out the door; for she had never experienced this delicacy before, and I vividly recalled the first time I had tried caviar. I had also wondered how anyone could even like it. Pointing to the caviar, I said "Sakana". But it was to no avail. Miss Okinawa would likely never eat anything that looked like this 'sakana' again.

Occasionally a neighborhood acquaintance of Ms Okinawa would walk past her front door, and would stop momentarily to ask of her welfare. She was not embarrassed with my presence, and would always gesture in my direction and say "Watakushi-no 'Kinpatsu', and smile happily. I always arose from my zabuton to bow slightly.

As during the first visit, the time to say goodbye suddenly was upon us, and I left Ms Okinawa. Going to the corner of the main alley, I looked back to see her still standing there waving goodbye and smiling. I waved back, and couldn't help but think being old must be so lonely. I felt I had communicated with her during this visit, and knew I would be back again soon, to make her day, and mine, and was already making plans to bring something other than caviar for her palatal enjoyment.

My intentions were good, but with military duties being what they were, I was unable to make it back to Black Market Alley for about 6 weeks. I stocked up again, but instead of caviar, I brought a small jar of peanut butter and another jar of strawberry preserves. The walk to Ms Okinawa's place seemed very short on this occasion, and I arrived in record time – but was surprised to see that her home was closed, and that a single nail now held the door shut tightly. This was the door that always seemed open to welcome guests at any time. A few people milled around, and from among them, a small boy approached me and said a few words in Japanese. I didn't understand

his sentence, but translated the word "O Baa-san" as "grandmother."
I nodded my head eagerly, and the child looked down, staring at the
ground. He responded with the single phrase "*nakunarimashita*". I
immediately recognized the Japanese phrase for "lost", but wasn't
sure what I was hearing.

"What?!" I exclaimed in disbelief, "*Nan-ni?*"

He repeated the phrase "*Nakunarimashita*", and when he looked up,
I saw the tears streaming down his cheeks. For a fleeting moment
I even saw a strange resemblance in the face of this child to that of
and Miss Okinawa. I found myself weeping shamelessly. I placed
my bag of "gifts" on the ground, knelt and took the young boy in my
arms. When he finished sobbing, I noticed we had drawn a crowd,
and the boy ran to the arms of a middle-aged man standing nearby.
I then noticed a small black piece of cloth pinned to the gentleman's
sleeve, and then recognized the same facial resemblance between this
older man and Miss Okinawa as well. The boy gestured toward me
and said something in Japanese that I did not understand. Father and
son then led me to the door of Miss Okinawa's home, and the father
pulled the door loose. He gestured for me to come inside, and I did.
On the small shelf were two loaves of bread, an opened cracker box,
and two empty caviar containers, washed perfectly clean and placed
on the shelf with the rice bowls.

I was empty - saddened by the loss of a friend.

As I continued on my mission of life, I was perhaps a little more
learned as to how delicate, how fragile we are; and how life must go
on. I think of Miss Okinawa now and then, and will always remember
her. It has been many years since she passed now, but I cannot think
of Okinawa without recalling her near-toothless smile and hearing
her voice – "*Kinpatsu.... Kinpatsu. Oooh watakushi-no kinpatsu...*"
(Oh, my Goldilocks......).

Acknowledgement: Now, years hence, I travel as often as possible
to Asia, and occasionally have dreams taking me back through the

decades to the times when I was actively involved in the Asian languages, the history, the customs, and the people. I am certain without a doubt that my brief encounters with Miss Okinawa played a very positive role in the love I developed for the people and the lands of that unique and exotic area of the world. My eagerness as a young man, my patience as an older man, combined with my unending desire to keep going, to learn, and to personally develop within the my chosen career field, led me through the most fulfilled professional career possible.

Thank you, Miss Okinawa for coming into my life, and for providing me with that lifelong impression. You gave me the strength and courage to pursue my studies and lead me along the path toward success. Little did I know that I was about to embark on the most intriguing aspects of espionage.

Throughout my tour in Okinawa, I continually sent Mom copies of photos depicting the Americanization of Okinawa, including McDonald's, Kentucky Fried Chicken, and Dairy Queen. More photos of well-known, varied American entertainers at the military clubs on Okinawa were designed to ease her mind. Not once did I ever discuss my duties, the alcohol consumed, the bars and strip joints, the gambling and slot machines, and the varied nightlife of Okinawa, as I'm sure it would have sent her on a tirade of how sinful, how dangerous, and detrimental to her teachings the assignment was. She had made me promise that I would always attend church services, whenever possible. I kept that promise, utilizing of course my own definition of the term 'whenever possible'... I did however tell Mom the story of Miss Okinawa, and how my brief association with Miss Okinawa had helped stimulate my personality and my love for Asia.

I was nearing the end of my second month on Okinawa when I received a package from Fort Holabird. As the return address read simply: 'Headquarters, US Army Intelligence Center and School, Fort Holabird', I had absolutely no idea what was in the package, or who had mailed it to me. At first opportunity, when I was alone, I opened the package. As I began to remove the wrapping, I found a hand-written note on a sheet of yellow note paper. It was from Ed. It read:

Master D. W. Bradshaw, My Dear Friend.

This package holds three gifts for you. The first is a brass casting of the golden Sphinx, and the mascot of Fort Holabird. Someday, I hope to be able to see it on your bookshelf, in your library, or in another place of prominence somewhere among your personal memorabilia.

Secondly is the camera. It is an East German, 35mm Praktica, and the very one you held in your hands. It was utilized by Oleg Penkovsky. I had three more in the closets here at the museum, and was instructed to give all surplus items away to institutions and to send them (at my own discretion) to locations where they will be preserved, in preparation for the reconsolidation of our new museum. I know you will take good care of it.

Books are being written of Oleg Penkovsky's efforts on behalf of the West, and they will contain photographs of this very camera. Please keep the enclosed copy of 'The Penkovsky Papers' also as a gift from an old friend, a "comrade" who will never forget you.

Your friend, Forever, Ed.

The items he sent me are in fact on the shelves of my small library, where they shall remain.

My friend, Mr. Edison Nieman died at the age of 79, in 1977, while I was attending Japanese Language training at DLI in Monterey.

CHAPTER 7.
ENTER IVAN - THE DOSSIER.

Duties on Okinawa had begun with my assignment to the Naha Field Office of the CIC, located in a district called "Higashi Machi", adjacent to the Bank of America in downtown Naha. Our primary duties fell into the category of "Overt-Sensitive" in that we worked in tandem with the Okinawan Police and other official contacts.

My specific duties consisted of identifying sources as possible legal travelers, and focused primarily on third-country nationals who traveled frequently between China and Okinawa. Our office Deputy for Operations, Chief Warrant Officer Dan Johnston, was also a Chinese linguist. When I first arrived, he took me aside to explain how happy he was to have me come aboard. He humbly explained that his Chinese language had never been good. He explained that due to his lack of fluency, and the fact that he was busy performing the duties as D/O, he had not been able to spend as much time focused on the Chinese community in Okinawa as he would have liked. As the new Chinese linguist on the ACE (Aggressive Counter Espionage) team, my primary target would be China.

At that time, there were approximately 12,000 mainland Chinese residents on Okinawa. The majority of them were legal travelers, involved to some extent with cross-straight business negotiations between Okinawa and China. It was believed possible that many were involved in intelligence activities directed against the US Forces on Okinawa. The acronym for those activities was 'SAEDA', which stood for Subversion Attempts of the Enemy Directed Against. The Nationalists and Communist Chinese were of course targeted at each other. Okinawa was also the home of the USARPAC Intelligence school where all our Asian counterparts were trained in US Intelligence methodologies.

One of our additional duties was to brief US military personnel annually on SAEDA, and to explain their individual responsibility to report suspicious elicitation attempts and activities to CIC. SAEDA reports resulted in about 25 percent of our leads, most of which turned out to be dead ends, and were precipitated by young, naïve soldiers with a good imagination, and a lust for intrigue. Every lead required at least one follow-up activity and an operational report by one of our Case Officers. Thus, I found myself quite busy just keeping up with SAEDA leads and reporting.

Among our operatives was an older agent nicknamed "Rad". Army Sergeant Major Richard (Rad) Radislovsky was the lone native Russian linguist assigned to ACE.

Another source of leads to which we had access was through a joint, US – Okinawan Intelligence Service known as 'Pontiac'. In our counterpart relationship with Pontiac we were required to board ships about to visit Okinawa's Tomari Port. When I say 'we', I generally mean 'Rad and I'. We, along with US Air Force medics, would board the ships while still in international waters. The medics would perform medical examinations of crew members who had been reported ill over the past 30 to 90 days at sea. While exams were being conducted, CIC agents had the responsibility of reviewing the passports and other identifying documents of all crew members, and matching that information with a 'watch list' of undesirables which had been provided by 'another agency'. If a match was made, we would then report the information to 'Pontiac' and they would take appropriate action to insure those identified crew members were not allowed to come ashore during the stay. On rare occasions, the medics would have the individual 'quarantined' during the period the ship was docked. On even more rare occasions, an individual identified as 'undesirable' would be allowed off the ship only after he had been specifically identified for surveillance purposes. In those instances, 'Pontiac' would conduct the surveillance.

This operation seldom produced leads which could be used by the US CIC, and was used primarily as a "traffic control" tool, conducted as a courtesy for our Okinawan counterparts. Sometimes, the ships' Captains would elect to remain in international water, and would be gone by the break of dawn to their next destination. If they moved North, with identified 'undesirables' on board, we would alert our Japan offices. If they moved southerly, we would likewise notify the respective Taiwan or Philippine detachment. If they required only refueling, they were allowed to come into port during daylight hours, refuel and then were escorted back into International Waters to continue on their way.

It was during one of these routine traffic control initiatives that I first came across the name of Ivan Romanyev. Of particular intrigue to me was that he was listed as dual – US/Russian - citizen. After seeing and observing Romanyev's name on a particular manifest four months in a row, I typed up a memo request for operational interest, passed it through my D/O, and then hand-carried it to the CIC Operations Officer, Mr. Howard Lucier. He endorsed my request, and asked for additional information from the 'other agency', for operational reasons. Two weeks later, I was called to their office, where I was given a short briefing, was allowed to peruse his dossier and they gave me temporary Operational Interest in Ivan Romanyev.

The dossier was primarily regarding Ivan's father, Sergei; however, it also contained ample information on Ivan to initiate a separate dossier on him and his activities.

Ivan Romanyev was born in San Francisco California of Russian Diplomat parents, in August 1941. His father, Sergei, was assigned to the Consular section in San Francisco, and there Ivan remained with his family through the period of WWII. Ivan had returned with his parents to Vladivostok in 1948, where his father was designated the head of immigration affairs at that rapidly expanding port city. For eight years, the senior Romanyev traveled between Moscow and Vladivostok, maintaining offices in both cities. Almost without exception, in Moscow, Sergei's office was located in the first floor basement of the famed Gorkiy Street address, which officed SMERSH, the Counterintelligence School. In 1956, Ivan returned with his parents to the US (Washington D.C.) where his father, Sergei had been given the title of Assistant Deputy Consul General.

Excerpts from FBI reports attached to the Romanyev dossier indicated that his father had been suspected of conducting espionage or low-level subversion activities while assigned to both San Francisco and Washington; but surveillance of his activities had turned up nothing substantial. The senior Romanyev's name had surfaced more than a few times over the years, as he was active in attaché operations and often identified at embassy functions.

The dossier contained surveillance photographs of young Ivan in San Francisco with his mother and father, the private school he had attended on Leavenworth Street halfway up San Francisco's Nob Hill, the Romanyev family picnicking in Golden Gate Park, visiting the Golden Gate Bridge, Fort Funston and the beaches along the Presidio and up into Marin County. Just as I was beginning to wonder why Mr. Romanyev, the primary surveillance target, was not in all of those photos, I found a note from the surveillance team stating that Mr. Romanyev apparently had a knack for eluding surveillance for periods of 1 to 4 hours at a time. He could slip away unnoticed, and apparently return at will or simply show up at his rented flat in the Union district, and was Very near the Presidio, and convenient to the Soviet Mission. To me, I felt these incidents to be excellent examples of Sergei using his family as a decoy.

From 1948 to 1956, few photos existed of the Romanyev family in Russia; the exception being that there were photos in the dossier of the Romanyevs attached to Christmas cards. The cards had been mailed from a Mr. Ilya Svesdenkov in Vladivostok Russia, to the cover name of a Senior FBI agent, at a PO Box address in Chicago.

This indicated that the FBI, or the other agency had maintained at least limited coverage of the Romanyevs while they were back in their homeland.

The next document was a translated copy of the special instructions for Sergei Romanyev to return to the US. His wife and teen-aged son Ivan were to return with him, and arrangements had been made through the embassy for Ivan to attend High School in Washington. Attached to the translation were notes and directions from a local FBI office, indicating that the project would be reinstated, and close surveillance would be reinitiated when Mr. Romanyev and family arrived at the airport.

Photos of Ivan now depicted a more recognizable, matured young man, who could pass for an American High School or College student on any street in the US. As I read, I learned that apparently, Ivan finished his last years of High School in Washington, DC, and then struck out on his own. At age 18, Ivan became eligible to change his citizenship to that of a US person. In the meantime, he could travel freely, find employment at will, and an FBI informant had logically opined that Ivan, as a dual citizen, would migrate his parents to the US when the senior Romanyev retired. (Apparently that was not his plan). When Ivan returned to his childhood stomping grounds of San Francisco in September, at age 19, he enrolled in San Francisco State University, to major in journalism; he still had not selected his citizenship.

As I read, I wondered if our paths had crossed during those periods we were both in San Francisco, and found myself going back to look at his photographs again. No lights lit up.

On his application for college, Ivan's stated goals were to become a foreign correspondent and journalist. Languages listed with fluency were: Russian, native; English, native; and Chinese, fluent. It was noted that during the period Mr. Romanyev had been stationed in Vladivostok, Ivan had studied Chinese Mandarin both at the Foreign Language School in Leningrad, and when he traveled to China to hone his Chinese language for one year at a school in Ch'ing-dao, Shan-dung Province China. Hobbies included hunting, boating, fishing, tennis and chess.

Also included in the dossier were fingerprints of all 10 fingers, taken from a wine bottle and a drinking glass, and a recording of an interview administered to Ivan at the University in San Francisco. I popped the tape into the provided recorder and listened. I was absolutely amazed at his English. There was no hint of any accent whatsoever. The diction, grammar, pronunciation, enunciation and delivery were all absolutely perfect.

Ivan had purchased a turquoise and beige, 1959 Ford Convertible. Photos of the car included in the dossier depicted the placement of technical equipment designed to track and record his travels and conversations. A listening device with a range of two miles was placed under the dash, and behind the glove compartment, completely out of sight.

The device could be conveniently removed or replaced within seconds, requiring minimal access to the vehicle. This was accomplished regularly by a service garage located on Lombard Street in San Francisco. The garage held a contract with the Soviet mission to regularly service the personal and diplomatic vehicles for members of the Russian diplomatic community.

Audio samples of conversations between Ivan and his few classmate friends were not good, as almost without exception he would put the convertible top down when he was with his friends, and interference from wind and traffic made the tapes nearly inaudible. FBI tech support offices had attempted to remove distortion from the tapes, but even those considered barely audible turned out to be of no interest to FBI investigators.

The last documents were a packet of chronologically filed papers and photos documenting Ivan's weekend trips, south from San Francisco, approximately 130 miles to the Monterey Peninsula and the Big

Sur area. Accordingly, Ivan traveled approximately 275 miles on every other weekend, gassing up at the same stations, and residing at the same motel in Seaside. He traveled alone, walked alone on the beaches near Monterey, visited an old classmate friend in Carmel, and returned to San Francisco. The classmate was the son of a Russian immigrant who taught the Russian language at the Monterey Institute of Foreign Studies in Monterey. To the FBI's knowledge, Ivan never traveled with any female companion.

On one notable occasion however, in preparation for a long, July 4th weekend, Ivan varied from that routine. After making several phone calls to Washington to speak with his father and arrange some time together, Ivan made the same trip, breaking slightly from his habit by driving to Monterey before gassing up and by staying at the Presidio Park Hotel in downtown Monterey rather than the usual cheaper motel along the strip between Fort Ord and Seaside. The elder Romanyev flew into San Francisco, where he had reserved a rental car to drive to Monterey. As though he knew the car would be bugged (and it was), upon arrival at the hotel, Romanyev left his rental car parked at the hotel, and had Ivan drive him to a nearby HERTZ dealer, where he rented a third car which they used for the duration of their stay. Audio surveillance while they drove together was rendered virtually useless.

Every morning when they departed the hotel, the senior Romanyev would remove the HERTZ rental from the lighted parking slot just beneath their room window; Ivan would move his father's first rental into that same parking place to make sure the slot was available when they returned in the evening. On Friday, Saturday and Sunday evenings, they returned to the hotel late. When parking their rental under their room window, they would look over their respective cars, taking a little extra time to insure they'd not been scratched, damaged or tampered with. Although their room had also been wiretapped, their conversations, generally in the Russian language, turned out to be of no interest to the FBI. Since they had almost always eaten at fast food stops on the road, and occasionally at the Royal Cone Fish & Chips in Carmel, they did not take any meals or drink at any of the hotel facilities. All recorded conversations were considered to be of a non-operational nature. They always turned the room sound to a local, radio music station as soon as they walked into the room, and the music would remain on until they departed the next morning. Leaving the sound on continually would deplete the tape of the voice-activated recorder within minutes. The security precautions they took made them appear even more suspicious to the FBI.

On the morning of July 4, the surveillance teams had one 20-minute streak of luck when Ivan drove his own car for a short trip to a nearby *Sambo's* Restaurant. On this single occasion, from the listening device planted in Ivan's car, a clear transmission was overheard as Sergei broke the news that he had been diagnosed with lung cancer. A spot had been located on his right lung, and a biopsy had revealed the malignancy.

He received Ivan's promise of confidentiality, and told Ivan not to be concerned, as the biopsy had removed the entire lump, and no immediate treatment was planned. He promised to do his best to quit smoking and to change his diet in accodance with the Oncologist's guidelines. Sergei promised to keep on top of the situation.

During those few minutes, the elder Romanyev also told Ivan how proud he would be if Ivan were to follow in his footsteps and enter the Diplomatic Corps if he were so inclined. The short discussion was more of an encouragement to do well than an effort to persuade Ivan to take up the career of espionage.

In the Agent's notes, this was thought to be of importance because Ivan had always seemed to admire his father, and this quick discussion was our first indication that Ivan may consider a different career path. This was the only recording of value throughout the entire surveillance period.

As I looked over the surveillance reports and photographs, I was convinced I could have done a better job had I been tasked with the surveillance portion of that operation. For one thing, I would have anticipated a degree of counter-surveillance activity, and in particular, I would have permanently parked automobiles beneath the single window of the Romanyev's room to prevent them from parking in such close proximity; and would have rotated my surveillance cars regularly while they were driving elsewhere. After all, it was obvious the FBI knew which room the Romanyevs were to be using, because they had already arranged eavesdropping activity within that room. But, I decided, hindsight is 20/20.

Following day 5 of the 4th of July meeting, Ivan returned to San Francisco and abruptly made arrangements to suspend his course of studies. His school advisor, a paid FBI informant tried to talk Ivan into remaining for at least two full years, explaining that he had an excellent background, and with his 4.0 average, could look forward to an even more exciting career. Ivan however informed his advisor that he wanted to get away from the routine of studying for awhile, and would make every attempt to come back to college once he had "seen some of the world".

I glanced at my watch. I'd been reading for over two hours. It seemed like 20 minutes.

As I continued to pore over the dossier, reports indicated that Ivan had applied for work as an Able-Bodied Seaman (ABS) with several shipping lines, and after passing the exam as a radio operator, contracted with a San Francisco-based, free-lance company (Hi-Seas Shipping and Transportation), who could sub-contract their employees with other shipping companies at will. This seemed to be ideal for Ivan, who preferred Liberian Tankers to regular cargo ships. Ivan was employed full-time over the next few years. As I glanced through his travel documents, I recognized the ports he consistently visited. Most were of strategic importance to the US, and at locations where US Forces were stationed. Now, possibly as a US person, he would be allowed ashore at any of those ports, without question. A pattern was emerging.

Ivan corresponded with his father regularly while employed at Hi

Seas, sending occasional photos, documenting his travels. Sergei's mail was regularly monitored.

As I neared the end of these pages of the dossier, I was surprised to notice a document dated just 15 days earlier regarding his visits to Okinawa. Attached to the 1-page cover-document from the 'other agency' was a copy of the memo from the CIC; and at the very bottom of that memo was the signature block: 'Special Agent D. Bradshaw'. *'Wow, that's me... Finally!'*

I returned to my office and talked with Dan and Rad. They Listened to every word, and found my theories regarding Ivan to be fascinating. I believed without a doubt that Ivan was building his background, and would eventually be involved in the same subversive activities for which his father remained under suspicion.

The next step would be to make a list of ports that Ivan was visiting regularly in order to establish himself as a 'routine visitor'. Requests were sent to the various embassy immigration offices to compile this information. Such requests are initiated through files checks conducted by our counterintelligence agents, and require the cooperation of host country immigration offices in order to obtain the information. Care was taken to include Ivan's name on lists of 15-20 known, target country crew members' names in order that we not arouse any suspicion by singling out or identifying our specific target.

Over the next two to three months, responses began coming in, and our office was able to compile a comprehensive list of most of Ivan's movements. We were also able to alert our local Air Force (OSI), The Office of Naval Investigations, and 'other agency' offices for assistance, to arrange surveillance of Ivan on occasion. Over the next year, Ivan continued his travels, but to the best of our knowledge, he never involved himself in any espionage activity while working aboard ship. We were convinced that he was acting according to instructions to establish an innocuous cover. He remained listed as a 'dual citizen'.

In the meantime, I was also kept extremely busy with normal counter-intelligence duties on Okinawa, and tracking Ivan's movements became more of a routine, but extremely interesting pastime.

In late November, to my dismay, I received instructions for a permanent change of station. I was to return to language school (now re-designated the Defense Language Institute (DLI)), to study the Vietnamese language. The thought of returning to Monterey was to my likening, but I soon discovered that a special school had been set up at Biggs Army Airfield in El Paso Texas, specifically for the training of military students destined for Viet Nam. Another 47 weeks of foreign language training was now in store. After some thought, I attempted to contact Major Fletcher, hoping that with his support I could at least temporarily avoid the inevitable Viet Nam assignment. My letter to now Lieutenant Colonel Fletcher was forwarded to a small advisory unit in Viet Nam which was involved in counterpart activities in Saigon. His response was formal, and he stated clearly that he was no longer in position to influence, postpone or change the desires of the United States Army. Since Lieutenant Colonel Fletcher himself was serving in Vietnam, I was not surprised. My disappointment faded as I decided to face the reassignment and hope for the best.

As I bade farewell to my friends in Okinawa, Dan and Rad both informed me that they had submitted their retirement papers. The 'Ivan project', Johnston explained would continue, and 'the other agency' had decided to reassume operational interest, based on our input. That meant they would take it back under their control. They had promised that they would submit updates at the request of CIC, as long as the project remained active. They were quick to point out though that due to inactivity on the part of Ivan, it was not likely they would remain involved full time in his surveillance. I complained that this is just what Ivan would want – to be left alone. Dan and Rad both agreed, and the three of us further agreed that for the time being, the trend of counter-espionage focus would probably be on Viet Nam. That, they explained was why they were both retiring.

Ivan, our paths will cross again.

CHAPTER 8.
DEFENSE LANGUAGE SCHOOL

Enter Robert (Bop) Cooney and DLISC

I had made up my mind that I would do my best to excel at language school. After all, if I didn't apply myself, I could fail and go directly to Viet Nam. I could think of nothing worse than going into a war zone prematurely and without proper language proficiency. I requested no leave in route to school, and arrived in El Paso in mid January 1967. I processed in through the DLI Support Command (DLISC) at Biggs Army Air Field. A few classes were now in session, but my class would not begin for another ten days due to an unexpected shortage of instructors following Christmas break. All students would be in uniform. On reporting in, I met with the Company Commander and First Sergeant, who advised I take the 10 days to find an apartment or small house to rent, as on-base housing was not available for single Senior NCOs at Biggs Field... unless I desired to live in the barracks. I didn't.) I was told that nobody had yet failed the Vietnamese Language course.

Over that weekend, I located a small, 2-bedroom, partially furnished duplex on Dyer Street, and signed a one-year lease for the unit. Having transferred the utilities to my name beginning on the date of the lease, I called the Base Transportation Office on Fort Bliss to inform them of the delivery address for my hold baggage from Okinawa. They informed that the baggage had arrived and could be delivered next Friday morning. That was great!

DONALD BRADSHAW

Late Monday afternoon as I returned from shopping for the basic staples required to sustain my tired body, I encountered and introduced myself to my new neighbor. Bob Cooney was an Army Sergeant, studying Vietnamese at Biggs Field who had rented the other half of my duplex three months earlier. As we talked, it seemed that Bob didn't have much interest in my past or background, which was fine with me. He was however interested in trying to impress me immediately with his own military experiences. He had joined the army to fight "commune-ism". (His pronunciation).

Without any hesitation, Bob invited me in for a beer. I accepted, because it's always good to know a little about your neighbors. I took the opportunity to look around just a little inside. Bob's 'hooch' was exactly as I had pictured it......total unadulterated disorder and confusion. Suffice it to say; sometimes 'to know a little' is too much, already.

I was still drinking from my first bottle when he opened his fourth, and the more he drank, the faster he drank. He talked about himself for 45 minutes, consuming approximately one beer every 10 minutes. Bob had been married twice – both times to "floozies", whom he described as "oxygen thieves", who couldn't live with his Army life and personal habits. They just "didn't understand" him.

He amazed me with his stated ease of studying Asian languages, and appeared anxious to make friends. Bob was one class ahead of me. He was proud, and bragged constantly of his military occupation specialty, which was that of an Intelligence Analyst. He consistently shocked me with the details of his classified duties. Not one day passed without Bob quoting his favorite philosophical phrase: "If you can't dazzle 'em with details, then baffle 'em with bullshit." I thought it better to keep my personal views to myself, choosing only to say I was also in the army, and had just returned from Okinawa.

I had heard that Juarez, Mexico was the world's shopping center; the haven of Satan; the eternal well of tequila and beer. Those titles are all a soldier needs to hear in order to develop at least a limited

78

interest. I decided to spend Thursday discovering the bargains and entertainment of that town.

Although I tried to sneak out of the duplex before Bob woke up, as soon as I started my car he was knocking on the passenger window, asking "Where ya headin?".

I told him I wanted to cruise through Juarez just one time to see what it was like. Inviting himself to go along, he opened the door and jumped in, saying, "I thought you'd never ask." It was obvious that he was awake only because he'd not gone to sleep.

On our way to the border, we decided it better to park on the US side. My car was a 1964 Plymouth Valiant convertible, and the thought of having to replace the top after a day in Juarez was not to my likening. When we walked though the checkpoint into Juarez, I was not at all surprised to see that the 'ladies of the evening' had already claimed their posts, and would call out, beckoning as Americans passed through the gate. At 0930 hours, they had become the 'ladies of the morning after'.

Shopping was fun, bargaining for unneeded souvenirs. Excellent food and drink was just a little too available. We had no more than consumed healthy breakfasts, when Bob announced that it was time for a beer. At his insistence, we walked into a small lean-to stall where he ordered two *Carta Blanca* beers. During the thirty minute visit Bob managed to drink three while I sipped on one. I complained that it was too bad I had to drive. We left the first stall to walk around the city of Juarez, and Bob insisted on taking up conversation with every hooker on the street who would glance in his direction. That was almost all of them.

Bob had an approach which I found very amusing: He would walk directly up to any girl who had spoken to him and say something like "Weren't you in my freshman class at the University of Idaho?" They would look at him, puzzled by the question, pause, and then answer, saying something like: "Yah, tha wass me…., Wats your name?" He

79

would usually answer truthfully that his name was Bob, and the girl would always reply "Hey 'Bop', you wanna go my room?" And the ensuing conversation would go on for five minutes.

I assumed "Bop" was broke, because he refused to partake of their offerings, but he did enjoy the quick, teasing conversations. As for me – it was easy to see that Juarez was not the world's cleanest city, nor could it by any means be considered free of sexually transmitted disease. I am not a fan of Russian roulette.

We shopped and bargained throughout the afternoon, pausing occasionally for a sip or two of the requisite refreshment - beer for Bob, and lemonade for the driver. After an evening meal at *Martino's Restaurant*, where Bob was finally able to drink something other than beer, we spent 4 minutes in a standing-room-only strip bar, before returning to El Paso and to our 'hooch'. Enroute, I gassed up at a *Quick Stop*, and Bob purchased another case of beer to get him through the weekend. I excused myself from Friday beer activities, telling Bob that I had to wait for the delivery of my hold baggage the next day. He seemed to understand the concept, but didn't know what drinking had to do with receiving hold baggage. He promised me that he would be over to spend some time on the weekend helping me prepare for the first day in class. Wow... Lucky me!

I spent Friday unpacking my hold baggage, and as promised, there was no sign of Bob for the entire day. Everything had come through without a scratch. I had time in the afternoon to go to Headquarters Company and sign for my textbooks in advance. Checking my mailbox, I was happy to see that the package I had mailed by surface from Okinawa had also arrived. In the car I opened it and found my prized gifts from Ed Nieman to be intact.

As promised, at 1000 hours Saturday morning, Bob showed up with what remained of his case of beer. Try as I would, I couldn't convince Bob to forego the Saturday binge; but he promised to just hang around, watch TV, and stay out of my way. He did. I learned quickly that as long as he had his beer, my hamburgers, snacks and toilet to use, he could entertain himself alone in my living room. I sat in my very small dining area and read the class introduction to the Vietnamese Language. Sometime after midnight I helped an unsteady Bob back to his duplex for the night.

On Sunday, I readied myself for Sunday service in line with my promise to Mom. As I was about to walk out the door, I was interrupted by a loud knock. I opened the door to find Bob, dressed in a three-piece suit. His appearance was so neat I hardly recognized him. I was shocked beyond speech. He said "We goin' to the chapel?"

Throughout the services, I was impressed to see Bob participate in singing hymns and during the sermon, interjecting a timely and occasional "A-men!" On the way back to the hooch, Bob never mentioned beer or Juarez. I thought *"He must have gone totally insane!"* When we arrived, he excused himself and said he'd be right back. *I knew it, now's when he reintroduces the beer.*

To my delight however, Bob returned in 2 minutes. He had shed his coat and vest and had loosened his tie. He was carrying some well-used language books, and a notebook on which he had written the title "MUST KNOWS".

As I made room for his books on the dining table, Bob sat, looked at me and said "I don't know if you've ever studied a foreign language or not, but" he went on to say, "I have a fool proof method." Bob went on to explain that he never intended to learn anything more than that which he 'needed or wanted' to say, so he had written a list of phrases, which were designed to get him through the course. He opened his 'Must Knows' notebook to page one, entitled "List of phrases". The title was followed with Bob's list – probably in order of priority, along with their translations in Vietnamese. Page one included:

1. Where's the bar?   2. Beer   3. Toilet?

4. Don't shoot   5. Friend   6. Girl

7. How much (money) 8. Too much 9. I'm an American

10. Russian 11. Polish 12. Japanese

13. A medic; and finally, 14. It hurts here.

Bob had an additional 119 pages of his dictionary in his notebook. He planned on alphabetizing the book at a later date. He felt it important to be able to say "Are you sick?", and in the same phrase group, he could ask "Are you tired," or "are you sad", or "are you hungry?" simply by changing a single word. To the right of this group Bob had written the phrase "Are you horny?", but he explained that he had not yet found a Vietnamese instructor who was willing to provide him with the translation.

"As you can see, Donald", he explained, "As an Intel Analyst, I'm preparin' myself for every contingency."

I could see that! No doubt, Bob had his priorities in order. I told Bob that I had in fact studied a foreign language before, and had used a method somewhat similar to his which I called "study ahead".

"That's it!" He exclaimed, grinning.

Actually, I had lied, and personally could see no resemblance between our two methods.

Looking me in the eye for a moment he then said "You know something Don, you're a smart guy. Now, how about a beer?"

Bob definitely had his priorities in order.

Vietnamese Language Training:

A few days later, the class schedule began, and as the daily routine of the first week unfolded, it was obvious that I was the only student who had reported in early. My classmates arrived over the next three days.

The Army was so busy filling quotas for Vietnamese linguists that class assignments were not designated until enough students showed up for duty – only half of my class had arrived by Wednesday.

Thursday morning the class actually started, and we were introduced to the other 6 students in the class. Coincidentally, an older Warrant Officer, George Moore was initially designated our class leader. I had served with George in a manner of speaking for the first few months I'd spent on Okinawa, as he was working with the CI Detachment Technical Section. Although our contacts had been minimal during that period, it was good to know someone from a previous assignment. George and I became fast friends, and the friendship remains to this day. I had decided to study ahead. The language class was no challenge, and I quickly learned that I did not need to memorize the morning dialogue in advance. If I was aware of the story, I needed only to know the vocabulary in order to bluff my way through the first hour.

Although I remained quite busy trying to maintain my lead, Bob would frequently call on me unannounced after class, carrying a half case of ice-cold beer and announcing that the game was about to start on TV. He didn't need a real excuse to drink, as any game would suffice. Bob often forgot to eat, or perhaps he was already full, or intoxicated. I thought it wiser to retain him as a buddy than to treat him as a remote acquaintance – at least for the time being. More often than not, I would help him stumble back to his apartment after a couple hours of putting up with TV basketball. Whatever the case, there was never any beer left. There were times when I encouraged him to drink, knowing that he would finish his half case, and I would still have time to study after he left. He was a harmless personality, with a seemingly unending repertoire of good jokes.

In class we learned early on that our so-called 'teachers' had little to no experience teaching, and had been selected from among the local, unemployed Vietnamese immigrants for teaching at DLISC. Additionally, I quickly learned that two of our instructors were Chinese Vietnamese, both of whom spoke fluent Mandarin. Occasionally when we were required to write our dialogues on the blackboard as a way of testing our spelling, I would use Chinese characters, just to impress the Chinese teachers. I quickly became the 'teacher's pet", and would quite often find myself giving the English explanation when a student would ask a difficult question of the teacher. None of the teachers would hesitate to refer a student's question to me, and one in particular, Mr. Nguyen, often jokingly referred to me as his 'assistant instructor'.

He loved to say "That's such a simple question, I'll just pass it on to my assistant..." and he would call my name.

Seven months into the course, my good grades became an advantage. The teachers had gone on strike, and planned to stay on strike as long as needed. They were striking for programmed pay raises, longer contracts, and a medical program. I found this despicable. I could not fathom how a group of unqualified teachers could take advantage of such a crucial program, with their demands. I was angry; after all, most of the male teachers were of draft age in Viet Nam, but had managed to migrate to the US. Many of the women were qualified medical staff. American soldiers were dying daily in Viet Nam while these 'teachers' held relatively well-paid positions here at DLISC, and were in a way evading the draft.

We students had been instructed to continue reviewing and studying on our own until the strike was over. One lazy afternoon as I sat poring over my textbooks, I had a brainstorm. The next morning I found myself standing in front of the School Sergeant Major and Commandant with my idea. I simply volunteered the services of those senior students who had maintained a proficiency level in the 90 percent bracket, to teach the language to incoming students. I explained that I had already discussed the idea with many of the senior students, and all had agreed that we could teach four to six hours a day, and still continue with our own studies. I guessed that the Vietnamese instructors would return to work within a month.

The Commandant, an old Army Colonel with a Texas drawl, jumped on the proposal.

"Hot Damn! Why the hell didn't I think of that," he exclaimed. He turned to the Sergeant Major and asked for a list of advanced students. After seeing my GPA, he put me in charge of conducting a few quick interviews, and making selections for temporary language instructors. Most of those I recommended were from my own class. Although I felt Bob would be fun to have as an instructor, I decided not to recommend him for fear of sending a classroom of alcoholics to Vietnam.

The program worked even better than I had anticipated, and the instructors came back to the classroom in three weeks. They had returned to the Civilian Personnel office virtually on their knees, agreeing not only to taking back their jobs, but also to accept the same wage program and privileges they'd had before.

Coincidentally, the officer class to which I was assigned to instruct included a very senior Lieutenant Colonel by the name of Glen Spradling. He recognized me immediately, and proudly told his classmates that I had served under his command seven years earlier. LTC Spradling and I reacquainted ourselves at lunch time that first day, and played our long-awaited game of pool. He won, of course.

Nearing the end of October, one quiet Thursday evening, a solemn Bob knocked on my door. He informed me that he had received his orders, and was being assigned to the Big Red One – The First Infantry Division. He would be leaving the end of the following week. I sincerely believed that Bob, who always seemed to survive under an umbrella of denial, was just now accepting the realization that he was going into a combat situation. He had always seemed alone and without a true friend in the world.

"Come in here", I said. "Sit down. Can I pour you a Rye?"

He accepted the invitation, and I poured him a double on the pebbles. He began to sip. He sat motionless for a moment; then took another sip.

"So," I started, "Are you looking forward to getting this Viet Nam thing over with?"

"Yeah, that I am," he said positively. "That I am." He then changed the subject. "You know Don, you're probably the only friend I have on this side of the earth."

"I find that hard to believe, Bob." I lied.

"No Sir, It's true!" He came back. "From the start, you accepted me for what I am… an alcoholic, a bum, and a loser."

"Aw Bob," I started, pouring myself a drink.

"No, Don, don't interrupt me please. I gotta get this out." He went on. "You never tried to tell me what to do, or to change my ways. You accepted me, and I appreciate that."

Bob went on to describe his life. He was born to an alcoholic father and a drug infested mother. They had lived in government project housing in Chicago until he was 14 years old. A freshman in High School, Bob returned home one afternoon to find his mother shot to death in their living room, and his father lying on the bed with a gun still in his hand, and the top of his head blown off from the suicide.

"What a helluva way to die, and what a helluva way to leave a 14 year-old kid." Bob described his father as physically abusive to both he and his mother.

As a small child, he had dreamed of finishing school and finding a good, steady job or joining the army. He wanted to take his mother out of the slums and provide for her. "Now, I realize that her drug problems would never have allowed that to happen." he sighed.

"As for my two wives, well, the situation wasn't completely their fault." He now admitted. "I was already an alcoholic when I got married the first time. Thank God'" he continued, "I never had any kids."

"You know, Bob," I started. "It's good that you recognize alcohol as a problem. The next step would logically be something like 'AA'".

MEMOIRS OF A COUNTERSPY

Now I was doing exactly what Bob had not wanted: Giving advice.

Bob poured himself another drink over ice that had barely begun to melt. "I can't go to AA now," he complained. "They'd think I was trying to get out of going to Nam. Maybe I can get over this problem while I'm over there." He mulled, "Sometimes booze is hard to come by, you know."

I realized he was only blowing smoke. Perhaps that remark was a little wishful thinking.

We sat for another hour, while Bob held on to the bottle of Rye, and I listened to his life story. I learned that he had quit high school, and at the tender age of 17, had gotten in trouble for attempting to hold up a liquor store in his own neighborhood. His 20-year old comrade in crime had shot and wounded the owner, and had gone to prison for the crime. Due to his age, Bob had been sent to Reform School, and directed by the judge to join the army when he turned 18.

Bob insisted on leaving at 0130, and walked back to his side. He had drained the Rye.

I showered and retired, but was startled awake at 0313 hours. I shall never forget that exact moment. I sat up immediately.

"Was that gunshots?" I asked myself out loud. I reached under my bed to the metal compartment that I had clamped to the bed frame. My old S&W 38 was still inside.

"No," I told myself. "only one gunshot. Call the cops!"

I dialed the number, and the desk answered. I identified myself, and told them I'd just been awakened to the sound of gunshots. "No, a single gunshot," I corrected myself. As I was giving my address, I began to realize that the sound had likely come from Bob's place, next door. I clamped my 38 back into the box, and awaited the police.

It seemed like hours; then at 0324, two police cars pulled up in front of the duplex. A third was parked a half block away, down the street. The police approached my door with their weapons in hand.

Opening the door, I said "I'm the one who called you guys. Probably you should check next door."

Per their instructions, I waited inside while the police entered Bob's unlocked apartment. Within one minute, they were calling for an ambulance, saying they had one apparent suicide in the apartment.

My heart sank.

One of the policemen, along with the two that had parked down the street, came to my apartment. Could I identify him? When had I last seen Bob? Was he alive at that time? What was the nature of our relationship? Did I know of any relatives?

"We were friends," I told them, "fellow students and fellow soldiers."

The noisy ambulance arrived, and Bob was covered, placed on a gurney and rolled inside the vehicle. Curious neighbors and onlookers were beginning to gather. The police informed them that all was taken care of, and they should go back to bed. That's just their polite way of saying "Mind your own business."

Before departing, one of the policemen, whose nameplate read "Crandall", asked me to avail myself Friday afternoon to make a statement. I could. I would.

By 0350 hours, all was quiet. It was too quiet. I felt as though I had to wash my hands, and scrubbed for at least 10 minutes. I lay in bed and kept asking myself "Why?" "If there's really a God then why would he let such a tragedy occur? Had Bob been tried? What had this harmless soul ever done to hurt anyone?"

Unable to sleep, I arose at 0500, and took a long shower. After a very fast-paced morning in class, George Moore approached me asking "What's wrong, Don? Something's bothering you, I just know it."

As I told him of the events of the early morning hours, I began to realize this was my first casualty of the Viet Nam war. I said. "It has really opened my eyes."

After class, accompanied by George, I went to the police station and filled out my statement regarding Bob. Officer Crandall, who had just come back on duty for the evening shift, asked a few more questions, and informed me that Bob's fingerprints were the only marks on his weapon. It had been categorically determined a suicide. He asked me to stop by at Bob's Apartment, and said that the suicide note found early this morning had indicated that his belongings were to be given to me for disposition. His note had indicated that he had no living family or next of kin.

When George and I arrived at my duplex, I noticed two policemen at Bob's apartment. I walked over and introduced myself, and Officer Schmidt asked me to come inside. I was shocked. Bob's duplex was immaculate. He had cleaned, polished, vacuumed, and waxed everything. Except for his bed, there was no mess; and even then, he had covered his head with a large pillow to prevent blood from splattering everywhere. There was not a beer bottle in site.

Schmidt said that the apartment was only partially furnished, and that I was to take care of Bob's belongings. As I walked back through the apartment, I noticed Bob's watch lying on the coffee table. I picked it up and stared at it. *"Strange,"* I thought. *"It's still ticking."*

"I'll only take this." I told them. "Please give everything the landlord does not claim to the Salvation Army. His bank accounts and cash will likely take care of any funeral expenses." I mentioned that Bob would be entitled to his veteran's privileges. "Please keep me posted as to the disposition."

There would be legal documents to sign.

"What about the old Studie?" Schmidt was asking of Bob's old 1954 Studebaker.

"I'll sign the release after I look it over," I answered, "then you guys can take it to the impound lot and dispose of it." One of the police officers informed me that they would be in touch in a few days with an official *Record of Disposition* for legal purposes. I was glad George had decided to come along.

Bob's old watch remains with me. Occasionally I pick it up and give it a few winds. It still runs and keeps good time. I've often wondered why I still cannot forget those days; why I cannot put them to rest. I also wonder - if I threw the watch away, would the memory of Bob somehow disappear? Yet, I could no more throw it away than I could forget someone who considered me to be his only friend; who told me so; and died. The reason for his death, I've decided is no more valid than that of going to war without a valid reason – especially to a useless war. Only he and God know why he died. May he finally rest - in peace.

Bob's bank account was ample to pay for his well deserved funeral, and make a generous donation to the Veteran's Administration.

At the end of the course, I was honored to graduate as Distinguished Graduate, and was also given recognition for organizing the program that brought the Vietnamese instructors back into the classroom. I assured that the rest of the volunteers for this short-lived program also received recognition.

As I walked through the halls of the school one last time, I happened across LTC Spradling. We shook hands and wished each other good luck. He actually embraced me momentarily; then stepped back, clicked his heals and walked away. We were never to meet again.

The relationship between two soldiers, two friends, comrades, in wartime requires no explanation. The term "Comrades in Arms" is self explanatory to anyone who has ever served.

CHAPTER 9:
THE INEVITABLE VIET NAM

Of course, before heading to Viet Nam, I made the requisite trip back to visit Mom and my stepfather. This time, it was more difficult to convince Mom that I would be going to a peaceful location. She wondered why I was even going, since I was no longer in the army; and I explained only that there were many civilian contractors in Viet Nam, and that most were given jobs away from the front lines. It wasn't exactly a lie, just a statement of fact that probably didn't apply to me. My chance of going into a combat position was as good as any other soldier, but there was no need to explain that to my Mom.

I tried to talk of a year later when I'd be reassigned away from the war zone, but Mom's worried face told me she didn't want to be involved in any conversation which included the word "war".

For some reason, Mom seemed to have grown much older the past year or so. Her brown hair had turned to a shade of ash; wrinkles were deepening around her eyes, and across her brow. Her gray eyes were not as clear, nor as blue as I had remembered. My stepfather, probably realizing that I no longer desired to work on the farm, talked more of leaving the farm and moving into town to be near his own aging parents. His Railroad retirement was ample, and the money left from the sale of the farm would carry them into retirement. The world was turning constantly, and it was time for me to move along with it.

The trip back home was quick. I spent most of the time with Mom and my stepfather, but made the final trip to visit my adopted grandparents with the entire family before my departure. Seeing Larry and Loretta shocked me into reality. How they had grown since I last saw them. Aunt Jo was back to teaching elementary school. She looked exactly the same. We talked of foreign languages and culture barriers.

Uncle Everett left me with a piece of advice: "When you go to war, the conditions are not like anywhere else or any other time in your life. You will make friends." He defined 'a comrade' as 'a loyal friend for a lifetime'.

"You'll share life and death with them." he continued, "If you can, keep in touch with them forever, for you share something that's not easy to explain to anyone who has not experienced war. The experience is forever. Make it last as long as you can."

Larry was still in High School, but was anxious to get on with his life. He had a myriad of questions regarding the military. Loretta had blossomed into a beautiful young lady. I couldn't take my eyes from her. She was talking of college in Bellingham and of course of her beau "Lucky", who was just that - lucky. I couldn't help but think that somewhere along the way I'd missed the boat. After all we were cousins only by marriage. Alas, time and fate are not always kind to us. Farewells were extremely difficult this time, and hugs were a necessity.

Before leaving for Vietnam, I out-processed through the Oakland Army Terminal, and while there, I changed my emergency notification procedures form, removing my Mom's name and replacing it with my brother's name and address. I felt that if something were to happen to me, he should be the one to break the news to my Mom, rather than to have her receive a phone call or a visit from a stranger. I called and informed Bob of this decision and he agreed.

Regardless of what unit we had been assigned, we all flew by civilian contractor, commercial aircraft to Tan Son Nhut Air Force Base. It was just before Christmas 1967. We were then transferred to our branch-respective replacement stations for further disposition.

When we arrived at Camp Alpha, we were informed that our final destinations were all being changed. Priorities had been altered in the past few weeks. I glanced around for anyone I might know, but to no avail. It seemed that although we were all 'comrades in arms', we were all perfect strangers. Here we would remain until our new destinations had been decided. We took our turns standing guard and walking our posts, commensurate with our ranks, and then, on day three, I heard a familiar voice behind me.

"Hey soldier, what are you doing here?" It was George Moore – my first familiar face.

George was a veteran of both World War II and Korea, and I felt relieved just to see his face. Our paths had now crossed for the third time in three changes of station. George, who had been destined for the Military Assistance and Advisory Group (MACV) in Saigon, was being diverted to an MI Battalion. I, who had been destined to go to a Military Intelligence Detachment in Cu-chi, was also being diverted. On that very evening, when we attended the call-out, our names were called together, and we learned that we were going to the same team, where we would be assigned with duty as advisors to the Vietnamese Military Security Directorate (MSD), in Saigon. I had hoped of an assignment to MACV, with an opportunity to work in the Phung Hoang (Phoenix) project, as I had been reading about their collection successes for nearly two years. I felt that it was the place to work. As it turned out, the MSD was a much more appropriate assignment, allowing me to operate as a linguist Case Officer.

That last night at Camp Alpha was another eye-opener. At one point, I was listening to radio transmissions from Cu-chi where I had originally been assigned. Apparently, a group of new arrivals bound for Cu-chi had taken fire and was under ambush. Before that night was over, they had lost 80 percent of those new arrivals. Information is food for thought.

There was very little in-processing to do, and the next day, we arrived at the Headquarters of the MI Battalion. Checking in consisted of verification of our overseas replacement qualification records, language training verification, drivers licenses, and in-processing through the army finance center in Saigon. Transportation to our new units was promised in three days, and we would perform usual military duties while waiting. The 'three day' wait stretched into nearly two weeks, as rumors of the offensive increased. Daily reports were increasing, and some were completely ignored regarding the buildup for the 1968 "Tet" offensive.

The office to which George and I were eventually assigned was called the Military Security Directorate, Operational Assistance Team. (MSDOAT). This assignment to MSD would take a little longer than normal. For security reasons, most of the operational personnel assigned to MSD were processed through the 902nd MI at Fort Meade, Maryland. We were assigned a Department of the army Special Roster (DASR) control number. All administrative actions to include special orders, decorations, and disciplinary actions taken and even medical treatment given on behalf of anyone on the DASR, would be accomplished without direct reference to their true name. With the exception of finance records, the 902nd would maintain our personnel records At Fort Meade, Maryland.

Enter, Major Bach Van Ho

Ours was a small office, but our counterpart's office constituted the Headquarters of the Military Security Service (MSS), Viet Nam's equivalent of Military Intelligence/Military Security. At the time of our arrival, Brigadier General Nguyen Ngoc Loan was the Vietnamese Commandant of MSS, and maintained an office at the Directorate. Loan also wore a second hat as the Commanding General of the National Police. Our Commander, Lieutenant Colonel Lewis K (Col K) was Loan's MSD counterpart. As I was considered to be 'quite fluent' among our Vietnamese Linguists, I was assigned to the office of Major Bach Van Ho, the chief of the Collection Bureau of the MSD. Major Ho was responsible for the coordination and control of human sources within the entire MSS system. Ho, who spoke little English, and had never accepted the assignment of any advisor, was a little aloof at first. After our initial meeting and his realization that I had achieved a working level of fluency in his native language, he agreed to have me come aboard. He even set up a separate office for me adjacent to his own, and insisted that I spend at least one-half day every day in the advisor's office - the *'Phong Co-Van'*. I became his runner so to speak, and the carrier between his office and ours. Ho had made it clear he wanted minimum direct contact with US officials.

It was one of Ho's sources who reported in January that the North Vietnamese Army (NVA) had the capacity to deliver 250 lb bombs. While that report was looked at with some doubt and apprehension, it was a frightful upgrade from just three months earlier.

After approximately one month at the new assignment, I had learned of the long-arm reach of the MSD. Major Ho's Vietnamese Case Officers were all members of the MSS who had been trained at the United States Army, Pacific (USARPAC) Intelligence School on Okinawa.

It was against MSD regulations for foreign advisors or counterparts to meet directly with the Human sources of MSD, so I was not allowed to meet personally with Major Ho's sources. Ho was extremely cooperative however and provided me with a list of those sources, along with their placement and access. He asked only for tasking of specific information requirements to incorporate with his own tasking to his sources, and promised to provide the results of their collection efforts to me. Of course the highest priority placed on any requirements at that time pertained to information on the imminence of hostilities such as the "Tet" Offensive, and from the very start, all of my attention and tasking was focused on that particular area of interest. Ho's reports joined the mass reporting efforts of MACV and "other agencies" in Vietnam.

CHAPTER 10:
REENTER - IVAN

Following the Tet offensive/counter-offensive, the sounds of firefights within and around the city of Saigon, and the Chô-Lớn area where I resided became less frequent, and an occasional full night's sleep was no longer impossible. By early April, there was a temporary lull in reporting activities coming from MSD, and I had already begun looking toward my departure from the war zone (260 days to go). Then, on a whim, I retrieved the original source list from Major Ho, and began searching. I was pleased to learn that one of Major Ho's sub sources was a Vietnamese Navy Lieutenant, assigned to the Port Authority in Saigon. I discussed this source with Major Ho, and learned that his source had access to the crewmembers lists for various ships arriving in Saigon. I immediately tasked him for the list covering the past 30 days.

Within two days, Major Ho called me to his office and provided me with the list. I searched the list for Ivan's name and was disappointed when it did not appear. Major Ho did not know who or what I was looking for, and I felt it was not necessary to discuss the project with him; after all, I had relinquished Operational Interest in Ivan when I left Okinawa more than a year earlier. But as I left Ho's office, I asked him for one more additional favor – for the same list going back an additional three months. He agreed, but it would take awhile. After all, with the advent of the war, Saigon was probably the busiest seaport in Asia. As we talked, I refined the list to include only those cargo ships on which I thought Ivan might serve.

Another two weeks passed, while unending reports of another impending offensive were beginning to emerge. I continued my routine duties of tasking, collecting, translating as needed, and reporting. Then one day, Major Ho called me to his office again, and when I arrived he gave me three boxes of files pertaining to the crewmembers of non-military foreign ships, including US Ships which had called on the Port of Saigon over the past six months. I began with the most recent list (1-31 March, 1968). The list had been printed alphabetically, and voila! Ivan's name was easily located about halfway through the R's.

The rest of the week, I sat in my "phong co-van" going over the boxes of lists. I learned that Ivan had also visited Saigon approximately once every six to seven weeks over the past four month period. Occasionally, he changed his ship assignment, and was allowed to remain in Saigon awaiting his reassignment. During each of his visits to Saigon, without exception, Ivan would spend a minimum of five days on shore leave. Immediately I decided this was unusual because in that timeframe, only rarely would any crew member consider taking five consecutive days shore leave in Saigon – the war zone. Most saved their leave time to use at other, more convenient and secure Asian ports of call, such as Naha, Kobe, Yokohama, Pusan, Seoul, or the Philippines. I took my compiled list back to our office to discuss the finding with Col K. Calculating Ivan's last visit at about 5 weeks earlier, I felt an urgency to expedite my actions, in that Ivan could be scheduled to return as early as within a week or two.

The next day was a Sunday, and I talked with Col K at my earliest opportunity. While he was excited at my findings, he was not as enthusiastic as I; and as a matter of fact was initially quite discouraging. He stated first that I had tasked my counterpart for assistance in something unrelated to the current situation in Viet Nam; secondly, there had been no coordination with the 'other agency' involved, who thirdly had probably maintained Operational Interest in the target personality - Ivan.

Because I had been careful not to identify Ivan to my counterpart as a person of interest, Col K agreed to take it to the Agency in the coming days, but was not optimistic about their expected response. He was certain they would not and could not on such short notice, put together a team to follow Ivan's activities while he is in Saigon, and said in a very matter-of-fact tone, "After all, Ivan is probably already a US citizen".

As I left his office, Col K apparently noticed my disappointment. He patted me on the back and said "Donald, you did well!" He smiled, and then added "Never give up that conscientiousness, little buddy."

Col K stood all of only 5 feet 8 inches; but I had already learned early in my career that the little bosses, as tough as they seem, have hearts of gold. He understood my anxiety.

CHAPTER 11:
THE MAY OFFENSIVE (21 APR – 9 MAY 1968) AND "HO'S REVENGE"

LK traveled to the scheduled briefing with me in tow. Although he had a driver, LK preferred driving his personally issued jeep when there were other Detachment Personnel aboard. Enroute, Col K stated that he would brief the "other agency" on what we now called "The Ivan Project", and tell them that I had just recognized the name while in the conduct of my routine duties with MSD.

But when we arrived at the MACV compound, we were met with an unusual degree of hustle. The guards hurriedly checked our identification, checked our appointments, and rushed us into the main building. Inside, people were running through the corridors, darting from office to office with much more urgency than normal, and a sign hanging on the "other agency's" office door indicated "conference in session". We learned that another offensive was imminent, and that all meetings had been canceled unless there was information to be passed that was significant to that particular offensive. The importance of the Ivan Project had just been relegated to the bottom of the list. One of Mr. Colby's assistants met with us for only a few minutes, but the subject of Ivan did not surface. Instead, we discussed tasking of intelligence requirements regarding the May counter-offensive, now underway.

On the way back to MSD, Col K and I discussed tasking for the counterparts, and just as we were turning the corner by the Saigon Zoo, he added that he would still like for me to keep track of Ivan as an additional duty, and keep him informed. He promised to brief the 'other agency' as soon as there was a break. It was an open statement, but I appreciated his attempt to keep me happy.

In the following days, nothing transpired regarding Ivan. But a few weeks later, during a routine team meeting, we were discussing sources and reviewing periodic source evaluation reports. Our headquarters had recently expressed strong interest that my counterpart Major had a new source at the Polish Delegation. The new source was a Vietnamese Army Captain Phan, who had been selected by Major Ho for the special operation within the Polish delegation. Ho had trained his agent extensively in communications to include secret writing the use of microdots, and dispatched him to seek a position, any position at the delegation. Phan did as directed. He was offered, and accepted a low-level position of Janitor.

Once Phan was accepted for his cover position, all debriefing meetings between Phan and Ho were conducted in a clandestine manner. Major Ho arranged for dead drops, cut-outs and courier support for sending and receiving reports and tasking, and to ensure that the Captain's military salary was provided to him regularly.

According to Ho's reports, Phan had detected surveillance of himself to and from his home sporadically during the first few weeks of his employment.

In accordance with MSD regulations, Ho would not allow foreigners to make contact with his field agents, and there were absolutely no exceptions to this rule – there were two primary reasons for Ho's steadfast adherence to this regulation: 1) because Major Ho himself was the senior operating Case Officer for each sub-source, and 2) Ho had expressed very little regard for any foreign involvement. I had no reason to argue these points; after all, Major Ho had always allowed me to read every report when received, and to participate in the preparation of tasking for his agent. Ho also understood that I would brief my Commander on these activities and the results.

While translating and reading Ho's contact and information reports as pertained to this agent, I discovered that Phan's duties called not only for him to clean the delegation's conference room daily, but immediately before and after staff meetings on a regular basis. Phan had established good rapport with the members of the Polish delegation, and after a period of time even found members of the delegation to be likeable and amicable. Phan remained in his place, and felt he was treated better than the average employee.

Per my recommendations, Major Ho decided to put Phan to work collecting, and we provided him with a concealment device. The device, designed to conceal 10, 8.5X11 inch standard pages, was a case in which he could openly carry his identity documents, his lunch, a small thermos, and a book. Phan liked reading novels and had been carrying his book in an old broken lunchbox up to this time.

He began using the concealment device, which was originally designed as a small satchel, as his new lunchbox. Initially, he did not attempt to conceal anything inside. The first few times he entered the compound with the new lunchbox, the guards examined it thoroughly. He observed their inspection, and noted in his reports that they never observed the concealed opening along the inside seam of the case, which allowed access to the pocket wherein he would place documents. Later, as the guards became accustomed to the new item, they would simply open it and glance through the contents. They paid no particular attention to the container itself.

Now was the time to put it to the test.

With his very first successful trip, Phan provided a schedule of meetings to take place in the conference room. It was stamped *'CONFIDENTIAL'*.

Major Ho and I discussed the utilization of a concealed listening device that Phan could place in the conference room and easily service in the conduct of his janitorial duties, and I told him that while our office did not have such a device readily available, I felt sure that the 'Other Agency' could and probably would provide one. Major Ho was extremely hesitant, and stated outright that he had very little respect for the 'Other Agency', and was acutely aware of their 'cowboy' reputation. I assured him that they would not have to be in direct contact with his agent, and would likely be happy to provide the logistic support needed, as they would certainly be on distribution for any information of value obtained through the use of their device.

I had stuck my own neck out for the sake of the operation, and based on those promises, Major Ho agreed that we could approach the 'Other Agency'.

I briefed LK that very day, and then put together a packet of information regarding the source, his placement and access. It was time for another trip to MACV. Another appointment was arranged for the next day.

We arrived at the MACV compound just at lunchtime, and after passing through security were met by one of the 'Other Agency's' deputy officials. As the three of us had lunch, we briefly described the purpose of our visit, and he seemed eager to help. We also learned that a newly appointed Station Chief was a subject matter expert on Polish affairs, and would likely take a personal interest in the operation. After lunch, we followed the Deputy into their conference room, but learned that the new Chief would not be available for the meeting.

Another Agency Case Officer who also held a primary interest in the Saigon Polish Delegation was in attendance at the second meeting. It seemed to me that he wanted to take charge of the meeting. He asked more than just a few questions relative to the operation, and LK and I answered with the maximum truth we felt we were allowed under the circumstances. By the time the meeting was over, they knew of the Captain's placement within the delegation, the extent of his background, training and experience, and we assured they were acutely aware of the MSD regulation prohibiting foreign contact without the explicit approval of Case Officer, Major Ho.

We were shown photographs of the various devices, and tentatively chose the 'trash can' device, which was designed to tightly conceal a voice-activated recording device with a 90 minute tape in its base. This device required only a ¾ inch deep space in the bottom of the false-bottomed container. Two recorders would be furnished with the trash can, and servicing could be accomplished in 10 seconds.

At the last minute, they insisted that Major Ho be brought to their office so he could be trained in the use of the device. Immediately, I took exception to that demand, stating that we could certainly provide the training to Major Ho; adding that Ho was a graduate of the USARPAC Intelligence School in Okinawa, and certainly had the intelligence to grasp the operation of any device they could design. My statement was not completely accepted by the 'other agency' personnel in attendance.

LK signaled for me to relax, and spoke up, saying that Major Ho would likely not want to come to their office for security reasons, but added that we could possibly work something out if they did not trust in our ability to provide the appropriate training to him. LK had always been an excellent off-the-cuff speaker, and his statement was much more tactful than mine. They accepted his clarification, saying they would be in touch as soon as the device arrived.

We left without a listening device, but with the promise that they would request one from "Virginia" and that it should arrive within a few days. On the way back to MSD I apologized to LK for being so blunt. He responded, saying "I understand. We and the 'Other Agency' are supposed to be on the same side, although they are not as cooperative as we would often like." He explained further that the 'Other Agency' actually has the final say, particularly when it comes to the utilization of their technical devices. When I suggested we rely on our own Headquarters' tech services branch, LK was convincingly clear that we did not possess the expertise to build as good a device as the 'other agency' could provide on such short notice. We decided to wait and see.

Early on Monday morning about two weeks after the meeting, Major Ho called me to his office. I could tell by his tone that something had gone drastically wrong. As soon as I walked into Ho's office he said to me "My Captain no longer works at the Polish Delegation." His voice was stern; his expression cold and angry.

"Why, what happened?" I was shocked.

"Sit down, please", he asked. I sat.

He told me that very late Friday night this past weekend, Phan had contacted him, using their previously established emergency contact procedures. Because of the urgency and security procedures required of such an unusual meeting, they were not able to meet until Saturday evening. When they met, Phan explained that late Friday afternoon, an American, identifying himself as a member of "another intelligence agency", came to his residence uninvited. Phan had immediately ushered his wife and two children into a back room while the Vietnamese-speaking American stated that he was aware of the Captain's activities with the Polish Delegation, and that he was there to offer him the technical device and training he needed. The American further informed Phan that he could be his intermediate Case Officer for any future activities involving the Polish Delegation; explaining that by doing so, they could eliminate the middle man and that reporting of information would be instantaneous. Phan said that he initially disavowed any knowledge of what the American was discussing, but when the American used Major Ho's name as his "point of contact", Phan told him he would have to speak with Major Ho first and could not make such decisions on his own. He dismissed the American who scribbled a telephone number on a piece of paper. The American then gave his name as "Mr. Adams".

Major Ho handed me the piece of paper.

Ho explained that Phan was very upset, and understandably worried about the security and safety of his family, who were at his residence when the American arrived. Phan was sure his family members had not overheard the conversation. Phan wondered if the American was Major Ho's counterpart (me), and Major Ho assured him that it was not the case.

I told Major Ho that LK and I were not aware of any such person or any such activity on behalf of the 'Other Agency" regarding Phan. Per Major Ho's request, we had not provided Phan's true name to the 'Other Agency' during our initial contact with them regarding the recording device. We further did not know, nor had we provided Phan's address or whereabouts to the 'Other Agency' when we had met with them two weeks earlier.

Although, I can now admit that it would not have been difficult to ascertain his identity and location with the placement and access information we had provided them. It was unacceptable that they would make such an unprofessional contact with this agent, as they would have to be aware of the danger they had bestowed on him and his family by virtue of such a reckless act.

By the time I returned to LK's office, it was about 0930. He was in a scheduled meeting with some of the other members of the detachment. I poked my head in saying "This is quite urgent, Colonel". He dismissed the others in less than two minutes. I entered, and asked if he'd heard anything from the 'Other Office' over the weekend. He had not. LK gestured for me to sit, and I did. I then told him of my meeting with Ho. As the story unfolded, I could see LK's expression change and his face turn beet red. The little boss was livid.

LK picked up the phone and called our headquarters. Over that insecure line, he made every attempt to be cautious in his conversation with the Battalion Commander, and eventually asked for a meeting at the Commander's earliest opportunity. The meeting was arranged for the moment LK (and I) could arrive.

I called Major Ho and informed him of the meeting. He of course refused my invitation to attend the meeting at Battalion Headquarters, but when I told him that we would be meeting with the "Other Agency" very soon, he immediately insisted he be given the opportunity to address the Chief and the so-called "Case Officer" who had met with his Captain. He stated he would be ready first thing the next day. He hung up.

LK and I met with the Commander in less than one hour, and after explaining our dilemma, our commander immediately called the "Other Agency" and arranged our meeting. Although we invited him to join us, the commander insisted LK and I take care of the meeting ourselves, reminding us to use the utmost courtesy in addressing the issue at hand, and advising that we coach Major Ho to try his best to be cooperative. We tried.

The next morning at 0730, LK and I picked up Major Ho, and departed for MACV. LK insisted I drive, saying he was too angry to make the effort to be a courteous driver. Enroute, he apologized profusely to Major Ho who sat quietly in the passenger seat. After passing through routine security at the compound, with Major Ho presenting his credentials, we were taken to a rear entrance near the "Other Agency's" office, where we were issued special-entry badges. We sat alone in the conference room for about 3 minutes awaiting the arrival of the Deputy and the Case Officer.

Finally, Major Ho spoke. "When they come in, may I speak first?"

(I must admit I was surprised at Ho's English. It was completely understandable.)

LK responded, saying "Of course you may, Sir! If you don't mind, I'll introduce you first thing."

I started to translate, but Major Ho put up his hand, saying "I understand."

As they entered the room, the three of us stood. When introductions were made, the Deputy introduced the stranger as "Case Officer Adams". As Major Ho was introduced, he did not shake hands with them. When prompted by LK, he simply walked to the small podium at the front of the room, opened the manila folder he was carrying and began:

"Good Morning," he read. "I am Major Bach Van Ho. I am Chief of the Collection Bureau for all of the MSD. We are the Headquarters for the MSS, completely. That means we are in charge of all military security collection in all of Vietnam."

He continued. "First, I wish to tell you about my source, the army Captain who *was* employed at the Polish Delegation"...

At this point, Ho paused and I noticed that the word "was" had caught the attention of both the Deputy and of Mr. Adams. Their eyebrows raised in anticipation as Major Ho continued.

"On last Saturday I relieved him of those duties, and have sent him to the front lines where he will become a regular army officer, and will not have to worry about the safety and security of his family. I did it for two reasons. One, because of your agent's illegal contact with him last Friday night, and two, because I am his commander, I have that authority. Thank You. That is all." Major Ho calmly closed the manila folder containing his one-page speech, and walked toward the door. Adams' face was turning red.

"Wait!" the Deputy called out, "We need to talk!"

Ho stopped and turned, facing both Adams and the Deputy and said firmly "No, we do not." Then he calmly added "I have said all that must be said. This is my country."

As Major Ho walked through the door, I immediately arose and joined him in the corridor. I knew LK could handle the rest of the meeting. Major Ho and I exited the building, giving our passes to the guard on the way to our jeep. As we reached the jeep, I could wait no longer. I shook his hand enthusiastically, congratulating the good Major on his 'wonderful speech'. He smiled and said in Vietnamese, "You see, that's why I just don't like these people." Within just a few minutes LK came running to the jeep. He apologized to Major Ho for keeping him waiting, and repeated my congratulations for a good speech.

On the way back to the office, the three of us stopped for a *"33"* beer - with ice. We didn't say much, our smiles were enough.

Back at the office, LK and I discussed the violations:

They had made direct contact with Major Ho's confidential source. Since they were fully aware of the MSD's restrictions against such uncoordinated foreign contacts they were acting against existing bilateral and protocol policies.

They had endangered the life not only of a counterpart agency's source, but also that of his wife and children.

They had caused the premature termination of an agent with highly desirable placement and access within a target facility.

They had caused a riff between a counterpart agency and another US agency by virtue of this one single, careless, unwarranted and unprofessional contact.

They were without question, acting amateurish and unethical.

The list continued, but LK and I agreed that somewhere along the line, this problem evolved when someone at the 'Other Agency' decided that they should own this source, regardless of local protocol and restrictions. Unfortunately much of this type animosity still exists among the agencies.

I believe these short conversations were the first and last time LK and Major Ho talked. LK departed the detachment later that month for his normal rotation back to the US, and was replaced by LTC Michael Smith. MS was the precise opposite of LK.

Major Ho was legally married to two wives, and had fathered a total of 23 children. He was a rare Catholic. He maintained a home at the MSD compound, where one of his wives resided with about one-half of his children, while the other wife resided in his permanent home near the Phu-Tho Racetrack on the outskirts of Saigon. The wives were best friends, and visited each other's homes regularly. They seemed to mix their children at will.

Throughout the remaining months of that tour in Viet Nam, Major Ho continued to cooperate with the US counterparts of our team on a regular basis. I departed Vietnam heading for a follow-on MI assignment to Fort Meade, Maryland, in December 1968. My plan was to travel directly to my new assignment and return home on leave during the spring and pick up my little Valiant convertible to drive back across the US. However, during in-processing at the new unit in Maryland, I was filling out the paperwork to have my household goods brought to Fort Meade when I learned that the Department of the army had sent out a bulletin requesting volunteers to return to Viet Nam. The message offered choice of assignment to those with a demonstrated fluency in the language. I immediately requested reassignment back to Vietnam, was granted that request, and returned in late January 1969, to serve back to back tours – this time, under the command of COL Fletcher of Ft Holabird fame. My belongings would remain in storage.

On arrival, back in Vietnam, with Colonel Fletcher's permission, I took a 10-day leave to revisit with the old counterparts at MSD and a few remaining friends from the previous year. During that short period, I was able to visit with Major Ho and thank him for his cooperation during my first tour. Ho had fulfilled his promise to cooperate after my departure, but had no plans to accept another Co Van. I knew then that although he respected our team, the confrontation with the "Other Agency" had left him with a sour taste for Americans.

During that first 10-day leave, I discovered that most of my American acquaintances from the old detachment had rotated back to the US. Other Vietnamese contacts were busy doing their best to control their personal situations within the parameters allowed by war. I returned to my new unit set about getting involved in the counterinsurgency mission in my new area of operations.

Within that first month of 1969, while accompanying my source on a cordon search, the village to which we had traveled was suddenly under attack. We were not prepared for "Charlie" – at least not during the daylight hours. We took cover in the nearest available hut. We called in air strikes, and Charlie retreated into the surrounding jungle. Before he bid us farewell though, Charlie set fire to all the small huts within our perimeter. In addition to being quite severely burned over a good portion of my body, I took seven pieces of shrapnel in my legs, up to the level of my crotch. (Much too close).

Several of my comrades were also wounded in the same operation. Although the wait for evacuation seemed to last forever, I later learned that choppers arrived to evacuate the wounded within 20 minutes. We were flown to a field hospital, where I was accompanied by burn specialist SP4 Thomas Jones, and evacuated to Japan, and to a small burn unit established at the Sagami-Ono Hospital, not far from Yokota Air Force Base. The burn unit had been set up to care for the Viet Nam evacuee overflow from the Yokota AFB and Yokosuka Naval base hospitals. I never forgot Specialist Jones.

Footnote: Much later, I learned through Ms. Nguyen Thi Loan, a Vietnamese teacher From Texas whose family resided at the Saigon Radio Station complex, across the street from the old MSD office, that Major Ho and the members of both his families were assassinated during the 1975 Communist takeover of Saigon.

At that time, I never dreamed I would some day return to Japan to work as a Case Officer, and that the area around Sagami Ono would become as familiar as the back of my hand.

As my condition was downgraded from 'critical to 'serious' I was further evacuated from Sagami Ono Hospital to a temporary burn unit at Fort Ord California. From there, I was once again moved to the burn center in Ft Sam Houston, Texas. During the initial interview, I requested again that only my brother be contacted for purposes of family notification. Mom need not be bothered. After 90 days of healing, grafting, re-healing, and convalescence, I found myself on my way back to Vietnam – to complete my tour.

In the interim, I went home to see Mom. She had heard from Bob that I was back in the US, and was in Texas. I told her that I had gone to Texas for business, and quickly changed the subject. It didn't take long for her to become suspicious though, as within the first few days, she caught me coming from the bathroom wearing a towel. Immediately she began to cross examine me about the semi-fresh scars on my legs, and never fully accepted my explanation that I had gotten a few scratches in a minor car accident. The next day, I found her going through my medical records which I was hand-carrying to my next station. She had read the evacuation orders describing my condition as 'Critical', then later as 'Serious', and finally as 'Stable and fit for duty'. Mom was not angry, but when she asked why she was not notified, I told her that it was never that serious, and managed to change the subject. While she never completely forgave me for that little white lie, she also never raised the subject again. I processed again thru the temporary facility at Sagami Ono Japan, and after 72 hours, found myself bound for Tan Son Nhut Air Force Base in Saigon Viet Nam.

CHAPTER 12.
"NUGENT"

It was during the remaining few months of this short tour at this remote detachment that I became acquainted with "Nugent".

The Vietnamese surname "Nguyen", is the English equivalent of Smith or Johnson, in that it is probably the most popular and common surname in the language.

Throughout history, English-speaking foreigners have adapted to foreign - and particularly Asian - words in their own way. For example, The Chinese term "yang-guei (dz), pronounced 'yang-gway dz' which means 'foreign devil', long ago became "Yankee". Foreigners not familiar with the intricacies of any language, will always come up with a new name or phrase; thus 'don't touch my mustache' became the American-GI contrived substitute for the Japanese "Doi-tashi-imashite" or 'you're very welcome.' The GI slang word "dinky-dow" was simply a replacement term for the Vietnamese 'Dien-kai-dao' for 'crazy', and so on.

Nguyen, when pronounced properly begins the n-g sound in the word 'singer', followed by the long vowel 'ū' and 'yen' sounds.... Ng + ū + yen; and as simple as that may seem to be, it will always be pronounced "Nugent" by many an American G.I.

"Nugent" came into our camp and hearts following a mid-1969 counter-offensive. About to collapse, he was hobbling on his left foot and leaned on a home-made crutch, as his right foot had been blown apart in an unidentified explosion. Our Medics recognized the signs of infection immediately; and after sedating Nugent, went about amputating that portion of his right leg, about two inches below the knee – and hoping for the best. With an inordinate amount of broad spectrum antibiotics and TLC, Nugent recovered, and within five or six weeks was hobbling around on a pair of real crutches; even occasionally trying to compete in foot races with his newfound companions on the local dirt-tract hundred-yard sprint/dash trail we had dug out of the side of the hill. He never won, of course, and was constantly ribbed by all of us who knew him. Considering his handicap, his sense of humor was intact.

Nugent was not a leech, and kept himself constantly busy paying his room and board by shining shoes and washing laundry for those of us who would let him in the hooch. There were plenty of members among our staff who would not trust Nugent out of their sight, and would rather he not even be given food or C-ration scraps; and certainly the "heathen shouldn't be allowed to eat with us in the mess hall". But, even those hard-core stereo-types eventually came to accept Nugent into the camp.

Some of them, in clumsy attempts to create a 'new and improved' Nugent, tried to correct his favorite word "shit!", instructing him to use "shucks!" or some other inadequate replacement for his favorite vocabulary. This caused his original teachers to teach him the words "Dumb shit" to use whenever convenient for making reference to those less adequate teachers.

Nugent adopted the old, black, garbage-can bitch dog that had inhabited our camp and he basically kept her alive with table scraps cleaned from the mess area. The old dog, in turn, kept her wild, hunting fantasies fulfilled by chasing and killing local rats who tried to claim her territory. She never ate the rats, but occasionally left them as gifts for someone who might have given her a chocolate-rice snack from the C-rations. The dog had a sweet tooth.

If you saw Nugent, his dog companion - GI-named 'Dammit' - was generally nearby. The humor of Dammit's name was lost however when Nugent would call her, as he could only pronounce *"Dom-ich"*. The words 'Dumb shit' worked just as well when calling Dammit.

On Sundays, when the local chaplain would visit our camp, Nugent always sat in, and when we prayed, he would always bow his head – likely in thanks for his GI family.

As the chaplain walked among us one muggy Sunday afternoon, he remarked that it was too bad Nugent didn't have a prosthesis for his right limb. Leroy Johnson, our local supply sergeant then donated his pride hickory baseball bat to anyone who could carve it into a stump for Nugent, and before long, our resident sniper and wood carver - nicknamed 'The Tennessee Stud'; or just 'Stud' for short - examined Nugent's partial limb, and announced he would give it a try. It took a few weeks working in his spare time, carving, fitting sanding and fitting again. 'Stud' managed to carve and fit the prosthesis with a padded leather garter strap to hold it in place, cinched above the knee. 'Stud' added a foot, riveted at the ankle for some pivotal movement, and permanently attached a size eight combat boot to match Nguyen's good left foot. We created a birthday for Nugent, guessing him to be 13 years old, we gave him August 13 as a birthday (numbers 13 were significant to his run of luck), and presented him with his new stub, autographed by everyone in the unit. Even though he was aware of the prosthesis plan, once it had been attached, he cried into the night. Early the next morning Nugent hobbled his way to each bunk in every hooch, personally thanking everyone involved. He would reluctantly unfasten the stub each night and anxiously reaffixed it early the next morning. He suffered obvious discomfort from the prosthesis, and rubbed Vaseline on his own stub daily until calluses began to surface; but he was forever grateful for the efforts of those among us who had tried to normalize his existence.

Nugent could now wear full-length trousers, and with a little practice could walk quite well. After a week or so, Nugent ceremoniously threw away his crutches. The next day they were back under his bunk.

On one occasion, nearing TK day, our unit scrounger, Leroy received a fairly large package in the mail. It had been mailed from New Orleans a month earlier. It contained a single-speed bicycle. Leroy set about with the assembly and lubrication processes and the next day presented it to Nugent, along with a full day of riding lessons – not a simple learning task for someone with a single functioning leg. With his usual stubborn enthusiasm though, Nugent was soon sailing around the camp area on his bike as though it were part of him; and of course downhill was his favorite direction. Nugent himself had fashioned a 'stirrup' to hold his 'bat-foot' in place on the pedal.

Nugent was normally up early in the mornings. Donning his stub, and putting on his 'uniform', he would walk his bike to the crest of the hill above camp with Dammit at his side. Ritualistically, he would wait until the changing of the guard, - about 0630; would yell and wave, then coast on the bike toward the camp gates. Gaining speed along the way, Nugent would arrive just in time for chow. It was almost a habit to look up towards the crest for Nugent as I left the hooch each morning, and to wave at him as he started his descent. As a matter of fact, everyone watched, almost in awe as this handicapped "unileg" or "monopod", Dammit trotting along side, would sail down hill, gripping his brakes to a halt just as he passed through the gate. Although the guards knew him, they often left the gate closed just enough to give Nugent the task of slowing down. Everyone would laugh and Nugent would join us for his favorite SOS breakfast.

He diligently kept the bike shined and spotless, and would always park it with kickstand, at the mess entrance during the meal. I believe he never missed a meal – at least not breakfast.

It was a relatively cold morning in late November that nobody in the unit would ever forget. On that day, neither Dammit nor Nugent had been seen in the unit area, and this conspicuous act was noticed by everyone from the Colonel on down. I was going to early breakfast, as I was part of the 0630 relief.

As several of us walked out of the mess tent, we looked toward the ridge in unison and then I heard someone yell "Hey there he is; there's Nugent!" Then, in utter silence, we stood in awe, watching the event unfold before our eyes.

Something was different this time. There was no wave, no smile... and no Dammit. It appeared as though Nugent had been tied to the handlebars, and was struggling to get loose. The bike lurched ahead, and Nugent could be seen shaking his head back and forth. It was somewhere about that time that we all realized what was happening. Nugent had been booby-trapped. He was wired. As he moved closer, a 'package' strapped to the crossbar became visible; a piece of twine was attached to the package, and voices could be heard shouting from the jungle growth behind him.

I could not imagine what was going through Nugent's mind as he bounced in our direction. He probably thought he was dreaming – a nightmare. He was bound to the bicycle and gagged. He couldn't warn us. On one hand he would want to let himself fall down and die, and the other side of his brain was signaling him to keep going. His GI buddies would save him......

The truth was he had no choice but to sacrifice himself for his American friends who had given him just a few more months of 'life'... as it was.

Several of us trained our rifles on poor Nugent, but as he began to fall, the twine was pulled tight and shots rang out from behind him. I habitually counted the four long seconds - and then the grenade exploded.

I saw the flash one-half second before hearing the grenade. Ka-WHUMP!

Nugent would suffer no more.

That evening the Colonel provided a moment of prayer for Nugent, and on Sunday, after hearing of the incident, our Chaplain also reminded us all how much his sacrifice meant, by dedicating a moment of silence.

Goodbye Nugent. You will forever remain in our hearts and memories.

Dammit was never seen again.

During that short, broken tour, I'd heard nothing of Ivan.

I departed Viet Nam in December for rotation back to the US, assigned to the Military Intelligence Detachment at Sandia Base New Mexico (SBNM) in Albuquerque. It was my duty station of choice.

I stopped briefly to visit Mom and my stepfather, and pick up my little Plymouth Valiant convertible which I lad left in their garage.

Expecting my arrival, my stepfather had taken the Valiant out, cleaned and serviced it for me. While I was gone, they had kept license and insurance up to date. It was ready to go.

For the fourth consecutive time in my career, my assignment fell under the management of the 'control group'. I was again controlled under the DASR. Assignments branch informed me that as long as I retained the primary military occupation specialty (MOS) title of clandestine case officer, the 'control group' would maintain control of my personnel actions at Fort Meade, Maryland. That was OK with me.

CHAPTER 13.
SANDIA BASE NEW MEXICO

My new Unit provided the entire sphere of CI support to a joint-service - Army, Navy and Air Force - command. There, I was promoted and assigned duties as the NCOIC of the Special Operations Branch under Captain Roy Harmon. My Commanding Officer was Colonel Fred Swatford.

Duties at SBNM were primarily CI focused, but as I began to get the feel of the surroundings, I was able to be involved in a few of the more exciting aspects of CI, and our Special Operations section was involved in several intriguing surveillance operations and penetration inspections. We were not involved in the boring, routine background investigations and security services.

I was approaching 11 years in the military, and although I wanted to remain active in Intelligence work, Stateside CI duties no longer appealed to me. I was anxious to change services. With the Ivan Project still haunting me, more than anything else, I wanted to go back overseas. I applied for a Case Officer position with the "Other Agency", and was interviewed. The interview included many questions about my personal life and professional experience, but the recruiter focused primarily on my language abilities. The next day, he provided me with a written test in the Vietnamese and Chinese languages, which I was allowed to take on my own time with the assistance of dictionaries. I never learned the results of those language tests. Within a month, I was given a battery of psychological tests, designed I presumed, to identify kinks in my personality. I was informed within two more weeks that I had been accepted and told that I could expect to be aboard within 30 days after I ended my military service. I was told that it was 100 percent likely I would find myself back in Viet Nam as a provincial advisor.

It is hard to believe I had decided to accept the position with the very agency with which I had encountered so much frustration, but I convinced myself that I could not blame the individual agents for their actions. Since the onset of the Viet Nam conflict, the "Other Agency" had been forced to accept many employees who were less than adequately trained and very inexperienced.

Perhaps I could make a change, I thought.

At the next meeting the recruiter handed me a contract which I decided not to sign at that time, as I wanted to discuss the decision with my commander before doing so.

The next day, I showed the contract to CPT Harmon and informed him of my choice. He arranged an appointment with the Colonel.

Col. Swatford had always seemed to like me, and the feeling was mutual. He was an excellent Army Officer and a true professional. He was less than impressed when I told him of my tentative decision. During the course of our conversation, he stated that he detected some reluctance on my part to make the move. I gave him a quick briefing of some of my encounters with the "Other Agency" personnel and volunteered my non-complimentary opinion of their expertise.

COL Swatford asked me point blank "What would it take to keep you within Army employment?"

Another Decision.

By that, I supposed he meant that I could possibly remain within the Department of the army as a civilian. My thoughts momentarily regressed to the decision I had made to end my military term of service. Actually, I had considered being a civilian case officer for the army; but had decided to try the "Other Agency" first.

I answered truthfully "Sir, at this point, there is but one assignment that would make me change my mind, and that would be an assignment to Taiwan."

We talked for a few more minutes, and COL Swatford stated he had some calls to make. Before dismissing me or even giving his tacit approval of my decision, he asked me how long I had yet to serve. I answered that I was now looking at 60 days.

One week later, CPT Harmon informed me that COL Swatford would like us to meet with him in his office.

Knowing he'd not yet given me his nod, I assumed it would be a meeting of the minds, so to speak. He would tell me that I'd made the right career decision, and would give me his advice to enter into this new phase with an open mind. I had already arranged an appointment with the "Other Agency" recruiter, and would be signing their contract within a month.

CPT Harmon and I walked into the Colonel's office and he asked us to sit. He quietly finished reading a single-page, FAX document that he had just received.

A moment later, he turned to me and said "You know Don, we really would like to keep you within our employ; and of course my first choice is to keep you right here under my own command." He continued "Unfortunately, I've been accepted as the new Army Attaché in Japan, and will be leaving this unit within 3 months." CPT Harmon was even more surprised than I. Harmon had once told me that the only reason he came to this assignment in Albuquerque was because he'd known Col Swatford from a previous assignment and had admired him greatly.

Colonel Swatford stated that since I did not speak Japanese, he could not take me along. I was flattered. Harmon and I both congratulated the Colonel for the coveted Attaché selection.

The Colonel went on to say that he had a good friend who now commanded the famous "Detachment T" in Taiwan. The (Clandestine) Taiwan Detachment was establishing a small CI element consisting of two positions – one military Senior NCO, and one Civilian GS-11. Both positions required persons with CI and positive HUMINT experience, and a working level in a Chinese dialect, preferably Mandarin. He went on to say that he had talked to the assignments office and they agreed that if I so desired, I could be assigned to that detachment.

I gasped!

The Colonel handed me the piece of paper which I assumed were his own reassignment orders to Japan. It was a draft Special Order assigning me to Detachment T; contingent upon passing the Chinese language proficiency exam, reenlistment in the army, and updating my Security Clearance. The Colonel then said he must respond with my decision in 72 hours.

He made it clear. "Now Don, it's time to 'Shit or get off the pot'!"

My mind was racing. This assignment was the epitome of all Army CI assignments. I had heard of Detachment T since I first went to Fort Holabird more than 6 years earlier. It was commonly known that within the Pacific-based MI Detachments, Taiwan was the first choice. Detachment B in Thailand was also considered to be one of the very best assignments in all of Asia. From the briefing by JK Jong years earlier, I knew that Detachment T had only a handful of positions, and therefore, only a few, elite personnel would ever be selected for those assignment.

Although I was nearly speechless, I didn't hesitate for even a fraction of a second. I told Colonel Swatford that I could be ready as soon as the assignment is available, following fulfillment of my current enlistment, now only weeks away. He was almost as happy as I, and while I sat in front of him stunned at this opportunity, he called the assignments office directly and told them of my decision. Moments later, the final copy of my special orders arrived by FAX. Extra copies were made for the purpose of processing, and I immediately began formulating plans for the reenlistment and language testing. My scheduled date of arrival was 60 days after receipt of orders. That meant I had two months to prepare. Colonel Swatford had turned out to be a true friend, and I felt certain that our paths would cross again. They did.

The next day I called the recruiter from the other agency, and informed him of my decision. "You've made the right choice." Was all he said.

During my tenure in Albuquerque, I had initiated and ran an operation directed at Chinese citizens residing in the Southwestern United States, who were suspected of collecting information on the US Defense Industry, particularly the Defense Atomic Support Agency at Sandia Base. The operation involved wiretapping, investigative monitoring and eavesdropping activities, and for the first time in the history of the detachment, we were successful in introducing a true element of clandestinity into the counter-espionage activities at Sandia. This operation was transferred to the "Other Agency" on my departure. This time, it didn't bother me to transfer operational interest, and I was still dreaming that one day I would be able to focus full attention on such as the Ivan project.

When military personnel are transferred, it is common courtesy within the Department of the army that they be assigned a sponsor whenever possible. The duties of the sponsor include helping the new guy settle into his new duty assignment, and to assist him in the conduct of administrative in-processing procedures. Within a few days, I received a letter from Lieutenant Colonel Blaise H. Vallese, the Commander of Detachment T, welcoming me to the unit and assigning Warrant Officer Juan S. Jan as my sponsor.

DONALD BRADSHAW

When I read Juan's name, I assumed he was Hispanic; but nothing could have been further from the truth.

Before I had a chance to write back to Colonel Vallese, I received a second letter - from Mr. Jan. I first examined the handwriting on the envelope. It was absolutely beautiful. The formulation of every letter was in perfect proportion to every other letter, as though it had been written by an artist. I anxiously opened the envelope and immediately smelled the scent of rose petals. The letter was written on personal, scented stationery. It read in part:

My new Friend, Mr. Don W. Bradshaw.

Let me please introducing myself. I am Juan S. Jan, your sponsor for coming to Taiwan on assignment to here.

So far, so good. It went on:

I am pleasingly in helping you with your arrival. I shall be at the Airport in Taipei when you arrive, and am easy to recognize – I am the Chinese who is wearing the grey slacks, checked shirt, baldness, and will be carrying my briefing case which is black like shoes.

About me I, am married to one wife Japanese, one son and one daughter who are both half and half. We have two little Shih-Tzu doggies. I will come alone for your baggage space, and you can meet all later.

I made arrangement for you to stay in Union Hotel on one block from Central Mountain North Road, at the intersection with the street. It is a short-time hotel ...

I mistakenly took this to mean that I would be staying at the hotel only a short time. He continued:

....and you can live only until you find a place to residing and *come to work. If you must contact me, my contact telephoning number for calling is......*

He provided me with contact numbers at the office, which had already been provided by Colonel Vallese. I smiled to myself as I put the letter away. I was certainly looking forward to meeting Mr. Jan. I spent a few minutes writing my replies that afternoon, and mailed them off the next morning.

The blur of the next few weeks went by uneventful. I was so excited about the upcoming assignment that I was constantly distracted, and recall spending the majority of my spare time brushing up on Chinese and mentally inventing Oplans. I had not used the Chinese language in several years and in the interim had studied Vietnamese and also served a Vietnamese language utilization tour; therefore, I caught myself continually mixing the words of the two languages. After a month of dedication to Chinese, I took the exam, and passed with over 90 percent. I was relieved.

I made but one phone call to Taiwan before leaving the US; and I spoke with Col Vallese. I wanted to insure they had my flight schedule and arrival times. Mr. Jan worked at a joint service debriefing center located several miles from the detachment office, but Col V insured me Jan would be waiting my arrival. I requested two weeks leave in the Philippines on the way to Taiwan, and it was telephonically approved by Col Vallese.

Over the following weeks, I spent time brushing up on Taiwan's recent history and the culture of Taiwan; and was privileged to attend a 10-day State Department seminar in Virginia on the <u>status of the political situation between Taiwan and Mainland China.</u>

Re-enter – **Frank V. Liles**

Within the last 30 days before I departed Albuquerque, the new Unit Personnel Sergeant arrived. He was an experienced Special Agent, and had served single tours in Korea and in Viet Nam before accepting the assignment to Sandia Base. Because of his personnel background, before going on the street, Col. Swatford had instructed him to spend some time straightening out the personnel files of the entire unit, aligning all of our operational personnel under the management of the control unit and assignment to the DASR.

The new arrival was none other than Frank Liles.

Frank and I renewed our acquaintance, and both of us reminisced about being overseas. Frank said he was "jell-us" I was going back overseas so soon. He hated personnel "administrivia". I told him that if he does a good job, he'll likely get a good assignment when he leaves Albuquerque in 18 about months. Hopefully, he found that encouraging. Frank arranged a farewell party for me at his home, where I was finally introduced to his family, and on my departure, he took over the NCOIC position of Special Operations Branch.

After a quick trip home to visit the family, I left for Taiwan on 31 July, passing through Manila - Clark Air Force Base - on leave as planned. I had envisioned two weeks on those tropical islands as a cheaper, more-exciting version of a Hawaiian Vacation; however, that was only half-right. It was definitely cheaper.

My timing was terrible. The Philippines at that time of year, was only a few degrees hotter and more humid than Okinawa, but living in New Mexico those few months had given me enough time to acclimate to the dry, cool evenings of the desert air. The Philippines was no comparison to the memories of Okinawa, and certainly not to New Mexico. During my 14-day stay, the humidity never dropped below 90%, and the daily, 24-hour temperatures averaged 110 degrees. I was permitted to stay in transient quarters, but two nights in that non-air conditioned situation forced me to seek local accommodations for the last twelve days. The musty, cold air flowing from the air conditioning systems in the bars and hotel rooms of Pampanga must have been at least part of the reason that soldiers taking R&R from Viet Nam often chose this God-forsaken location. As a matter of fact, I decided that any reason for selecting the Philippines when there were ample, and much more suitable destinations, would have to be of a self-gratifying, and almost masochistic nature. And I'm one-hundred percent sure, that any season would have been more exciting than summer.

CHAPTER 14.
TAIWAN-THE RIGHT DECISION.
ENTER: JUAN-SHIH JAN.

On August 15, it was mid-afternoon when I landed in Taiwan. And while it was considered to be the very hottest time of the year, compared to Pampanga, it was cool and refreshing. I was met at the airport by Mr. Jan. He preferred being called simply "Jan". I spotted him immediately as I was passing through the Immigration and Customs stations. He glanced at the ID photo he was carrying, and then ran over, interrupting me in line, calling out "Are you Mr. Don?"

I acknowledged I was Don Bradshaw. His disarming, perpetual smile caused us to become immediate friends, and he ushered me past the lines, expediting my processing. He carried my official passport, and flashed it discreetly but forcibly to those officials with whom contact was required. Within 15 minutes, we had picked up my waiting baggage which had already been taken from the carrousel. On Jan's advice, I purchased $250 worth of New Taiwan Dollars (NT) at 40-to-1, and then loaded the baggage into the trunk of the 1967, plain 4-door Chevrolet sedan which was parked in a lot marked "Official Use Only".

"Your mailing packages", Jan informed "are already at the office. We have alotta place to keeping them for when you have a permanent housing."

I understood.

On the way to the (short-time) Union Hotel, Jan did his best to brief me on the office and the personnel with whom I would be working. I didn't have the heart to tell him that if he had not sent the 'welcome letter' to me, I would have suspected that Colonel Vallese had dispatched a local national driver to pick me up. The more I listened to Jan however, the more I began to appreciate his version of English. Our friendship was bonding.

Jan asked "Do you liking spicy food?"

I hesitatingly responded that I did, but cautiously added that I'd just had lunch on the airplane.

Jan ignored my indirect plea and suggested that we go immediately to the restaurant where he'd already made "reservations" to introduce me to some authentic Sze-Ch'uan cuisine and a very necessary cold beer.

Since Jan had already made "reservations" how could I refuse? He took me directly to the *Sze-Ch'uan Fan Dian* (restaurant). I learned that "reservations" meant that he knew the owner personally, and had convinced him that his life-long friend - that would be me - was coming to Taiwan and would like to use his restaurant. I further learned that Jan was born and raised in Sz-Ch'uan province in China, and his palate was already accustomed to the outrageously hot, pepper-spiced, Sz-Ch'uan cuisine. The secret I learned was to simply go ahead and eat the hottest thing on the plate. After that, your entire mouth is burned, your taste buds are anesthetized and totally insensitive to anything that follows. I ate every morsel on my plate, followed with a medium bowl of extra hot, hot-sour soup. I ate as though I wouldn't be able to eat again - for another year - hoping, and begging to God that Jan would agree to try a different type of cuisine next time around. Maybe something sweet and sour – like Cantonese – would be more tolerable. Served cold would be nice. There is however something about Sz-Ch'uan cuisine that will bring you back time and time again, longing to burn your mouth, lips and other internal parts of your body with that everlasting masochistic pleasure.

The first cold beer lasted three large gulps. I was able to sip the second one.

We paid for nothing - again, Jan knew the owner. I left a New Taiwan (NT) 20. Dollar tip, neither knowing nor caring that it was only 50 cents. All I really wanted was to suck in some fresh, cool air. Inside, it was as though the air conditioning had ceased to function.

Following that second lunch; therefore dinner, Jan drove me through Taipei, taking the long route to the Union Hotel. Even the top of Jan's bald head was beginning to sweat – it was sweat, condensation, or perhaps hot pepper oil.

Jan was embarrassed when he briefed me on the meaning of "short time" and asked that I please not be uncomfortable if I should observe young men with their "ladies of the evening" also using that hotel. He even told me that because the walls were thin, I may occasionally hear couples being "noisy"; especially on weekends. Jan was relieved when I reminded him that I had just spent a couple of weeks in the Philippines, and assured him that nothing could embarrass me. When he saw me yawning, he informed that he would tell the Colonel that I was suffering from jet-lag, and that he would pick me up the next day after insuring I'd had ample sleep.

Jan had already checked me in at the Union, and with my key in hand, helped me directly to the room with my luggage. Before departing, he instructed me to leave any laundry and my shoes outside the door, and promised they would be taken care of. We agreed to meet for breakfast around 0830.

Although it was only around 1800 when I checked in, I went directly to the shower and fell asleep after rolling and tossing for 15 or 20 seconds. I awoke disoriented at 0135 hours, and as promised, listened to the sounds of the evening until I fell asleep again around 0200.

About five hours later, I awoke to a knock at the door. Not expecting visitors, I cautiously approached the door asking "Who is it?" in Chinese.

"Raundry." Came the English answer.

I looked through the peep-hole and saw a young man standing with a bundle in his arms. I opened the door. "Mr. Bai," he said, raising his eyebrows so I would know it was a question.

When I answered in the positive, he handed my laundry to me. I signed the chit and he left, bowing profusely. When I tried to tip, he refused, saying "Glatuity. It is incruded." I thanked him, and examined the set of clothes I'd left at the door for pressing only.

They had all been washed, to include a pair of tropical worsted-wool slacks; but were clean and pressed. The shoes I'd left at the door were so highly polished, I had to take a second look to insure they were actually mine. As I closed the door, the phone rang. A sweet voice at the front desk was asking if I preferred breakfast in my room. I told her I would have breakfast at the restaurant, sometime after 0830.

After showering, I dressed, locked my suitcases, placed them in the closet, placed my remaining soiled clothing outside the door, and carried my brief case to the restaurant. I was met by a waiter who asked my room number. When I told him I was in room 321, he ushered me to my reserved table, located privately in the rear of the dining area. There I was able to order a decent breakfast in Chinese. My gratis copy of China times was on the table, so I read the morning news while awaiting my breakfast. Moments later Jan arrived. As I saw him I waved, and he grinned broadly as I beckoned to him.

Jan sat and immediately asked of the accommodations, I told him they were more than adequate, but he insisted on apologizing for putting me up in such a "sleazy-bag hotel". He said that the Union Hotel had been picked because I would not be bothered there. He explained that my per-diem was ample to stay at any one of the more exclusive hotels, but in doing so I would have to put up with persons from other countries, as well as other Americans, who are always a little too curious. I realized he was talking about official and operational covers. I thanked him for his thoughtfulness. Jan had breakfast with me, and we departed the hotel by 0930, as he insisted on taking the rest of the morning to show me around Taipei. I picked up my briefcase as we departed, and stowed it in the trunk of the sedan. As we drove around Taipei, Jan gave me a brief rundown on Taiwan History, and I allowed him to show me his knowledge. I didn't have the heart to tell him I'd spent the last few weeks studying the history and customs of Taiwan.

We traveled first to the National Museum where we stopped only momentarily while Jan picked up tickets for me to visit at a later date and at my own convenience.

When we drove to the Presidential Offices Jan turned into a small alley and we were waved into the parking lot of the 'Foreign Affairs' Bureau. As we walked back to the entrance, he had a quick conversation with the security guard, and introduced me. The very polite guard told me that Jan and he were old friends who had migrated from Sze-Ch'uan during the same period, many years earlier. They were both members of the Taiwan branch of the Sze-Ch'uan Provincial Association. We then walked to the boulevard, where we stood while Jan gave me the history of the building, dating back to the turn of the century when Taiwan was under Japanese rule. He described the first stage of the design competition for the Ruling Governor's Office.

Note: Planning for construction of the Presidential building had begun in 1906 under the direction of Japanese Architect Uyeji Nagano, but the actual construction did not begin until 1912. In 1915, there was a large "Beam-Raising" ceremony for the building and it was finally completed in 1919. Although heavily damaged in 1945 by 'allied forces', reconstruction began within 24 months by the Taiwan Provincial Government of the Republic of China (ROC). In 1948, Chieh-shou Hall was completed and dedicated in honor of Chiang Kai-shek. In 2006, Taiwan President Chen Shui-bian removed the title "Chieh-shou" from the hall.

By the time Jan finished his historical review of the construction of the Presidential Offices, it was time for lunch, and he suggestd we have lunch at his favourite noodle shop, located in an alley off Roosevelt Road, near our office. As we drove back onto the boulevard in front of the Presidential Palace and Offices, we were met with bumper-to-bumper traffic. I aleady had no idea where we were, nor in what direction we were driving. I was relieved when Jan told me I would have to wait until I had a Chinese Driver's License before I would be allowed to drive.

Over a most delicious - and mild - beef noodle soup lunch, Jan continued trying to explain what I should expect at the office. In his broken - but not limited English, he explained the counterpart arrangement in Taiwan and made comparisons with the bi-lateral offices in Tokyo, clearly stating his personal preference for Taiwan. The Taiwan assignment was much different, because the American-side collectors actually provided training in operational techniques, advice to their counterparts, technical support when needed; and participated in liaison functions. Here, Jan was a member of the joint debriefing center, and was involved in debriefing of expatriates and other sources provided through our bilateral efforts.

Jan looked at his watch. It was 1:30 PM, and time to go to the office. We turned off Roosevelt Road onto Hsin-sheng Road, and within 3 minutes were parking at the office. I was impressed. I also made it a point to remember the location of the noodle shop.

The office was a Residence which had been converted to an office for use by Viet Nam as an embassy/consulate, before the Viet Nam conflict; and the plaque on the outside wall still identified it as such. As we parked the sedan on the grassed island between the sidewalk and the road, the guard/custodian 'Lau Chen' (Old Ch'en) opened the gate and allowed us inside. As soon as we entered the gate I also observed a very large German Shepard watching our every move. The dog (Lily) was being "held back" by Lau Chen's wife, 'Hsiao-Mei' (Little Sister).

Enter: **Col Val.**

Lieutenant Colonel Vallese, hereafter referred to as Col Val, greeted me immediately with a firm, two-handed shake. Still dressed in uniform from an earlier meeting with the MAAG J-2, he ushered me into his office, closing the door behind us.

"Sit down, sit down." He insisted as he slid a chair closer to his desk.

The first words out of his mouth were "Tell me, how was your trip, how was the Philippines and how is my good friend Colonel Fred Swatford doing?"

I responded "Great, hot and great!" adding "As we speak, Col Swatford is on his way to Japan for the attaché position."

Col Val had spoken to Colonel Swatford on Wednesday, and already knew of the reassignment. He told me of their corresponding, careers in Military Intelligence, how they had become good friends, and had kept in touch over the years.

Col Val asked the normal questions, and we engaged in casual get-acquainted conversation for the entire afternoon. I knew from the start that my relationship with the Col Val would be a lasting one. He had a natural gift for establishing an element of camaraderie at first encounter and I immediately recognized his leadership qualities. Like LK, Col Val stood all of five feet eight inches tall, and was in excellent physical condition.

His uniform was beyond neat. Every platinum button and piece of brass shined brilliantly and was perfectly oriented. Medals and commendation ribbons were faultlessly aligned with absolute perfection. His shoes were polished with spit-shined excellence. My first and wrong assumption was that like Colonel Spradling, he also was a West Point graduate. He cautiously spoke with selective eloquence, humor and impeccable timing. His most striking characteristic were his piercing blue eyes. He was continuously curious and cautious, yet totally cognizant of his surroundings.

Col Val told me to take my time selecting suitable civilian quarters and familiarizing myself with the environs. He gave me a plastic-laminated map of Taipei and the surrounding area, pointing out the areas where he and most of the office personnel resided. Since I was documented as a Department of the army civilian, he made suggestions commensurate with that level. But first, I would have to get my driver's license, and accomplish in-processing, taken care of at Taiwan Defense Command. He called Jan into the office, and instructed him to take a few days off to help me get oriented. He also told Jan not to bother me in the mornings, and allow me to catch up. He winked. I joked that without the business card from the hotel, I would be hard pressed to even find my way back to my bed each night.

After walking me through the office and assigning my desk, Col Val introduced me to the Operations Officer, Danny Davis and the Assistant Operations Officer, JK Jong. I reminded JK of his presentation to my class years earlier, and he clearly recalled the occasion. Having only done that on one occasion, it was easy to recall, but I was not sure he had specifically recalled our first discussion. This assignment would not be the last with JK Jong, and over a short period, we also developed a relationship which resulted in a lifelong friendship.

The office lobby and first floor offices were decorated with locally purchased furnishings, with the exception the safes, which were of regular military issue. Flooring on the entire first level of the office was pieced together with a herringbone pattern of mahogany parquet'. It had been waxed and buffed to a high shine.

Most of the other personnel in the office were out on "errands", so Col Val told me to have a nice weekend. I thought it was Thursday, but then I had lost a day enroute to Taiwan, either by sleeping or by virtue of crossing the international dateline. It didn't matter, because I was already suffering again from jetlag, and was anxious to get some more sleep.

As Jan and I drove from the office that Friday afternoon, he suggested once more that he introduce me to yet another Sze-Ch'uan restaurant. Still suffering from the aftereffects of overindulgence from the first encounter, I told him that I had already eaten too much good food for the day, and really needed to shower and nap. Jan agreed to introduce me to the Tien mou American real estate offices the next day.

Jan drove past the Taiwan Defense Command, pointing out where I would be in-processing on Monday morning. We drove south on Central Mountain North Road, then around the corner to the Union Hotel, which to my surprise was only a 15 minute drive along the river from the office. He dropped me off, promising to pick me up after lunch the following day. As I passed through the lobby to pick up my keys, I noticed that the forewarned weekend activities were already beginning to pick-up. The bar was already open for business, and scattered couples already occupied most of the booths in the bar area as well as the tables in the restaurant. I decided to have dinner in my room, and after making selections from the menu, ordered delivery from the service desk for 7 PM.

I went directly to my room and took advantage of the hot shower, cleaning the humidity that had caused my clothing to stick to my body during the day. At precisely 7 PM, a knock came at the door, and a soft, sweet voice announced "Room Service, Sir."

It was not the "raundry" boy.

She moved in as gracefully as an angel. Converting the tray to a TV table with a push of a button on the tray, she plumped it down next to the desk. She poured my beer as she informed me there was a complimentary bottle of champagne reserved for me and still waiting at the "front". She would be happy to personally deliver it at my request. I told her that I was aware of the champagne, as they had informed me of the hotel custom when I checked in the first day. I promised that I would certainly partake before checking out in a week or so. She smiled and said how happy she was that I was not staying just for "short time." She gave me her card which identified her as "Hotel Entertainment Director".

It sounded like a military title.

Walking out the door, she turned and half-whispered "anything for you, any time, sir." She walked down the hall, turning once more to smile before disappearing around the corner toward the elevators.

What an ANGEL!

Her arrival had made it difficult to think and speak in Chinese. I seemed to have temporarily forgotten much of the vocabulary I had learned just a few years ago. After she left, I wolfed down the dinner, took two more showers - the second one cold - and went to bed.

My slow-motion dreams were mixed with exotic food, strange drink, and bizarre strangers. From nowhere, entered an angel, who danced gracefully circling around me; then glancing at me over her shoulder, she disappeared into the hallway.

My clown sat at the end of the bar, grinning like a Cheshire cat.

Sometime around midnight, I woke with a start. In a half-awake daze, in temporarily unfamiliar surroundings, the sounds of the night surrounded me. As I adjusted to the room, I clearly recalled Jan's cautious warning of the sounds. I tried with some difficulty to fall asleep, and when I realized that the longer I stayed awake, the more apt I was to remain that way; I got up, rinsed my mouth, and inhaled a miniature JW black from the mini-bar. Within 10 minutes, I found myself unable to fully focus, and after another half miniature, I was ready to sleep.

I slept through the remainder of the night waking at 0600 to utter silence. The jetlag was over at last, but my head was pounding like a pile driver. By sniffing the remaining half miniature of JW, I realized that I may have been duped; that it was not a true JW product; and likely a cheap copy. I should have noticed the difference. I reminded myself to pick up some real JW miniatures at the class six store. Or, maybe Chivas.

After morning rituals, two *Excedrin* and breakfast, I decided to walk to Central Mountain Road and explore the surroundings. Jan would be here in about 4 hours, and I was anxious to begin learning my way around – just a little.

The hustle and bustle of Taipei was picking up by 0715 hours Saturday. Motorcycles with stacked bowls of gruel or hot noodles, and small delivery vans were making their stops at back doors of restaurants, bars and small businesses; while larger trucks made their weekly deliveries at grocery stores, garment outlets, souvenir and tailor shops along the way. Most front entrances were not yet open, and their steel doors were pulled down and locked. I walked along the boulevard, watching store proprietors and shop owners as they were gradually beginning to emerge. They swept the night's trash from the sidewalks, rinsed, cleaned windows and prepared for another day of business. As more doors and shutters were lifted, a wide variety of souvenir and art-filled interiors were revealed. Shops were decorated quite attractively and most of the sales persons were anxious to make the first "good luck" sale in the morning. They were even willing to bargain down to a lesser profit margin in order to make that sale. Regardless of how well I bargained, I knew that they would still realize a reasonable profit.

Tien-mou, an area situated in North Taipei, was where the majority of Americans assigned to northern Taiwan area resided. Tien-mou Number 1 road, an extension of Central Mountain North Road, ran generally north - south through the entire Tien-mou district. Jan picked me up on schedule and drove. As we passed north into Tien-mou, I immediately began to realize that this district would be the most convenient area in which to live. There were two Chinese theaters displaying English language marquis, a small US military sub-compound, which housed the US Army's Dependent Youth Activities sports field, a recreation area, a swimming pool and a small exchange. The US Navy hospital was located about five minutes drive west into the town of Shih-pai (virtually across the street from the Chiang Kai-shek Memorial hospital). Along the main street there stood a multitude of Chinese shops carrying what appeared to be an unlimited supply of US-made (and Chinese copies of US-made) kitchen supplies, hardware, food items and home appliances. There were even two large automobile repair shops advertising "US and Japanese Car Specialists". The most prominent and attractive repair shop displayed the sign identifying "Joe's Garage." Fresh produce markets were scattered throughout the area.

Jan pulled into a small lane and parked the car. He did not like to park our government owned, yet unmarked vehicles on the main street, and explained that his own car had been in several accidents while parked on such busy streets. He wasn't anxious to pay for an accident with one of the large sedans. We exited, walked to the main street and entered a real estate office located across the street from Joe's Garage. It bore a sign identifying the business as "John Mau's Real Estate Exchange". I was still smiling at the sign as we entered. Inside the shop, proudly displayed for every customer to observe was a famous photograph of Madame Chiang.

"Hey, Mr. Jan, Long time no see me". An English speaking voice in the rear of the office called out. "Is this the friend you told us was looking for a house?" John Mao resembled a dried pea on a tooth-pick. His face was small and skeletal, his large mouth and complete set of good, large teeth overwhelmed the rest of him. At about 65 inches tall, I estimated he weighed in at around a hundred pounds. His mannerisms are accurately and simply described as 'gay'.

Before Jan had a chance to answer, the gentleman turned to me and said, "I have a special, number-one house, on the hill, just for you! - Just a moment, I have the picture!" He smiled.

Again, Jan began his introductions, but before he could finish, the man interrupted him, gesturing and speaking to me, "Here, come here and see this mansion!"

As Jan finally finished his introductions, John Mau's wife entered the main office from their living quarters in the rear, carrying a tray with tea for all of us. Apparently my first impression of John Mau was incorrect. We were seated while Mr. Mau handed me a photo album with photos of the homes he had listed for rent.

I selected the homes I would like to see and all were within a ten minute walking distance of the Mau's office. After tea and biscuits, Jan and I walked with the Maus to look over the three selected dwellings. After viewing just those three, I chose to rent the one John Mau had originally introduced.

It was a fairly large, three-bedroom home with a glassed-in foyer, and balcony overlooking a small farm behind the house. The front yard was terraced, sloping downward to the driveway. The home was surrounded by a 6 foot stone fence across the front, and with wrought-iron, spear-headed colonial fence on both sides and across the back. The stone fence was topped with large shards of broken glass which is said to deter thieves. The large, red, wrought-iron gate opened into the drive and front garden area. The selling point was a large stone fireplace in the living room, and about two cords of wood, cut, split and stacked under the deck in the back yard.

Included with the $90 a month rent, was a caretaker to cut grass, trim bushes and shrubs, wash windows once a year, and arrange for electric and plumbing services on my behalf. When I signed for the home, I was told it would be ready in 14 days. John Mau insisted I sign for the home using my Chinese name. I did. The contract began on the 15ᵗʰ day, following signing.

As we drove back toward the Union Hotel, I insisted that I not interfere with the rest of Jan's weekend with his family. He appeared relieved, saying he would meet me for breakfast at the hotel on Monday morning at 0830.

I spent the weekend learning how to take the bus to the Taipei Train Station and to the West Gate markets, discovering that the Presidential Office was only minutes from the Union Hotel, if one catches the correct bus. The bus ride from down town to Tien-mou took about 30 minutes. While walking I discovered the pedestrian underpasses that make crossing busy streets quite easy, particularly during heavy traffic hours. The rush hour in Taipei started at 0600 on Monday morning, and pretty much ran through 2200 on Saturday night. Bars and night clubs remained open until the early morning hours, daily.

After a relaxing weekend, I was ready to get to work. On Monday, Jan showed up for breakfast and afterward we drove to the office via TDC, where I began in-processing. On arrival, I provided the personnel clerk with a copy of my cover orders for this assignment, forgetting momentarily that my true military occupation specialty was not indicated on the documentation. Instead, I was listed as MSG Donald W. Bradshaw, with primary duties as a military driver. Originally, this had seemed innocuous enough, but as I handed him my orders, to my surprise, the clerk said "Great! We've been expecting you."

The clerk called the personnel officer to the front desk and said "Might as well tell 'The General' that his new driver has just reported in."

What?!

The personnel officer, Lieutenant Ingram informed me that there had been a change in assignment, and that I was being retained at TDC as the General's new driver. When I informed him that there must be some mistake, he disagreed, saying "Tell it to the General." He went on to say "The General learned that Lieutenant Col Vallese was getting a driver over a month ago, and had decided to make the change himself. After all, 'The General's own driver rotated back to the US and 'The General' felt he needed a driver more than any Lieutenant Colonel."

Every time he pronounced those two words "The General", Ingram emphasized the words as though it was synonymous with "God."

Jan was immediately on the phone to COL Val, explaining that TDC was taking his "driver". COL Val instructed that I should not go anywhere nor sign anything until he arrived. I looked closely at my original orders. They assigned me to TDC, with attachment to Detachment T. Simple enough. The clerk handed me a copy of new orders amending my assignment from Detachment T to TDC headquarters. I noticed immediately that an information copy had not been sent back to Ft Meade for the control group.

When COL Val arrived about 15 minutes later, he was already in uniform. After looking at the reassignment orders, and hearing my explanation, he demanded that the clerk make way while he spoke with the General. As he walked toward the General's office, he wadded the reassignment orders and started to throw them into a wastebasket; then on second thought, decided to throw them at the General as he exited his office. I was surprised, but learned immediately that Col Val and the General were old golfing buddies.

"Hi Val, surprised to see you here. Where were you last Sunday? I expected you at Guo-hwa." (one of the local golf courses).

Col Val smiled and said "I was busy welcoming **my new driver** to the unit." He turned and winked at me as they walked into the General's office. I continued executing my in-processing forms while

Jan waited, pretending not to notice the intermittently loud exchange emitting from the General's Office.

The first line was from the General, "...no Lieutenant Colonel...blah, blah .. driver!"

Col Val was next "Blah...stupid... shoulda known better...blah-blah..... **MY** people...!" I prayed that rather than blame the General, Val's complete sentence would have sounded something like "Your stupid Personnel officer should have known better than to touch my people."

Moments later, as they exited the office, they were laughing, telling golf jokes and shaking hands.

Col Val talked momentarily to the clerk, saying that the General was aware of the misunderstanding. The clerk was trembling, and handed me back the forms, saying he would personally take care to insure everything was in order. While there, they took an ID photo and issued me a Chinese Drivers License for which I had taken no exam. Oh, great!

We picked up official distribution then drove directly to the office. Jan still drove. I was given the day to sit down with my new co-workers and listen to their spiels regarding the detachment. Most of their briefings were completely in line with what I had read and envisioned – with very little exception.

The duties of this office dealt exclusively with the collection efforts of our Taiwan counterparts directed at mainland China. With a primary focus on the PRC Liberation Army capabilities, we were also interested in contingency plans and collection efforts directed at Taiwan. The requirements pertaining to the Viet Nam conflict also remained a priority. Our activities were directed by our headquarters in Hawaii and coordinated through our Chinese counterparts. It was understood that we would not be actively involved in their operations, but we funded them in part, provided guidance and expertise insofar as the operations were concerned, and provided them with technical support and training. In turn, their efforts were directed in accordance with existing US requirements which were basically in line with their own. To document our efforts, we prepared translations of all of the counterpart operational plans and coordination activities, which were forwarded to our own headquarters along with our detachment comments for coordination as though they were US-directed operations. In turn, they provided us with the produced intelligence resulting from our joint operations. In this way we could rationalize funding, coordination, training and occasionally costly technical support. Under any given, approved Oplan, once funding and logistics were provided to the counterparts, it was considered expended and was written off. Incentive supplies used for inducement of cooperation were purchased either through our local, official supply channels or on the local market in Taiwan. Other Incentives ranged from cigarettes and bottles of various wines and liquors, to the purchase of small radio transmitters used in joint operations, and even enormous radio transceiver towers to be used for propaganda broadcasts aimed at the mainland.

As primarily a counterintelligence specialist, I would be providing CI support to the office in the form of Security Officer, and would be expected to perform those functions relating to security, security clearances, and evacuation plans in the event of hostilities; and assisting office members in their preparations for background investigations. As additional duties, I could be called upon for input to the planning of offensive CI operations, and could be involved in the finalization of planning documents and final reports for the Colonel's signature, as required. That could mean proof-reading and typing.

Initially, I was disappointed. I explained to JK Jong that it was true - I was a CI Special Agent; but that I had spent most of my career so far as a Case Officer dedicated to more positive collection efforts. My primary interests were Counterespionage oriented.

When asked, I told him of the operations on which I had focused my attention. From the initial tasking on Okinawa, the port watch-list service for the "Other Agency", the Ivan project, the assignment to MSD in Viet Nam and the DASA project directed at Chinese residents, etc. I described the echelon of counterpart activities in which I had been involved.

JK smiled, saying he understood my position as he himself was primarily CI when he first came to Taiwan. He volunteered to address the subject of my background with Col Val, and said he would do what he could to help me move along in my career path. He was confident though that I would find the assignment both challenging and rewarding, and was willing to bet that I would extend my tour once I became completely entrenched in the functions of the office. Intrigued by the Ivan project, JK said he would examine the viability of following Ivan's travel activity, but warned me that it would not be an official, reportable request for coordination, since it did not involve our counterparts' explicit goal of collecting information on China. That made sense and I felt a little better, even with only a remote possibility that I could at least keep track of Ivan's movements in Asia.

JK was right of course, and the ensuing assignment turned out to be among the most beneficial and productive of my career. Days turned into weeks, and weeks into months in rapid succession. Under the command and control of Col Val and with the operational guidance and control of both JK and Danny, our little detachment continued along the path to success. The assignment was truly the best kept secret in Asia.

Col Val turned out to be my favorite of all commanders. Every morning he would walk through and speak to every person present. His greetings were personal. He would ask how they were doing, both professionally and personally; and if any one needed time to discuss their status, he would immediately provide private time for conversation, counseling and advice. He was always there when needed. Danny and JK also fell into line with the same tradition. The interpersonal relationships within our small office left nothing unstated. We functioned together as a single entity. Still, confidentiality was always guaranteed.

Col Val left me alone during the first few months, allowing me to function under our Operations Officers for duty assignments, which consisted mostly of translating our English language reports into finalized, workable production. I also learned how to make coffee Val's way.

One afternoon, JK took me aside to tell me he had talked with the counterparts earlier that morning and had broached the idea of using the port authorities as a source for spotting potential operatives from among the legal travelers who were listed as crewmembers aboard cargo ships and tankers visiting Taiwan's various port facilities. Since it was just a conversation, no specific report was required. He asked the counterparts if they had the contacts with the port authority who could obtain ship passenger manifests, if he should ever want them. They confirmed that they did, and after a short discussion agreed to come up with some recent samples for JK, covering the past few months.

JK swore me to secrecy about this effort, reminding me that my interest in "Ivan" was not in line with our counterpart's interest in China and current Intelligence requirements on the PRC. He smiled and added that he would love to go over the crew manifests with me, and went on to suggest that If the Ivan project was still going with the 'Other Agency", we could pass any positive information on to them as though we had "stumbled across" it during routine source acquisition activity. JK was fully aware that Ivan was <u>probably</u> a dual citizen by now and <u>may</u> be traveling with US travel documents. Therefore, he may already be considered a US subject.

Two days later, the first manifests arrived. They were voluminous, going back 180 days. JK and I managed to eliminate about 90 percent of them right away. After spending about four hours poring over the manifests – voila – eureka, Ivan's name appeared. He had visited Taiwan on every trip between Viet Nam and Japan. He had also requested and was granted shore-leave a few days each time. The manifests listed Ivan as a US 'subject', and since his personal information identified his place of birth as San Francisco, there was no reason to doubt his status and no restrictions on his movements in Taiwan had ever been imposed. I was aware though that it was also equally possible that he was traveling on a Russian passport, and probably using US employment documents for processing in and out of Taiwan.

JK was ecstatic, grinning from ear to ear. Our counterparts had no way of knowing who we could have been interested in, and JK decided to keep it that way. He would pass the manifests back to them at their next meeting, and show them how easy it would be to identify PRC crew members by the codes provided for their passports, and the counterparts could take it from there.

As we descended the stairs back to the main office with manifests in hand, Col Val was coming up the stairs. Noticing the grin on JK's face, Col Val looked at us and asked jokingly "Now, just what are you two renegades up to?"

JK Jong responded for both of us, waving the manifests at Col V, he said "I was just testing Don on his ability to read Chinese names. You know Colonel, he's pretty good!"

"Of course he is!" the Col Val whispered. And then in a secretive tone "He's one of us. And I'm going to teach him to play golf too."

I wasn't sure of the relationship, if any between those two statements, and decided to let it go for the time being.

My single inspiration at this moment was the knowledge that Ivan was back in my scope – at least figuratively speaking. I could now keep track of his activities although my efforts would be somewhat limited. I realized that if Ivan was following in his father's footsteps, he would probably work his way into the diplomatic field and could eventually be posted to a location where he could function as an intelligence agent.

That night I dreamed of Ivan again. *My nemesis, my opponent, my adversary Ivan was walking around freely in Taiwan as a US citizen, driving fast cars, drinking, carousing, and blowing up military bases................. and with every sighting of Ivan, I saw my clown watching Ivan's activities from a distance, through binoculars.* I woke with a cold sweat.

The first year passed quickly, while I continued to provide the requisite CI support to the office. I was busy ensuring that all assigned persons' security clearance information was up to date. JK would occasionally provide me with the manifests, and together we would speculate on Ivan's activities. The 'other agency' was retaining OI.

Madame Chiang's speech.

October is a full month of three-day weekends. One of the most important events in Taiwan is the 'Double-Ten' (Independence Day) celebration. On this holiday, tens of thousands of people gather in the 16-lane boulevard leading to the Presidential Palace, and listen to The "Gimo" (Generalissimo) Chiang Kai-shek and always hopefully to Madame Chiang, as they make their annual public appearances.

Our office was extremely lucky to have a few seats with our counter-parts only a few feet from the platform; and as a newbie, I felt privileged just to be in attendance.

Total silence fell over the crowd as President Chiang Kai-shek gave his speech. Standing tall and proud, The Gimo's words lasted a full 30 minutes. Other dignitaries took their turns, and at long last, Madame Chiang stood and approached the microphone.

I was spellbound; not only with her grace and beauty, but with the eloquence of her speech. The Madame welcomed the public, and then spoke of the recent successes of Taiwan both politically and economically over the past year. During her 30-minute speech, she injected more than just a few English phrases along the way, and then personally welcomed the US Ambassador, Walter P. McConaughy and his entourage.

When her speech ended, the crowd gave a loud round of applause; and in that moment, those of us seated near the front were allowed to line up and greet the President and Madame. I fell in line behind our counterparts and JK, and then approached the platform. I spoke first to the president, and was allowed to shake his hand. I then moved ahead and spoke to Madame Chiang. "Jyou-yang, jyou-yang" I said, in a humble greeting signifying my pleasure for just being allowed into their moment. She reached down and shook hands, then reached out and ruffled my blond hair. "Goldilocks," she said. "It's nice to meet you". For just a fleeting moment I thought of Miss Okinawa.

I was speechless. I trembled like the last stubborn maple leaf on a tree in the midst of a winter blizzard. I was absolutely positive that my burning face was glowing beet red and that my entire head would explode any second. I knew not what to say. I couldn't even speak English. Temporarily, I had no breath, and my thick, immobilized tongue seemed stuck to the roof of my mouth. Finally, I mumbled "Gapless turtle placards", or something to that effect. Nothing was coming out right, and my face burned even hotter. She smiled. I just wanted to disappear.

Driving back to the office, JK kept telling me how lucky I was, saying that the Madame normally did not speak individually with anyone. She would sometimes shake hands, and smile. Back at the office, the only person present was Danny, and JK immediately related the story to him. I was too embarrassed to talk to anyone about it for a long time.

A full 15 months passed, then early one quiet morning I arrived at the office and was going through the morning ritual of making coffee. Col Val called me into his office. He had picked up our classified distribution at TDC, and had been reading through it. He handed me a set of special orders pertaining to GS-11 Gary Sandell, a CI civilian. Gary and his family would be arriving in a month from a CI assignment in Hawaii. I was hereby appointed as his sponsor. While Col Val was not particularly excited with the idea of having a CI element (albeit a small, two-man team) assigned to his clandestine unit, he understood the necessity.

It was during this quiet, private meeting that Col Val informed me he would be going back to Hawaii for the Commander's Conference, where he would be meeting with all the commanders of the units within our Group Area of Operations. The Headquarters was hosting the conference, and many other commanders and operations officers from around the world would also be in attendance. He hoped he would have an opportunity to spend some time with Col Swatford, from Japan. He further confided that there had been some high-level discussions on the possibility of an eventual "purple suit" intelligence reorganization wherein all defense department HUMINT services would be merged and collocated at various locations around the world. He asked for my personal view of this idea.

I was initially dumbfounded, but flattered that he would consider my personal input of any value whatsoever. Col Val explained that the envisioned plan also called for the inclusion of some CI elements as well. A portion of the Commander's Conference was scheduled to be dedicated to the discussion of inter-service merging. Col Val showed me a classified, two-page memo signed by then Defense Secretary (SECDEF) Melvin Laird, regarding the subject of inter-service consolidation.

We discussed some of the history of the personalities involved, beginning with the tenure of Secretary Laird:

According to Col Val, there was also a possiblity that Mr. Dick Cheney and Mr. Donald Rumsfeld were also involved in the inter service deal.

I told Col Val that to begin with - due to the respective positions held by both Rumsfeld and Cheney, there was a good possibility that they were looking at the merging of the service intelligence agencies from an economic - possibly cost-vs-gain - standpoint, without regard to the long-standing service compartmentalization of sources and tasking requirements. After all, it was clear that the Defense budget was a consideration in the organization of the joint-service Defense Investigative Service also established under Secretary Laird. We discussed our personal views of the idea, and concluded that it was not likely to happen during our respective military careers.

Had we talked long enough, we could have solved even more of the world's problems.

This was our first professional discussion. Over the next few months as our conversations became more frequent, I developed a deep respect for Col Val, his knowledge and professional opinions. To some extent, we became trusted confidents to each other. He was also a very good golfer.

That same afternoon, JK informed me that he had tentatively scheduled a Surveillance and Counter-surveillance class for our counterparts. It would take place sometime during the period Col V would be at the Commander's Conference. By this, I knew that he also had been informed of the upcoming conference.

The next morning, Col Val called the office together and officially informed us of the upcoming conference. He outlined the conference agenda, and the resultant discussion surrounded the remote possibility of the downfall of the detachment as it now existed. All in attendance were opposed to any further Air Force or Navy infiltration, although some of the younger members of the detachment didn't care one way of the other. The translators were already collocated with Air Force translators, and decided it would probably make no difference to them.

Col Val was well prepared. I don't recall the exact month of the Commander's Conference, but it probably began in late October.

During the Colonel's absence, JKJ had scheduled me to present a training class on surveillance to our counterparts, and had obtained a surveillance film from Headquarters for the presentation. The movie was in English, and JK requested I translate the 60-minute film and write a Lesson Plan.

With some reluctance, I agreed, and began working on the LP. Without a complete translation I struggled for about one full week, and then gave my draft to JK. After looking it over, he came to my desk and told me he was impressed with the lesson plan, but thought it could be honed a little. He handed me the complete translation of the film, suggesting he would give that portion of the class, and I could narrate as we progressed through the film. It was an excellent idea. We worked on it from that standpoint and had the presentation ready within the next week.

We traveled to Keelung, in Northern Taiwan for the presentation. There, we met in the counterpart's conference room and gave the class. Including lunch, the class lasted about 6 ½ hours. They had provided an audience of 20-25, mostly field-grade officers. After the presentation we entertained their questions and listened as our counterparts commented very favorably on the format. They were also impressed at how informative and entertaining the class had been. The counterparts stated that they would be extremely happy if we could provide more classes on a regular basis.

To our surprise and delight, General Lai, the Taiwan Minister of National Defense approached us after the class and complimented the presentation. He explained that his visit to the Keelung office had been planned as a courtesy call on our senior counterpart General Ch'ien and he had not expected to spend so much time there; but he found the class so interesting that he couldn't break loose. He turned to me and asked if we had ever considered providing English Language classes to our counterparts. JK answered for me, saying that it was common practice to spend personal time with counterparts wherein English language terminology is defined and explained. He volunteered that he had been giving some consideration to formal language classes since I had arrived a few months earlier.

I drove the unit car from Keelung back into Taipei, and along the way, JK expressed his approval of the surveillance class. Although much of the class was given in English or with the incorporation of much English terminology, JK had obviously carried the ball through the Chinese language presentation.

JK was born in Massachusetts in 1928, and had traveled to Hong Kong as a child, as his parents wanted him to attend a Chinese School. He returned to the US to complete his formal schooling through High School, and joined the army in 1949. As a result of his educational background, his English and both Mandarin and Cantonese Chinese language abilities were considered of native fluency. He was a perfect candidate for intelligence training and assignment.

During that drive back, JK told me that when I first arrived in TW he actually didn't recognize me from Fort Holabird; but sometime during this training presentation, he specifically recalled our conversation years earlier when he told me it was "too bad" I was Caucasian. He now stated that he took that statement back. He felt that I had progressed in the Asian theatre to the point where I probably could do very, very well. Then he followed up joking that it really was too bad I was not Chinese…. "Someday", he promised, "I'll make you an honorary Chinese". We both laughed. Many years later, he did.

By virtue of an established mutual respect, we became both personal friends and professional colleagues. As trusted friends, we would occasionally have a drink together over our extended, secret conversations and over the years we exchanged well over ten thousand bilingual jokes (well…. almost). It was JK who taught me how to tell Chinese jokes, and to translate English Jokes into Chinese (a most difficult task when the punch line is a play on English words).

I worked for and with Mr. Jemmie K. Jong for a total of 20 years, over the remainder of my career. We had planned to retire close to each other. JK retired from the intelligence service in 1993. Before retiring, he announced my membership in the (non-existent) Honorary Chinese Association. Unfortunately, he passed away while on vacation in Hawaii in the early winter of 1995, and it was several more years before I could realize retirement. He is sorely missed. My family and JK's family are in touch occasionally. We share the sorrow of our common loss.

On a Thursday afternoon, six months to the day after my arrival, Gary Sandell and his wife Susan, accompanied by their daughter Kelly and newborn son (nicknamed "Tug") arrived, and I met them at the airport.

On the way to his temporary lodging at a hotel, Gary, who is one year older than I, gave me a quick rundown of his past CI experience. He told me that he had known JK for several years, as they had once served together in the US while assigned to the Seattle Field Office of the CIC. There were enough similarities in our respective personal and professional backgrounds and ambitions, that we became immediate friends. Gary too played golf quite well. I can say that about most of our golfers, because as the least experienced golfer in the office, I maintained a 36 handicap throughout the assignment. Gary fell into the routine of our office duties, and as a GS-11, became my immediate supervisor.

Keeping my promise to JK, I did not pass the information on the Ivan project to anyone – not even Gary. And neither did JK.

One of the detachment's local liaison contacts in Taiwan was the Office of Naval Investigations located at the military service complex on Central Mountain North Road, not far from TDC. Special Agents William McGinnis and Thomas Schedlick were the representatives at that office with whom our office maintained regular contact. Our weekly outings to one of the local golf courses often included one or both of them.

When Col Val returned from the Commander's conference, he first spent a few days in quiet isolation, putting together his after-action report, and then called us all together to brief us on the discussions of the conference.

Detachment T was still safe, and there were no more rumors of its imminent demise. The idea of the total emergence of the HUMINT services was still a pipe dream. Col Orlando Upp, the commander of the MI Group was being promoted to Brigadier General, but would remain at the headquarters as commander until his normal rotation, and Col Hughly would retire and fulfill his same Operations Officer position as a civilian, GS-14. General Upp was on his way to Taiwan for his annual visit, and we were expected to assist him in all ways possible in accordance with established military protocol.

Col Val passed around his after-action report and over the next few days we all had an opportunity to read it and to acknowledge having done so by initialing the front cover. Suffice it to say there were no earth shattering revelations in the report.

Enter Betty.

Although we were a clandestine unit, it was important that we also remain qualified insofar as our annual military physical fitness examinations and weapons firing were concerned. Our Physical fitness exams were given with other military organizations, but firing ranges had to be coordinated through the Taiwan National Police. The Police force consisted of two separate agencies: 1) the National Police, and 2) the quasi-military Self Defense Forces. In Shih-lin, the district bordering Tien-mou on the West, the Taiwan Self Defense Forces had a training facility, and through cooperation with our counterparts, we had arranged to conduct annual arms qualifications and firing regularly at their indoor range. Our basic weapons were the 38-caliber, snub-nose, revolver, which we absolutely never carried. I traveled with Jimmie Song, one of our designated intelligence clerks to that compound to make the arrangements.

On arrival, we were met by Captain (Navy rank) CHEN, Ji-tsai, who was the Battalion Commander. As we entered his office I noticed a young lady seated in front of his desk, and he immediately dismissed her. On her way out I noticed she called him "Baba". In the 30 seconds I saw her, I couldn't peel my eyes from this strikingly beautiful little girl. I finally decided that she was probably about 16 years old, and resolved to pull myself back together. It was best not to ogle the daughter of our official contact anyway.

Within a week, we were back at the SDF compound, where we spent about one hour going through the routines of standing, kneeling, rolling, jumping and shooting at our designated moving targets along the cork-chip filled walls of the indoor range. I found myself constantly looking to see if Captain Chen's daughter might be standing around – but sadly, she was not to be seen. In all likeliness, she'd not even noticed me.

As time went by, the memory of Chen's daughter had all but faded, when one day out of the blue, my neighbor across the street asked if I would be interested in joining him on a double-date this coming Friday night. He was truthful in saying that his car was at Joe's Garage, and asked if I wouldn't mind driving. Although somewhat reluctant, I agreed, and on Friday, I prepared myself for this "blind date", promising myself that I would have a good time regardless of the outcome. On the way to pick up his date, Ernie told me that he had met both the girls previously, when he stopped in pouring rain to give them a ride. They were cute and friendly, and he had made this date to take them to dinner. He had promised to bring someone along for Betty. His friend's name was Helen.

We picked up Helen, and on the way to pick up Betty, in somewhat broken English, she warned me that I had better be good, because Betty's father "is a General".

Her English was a relief, as her sentences had no hint of slang or other indication that she had learned it from any source other than through formal education. She was surprised when I answered in Chinese that I had no reason to fear Generals after all, I was a good guy, with no bad intentions. I made them both promise not to tell Betty that I spoke Chinese. She was happy for Betty's sake, and said "I can't wait to introduce the two of you."

I was shocked when we arrived at Betty's place. She was Captain Chen's daughter. (Well, he was almost a general). I found it very difficult to remember the promise I'd made to Helen to be a "good guy", but was able to maintain my composure.

When Betty first entered the car, Helen made the introductions. She took the lead one step further and asked Betty (in Chinese, of course) "So, what do you think?" (Meaning – what did she think of me).

Betty looked at me and replied to her in Chinese "He's not bad at all."

To my slight disappointment, there was no hint that she recognized me from her father's office. I must not have made any impression at all, so there was no reason for me to mention it either.

We drove to the Hoover Hotel Restaurant, and enroute Helen talked with Betty in Chinese, asking questions on my behalf, and laughing constantly at Betty's open, unguarded replies.

Ernie, who was being left completely out of the conversation, could take it no longer. He finally blurted out to Betty "You know he speaks Chinese..."

Silence fell upon us. Betty asked in Chinese "Really? You speak Chinese?"

"Yes, I speak a little", I responded in Chinese. Her face turned bright red, as she recalled the conversations Helen had guided her through. The two of them laughed at the situation. Then I went on to talk casually in her language, and suggested we restrict our conversation to English for Ernie's sake. They both agreed.

Betty was adequately impressed; and this was just the beginning of a relationship that would last a lifetime; a relationship with unending love and devotion. A few years later, Captain Chen would become my father-in-law.

How fortunate I was to have accepted that single invitation from Ernie. Had I not gone along, chances are that I would never have met Betty face to face. Ernie transferred from Taiwan a few weeks later, and it is my belief that he never had the opportunity to meet with Helen again.

Like clockwork, every 90 days JK would request the shipping manifests from our unwitting counterparts, and they would provide them to us. With this, JK and I were able to keep track of Ivan's Taiwan stops, and the counterparts had another source of Chinese leads for their operations. (The Ivan project was never an official project of Detachment T. Outside JK and I, no-one was ever the wiser).

After a year at Detachment T, Col Val called me in for one of our one-on-one meetings, and informed me that the previous Detachment T Commander, Colonel D R, who was completing his Viet Nam obligation, would now be returning to take over command of the office. I had heard stories relating to Colonel R many times over the years, but was surprised to hear the news. I did not hesitate to express my initial dismay. Col Val stated that he had suspected it would eventually happen, as Colonel R had spent the past year in VM, and it was common courtesy to offer high ranking officers their assignment of choice, if possible when they returned from war zones. Colonel R, who like JK had spent the majority of his career at Detachment T and owned a home on Yang-ming Mountain, had of course chosen Taiwan. Col Val confided that his own tour would be complete within a year, and he would be transferred anyway, so this was a likely transition. He stated that with the arrival of Colonel R, his own position would be downgraded to that of Deputy Commander for the duration of his assignment.

Col Val also confessed that he was somewhat relieved Col R was returning early, as Col Val's wife (Leona) had not been well over the past years. She had been suffering from an unknown infection on her foot, and was taking medication for the resulting, excruciating pain. She would undergo a biopsy within a few weeks. Col R's arrival would allow Col Val more time to assist Leona traveling back and forth to the Military Hospital, and hopefully eliminating the problems before they rotate back to the US.

Note: As though there could be no further problems, and with the assistance of Murphy's Law, Leona Vallese passed on while in the Navy Hospital undergoing the scheduled series of routine examinations and biopsies. Now Val would have the additional tasks of escorting her back to the US for memorial and burial proceedings. Local members of the US military Blue-bark program were instrumental in assisting Col Val with each and every detail of the travel and transportation in conjunction with the escort.

The detachment shared Col Val's loss and we all did our best to assist him and his family through their sorrow and the grief over the loss of a beloved family member.

In the last few months of my tour, a memo arrived from headquarters asking for volunteers to provide assistance to returning wounded soldiers and prisoners of war from Viet Nam. The sole purpose of this program was to support the POW returnees with psychological nourishment while they attempted to blend back into society and a normal environment following their extended incarceration or hospitalization. While the term Post Traumatic Stress Disorder (PTSD) had not yet become designated as military terminology, the effects of that disorder were specifically outlined in the memo, and those of us considering volunteering were warned that many of the POWs had undergone extensive interrogation, extreme mental and physical torture and illnesses never before documented. Although the war was not yet over, a temporary processing station was established in the Philippines. It would be their first stopover on their way back to the US to rejoin their respective families and merge back into their previous lives.

I volunteered for this opportunity and after attending a two-week seminar on the conduct of this vitally important undertaking, spent six weeks working about 14 hours a day, holding both group discussions and one-on-one personal conversations with US soldiers whose lives had been interrupted by the circumstances of war.

Although the temporary duty position had little to do with Intelligence collection, that six weeks was one of the most rewarding experiences of my entire career. And the extreme heat and humidity of the Philippines didn't seem to bother me during that period.

When I returned to Taiwan for those last few months, JK and I went over the most recent of the ships logs and crew lists. Ivan had not recently been among the crew members. We made a quick trip to the "Other Agency" liaison office, and after briefing their HUMINT representative on our previous findings, urged them to make an unofficial records check for information on Ivan. Their Virginia headquarters returned their enquiry that same day. Over a Secure FAX they sent the last portion of Ivan's dossier, updating our information.

The FAX informed that for a ninety-day period in 1971, Ivan had returned to San Francisco to complete the last few months of his pursuit of a degree in International Journalism. Ivan had decided to retain his Russian citizenship, and had enrolled as a foreign student. This answered our questions. JK and I agreed that Ivan was probably preparing to pursue an Intelligence career, following his father's established path. We guessed he would soon enter the Russian military or apply for the Diplomatic Corps.

Knowing that Colonel R was due to return in a few days, and that Col Val was Preparing to retire in place, I had suddenly, but temporarily lost interest in the Ivan project. It seemed that Ivan was out of my reach.

It had been a full year since Leona had departed.

When Betty and I became officially engaged, Col Val confided in me that he had proposed to his long-time friend Hsiou-mei. I was not surprised. The two were perfect for each other. Their personalities were almost identical - alike in so many ways, yet different enough to make their relationship extremely interesting. Both Col Val and I would now go through the formalities of marrying foreign nationals.

My reassignment instructions had been received, and I was being assigned stateside to the most useless assignment of my career - Fort Bragg North Carolina. I had unofficially requested assignment to a known vacancy in Okinawa through LTC Perry who commanded the Okinawa MI Detachment at that time. But when Colonel R. learned of my endeavors, he took me aside and informed me that he had gone to some lengths to get me into the Ft Bragg assignment as well as into the NCOES (a Senior Non-Commissioned Officer Advanced Course). Col R. explained that Ft Bragg-type assignments are something that everyone has to deal with; and the NCOES would be advantageous to my career. I did not/could not argue the point.

I submitted an application for the army Warrant Officer program, and both Col Val and Colonel R provided me with their respective letters of recommendation. I traveled to Japan to attend the promotion board, and passed with recommendations from each member of the board.

Occasionally throughout the Taiwan assignment, exciting operations came to pass. I am not at liberty to discuss the details of those successes; however, suffice it to say: Our counterparts reported frequent successes with their infiltration operations and repatriation efforts, along with the loss of an occasional source. There was much speculation as to the disposition of those sources who never reported back - ranging from being captured, to changing their minds - but our counterparts' reports always included some evidence of their disposition. To the best of my knowledge, no American members of our detachment were ever identified or compromised in any way. Our counterparts continued to launch their operations directed at the PRC, and we continued to provide support.

Val was spending his time and efforts on his post retirement plans, and was applying for various positions in Taiwan which would keep him there for a period, following his military service. He was bound to do well.

On my way to Fort Bragg, I stopped to visit my Mom and my stepfather. Mom had not been feeling well, and two days after my arrival, she suffered a major heart attack. I extended my leave by calling Ft Bragg. I also discussed the pending application with branch, and learned that the Warrant Officer field would be closing in just eight more days. I had been selected, but in order to be promoted, I must report in at my new duty station within that period. My conscience would not allow me to leave my mother in the hospital, and I elected to postpone the promotion and remain with her temporarily. MI Branch was encouraging and promised my name would be at the top of the list for the next series of promotions to Warrant Officer... Right!

CHAPTER 15.
FORT BRAGG.

During my rather limited duties as the NCOIC of the Ft Bragg Field Office of the MI Battalion, I befriended as many people as possible serving under me. I quickly learned that I was not habituated to being a uniform-wearing, combat soldier; but the Battalion Staff did everything within their power and on a regular basis to remind all of us that we were "soldiers first" and unfortunately, spies last.

About halfway through that 24-month assignment, I was able to take one trip to TW to visit with Betty and her family. It was probably the most essential vacation of my career. While there, I occasioned to talk with JK who informed me that the "other agency" was still involved with keeping track of Ivan, and on his occasional request, would send status reports. The 'other agency' retained Operational Interest in the project. Ivan was not currently traveling.

Col Val had already found employment and was working with the Youth Activities Program; still residing in at his original residence on the mountain overlooking the Tam Sui River.

Back at Fort Bragg, the stated mission of the MI Battalion was to provide advanced individual training to soldiers carrying the CI Military Occupation Specialties. After all, things were winding down in Vietnam, and MOS's once showing a tremendous shortage, were now flaunting an excess of over 100 percent. The truth be known, the

MI Battalion seemed more like a temporary basic training facility designed almost exclusively for soldiers returning from Viet Nam.

Some of the younger soldiers had not yet served beyond basic training or initial advanced individual training at Fort Huachuca. To them, this assignment to Fort Bragg was very much like that which they had been going through for the past 6 months of their extremely brief careers. Others were seasoned NCOs who had reached a turning point in their careers, and were wrestling with the decision of continuing on with this career or getting out and seeking employment in the civilian world. For me, I was merely concerned with getting this required assignment "that everyone has to deal with" out of the way and had decided to take advantage of any educational opportunities I could grasp along the way.

Entirely out of my element, I struggled to spend most of my fort Bragg tour on temporary duty at Fort Huachuca, the new home of the army Intelligence School. While attending NCOES, I volunteered for and was immediately accepted to attend the 16-week long HUMINT collection course. Following graduation from that course I remained at Ft Huachuca on the teaching staff for a full six months temporary duty. While still assigned to Ft Bragg, I was also pleasured to attend the State Departments Southeast Asia Area Studies Course in Virginia, and the drug recognition portion of the Alcohol, Tax and Firearms course in Washington DC.

With the realization that the Fort Bragg environment was neither to my personal liking nor in line with professional advancement, I knew that the longer I remained at that location, the more I would find myself drifting, backsliding from the career I had envisioned and come to love. I found solace in the form of a weekly letter to my beloved Betty, and in waiting for her replies. As much as possible, during my spare time, I avoided Ft Bragg. Weekend trips out of the immediate area were often another break from the uniformed rituals. I also made two lifelong friends while at Ft Bragg:

The first was Staff Sergeant Fred Loren'. Fred, a year or two younger than I, was also born in Michigan. Fred had served about 9 years in the military, and the tenure had included an assignment to Thailand where he served in an Army unit with a support mission to the Vietnam effort. He had also served in a CI assignment to Kobe Japan, under the same MI Group to which I had been assigned.

Fred's father, an ordained minister had wanted Fred to become a medical doctor, and Fred had actually begun that career, attending two years of pre-med before succumbing to the requisite military service. Fortunately for me, Fred selected Military Intelligence, and his service eventually brought him to the unit at Fort Bragg.

During his short career, Fred had also served with (then Captain) Blaise H. Vallese in Boca Raton FL, and was therefore acquainted with my favorite Commander.

For hobbies, Fred enjoyed music, playing trumpet, piano and even the banjo. Our friendship remains intact today.

The second new friend was Sergeant Timothy May. Tim, from Rison Arkansas, and Fred were the same age, and while at Bragg, they resided together on the economy for the majority of their assignment. From Ft Bragg, Fred was transferred to Dallas TX where he served as a CI agent.

Tim had met Michele (Mai) while serving his tour in Viet Nam when she worked within the Intelligence Community. Previously, Mai had worked as a photographer and as a photo-journalist for the *United Press International*, covering military operations as well as the political aspects and opinions of the war. Her duties caused her to cross paths with such well-known personalities as General Westmoreland, as well as such famed media representatives as Mike Wallace, and a young CBS reporter, Dan Rather. Among her photo collections are pictures of many international leaders of the time. Some of her incredible combat photographs were published in the Time/Life series *The Viet Nam Experience*. She has now been a US citizen for more than three decades.

Tim, a Counterintelligence Special Agent, had served in various duty locations while assigned to Counterinsurgency positions in Viet Nam, primarily as a Phung Hoang, Phoenix Program advisor to the Special Branch of the Vietnamese National Police. He spent the last five months of this assignment in the beautiful, soil-rich area of Dalat. There he met 'Mai', and fell instantly in love.

Prior to departing Viet Nam for Fort Bragg, Tim made his 'honest intentions' known to this young Vietnamese girl, and at her mother's request visited Mai's family home for a farewell dinner.

While at Fort Bragg, Tim wrote to 'Mai' regularly, courting long distance by letters, tapes and telephone calls. At one point, he mailed her a tape, proposing marriage. They had become formally engaged. Tim proudly carried her picture with him wherever he went. And, he could be seen occasionally opening his wallet just to feast his eyes for a few moments on her photograph.

He also realized some comfort by divorcing himself from his military duties at Ft Bragg as often as possible. One of Tim's hobbies was also music, and he played the piano whenever he had spare time.

Just prior to moving in with Tim, Fred had rented a one-bedroom home in Fayetteville, close to Fort Bragg. Fred told me that his mother and father would be visiting him, and he wanted them to meet Tim and me during their visit. He invited both of us to his home during that week. He asked (but didn't need to) that we not discuss his propensity to tip an occasional sip of 'recipe', and to occasionally visit one of the local bars to play pool and drink into the night. Of course, we both agreed and adhered to his request.

Fred's parents were wonderful people, and treated Tim and I with grateful applause for helping Fred cope with the consequences of an unsuccessful marriage, as well as with the Fort Bragg situation.

With all that he had gone through I wondered how Fred could even begin to muddle through the daily harassment of military life at Fort

Bragg; but then, after meeting his parents, I realized his solution. Fred is basically a religious man who believes in God with little reservation. His father, once a fortune 500 member) who had owned and ran a tool manufacturing company in Michigan and had therein realized an acceptable degree of success, was always on hand to provide the requisite moral support with psychologically sound, fatherly advice. His Mom, simply a loving, doting, completely dedicated parent, who cares unendingly for her children, was present to reinforce the family in its entirety. Fred's close relationship with his parents, and the loving, caring aspects of this family's interrelationships obviously supported the successful revitalization of Fred Loren, following the tumultuous episode of a broken heart. Fred was able to piece his life back together, and move forward with vigor. Now, a successful Doctor, Fred has remarried and continues on the road to success within the VA system. We keep in touch.

Following his parents' visit, Fred and I celebrated by overindulging at our favorite neighborhood bar. On that particular night, we played pool, watched the "dancer", drank too much beer and talked of our plans for the future until the bar closed at 0200. Fred would not allow me to drive back to Fort Bragg in my inebriated condition, and insisted I stay at his home, just a few blocks from the bar. I secured my car at the bar parking lot, and rode home with Fred. I remember that Fred stretched out on the sofa and immediately began to doze. By the time I washed my face, he was absolutely sound asleep. I urged him into his room and returned to the living room where I too passed out.

At 0630 Sunday morning, I arose feeling quite proud that I had very little hangover from the previous night's immoderate consumption. I had slept only four hours, and had probably risen too early to allow a hangover to kick in. After rinsing my face in cold water, I went into Fred's kitchen and made a pot of very strong coffee. As the coffee perked, the delicious aroma filled his house, stimulating my appetite. I was searching for eggs, ham/bacon, hash, Spam or anything with which to put together some breakfast when I heard Fred moving around inside his bedroom. I finally decided to settle for coffee, poured a cup and sat on the sofa. Moments later when Fred emerged, I spoke. "Hey Bud – you sleep well?"

"WHAT?!" he screamed. "Oh - God! Where the hell...? Man, you startled the shit outa me!"

Not only did Fred not smell the coffee or hear me rustling around in his kitchen, he had completely forgotten he had a houseguest.

After a few cups of coffee and some good conversation, we drove back to the bar to pick up my car and convoyed to our favorite breakfast restaurant in Spring Lake. Over breakfast, we laughed and joked about Fred's reaction and our mutual embarrassment. We still talk of those times today.

Tony B and the photo

Within the personnel assigned to the Ft Bragg field office, there were two black staff sergeants.

Tony B was an outgoing, soldier, who got along famously with everyone. A career soldier, Tony was destined to become a successful Warrant Officer before he retired. Tony outranked Staff Sergeant K by only one month time in grade. Since I had four teams at the Office, and four staff sergeants, Fred, Mark, Tony and K became Team Leaders. Everyone got along perfectly, except for K.

One weekend, I was visiting the Sears store, and ran across Tony with his wife Kay and their two beautiful children. They were having their family photo taken in the Sears Photo shop for the upcoming holidays. Tony explained that they were planning on having the Sears printers make Christmas cards with the photos to send to family and friends. They had taken 9 of the 10 proofs already, and would take one final shot. Then, in an attempt to be even more humorous than usual, Tony suggested I take a photo with his family. I assumed he meant with all of them, but Tony wanted a proof of me with his wife and children. I went along with his suggestion, and sat with his wife and children for the last shot.

I had completely forgotten the incident, and when Christmas arrived, I received a card from Tony – you guessed it. The card, which was imprinted with a photo of Tony's wife and their children, included the proof he had insisted I make. I cut out the 'family' photo which had been signed "With all our love" by Tony's wife, and put it in my wallet, facing the photo of the four of us. A joke to remember. Tony transferred out on Easter Sunday in late March, and was reassigned to San Francisco.

Let me regress a little. Throughout my life, I had always been interested in tying rope knots. Among my favorites were the "timber hitch/half hitch" combination, usually used for tying an item to a hanging hook; and the "half-hitch/over pin", used for tying such items as poles to a post in a semi-permanent manner. But above all, I could tie a perfect hangman's noose in less than 30 seconds. I had no specific reason for learning those knots, but being raised on a farm may have influenced my interests.

As a matter of habit, I would often sit at my desk and test myself by tying a hangman's noose, and show my skills to friends if they were curious.

Early one Saturday morning a few weeks after Christmas, SSG K entered my office and we talked about the day's motor stables assignments. Saturday mornings were often reserved for motor stables. We would service our unit vehicles, touch-up the paint, and insure they were in perfect working condition – something we already knew. Once every two months, this activity included a full field layout - a complete inspection of our combat field gear. The bi-monthly ordeal took the whole workday. If possible, the command offices would schedule this activity on a 3-day weekend, just to interrupt any 3-day free vacation plans the troops may have wished for. This was the commandant's way of insuring the atmosphere of basic training, and probably was an important integral part of our peacetime training mission.

SSG K spied the beautifully-tied, bleached, white hemp-rope hangman's noose dangling from the desk lamp, and immediately commented on it. When he asked me what it meant, I began explaining that it was a "hangman's noose", often used back in the 19th and early 20th century by cowboys and town sheriffs for hanging undesirables such as horse thieves and bank robbers. I told him that my grandfather had been a town sheriff in the Dakotas back in the early 1900's and it was he who taught me to make them so perfectly.

SSG K left my office immediately without excusing himself, without explanation, and without finishing our conversation. I attributed his departure the normal SSG K, anti-social attitude, and dismissed it.

About 10 minutes later, I observed SSG K and our Commander Major G coming across the parking lot, into the Field Office. As I was passing the word of MAJ G's arrival, the Major entered the building and asked if he could speak with me - alone. SSG K remained in the lobby area. As we entered the office, MAJ G closed the door and then located the noose. He removed it from the lamp and asked loudly "Just what is the meaning of this?" I began to explain the noose, its origin and my habit of tying knots, when he interrupted me saying "This is why I'm here."

It sounded as though I had somehow interrupted his Saturday workday. "I'm not quite sure I understand." I said.

Again, speaking in an exaggerated loud voice, the Major continued. "SSG K brought it to my attention that you were intimidating the non-whites in the Field Office by displaying an 'Arian' symbol of hate!"

Knowing SSG K was in the lobby, I kept my voice low, explaining that I had absolutely no idea whatsoever that this simple knot had an "Arian Nation" undertone or feeling, and explained immediately that I had no racial or prejudicial blood in my veins.

The Major lowered his voice, almost to a whisper, saying "I know you don't, but SSG K wanted me to take action. I cannot afford to allow such an issue to have any effect on this unit's reputation."

Maybe the Major was on my side.

He opened my office door and beckoned K into the office. We all sat; while I listened to SSG K tell the Major that I was "as racially prejudiced as they come."

Major G asked K "And how did you come to that conclusion?"

To which K responded "Just look at him – with that blond hair, those blue eyes, starched fatigues and spit-shined boots, he even **looks** like Gestapo!" This was coming from a black guy, with bright red hair, hazel - near blue eyes, a freckled face and an Irish surname.

MAJ G looked my way and winked. Now, I knew then that he was on my side so I took the conversation to another level. Taking out my wallet, I showed the picture of myself with Tony's wife and children. "You've obviously never seen these photos of my fiancé and children." I handed the photo to the two of them.

I saw the surprise in MAJ G's expression, as he handed the photo to SSG K. K's mouth dropped open, and he could have been bought for a nickel.

After a pregnant pause, K looked at me and said "Sorry, bro. I didn't know." He then followed the apology with the ultimate insult, when he looked in MAJ G's direction and said "But it was an honest mistake."

I said nothing.

The Major dismissed K, who left the Field Office to go about his routine duties. G then turned to me grinning and asked "How the hell did you get Tony's wife to take that picture?" I explained the details, and we both had a good laugh. The issue was dropped, and never became an embarrassment. I had not damaged the Battalion's good reputation. I told Tony of the incident immediately.

Note: Tony and I kept in touch. He retired from the army in 1983, and subsequently worked for the federal government in a Federal vice intelligence position until his second retirement in 2005. To the best of my knowledge, and as testimony to their separate attitudes, Tony B and SSG K never spoke to each other either professionally or through any social gathering, and K refused to attend Tony's farewell party. That was probably a good thing, because K surely would have recognized my 'family' somewhere along the line.

I could not have known that years later, in 1991 when I traveled to Thailand, then on to Viet Nam to work on two iterations of the POW/MIA issue, I again ran into the Major who had retired and was employed at the Headquarters level as a representative for the POW/MIA effort.

After extensive coordination with my branch assignments office, I began preparing for my departure from Fort Bragg with a few mixed emotions. On one hand, I was truly looking forward to the marriage and spending the rest of my life with Betty; and yet I was saying farewell to some newly acquired comrades, and a life at Fort Bragg. Actually there wasn't much choice. Fred had already received orders for his reassignment to Dallas, and Tim was looking forward toward his marriage to Mai, and a civilian career.

Little did I know that three decades later, Tim, Fred and I would meet again and have an opportunity to relive the memories of our assignments to Ft Bragg.

My next duty assignment was to Detachment B of the Pacific-based MI group. I would be working in Bangkok Thailand.

Fred, Tim and I met for a farewell breakfast on my day of departure. Knowing my plan to drive across the US, Tim asked me to pass through Rison Arkansas and say hello to his parents. He handed me a map, showing the exact location of Rison, and after looking it over, I decided that it would certainly do no harm to visit with them, and it wasn't that far out of my way.

Once I decided to make that stop, Tim confessed that he had an ulterior motive for asking me to go to Rison. Since he was planning on marrying Mai, and had not yet told his parents of those final goals, he wondered if I could sort of drop a hint and explain what a wonderful, old-fashioned girl Mai was bound to be.

Before I had a chance to answer, Tim said "I've already told them you were coming, and they're looking forward to it." He gave me explicit instructions to their doorstep.

I paused only momentarily, and promised Tim I'd do what ever I could.

I never regretted the nights I spent with Tim's family. His parents were exactly as He had described them. I absolutely could not believe the depth of Southern hospitality they displayed toward me. Telling them about Mai was easy. I showed pictures of Betty to them and told them that I expected very little, if any problems with my planned interracial marriage. I was able to answer most of their questions with generalities, and by the time I finished, they were anxiously awaiting the arrival of their new 'daughter-in-law-to-be'. Personally, even I felt accepted as family, and before I left, found myself calling them "Mother and Dad May."

At the end of my visit with Tim's folks, on a Sunday morning his mom gave me two shopping bags full of fresh, fried chicken and freshly-baked soda biscuits. She filled my thermos with fresh, strong coffee and I regretfully had to hit the road. I had already stayed one full day longer than I'd planned, and was running late. Saying good bye to them was like bidding farewell to my own family.

I know Mother May used one (or perhaps two) of my favorite spices on the chicken: 1 - Xanthoxylon, and 2 - powdered star anise; because I was instantly addicted). I was about three minutes down the road when I began to gobble, and once I took the first bite, I just couldn't stop. The new plan was to finish both shopping bags while it was still hot.

Enter: The Cop.

Driving North out of Rison towards Pine Bluff, heading to Little Rock, I was cruising along, listening to classical radio and devouring the best chicken ever eaten in my entire life. I was paying no attention whatsoever to my speed. I heard the siren, and in the mirror saw the patrol car pulling me over.

As I made it to the shoulder, I stopped, adjusted the radio to a country station, rolled down the window and awaited the inevitable.

The biggest policeman I'd ever seen got out of the patrol car and slowly walked in my direction. He was all of 6 feet, 6 inches tall, and walked with the sideway amble of John Wayne. I'm sure he was between 25 and 30 years old, but he had the face of 13. My guess was he hadn't yet started to shave. I may very well have been his first speeding ticket.

He walked completely around my 1972 Toyota Corona one time and then stopped at my window. "You in a heckuva hurry there, Sir." He was trying to look older. His face was as stern as he could make it.

"Sorry", I said, "I was just trying to make up some time." I handed him my North Carolina Driver's license, Arizona Registration, and made sure he saw the military ID card in my wallet.

"Ya in the military?" He asked

"Yessir!" I answered, "nearly 15 years; Sergeant First Class".

"My Daddy was in the army." He bragged, "Served in Korea. He was a sergeant too."

"I was in Viet Nam," I told him, trying to establish some rapport, "Your Daddy come back OK?"

"Yeah, he's OK now." He was filling out my driver's license information on the speeding ticket. "He didn't talk about it much at first, but now he gets together with his buddies, and that's all they talk - 'In chon, Pusan, Pyongyang'."

While he was writing the ticket, I could see he was enjoying the music (Buck Owens was about halfway through singing *'Tiger by the Tail'*).

He was talkative. "What you doin' in Arkansas?" he asked.

I was ready for that one. "I'm on my way to Fort Huachuca, and then on to Southeast Asia - stopped by in Rison to visit some kinfolk."

He stopped writing. "You got Kin in Rison?" He asked. He'd suddenly lost the stern face, and his arched eyebrows made him look like a sugar-starved, inquisitive little boy in a candy store.

"Yup", I answered. "The May family."

"The Mays?" He was surprised, "Yer kin to the Mays?" grinning from ear to ear.

I took a chance. "Yes sir, Walter and Earline. They live down on Route 2."

"Don't know 'em, but I know of 'em." he said.

Buck had finished *'Tiger by the Tail'* and was wailing out *'Together Again'*. I turned the radio down just a little. My new friend was still enjoying the music. "Yer driver's license says yer from North Carolina."

"I been stationed at Bragg," I told him.

He looked at me with the utmost pride. Tears were beginning to well up in his eyes. "A soldier!" he stated, "with Kin in Rison." Then he went on, saying "My name's Johnson," He swelled his chest and pointed at his nametag. "I'm from White Hall, but my birth certificate says I was born in Pine Bluff. I wanted to join the army, but my Momma wouldn't let me."

"You're serving your country," I told him, "that's the important thing."

He stomped his foot and grinned proudly. His tears were about to burst loose and run down his cheeks. With exaggerated motion, he tore up the ticket, saying "Ya have a good trip now, Sir; and come back safely!" It sounded like I was about to go off to war.

I thanked him more than I probably should have, we shook hands, and I drove away slowly. Looking in the mirror, I saw him wiping the tears from his eyes with an oversized red handkerchief.

He'd done a good thing. He was proud of himself.

-

After a few months at Ft Huachuca, I Once again visited my Mom and Stepfather. I had called them from Ft Bragg and informed that I would be there in about three months or so, as I was driving across country, and was required to stop at Ft Huachuca for some briefings before going to Bangkok.

When I arrived in Chewelah, I stopped by the A&P Supermarket and purchased a trunk load of frozen meats and food supplies for them, and called Mom, saying I was on my way home. I drove directly to the house in five minutes, and Mom was waiting on the front porch.

"I just knew you were already in town," she said smiling, "and wanted to surprise us when you drove up."

I hardly recognized my own Mom. In the two years I'd been away, her hair had turned completely white, her back was no longer straight, bending with the slight stoop, she was now exhibiting the early stages of osteoporosis. She had lost about 20 pounds. After my hug, I asked her if she was OK. She smiled and said "Oh, sure. I'm just not the young thing I used to be." I made a mental note to stock her up on calcium-fortified multi-vitamins before I left. I quickly calculated her age. She was now in her late fifties – old before her time. My stepfather greeted me at the door. He reached out to shake hands, but then decided a hug would be better.

Since we'd coordinated this get together, my brother Bob, his wife and new baby would be driving in from Petoskey, and would be there in a few days. We were all excited about the family being together. Inside, I saw a new, unopened bottle of '*Crown Royal Special Reserve*' on the coffee table. It was my stepfather's favorite drink – on the pebbles, of course.

I went to the car and retrieved the bags of groceries, filling Mom's freezer and refrigerator; and that first night we stayed up until late maybe 10 PM!, talking about old times and of old friends who had come and gone since we'd last been together. Later that night Bob called from somewhere in Montana to say he would be in Chewelah the next afternoon.

The five-day reunion with my brother whom I'd not seen in nearly 20 years was emotional to say the least. Bob and I spent a few hours each day going over the similarities we'd encountered in our respective lives – for example, we'd both bought Plymouth convertibles, both owned a red sports car, and of course our military experiences in basic training were not all that different. From that point on though, our lives had taken completely different directions. He had finished High School while serving in the army, and had worked for an oil company. We looked at family photos Bob had brought along, and I showed photos of Betty and I, along with the one of me with Tony's wife and children. I was forced to explain the circumstances surrounding that photo. Sadly, somewhere along the fourth day at Moms, the visit took on an air of obscure sorrow, as everyone knew that Bob and I would be going in separate directions, and our Mom and Stepfather would once again be left virtually alone. Bob and I drove around the town, noting that nothing had changed since we left years earlier. We stopped and bought a years supply of the calcium-fortified vitamins.

That evening, I noticed my stepfather frown as he divided the last three ounces from his bottle. Later, when he walked into the bathroom I dashed out to my car and retrieved the one-half gallon of *Crown Royal Special Reserve* I had purchased from the Class-Six store before leaving Ft Huachuca. I replaced my stepfather's empty bottle and awaited his return. He sat in his chair and finished his last sip. He was about to say something, when he looked at the coffee table – and saw the unopened half-gallon bottle.

"Wow, would ya look at that!" He exclaimed. "I guess I believe in God after all. This is a true miracle; it's a dream come true!" He looked upward and began to clasp his hands as though in prayer.

"I wouldn't do that if I were you!" Mom warned. "He just might send a lightening bolt down here and shatter your dreams." He changed his mind and quietly opened the bottle.

Over the years, I had been sending Mom and my stepfather a monthly allowance, and Bob reinforced their income annually at Christmas with a generous monetary gift. They were doing OK.

Bob and I said our farewells, promising to get together more often. We agreed not to leave Mom at the same time, or even on the same day, to make parting a little easier for her. I left first, bound for

California and the trip to Bangkok. I called later that evening and spoke to everyone.

At Oakland Army Terminal, one full day was spent processing my Toyota for shipment. I departed San Francisco for the trip across the pond, looking forward once again to spending the next two weeks with Betty and her family in Taiwan before continuing on the journey to Bangkok.

1974 was just around the corner and our plans to marry in the spring of 1975 were firm. My travel plans included a visit with Col Val who had retired in Taiwan, and was employed as the Director of the Taiwan Dependant Youth Activities Program for US Forces. The nightmares of Ft Bragg were rapidly beginning to fade into my distant past. I hoped that if I should ever have the misfortune to suffer a traumatic brain injury, it would affect only that portion of my brain containing the undesirable episodes of the memories of Ft Bragg. I could be normal again.

When I arrived in Taiwan I could sense the political changes taking place. Over the past two years, US President Richard Nixon had made his famous Acupuncture and *Mao Tai Whiskey* trip to China, Ping-pong diplomacy had begun, and the Chinese in Taiwan were greatly concerned that the United Nations would soon accept the PRC. It was felt that if this were the case, Taiwan would withdraw from the UN. Many in Taiwan felt that it would be the beginning of the end for Taiwan. An equal number blamed Nixon and Secretary of State Kissinger for these actions, as during his historic visit to China, Nixon had issued the Shanghai Communiqué, an official statement further severing US diplomatic ties with Taiwan.

Also, the 'domino effect' was on the move when the actions of Nixon caused several major countries to switch their diplomatic recognition from Taipei to Beijing.

When Nixon resigned in shame, President Ford took over the Presidency, and wasn't about to make any permanent changes in the

Nixon/Kissinger attitudes towards the China issues expressed during this undertaking.

Betty and I did not allow the potential political obstacle to interfere with our plans, and tentatively set our wedding date for April 10, 1975. Col Val readily agreed to stand up as my best man during the wedding, as he had during our official engagement before I left Taiwan. He and I had several discussions during that visit, and he told me that he was not sure what would happen to his position with the US military when the US pulled out, which seemed inevitable. I did not hesitate to suggest that he accept a civilian position in the HUMINT Field with INSCOM, and while he thought that was always an option, he would like to stay in Taiwan if at all possible. In retrospect, I was probably being selfish in making that recommendation, for I knew that if Val were to seek such a position, he would be readily accepted, and that would mean we would likely work together in the future.

Following two weeks of bliss with Betty, I bade my farewells to her family and to our friends, and headed for Bangkok. My preparations included plans to bring Betty to Thailand to remain with me for the duration of that tour. That gave me a little more than one year to get settled and establish myself in Bangkok before the marriage.

Historical note: In Dec 1978, U S President Jimmy Carter announced the termination of US diplomatic relations with Taiwan, effective Jan. 1, 1979; however, over the next 90 days, Pres Carter outlined the new US relationship with Taiwan in the Taiwan Relations Act. Under this bilateral US and TW agreement, the U.S. would hand over the responsibilities of its embassy in Taipei to a new non-governmental agency called the American Institute in Taiwan (AIT). The agreement further included the Carter Proclamation. This proclamation was specifically directed towards the mainland, with Carter announcing that the US President and Congress would take any appropriate measures - to include military action - against any aggression towards Taiwan, if Taiwan were threatened.

CHAPTER 16.
BANGKOK! (NOW THE FUN STARTS.)

On arrival in Bangkok I was met by my sponsor, Mr. Frank Liles. We had not kept in touch since I left Albuquerque. Frank had finagled an assignment to Bangkok and when he heard I was coming, immediately volunteered to be my sponsor.

Frank had not changed all that much, and except for the fact that he had gained about 70 pounds, he still moved at the same speed, walking and talking like a slow-moving Texan.

He took me to temporary quarters he had arranged within walking distance from our office. The Windsor Hotel was more than adequate, and was used exclusively by US government personnel. The hotel room bar had been stocked amply with a sundry of various liqueur miniatures and Thai beer Frank had purchased at the local Class-Six Store. After pointing out which were his purchases, and which were of Windsor Hotel stock, we had our first drink in over three years, and caught up on our respective experiences over that period. Frank told me that it had already been decided I would be assigned to his office – the OFCO shop; and seemed happy to have an old friend now in Bangkok. He did not hesitate to inform me that he and his wife had been having some limited problems since they arrived overseas. Bangkok was not to her liking, and Frank was not yet willing to give up such an operationally lucrative and exciting assignment.

The next morning on his way to work, Frank had breakfast with me and we drove directly to our office, located in the Chokchai Building on Sukhumvit Road. Our Detachment offices occupied portions of the third, fourth and 17th floors of what was then the tallest building in Bangkok. The entire building, with one exception, was leased by the US Government for office space. The exception being the 23rd floor, which was a well-known restaurant owned by the Chokchai Family. The Chokchai family owned the largest cattle ranch in Thailand; thus, the specialties at the restaurant were among the finest beef dishes known to man. The restaurant's filet' mignon was to die for, and always prepared in perfection, in accordance with the customer's specifications.

Frank introduced me to our Operations Officer, Mr. Parkington, who insisted everyone call him "Parky". Parky gave me the official unit briefing, and personally escorted me through the offices, making the appropriate introductions. Parky and I lunched together, and over lunch he asked if I had any preferences as to which area I would like to work. He was interested in my Chinese language ability, and mentioned that there was a vacancy in the "positive" side for a Chinese linguist Case Officer. Or I could work with Rick S., who was due to arrive any day from the US. Mr. S, Parky informed had been hand-picked for that position due to his experience and his fluency in the Thai language. I had known Rick S from Fort Holabird, as we had both worked on the Field Training & Exercise Committee, and occasionally as part of CAST. With the Ivan Project in mind, and on advice I had received from Frank, I asked if there were any vacancies in the Offensive CI Operations (OFCO) section. Parky confirmed that there was, and merely added "Great Choice!"

After lunch, Parky took me to the OFCO shop and introduced me to the section Operations Chief, Mr. Mike Henley. Mike turned out to be one of the most amicable, easy-going persons I ever worked for. He allowed ample operational freedom to the Case Officers, and readily welcomed new ideas. He briefed me on the ongoing operations, and allowed me to look over the files. The office currently had seven ongoing operations, all of which were in various stages of development and early recruitment.

Mike asked Frank to show me to my desk. Frank took me into my cubicle. I looked around and found my desk. It was the smallest desk in the office, and also the shortest. In order that my legs fit beneath the desk, it rested on 8 building bricks, two under each leg. The desk teetered on the bricks, so I four-folded a sheet of paper and placed it under the shortest leg. It still was not level. I told myself that I would probably not spend too much time in the office anyway. Stifled laughter was emitting from the outside office, as I told Frank right away that I wasn't too happy with the desk. He assured me that it was only a temporary arrangement. He said that the newbie in the office gets the LN desk, and that's just the way it was. He pointed out though that one of our C/Os would soon be out-processing, and would be gone in about 10 days. I could then move into the larger cubicle with a somewhat larger desk. I still thought it was a joke, but decided to go along.

As I examined my desk, I also realized that the drawers didn't fit, and that there was a crack running full-length along the top that was wide enough for a pencil to fall through. As I examined the contents of the single drawer, I found a single writing pad and numerous pencils and paper clips that had 'fallen through the crack', so to speak. I did not complain, and after a visit to our self-supply cabinet, began stocking up with pencils, pens, paper, typewriter ribbons and other supplies needed to complete my cubicle. My new calendar and writing pad covered most of the crack.

As I walked back into the main office, I noticed Franks Desk. It was a large, mahogany desk which curved around his rather stout body. "Nice Desk!" I said rather jokingly. Mike responded for Frank, saying "Well, he's been here the longest."

"Traditions!" I said, knowing that my desk would grow over the years as well. We all laughed.

With Frank sitting in, Mike briefed me that the Russians were very active in Bangkok, and that they were specifically interested in the contingency plans and capabilities of the US military. He outlined the

Russian modus operandi (MO) in Thailand, and told me that Mr. Leon Baensler, our Division Chief was attending the OFCO conference in Hawaii and would be returning in a day or two. Leon was definitely considered the local Russian expert. The more he described Leon, the more anxious I was to make his acquaintance.

Three days later, I met Mr. Baensler, who preferred being addressed as "Leon". Parky made the introduction, telling Leon that I had specifically requested the opportunity to work with him, and "wouldn't take 'NO' for an answer." Leon liked me immediately - probably because of Parky's introduction. It was mutual, and as our friendship developed, I found myself often in his company, having lunch and playing bumper pool in the recreation area located between the OFCO and traditional CI offices.

Once I had briefed Leon on the Ivan Project, he was excited about the prospects, but could not recall having heard Ivan's name in conjunction with any Russian activity in Bangkok. Just as a second thought though, Leon requested an updated Russian Embassy employee list from the "Other Agency". The list would also identify those employees suspected to be working under cover at the Russian trade mission.

I spent the next week going through all the operational files, learning much about the Russian attempts at SAEDA. Our office was supported by the CI services desk next door, and I requested an opportunity to attend the next annual SAEDA briefing, given to our own unit. I sat through that four-hour presentation the following week.

After the briefing, I returned to find a note on my desk that Leon wanted to see me. Leon was at lunch, and returned at one O'clock with Mike. We all went into Leon's office where Leon handed me the Russian embassy list.

'The list is here," he said, "now let's get to work. Go ahead. Look it over."

Re-enter, Ivan, full-time:

I gladly took the list, and of course went directly to the R's. Voila again! Highlighted in yellow was '*Romanyev, Ivan V.*' - Leon had already found it.

Obviously now, Ivan had followed in his fathers path. He was listed as an Assistant Cultural Attaché, and had been assigned just one month earlier. Other than age and place of birth (US), there was no additional identifying data on the list, so we went to work requesting Operational Interest immediately, and my name was given as the primary Case Officer. We further requested any available dossiers containing information on Ivan. I knew it would include Ivan's father, and was anxious to show Leon my name on some of the reports over the past nine years.

I prepared a temporary file folder on Ivan, listing basic information to include his hobbies and languages, along with any other identifying data I could recall. This was the only information we had until the copies of both Ivan and his father's dossiers arrived about two weeks later.

The father's dossiers now consisted of three files, and ended with a record of his death in 1971. Subsequently, Ivan had worked for another few months as a radio operator on board a merchant ship and in August 1971 returned to San Francisco for a short period to complete his studies at San Francisco State.

Ivan returned once more to Russia; this time to Moscow. He renounced his US birth-right opportunity and returned to Vladivostok for indoctrination following formal acceptance of his Russian citizenship. I still wondered then what type passport he had been using for his employment travels. There, he attended a six month course at the Diplomatic Society (their equivalent to the US State Department), and several indoctrination courses before being given his first official assignment to Bangkok.

I fantasized that *Ivan must have known I was coming to Bangkok and wanted to personally match wits with me......* Of course, that was a short-lived fantasy. I realized that Ivan had never seen me, and except for the fact that I have a belly-button, he wouldn't know me from Adam. He would have no personal axe to grind – yet.

After making copies of the documents we needed for our dossier, we returned the original documents to the "Other Agency", and I began formalizing my CI Operational Concept. With Leon and Mike tweaking my proposal it was submitted, and received local headquarters approval expeditiously. We received OI on Ivan and I began formulating plans for putting a US soldier in touch with Ivan, as a "dangle".

According to the dossier, Ivan still continued his hobby of playing reed instruments. His musical endeavors were considered by his peers to be of semi-professional quality, and he had made a few recordings of his work with a well-known San Francisco orchestra backing him up. He had focused his music primarily on the Russian classics, but enjoyed experimenting with western popular music as well. In Bangkok, Ivan was also employed by a local English-speaking Radio station as an international affairs consultant, and as a music teacher focusing on the reeds. Ivan had begun publishing some of his attempts at writing. His information series on foreign travel were printed in English and published in Thailand. They could be obtained through two of Bangkok's English Language bookstores.

On a Saturday afternoon after having lunch with Frank at the Chao Phraya Hotel, we were trying to entertain ourselves by not drinking; at least not drinking any alcoholic beverages. As we walked past a club near the near the Chao Phraya, we both noticed, a sign under the marquee headlining an "American performer". It read "DG Miles - live at the Kings Palace, Saturday Night". Since it was still early, at about 3 PM and we had no plans for this night. We decided to take in a movie at one of the local theaters, and then go see what this 'American performer' was up to.

Thai movie theaters are among the best anywhere. They are large, comfortable, clean and most importantly - Air Conditioned. We entered the theater, took the escalator up to the balcony level and made ourselves comfortable with ample snacks and soda. Frank warned me not to leave any opened candy lying on the empty seat next to me. From experience he had learned that regardless of how modern or how plush the theater, in Bangkok - rats rule. If any edible goods were left unattended, one of the rat inhabitants could snatch it from the seat in a matter of seconds. "Never, ever reach down to pick up anythin' edible ya drop on the floor," he warned. "Don't worry; the rats will take care of the mess for ya." I thought he was joking, of course. He wasn't.

We watched the movie *'Earthquake'*, which was exciting enough to deter our attention from any rats that may have come to pay their respects. As we left the theater, I paid particular attention, noting that not one morsel, not even one candy wrapper had been left on the floor. Apparently the rats had done their job.

Walking back down the street to the King's Palace with stomachs full of popcorn, *Baby Ruths* and *Pepsi*, we decided to forego dinner. If needed, we could dine later at the club. We entered and were seated at a table not far from the stage and ordered soft drinks only. We were on time for the introduction:

"Ladies and Gentlemen, welcome to the King's Palace. Tonight we have a special treat for you. Especially for your pleasure, please enjoy the musical talents of United States Army Sergeant D. G. Miles!" Applause erupted.

Enter, D. G. Miles

The lights dimmed and Miles entered stage right, carrying a saxophone. After a pounding rendition of *'Yackety-Sax'*, the Sergeant introduced himself as Doran G. Miles. The G was for Glenn, and he was proud to say his great uncle was none other than THE Glen Miles.

Miles went on to play different instruments, and sing many of the popular tunes of the day. He was an outgoing performer, an excellent musician and a better-then-average singer. He had superior stage presence. After a full 90 minutes of first class entertainment, Miles announced that he would be back after a short break.

Somehow, about halfway through the show, our non-alcoholic beverages had magically turned into Beer for Frank, and Scotch for me.

I turned to Frank and said "I've just had a brainstorm."

Frank responded by saying "Me, too!"

I asked "Are you thinking what I'm thinking?"

"Yup," Frank said, "let's get outa here and go get somethin' to eat!" He started to get up from the table, but I put up my hand, and asked him to sit for just a little longer. Competing with the sounds around us, I did not fear being overheard, and mentioned to Frank that this reed instrument player just might be a good selection for my "dangle" plan.

"Yeah......YEAH!" Frank exclaimed. "That's just what I was thinkin'." We sat for another 20 minutes while DG played a classic, 'Miles-ized' version of *Sentimental Journey*, and took requests from the audience. The first request was from a customer who must have heard him sing and play before. "How about '*I Couldn't Sleep at All Last Night*'?"

It was an excellent rendition. The *Big Bopper* would have been proud. This guy was a pro! What a match-up for Ivan. It was time for some vetting.

On Monday mornings, Frank always went to work early. It was his morning to call the recreation office and reserve the handball court for Monday, Wednesday and Friday.

I have to tell you, Frank's appearance was deceptive. He now weighed in at around 275 lbs, walked slowly, talked slowly, and managed to grunt even when he didn't need to. Anyone looking at him would never guess that he had played football on a college scholarship in Florida. But Frank could move with absolute grace and ease. He could dive, slice, back-off, and spike with the moves of a natural athlete. The word was out – 'Don't mess with Frank Liles'. And he was equally talented at almost any sport he desired to undertake.

I arrived early so I could look over Ivan's dossier once more, and as soon as Mike was present, I asked if we could speak for a moment. He of course had time, and we sat at his desk while I went over the plan I had put together. I began by suggesting that I visit the CI Investigations office to ascertain if their current list of ongoing Background Investigations (BI) were on anyone with whom DG Miles worked. If so, I would suggest they allow me to conduct a portion of that investigation involving character interviews with Miles. This would allow me a bona fide reason for the first meeting, and after two or three interviews, I could break away, and finish the vetting on my own.

Mike agreed with the proposal, and we immediately discussed the approach plan with Leon, who also readily agreed. I checked the MACTHAI personnel roster, and learned that DG worked in the personnel office. Among other things, he was in charge of maintaining alert rosters and aligning personnel by Military Occupation Specialty against requirements in the event of hostilities. He held a 'Top Secret' security clearance. He would be a prime target for any Soviet spy seeking information on US Military Forces in Thailand, deployments and contingency plans.

For Ivan, as a relatively new KGB operative, a contact with DG would certainly be a feather in his cap. And if Ivan follows through, it would be the final proof that he was, as suspected involved in espionage activities directed against US Forces.

Spotting of this potential source had begun. All I needed to do now was evaluate DG, and if he was acceptable, train and prepare him for the introduction to Ivan.

Our office also maintained regular contact with still 'another agency' that had set up electronic surveillance coverage at various strategic locations in Bangkok known to be frequented by KGB personnel.

Additionally, another ongoing umbrella operation conducted regularly by our Case Officers was called "Coverage of Local Establishments" (COLE). Herein, instead of surveilling official and commercial locations where the Russians conducted business, we would conduct random, periodic surveillance of establishments frequented by US military personnel, and Department of Defense civilians. The enviable COLE operation called for going to those selected establishments and hanging for one or two hours immediately after duty hours, identifying Americans, and conducting surveillance detection in search of Russian operatives. This was an extremely lucrative operation insofar as identifying the Russians; however, as often as not, the Russians were either enjoying the same entertainment, or not very interested in the American customers. At the very least, it left no doubt the Russians had been tasked to identify Americans who might be vulnerable.

After coordinating with CI Investigations Chief, Dick Flanagan, I called DG's office, identified myself as a CI Agent conducting background investigations on some of his acquaintances, and was invited to come at any time. He told me that there would always be someone in the office with whom I could conduct interviews.

DG's office was conveniently located on the 6th floor of the Chokchai Building, which housed the entire MACTHAI civilian and military personnel offices except the office of Finance and Accounting. When I arrived at his office, I was greeted by DG. Coincidentally, he was working on updating his US Army Contingency Plan rosters. He asked me to have a seat while he neatly put his files together, attaching classification cover sheets, placed them in folders and back inside his safe which he locked. He turned to me, and I handed him the names of the two individuals on whom I was running the Background Investigations.

He knew them both well, as they both worked directly under his supervision. We were able to conduct the full interviews on both men without interruption. At one point in the conversation, DG offered me a cup of coffee, and I accepted. For a few minutes I was able to ask some personal, innocuous questions of him in an attempt to establish some rapport and hopefully begin a personal relationship.

When I told him that he looked familiar, he made no mention of his outside employment. I must point out here that I was slightly suspicious that he had perhaps not gone through the routine request to work outside the US Government, which is a requirement for US Forces personnel with "Top Secret" security clearances who are stationed overseas.

The interviews finished without his having revealed his outside employment, although he had mentioned that he was a musician.

Before I had an opportunity to arrange another meeting, possibly for another interview, DG said that his own BI was also due. He had submitted the paperwork about two months earlier, and wondered if I might know the status. I told him I would get back to him, and he gave me his office business card on which he also wrote his home telephone number. Apparently, I had established his trust.

I returned to my office and passed the draft reports of the interviews to the CI office. Flanagan took them in draft form, saying that his office would finalize them for my signature. He was happy to have someone helping out, as they were temporarily short-handed on Special Agents.

At my request, he checked his lead sheet bank and found that DG had in fact submitted his request for BI, it had been processed, and was currently being done by one of his S/As. I asked him if I could conduct the subject interview which routinely occurs at the end of each investigation, and he said he would be happy to cooperate. He asked for a timeframe, and I told him I would probably have an approved Operational Concept back from HQ in about two to three more weeks.

I walked back to my office, floating on cloud nine. I was ecstatic that everything seemed to be working out so smoothly. I started filling out the forms for the lead development report (SLDR) and preparing a list of questions to be incorporated into the subject interview with DG.

That evening, Frank and I celebrated.. again. We ate subway sandwiches and had Thai beer at the Trolley restaurant across Sukhumvit Road from the Chokchai building. Most of the clientele were from the Chokchai offices, and everyone seemed to know Frank

Days later, my Proposal was approved, and I visited again with Dick Flanagan. DG's background investigation was now in the last phase, and it was almost time for the subject interview. He handed me the Lead Sheet and copies of the BI Agent Reports. I quickly browsed through them and noticed that most of DG's co-workers were fully aware of his outside employment at the King's Palace. He was well praised, not only because he was considered a well-organized, outstanding NCO, but also for his talents as a musician. All recommended him for continued assignment to his position of trust.

I called DG and made an appointment for his interview, and on Wednesday the following week went to his office. After assuring privacy, we went through the routine questions to be covered during the interview. At the very end, I asked about his outside employment, and he immediately opened his safe and pulled his request for the employment. It had been formally coordinated and his commander had signed off on the request. I also learned that DG's wife was a popular "belly dancer" who had been employed at the International Club in Bangkok since soon after their arrival in country a year earlier.

I made no mention of my intentions, as his utilization had not been fully determined, and the requests had not been entirely coordinated. I carried the results of the subject interview back to Dick's office. The investigation was now complete. After discussing DG with Mike and Leon, it was decided that he may be suitable, but they suggested I get together with DG on a social basis a time or two before pitching him. Leon reminded me that I must first coordinate with DG's Commander, for without his approval, there would be no utilization, thus no operation; and we would have to start over. Leon volunteered to accompany me to the office of Colonel Wilson, stating that he was acquainted with Wilson. Wilson, Leon stated was a gung-ho Colonel. Leon apparently knew Wilson quite well, and stated that Wilson had already procured his own, personalized "body bag" which hangs in his office and had once stated that he was prepared to make the "ultimate sacrifice" for his country.

I thought *"Well, aren't we all?"* But then I wasn't too keen about the body bag idea.

During the time I waited for the normal approvals from Headquarters, I remained at my desk every day, busy with planning, reading requirements and occasionally rubbing my knees which I was constantly bruising on the edge of the desk. I had removed the rollers from my chair as well as the middle drawer of my desk to give myself 4 more inches of space. It helped a little.

Then one morning, Frank met me for breakfast, and informed me that C/O John P. would be departing on transfer that morning. Frank suggested that I move into John's cubicle right away, because Rick S. was coming in and would be setting up his desk with us. I agreed and as soon as we got to the office, made the move. I couldn't believe it. It wasn't as enormous as Franks, but it was a standard-size desk; no more bumping, and crunching. I could use both my middle drawer and the rollers on my chair. I sat, leaned back, and rolled around – all to the applause of the rest of our C/Os.

Later that day, RS was brought to our office by Parky. He was introduced to everyone, and was told that he could use this office until such time as Dick had extra space on his side. That was fine with Rick. As Parky left the office, RS turned to Frank and asked "Well, where's my cube?"

"Right over here, Sir" Frank said, almost sarcastically.

Rick walked in and looked around. "But there's no desk." He protested.

"Sure there is." Frank replied, "Right over there – kinda hidden behind the filin' cabinet.

"That's no desk!" RS protested again, "it's just a small table. What're those bricks for?" Frank went on to explain that RS might want to raise the height of the desk, and was welcomed to use the bricks.

"I'll just get a better desk." RS was screaming. As he tossed his briefcase on the desk, the desk teetered, then tilted to the short leg. RS was furious.

RS walked back into the main office, and saw Frank now sitting behind his hand-carved, cherry-lacquer-finished mahogany desk. The matching mahogany in/out boxes, his personalized, hand-carved mahogany name placard and his 8-switch telephone-intercom all completed his desk-top ensemble.

He pointed at Frank and said "You're just a Master Sergeant, aren't you?"

Frank affirmed the accusation.

"Well then," RS yelled, "There's no problem here, I'll just take yours." He went on "After all, I'm a W. O. 1."

It was time for Mike to intervene, and he did so tactfully, explaining that RS was welcomed to go out and buy his own desk as many others had; or he could just wait his turn and move into a larger desk. "After all," Mike explained tactfully. "This is only a temporary arrangement."

RS tried one more time. Looking at Frank, he said "There must be some way I could maybe win a larger desk."

Not one to back away, Frank yawned, grunted and asked "Well, just what did you have in mind there, W. O. 1?"

"How about a contest of some sort?" RS challenged, staring at Frank. "What's YOU'RE pleasure, Master Sergeant?"

"Humph!" Frank grunted, "Well, how about a game of handball?"

"Great!" RS cried out, "When, where?"

To anyone with any sense at all, it should have been a hint when Frank responded, saying "I just happened to have a court reserved for Wednesday, lunch time." Frank went on "I could pick you up in the parking lot, say - 1100 hours?"

RS agreed, and walked out in a huff toward Dick's office.

RS had not yet recognized me from our Ft Holabird days.

Mike turned to Frank "You'd better be careful big boy. He looks pretty tough." He said winking.

"Yup." Frank said smiling, "Y'all just cain't tell a book by the cover now, can ya?"

Tuesday was a busy day, preparing for the appointment with Colonel Wilson, and on Wednesday, coincidentally nobody in our office had any appointments. We were all present for the Frank/RS confrontation.

We recruited our favorite analyst Dave from the 4th floor to go to the MACTHAI recreation center and watch the match. He agreed to report back by phone as soon as the match was over. Frank had said that the reservation was for lunch, so we all believed we would hear by around 1245.

At 1215 hours, Dave called. "It's over." He was saying, "Frank won. You guys should have seen it. RS couldn't get up off the floor after he collapsed. Frank rolled him over and was about to give him mouth to mouth, when he started gasping and spitting, and trying to catch his breath. Then Frank said 'Thank God I don't have to put my lips on that mouth'. All I could hear RS say was something about a rematch, and complaining about jetlag."

By 1300, Frank was back in the office, showered and fresh as wet paint. RS called in at 1330, saying he would be in the office by 0800 the next day. He had "things" to take care of. The next morning when RS did roll in at around 1030, he was not moving fast. He walked slowly to his cubicle. He never said another word about the desk and my best guess is that he never played handball again - at least not with a fat old Master Sergeant.

On Thursday, April Fools day, Leon and I visited with Colonel Wilson. As we entered his office, I saluted, reporting in a military manner even though I was wearing civilian clothes. Wilson ate it up. "Most of you CID guys" he said incorrectly, "try to hide behind their badges, and pretend to be something they are not. It's a relief to see a real soldier on duty. Some," he went on, "don't even want to salute. I don't mind the agents not wearing their rank, but when they walk into my office, we both know who we are. It's civility and it's tradition. Thank You, Sarge." he said earnestly. Instead of returning my salute, he shook hands, offered us seats, and told his secretary to prepare a fresh pot of coffee and tea.

Leon started the conversation. "Hey Frank, how are you?" They shook hands briefly, and as the Colonel offered chairs again, we both sat.

Leon made the proper introductions, and I began briefing the Colonel. The brewed coffee and tea arrived, along with pastry. As we talked, I began to notice a building curiosity in the Colonel's responses. He was wondering why we were briefing him. I decided to cut to the chase, and skipping the details, told the Colonel "We want to use one of your men."

"And just who would that man be?" the Colonel inquired.

When I told him it was Staff Sergeant DGM, he at first seemed hesitant. "Why him?" he asked, "He's just a sergeant."

I went on to explain that DG fit the bill. I informed him that I had officially vetted DG myself and found that he possessed the special attributes required to do the job. I was very complimentary of DG, stating also that he was a "good soldier", with excellent leadership qualities, and that his co-workers thought very highly of him. I could see the pride beginning to well within the Colonel. His chest swelled, he smiled and said "I guess it doesn't really matter what I say – you guys will probably go over my head anyway. Of course, DG can do the job."

The only stipulation was that DG not be given so much to do that he would be unable to accomplish his day to day duties. I assured him that would not be the case, saying that I would prepare every step of the operation myself.

Wilson was satisfied, and we shook hands again.

He turned to Leon "How's the wife?"

Leon answered that she was doing well, thank you; adding that his entire family was doing great.

They talked for a few minutes, splitting a bagel and drinking coffee. The Colonel drank tea.

As we walked out, the Colonel turned to me and said "If you're ever looking for a job, I could use a good 'Internal Affairs' man."

Both Leon and I had no idea what he was talking about, but after all, he had thought we were CID to begin with.

"Not on my watch!" Leon grinned as we walked out.

Once back in the car, Leon was as giddy as a boy with a new frog. During the 15-minute drive back to the office, he repeatedly remarked "Excellent, excellent!"

Over the next few weeks, the CI office conducted surveillance of DG to determine his habits. The results were boring. We learned that he nearly always had lunch alone at the Windsor Hotel, and often stopped to buy 'Chokchai' Burgers on his way home from work. He played three nights a week at the King's Palace, and his crowds were growing in direct proportion to his popularity.

Ivan was occasionally picked up by random surveillance, going to or from his office. He always carried his briefcase. It appeared to surveillance that he was taking his work home; or as I once opined "Maybe he's carrying his lunch." Ivan never left his office for lunch.

I timed my lunch hour to run into DG twice at the Windsor, and on both occasions was able to sit and talk with him. I told him of the status of his investigation. We became casual friends, and eventually he loosened up and began telling of his exploits, and of his previous military assignments. He was nearing the 10-year mark in the army, and would soon decide whether or not he was going to stay in. I selfishly encouraged him to consider a career, and when he asked about a career in Counterintelligence, I told him to think about it, adding "That might not be a bad idea!"

Over the weeks, I learned to my delight that DG was straight-laced. He never stopped for a drink, and never accepted co-workers' requests to join them after work for a drink. He did not smoke. He worked hard, was career oriented, and was without question devoted to his wife and his country. He was every mom's dream for a perfect son-in-law. To top it all off, DG was in excellent physical condition.

I received recruitment approval, called DG to set up a meeting at the Chao Phraya Hotel. I told him I had a business idea, and would like to discuss it with him. He agreed.

CHAPTER 17.
RECRUITMENT AND TRAINING.

The Chao Phraya Hotel (CPH) and Officer's Club was open to US Government. Like the Windsor, CPH was a transient billet for US Government personnel, and security was considered 'Good-plus'. Official US identification was required to enter the CPH. Non-US guests could be brought in, but were not allowed past the lobby or vendors' area without being escorted by a US government representative. Mike had rented a room for me to use for the recruitment, and had conducted the superficial tech sweep.

On a Thursday night, when DG's wife was performing at the International Club, I met with DG in the CPH lobby. We had dinner in the Dining "Champagne" Room, while engaging in casual conversation. Then about halfway through dinner I asked "I suppose you've been wondering about this 'business proposal' I have in mind."

"I have." He answered, "I assumed it had something to do with my music, or something along those lines." He paused, raised one eyebrow and then added "You're not......."

"No, absolutely not." I answered.

He didn't hesitate when I asked him to come to my room to discuss the idea.

I had laid the key to the room on the table, and suggested to him that he go up first, while I picked up the tab. He understood, and by introducing that minute' element of clandestinity into the relationship early on, he seemed already to be intrigued.

I picked up the bill, placed a few dollars tip on the table and lined up at the Cashier. In the mirror behind the bar, I watched DG casually pick up the key and walk to the elevator. He was not followed. The two-man CI surveillance-detection team I had requested were preparing for their departure.

After paying the bill, I walked through the vendor portion of the lobby, purchased a newspaper at the stand. I then took the elevator to the 3rd floor – and walked to room 345. I first tried the door. It was locked, and when I knocked, DG answered. I could see curiosity in his eyes, and his wide-eyed expression told me that what ever it was, he was extremely interested. "So, what's up?" he asked.

We seated ourselves at the desk, and I poured a drink. I asked if he would like something, and he said he'd like a coke. Dropping ice in his glass, and handing him a bottle of coke, I sat across from him and looking directly into his eyes, I went directly to the point, saying that I had wanted to discuss an ongoing intelligence project with him in hopes that he could lend a hand.

"Of course," he responded. "Anything I can do......well, almost anything?!"

The radio on the table was turned on just loud enough to interfere with any eavesdropping, as I continued to give DG an abbreviated SAEDA security brief, along with explanation of OFCO, and the more exotic and sexy activities within the realm of counter-intelligence. All was designed to perk his interests, but I maintained a reserved and serious tone throughout.

For the next 30 minutes, we discussed the proposal to use him in an operation. DG expressed serious concern about his own abilities, and as to whether or not his chain of command would have reservations. I did not tell him we had already coordinated with Col Wilson; instead I simply said that our organization "would take care of the coordination question."

I told him that the operation, if approved, would not require him to immediately make contact with anyone, adding that if he agrees to becoming involved, I would personally provide him with the appropriate training and guidance to be able to handle the job. "Future meetings," I explained will be handled in a more secure and clandestine manner."

Then, Murphy's Law intervened.

Just as DG was about to speak, the radio stopped. We tried changing stations, adjusting volume, shaking and eventually even slapping the radio around a little. It was dead. I called the front desk, and asked that they replace the radio. They agreed.

Before hotel maintenance arrived, I asked DG to step into the bathroom. I rinsed his glass, put it away and tossed his empty coke bottle into the trash - and sat.

Within two or three minutes, a knock came at the door. A young man with a tool box came into the room.

His name was "Jack", and he was there to "fik radio".

"I asked for a new one." I pleaded.

"No, no new ones", Jack replied. "Be only hab used-car ones". I assumed Jack worked days in a used car lot somewhere in Bangkok.

"OK," I responded. "But please hurry." I was thinking of DG in the non-air conditioned bathroom.

After about 15 minutes, the repairman was still unable to repair the radio. I complained that they should have spare radio. "No, no," Jack repeated.

"I know", I mocked him "You only hab used-car ones."

Jack tried to be helpful, saying "You can go club, suh. Down dare be hab music, dancing and *pu-ying* for comfort."

"Tomorrow." I answered. "Today, I just rest in my room." I found myself speaking pigeon with Jack who had just shocked himself, testing the electric line connection from inside the radio without having unplugged it. He jumped back, screaming in Thai and pointing accusingly at the radio, as though he was scolding it.

Jack then turned his attention back to me. "You no **want** 'pu-ying'?" Jack asked.

"No thank you Jack," I responded. "I have my own."

As though on cue, DG started the shower in the bathroom. I truly believed he was actually showering, as it must have reached 90 degrees in there by now.

"OOOOOOooh!" Jack exclaimed. "Pu-ying?!?" He was ecstatic.

I nodded, smiling.

Jack immediately took the radio and departed the room, saying "Jack be righ back."

DG continued to shower, and in 2 minutes Jack came "righ back". This time he was carrying a new radio, still in the original box. He had gotten it from hotel stock or from one of the main floor vendors.

He plugged it in, and adjusted the station to one with a semi-classical sound. He turned up the volume. Waving his arms and dancing toward the door, "♪Hab a nighz nigh♫," he sang.

"Thank you, Jack." I called out.

Jack was happy and so was I.

After locking the door, I noticed the shower had stopped. I knocked on the bathroom door.

DG responded saying "I be righ ow, Dahling." We both laughed.

That evening, DG agreed to accept the challenge, and was formally recruited.

Over the next few weeks, while I awaited final responses to my Concept and plan, DG and I entered into a full clandestine relationship. Our training sessions were conducted at various locations in the Bangkok area, but mostly in hotel rooms. I selected Officer's clubs, NCO clubs and military transient hotels for security reasons.

Initial training subjects included security, signals, personal meetings arrangements, and emergency meeting plans. We established a signal for initiating emergency meetings, as well as for aborting meetings that were already in progress. Locations and signals for follow-on meetings were already in place. At every opportunity, I tested DG without warning. He never failed.

Late one afternoon, after I had learned from the surveillance team that Ivan had already returned to his apartment complex, I drove DG past the Russian Embassy. During the approach, he observed the embassy, but as we drove by, he looked straight ahead, as I described the layout within the compound. At the next meeting, I showed him a video of the drive-by. I stopped action and we were able to identify the two of us quite clearly.

As I provided him with surveillance detection training, I cautioned him to never attempt to outrun or to ditch any surveillance he may detect. He should go about his normal day-to-day duties and travels, so as not to draw any undue attention. He should be aware of the presence of surveillance, but should not pay any noticeable attention. When he believes he is under surveillance, he should abort any plans for continuing on with operational activities involving USI. He needed always to consider 'plausible denial'.

We established a 'mission accomplished' signal for him to use when he had made contact with Ivan. The signal, a 2 to 4-inch long crayon mark would be made on the inside, glass wall entering the Chokchai building through the main pedestrian entrance. We further established a signal for emergency meetings, which could be used by either of us for setting up a meeting or contact when urgently needed. I gave him hands-on training for making the signals, to insure that he could accomplish those tasks discreetly. I explained that every Sunday, the windows would be cleaned, and his signal would be removed; and from time to time we would change our signals to another location.

We planned all meetings in advance, using appropriate safety and recognition signals, and abiding by the time constraints I had outlined in the sessions. At one point, DG asked "Why don't we have danger signals to give at our initial contact point in the event something suddenly comes up? You know, like they do in movies."

I complimented him for his thought processes, and told him that a danger signal would simply be the absence of a safety signal.

His response: "Well, duh!"

Time and again, we discussed how to break up a meeting, and how to change the subject of our conversations in the event one of us should observe possible surveillance. We discussed our mutual covers for being observed together in the event he should ever be asked. Throughout the training sessions I constantly encouraged him to feel free to ask questions. My philosophy was simply "A question gone unasked, is knowledge unlearned."

We talked of using the secure telephone units (STU) in our offices, and I would not rule out that obviously secure alternative. I told him that he should not hesitate to communicate over the STU, particularly when time is of the essence. We set up a code name for him to call me.

I briefed him extensively on Ivan; his likes, dislikes, habits, hobbies, as well as on the training given to KGB agents. When I explained the type of training Ivan had likely received, DG began to feel inadequate, fearing that he was not qualified to control his own situation. Encouragement became a routine portion of each session, and at one point I asked Leon to accompany me to a future training session with DG. The purpose of this introduction was for an additional, personal evaluation of DG, and to assist in building DG's self-confidence.

Leon came to the very next meeting. I had shown DG a photo of Leon, described his dress, (the usual pale-blue jungle suit) and arranged a recognition signal. As planned, Leon made the initial contact, displaying the signal, and after exchanging very brief bona fides, they walked to a pre-established intersection, where I met them. The three of us then walked to Barney's Restaurant, where we ordered the famous "Barney's Bouillabaisse".

After our meal, we traveled by taxi to the PM site. Once in the room, I began by telling DG that Leon was our foremost expert in the field of Soviet modus operandi. Leon continued by telling DG how fortunate he was so to have me as his "handler". For an hour, Leon and I put on a show for DG, stressing the importance of signals, and with Leon providing an extended explanation of the use of signs, countersigns and bona fides. To say that DG was impressed would be a gross understatement, and Leon's strong and perhaps slightly exaggerated Slavic accent seemed to add to his credibility.

Nearing the end of the meeting, it was Leon who explained to DG that his target, Ivan was only a suspect KGB agent. Leon said it would be DG's job to verify that suspicion, eventually allow himself to be recruited and manipulated to a controlled degree by Ivan – and

"Well...." Leon stated, 'hopefully this operation will make the big time." Smiling, Leon patted DG on the shoulder. "You'll do great!" he said. They stood and shook hands vigorously. Excusing himself, Leon departed the meeting.

DG was favorably impressed by this time. I told DG that should he run into Leon, me or any other agent from USI, he should not acknowledge our presence unless spoken to. We established a signal to allow emergency contact.

Over the next two weeks, I continued to prepare DG for his initial contact with Ivan. In preparation for this contact, DG was to begin studying some of the Russian Musical Classics. I suggested he go to The Bangkok International Times bookstore and purchase the sheet music from the Russian Classic "*Blue Mountain*" in order to begin learning some of the simple exchanges. He could use other sheet music if he so desired. I had suggested "*Blue Mountain*" simply because I had seen it at that bookstore. I also told him he would find Ivan's business card and telephone numbers on the bookstore's bulletin board as a referred musician. I instructed him to keep receipts, as I would need them in order to reimburse him for his operational purchases.

The week of his planned initial contact with Ivan, DG took five days leave. We met on Tuesday. Everything was arranged. DG was to visit the store the next day and shop for awhile. He could remove one of Ivan's cards or copy down Ivan's number and call the Russian Embassy from the public telephone inside the store. On the telephone, he would introduce himself and simply ask to speak to someone in the Consular section who may be knowledgeable of Russian classical music. DG would attempt to make an appointment for Thursday. If Ivan was not available on Thursday, then they would agree on a mutually convenient day in the near future. He was anxious to get started.

DG rehearsed his cover story. He would say truthfully that he was a US soldier, stationed in Bangkok. DG was acutely aware that this portion of his story was easily verifiable, so we worked on his reason for visiting the Russian Embassy. DG was planning on getting out of the military, because he was tired of the bureaucracy, and wanted to pursue his music and entertainment career. We were hoping that Ivan would be sympathetic to DG's decision, and would fulfill DG's simple request for some authentic Russian sheet music for him to work with. DG would show interest in the Russian Classics, but did not need to have much personal knowledge other than having an appreciation for the classics in general. The next move would be Ivan's.

The cover story was very simple. The simpler the story, the tougher it would be to make mistakes. Ivan could question him regarding his background, and he need not deviate much from the truth. I role played his first visit, trying to anticipate any questions that Ivan may have. DG did well.

On Wednesday, DG was on his own schedule; hopefully he was visiting the bookstore. At the office, I had long discussions with Mike and Leon. I would now await DG's signal. Whether he made the expected Thursday appointment with Ivan or not, I would be meeting with him on Saturday Morning for breakfast. The surveillance team called me at 1300 hours Wednesday to give me a preliminary report. DG had arrived at the bookstore at 0845 hours, and the store was still locked. He then went to the rattan furniture shop next door to look around. At 0900, he was observed entering the book store. At 0940 he departed and drove in the direction of his home. He was not followed; there was no reason.

On Thursday, I dwelled on the subject most of the morning, trying to decide if my training and dispatch briefing had been thorough. At 1315 hours, I received an encrypted message from the surveillance team that "Johnny had gone shopping." He was with the target.

Within the hour, I received a follow-up surveillance report. DG had entered the gate to the Russian Embassy compound at 1255 hours. He was challenged by a security guard, handed them what appeared to be a business card. The guard made a quick call, and then gestured toward the guest parking slots, and he was ushered inside. One of the guards walked alongside DG's car, pointing out the slot where he was to park. Then the guard entered the Consular offices with DG.

A little more than two hours later – before I left the office - the second call came in, saying that "Johnny has finished shopping". While DG was inside, the guard had returned to DG's car, looked it over, wrote down the license number, and tried both door handles once. DG had locked his car out of habit. No more attention had been given to the car. At 1548 hours, DG departed the Consular office building and walked to his car. He was waved through the gate, and departed the Russian Embassy compound at 1552 hours. DG drove toward Sukhumvit Road, and turned left, toward the Chokchai Building.

At 1715 hours when I departed the office, I walked out of the elevator and past the signal point. The signal was in place as I had hoped. I immediately noticed DG's car parked in the Chokchai parking lot. He had said that although he was on leave, he had made it a habit to check his official distribution/mail on his days off. Now, I had until Friday night to place my response signal. A response signal was not necessary since we had already arranged our next meeting, but was being placed as a test of DG's observation skills.

Before heading home, I took a side trip to the dairy store to pick up some milk. I had parked about 2 blocks west of the store, and walked easterly, up the right-hand side of Soi #49. With the piece of yellow tape inside my left palm, I turned north at the pedestrian-crowded corner, bracing myself against the cement telephone pole. My signal was in place. Once across the soi, I entered the store, picked up the milk and two ice cream sandwiches, and returned to my car. As I drove back to Sukhumvit road and reached the intersection, I glanced at the telephone pole. The small piece of tape was clearly visible.

The next day was very slow. I completed the reports leading up to the first debriefing, and then involved myself with the next project CIOC. I was confident the Ivan project was moving smoothly on its way to success. I'll be back, Ivan.

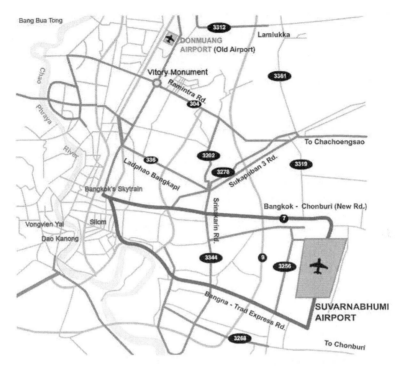

Road Access to Suvarnabhumi Airport

Construction of Bangkok's Suvarnabhumi International Airport began in 2003, and was to be the world's largest international airport when it was completed in 2006. It held that designation until Dec 2007 when the Hong Kong International airport was designated the world's largest; only to be outsized in 2008 by the new Peking International. The Peking and Hong Kong airports, at the time of the writing of this book were designated number 1 and 2 respectively. Donmuong, the old Airport is marked at the top of this map.

CHAPTER 18.
ENTER, ALEX TOPOV

The Bangkok Sports-men's Club was located on Airport Road, about 1 mile south of Don Muang Airport, which was the Bangkok International Airport at that time. The Sportsman's Club was open to those who could afford private membership, or to those whose companies, corporations or embassies sponsored their memberships. The elite club bragged of five-star quality accommodations and services.

Russian Consular Alex Topov was such a member. Within the Russian Diplomatic circles, Alex was considered to be the best all-around tennis contender, and of world class competition standing.

Alex Topov also coached Rugby at the President Country Club, as well as at the Bangkok Rugby Union, located at the Bangkok Patana School. The Patana School is listed at 2138 Soi La Salle, Sukhumvit 105, Bangkok, 10260, which meant that physically, it was located less than a mile from Sukhumvit Road, along Bang Na-Trat Hi-way – convenient to both MACTHAI Headquarters and the Chokchai Building. The Bangkok Patana School was also available to all tennis players and for Rugby tournaments for all educational, diplomatic, and foreign government personnel. The membership fees were less than 10 percent of that for the Sportsman's Club. If you were the member of a registered team, there was no charge for membership.

Leon was a member of the Rugby Union, and often referred to the union as "the Sportsman's Club", although there was no subordinate affiliation between the two. Leon would often invite one or two of the case officers to lunch at the "Club", which meant they would dine at Vic's # 3, a Hungarian Restaurant collocated with the Patana School.

Leon played no sports at all. He had no interest in sports. He could occasionally watch a tennis match or a basketball game, providing the game was exciting enough or if one of his two children was involved. Leon enjoyed chess, and was always open to a challenge at bumper pool, which he considered a "parlor sport".

According to the records of the "other agency", Alex Topov had been designated an aggressive KGB agent since his arrival in Thailand in the late 1960s when the Viet Nam conflict was still very much alive. His MO was to be where American Soldiers on R&R from Viet Nam were active. That meant he would hang in bars, massage parlors, clubs and other businesses open to the public, where he could attempt contact with Americans.

Every year, following the annual SAEDA briefings, soldiers would line up for appointments with our CI office to report contacts and attempted contacts by an individual who fit Alex's description; but to the best of our knowledge, his clumsy attempts had never realized any degree of success. Leon thought Alex was looking for a specific type of American Government employee. While I agreed that the dangles we provided did not have the desired placement or classified access that Alex found attractive, somewhere along the line, a mistake must have occurred. Nonetheless, Alex seemed always to gradually decrease contact with the 'dangle', and the US person would rotate stateside. Alex was definitely a "spotter". We had retained OI on Alex over the years, and virtually every one of our case officers had given him a shot. None of our 'dangles' were ever re-contacted following their rotations stateside.

It was now my turn to give it a try.

On this day, I had beaten Leon at two games of bumper pool in a row, and he decided it was his turn to buy lunch. He was aware that I had pulled Alex's file, and enroute to the "Club" briefed me about Captain Bill Tanner. A few months earlier, Leon had spotted Tanner as a potential lead for making contact with Alex, but had neither followed up on his idea, nor had he passed the lead to anyone else.

Enter Captain William (Bill) Tanner, US Army.

Leon had done some of the footwork and had read Captain Tanner's security file during the routine background investigation. He told me that when Bill was 27 years old, at his father's request, he gave up his then semi-pro tennis career to temporarily to serve his country. Once he had served his initial four years, Bill decided to make a career of the military, following in the footsteps of his father and grandfather.

After a full tour in Viet Nam, and following a one-year stint at the Defense Language Institute in Monterey, California, Bill's follow-on assignment brought him to Bangkok to serve at the "G-5" level as the MACTHAI Civil Affairs Officer (CAO).

A creature of habit, Bill visited the nearby Patana School almost daily as part of his physical fitness program, and would routinely play tennis for an hour, order lunch, shower, have lunch and return to his office on the 6th floor of the Chokchai building. His security clearance was TOP SECRET, with several special access designations.

Leon opined that if we found Bill acceptable, and decided to dangle him, the only problem we might encounter would be the approval of Col Wilson. Wilson, Leon explained was due to rotate in about 3 months. We had two choices: 1) expedite the paperwork, and try to bring him on board while Col Wilson was still cooperative, or 2) allow the paperwork to progress normally, and take our chances with the next Commander. This discussion was Leon's way of telling me he wanted me to run this operation, and how to do it. That was fine with me; after all, he's my boss. Since we had already paved the rapport-road to Col Wilson, we decided to act now.

We arrived at the "club" at 1030 hours. Leon strutted through the lobby area, showing me the sports trophies on display and we stopped to examine the pair of carved ivory tusks encircling the entrance to the adjoining Vic's #3 Restaurant. He smiled and spoke to every passerby as though they were long-time friends, turning to me several times to say proudly "They all know me." The maître d' escorted us to our table, asking our beverage preference. I ordered a beer, and Leon asked for a small 4 ½ ounce bottle of Rose' Mateus.

"Your waiter will be right with you, Mr. B". The maître d' was speaking to Leon.

Moments later the waiter arrived with our drinks, and took our orders. I ordered fish & Chips, while Leon struggled through the menu, and then speaking in a language with which I had no familiarity, placed his order. The waiter understood Leon's order, and then turned to me and asked if we would like the "special dessert menu."

Before I had a chance to say "no, thank you," Leon interrupted, saying "Of course." The waiter nodded, clicked his heels and departed. For a fraction of a second, I again thought of West Point.

Before our meals arrived, Leon spoke. "He's here."

"Who?" I asked.

"Bill's here." He had seen Captain Tanner arrive in the reception area, in uniform. Bill spoke momentarily to the maître d' then turned left and walked from the reception area into the lobby and turned right into the hallway toward the gymnasium and locker rooms, carrying a sports bag and two tennis rackets.

Our meals arrived. I could never have believed how mouth-wateringly delectable fish and chips could be. The filet had been marinated in a mild, garlic butter and a lemon-curry flavored sauce, battered and then fried in an extremely light virgin olive oil; drained over heated filters and wrapped in one single layer of pita to absorb any oil that may not have drained. The chips were obviously prepared by an equally qualified chef, and were delicately powdered with the exact amount of spices which included a pinch of Thai pepper powder.

My old Cajun MP buddy, LaFromboise from Baton Rouge, would have gladly died for this meal; and I wondered if Frank had yet satisfied his palate at this restaurant. Probably not; after all there was not a bottle of ketchup in sight.

Leon's lunch was equally exquisitely prepared. The thin slices of sautéed beef were sizzling on a stoneware platter to form a triangle. Each piece was scorched around the edges, and ranged from that small dark-brown border to a mild pink center. A generous serving of spiced, mashed potato filled the center of the triangle. A small mound of creamed corn finished the platter design. One clove of garlic had been squeezed; red pepper and white sesame had been ground. Those were then mixed into a sauce with just a hint of Worcestershire - or perhaps molasses-sweetened soy and vinegar - and poured over the garnishes. A generous tablespoon of wasabi paste was formed into a cone and placed in a small crystal bowl alongside his main dish. Leon smiled at the platter, and then demolished the cone, lavishly spreading the wasabi over his beef strips.

As we proceeded to devour our lunches, I noticed that Leon was constantly asking questions about my meal.

"Is it good?" he started; and later, "Tasty? And how about the spices - Are they OK?"

Finally, I asked if he would like to try it.

"Oh, thank you, thank you!" Leon answered, reaching over the table and cutting himself a generous portion of my filet.

He gently placed a small bit in his mouth. 'Why, that's absolutely breathtaking!" he proclaimed. "Isn't it wonderful? Exotic; almost erotic food such as this is both necessity and indulgence, all in one delicious package."

He obviously enjoyed eating; although I must admit he was right, it was 'breathtaking'.

"Imagine," Leon went on, "right at this moment, there is no-one in this world eating better than you and I." He was probably right about that, too.

I was totally focused on the meal, when I heard Leon say "Wow, look at him play!" He was speaking of Bill Tanner of course, who was 'in the zone'. He was destroying his opponent on the court. While eating, we watched him through the bay windows of the dining room which overlook the court. The game took about 30 minutes, and Bill's yet unidentified opponent was exhausted from chasing the ball back and forth across the court. Bill ran to him; meeting at the net, they shook hands. They spoke momentarily and Bill pointed at his watch. I tried to believe the opponent was asking for a rematch, but decided that was probably not the case.

Our special dessert menu arrived, and Leon selected the *chocolate mousse* for both of us. When I asked if we could simply cut one in half, complaining that the fish and chips had been a might too much, Leon blurted out "It's OK, I'll finish your uneaten portion." It was OK with me.

The desserts arrived within a minute. I understood at first bite why Leon ordered the mousse. It literally melted in my mouth. The blend of whipped chocolate with a hint of coffee constituted the most delicious air I'd ever eaten in my life. I almost regretted that I was going to give half to Leon. We topped off the dessert with a special cup of whipped latte made in part from Chokchai farm's special sweet cream.

By the time Bill entered the dining room and sat at his reserved table, his vegetarian meal was ready. Within a minute, he was being served. He looked our way, waved and Leon waved back at him. "He knows me too, of course." Leon whispered, grinning with pride.

As we departed the restaurant, I noticed Leon glancing around the room before he approached Bill's table.

"Hi Bill, that was a great game." Leon started.

Bill blushed. "Actually, it was not really a match. He's young, from London, and hasn't been playing long."

Leon introduced us, and then said right away "Don doesn't play tennis." His tone was almost embarrassingly apologetic.

I chimed in "We watched you during lunch. You play very well," I complimented him. "Do you teach or coach here as well?"

"Not regularly." He said, "But I do coach whenever I have time, and I play on their Rugby team. Next year, we're going to have a good soccer team too."

"That's good," I said "Keeps you pretty busy doesn't it?"

"I have nothing better to do at this time. We're not fighting any wars here in Bangkok!" He grinned.

It was time for us to leave. We shook hands. The introduction had been made – now the follow up was up to me.

We returned to the office, and on the way, Leon coached me on the approach plan, CIOC and SLDR I was about to prepare. He told me to use the same format I had used on the Ivan project, adding that he would prepare the appropriate comments, approvals and recommendations for expediting the requests.

At the office, I began consolidating the files for the project I shall heretofore refer to as "Alex".

During my free time I had located a small apartment at the corner of Soi 52 and Sukhumvit Road. The owner, a Chinese Thai, liked me from the start and went out of his way to expand my small studio into a one bedroom apartment. The cost was US$115 per month, plus gas. I could move in as soon as I had time, and the rent would not start until the first day. My hold baggage had arrived, and I had asked for an evening delivery between 1700 and 1800 hours.

When the hold baggage arrived, I noticed right away that the steel bands on both wooden crates had been replaced with yellow nylon bands. I asked the deliverymen why, and one said he did not know; the other said it was opened for inspection. They cut the bands and opened the boxes. At first glance, I believed most of my clothing was in the box, with the exception of my two very favorite, hand-made pairs of shoes. Almost everything else had been replaced with large rocks. I'd been ripped off, robbed; my hold baggage had been 'shanghaied'.

In the second box, I found that my stereo equipment was gone, all my cameras were gone, along with the developing equipment I'd sent, and a second look, with my copy of the inventory sheet in hand, revealed that a good amount of my clothing had been lifted as well. Wrapped in an empty, Thai rice bag were my 24-hour clock and barometer. Fortunately, the 35mm *Praktica* camera, along with the brass sphinx, had been mailed through the APO and were not included in the baggage. I was happy I'd decided not to send all of my belongings in these crates. My small book collection was sent separately, clearly labeled 'professional publications'. The steel bands were still intact.

I called the Military Police and filed a complaint. They made an appointment for me to come to their office and file a claim for the stolen goods. They asked me to bring receipts for goods I had purchased, and informed me that I could not expect to get a full reimbursement for used goods. I went to the MP office and talked with SGT Townsend. It appeared that they were more suspicious of my motives than they were interested in the truth. At first, they questioned whether or not the items had actually been stolen. This insulted me. Then as I handed over my packing inventories and described the theft, they finally began to believe my statement. But now they questioned as to whether the theft had taken place in the US or in Thailand. I handed them a piece of the yellow plastic binding and pointed out that the clasp was labeled in the Thai language. When they informed me that the clasp was no proof, I understood why I'd opted out of the MP Corps. I told them 1) that the box was full of rocks; and 2) if Thai authorities had opened a box full of rocks for inspection, surely they would have made some record of it, so they wouldn't be blamed.

I recognized the "Duuh!" expression as Townsend acknowledged my statement. He gave me paperwork to take home and execute. I didn't have to take it home, since I had most of the original receipts containing the serial numbers and cost for the items I had claimed. I filled it out right then and there. I also told the MPs that the stereo equipment and cameras had my service number engraved somewhere on each item.

On the way back to the office, I secretly hoped that the stereo items would not be found, as they were all 60 cycle, 110 volt, and Thai electricity is 50 cycle, 220m volt. I had already purchased the 60/50 cycle conversion kits and an electric converter, but they had also been stolen. I didn't want to use them anyway.

Frank had made reservations for me at the Windsor Hotel, and had stayed in the room on Friday night. I would use the room on Saturday for my meeting with DG, and Frank would stay in the room again Saturday night and then check out early Sunday. There was no need for dead drops, as Frank and I could pass the key back and forth in the office.

I walked to my office, arriving at 0745 hours Saturday morning, and waited for Frank to arrive. By the time he arrived at 0810, coffee was ready. He passed me the key to room 325 in the Windsor, and I called on the STU to DG's supervisor's office. DG answered, and using a prearranged brevity code, I told him that the reception would occur on March 25. That provided him the room number. The Windsor had already been selected as a meeting place. This time, there would be no public meal, a precaution we had initiated in the event DG was being followed. Enroute to the Hotel, I stopped at a Chokchai Hamburger stand and picked up four cheeseburgers. We would partake of Frank's beverage stock in the room fridge. Frank, who was remaining in the office to type his part of the surveillance report pertaining to the uneventful night at the Windsor, said he would await my return after the debriefing.

That morning, I walked to the Windsor Hotel. The 15-minute walk allowed ample time and distance for conducting surveillance detection, and I was more comfortable than I would have been trying to drive in this fairly new environment. My 1972 Toyota Corona had arrived the week before. It was now licensed and insured, but left-hand driving was completely new to me. I arrived at the Windsor Hotel and while passing through the lobby, picked up a morning paper, ordered a thermos pitcher of hot coffee and a bucket of ice. In the room ahead of schedule, I arranged the desk and table, checked the radio, adjusted the sound and waited for DG. The hot coffee and ice arrived at 1045 as requested, and DG knocked on the door at precisely 1100 hours. He was excited about his initial contact, and I knew immediately that all had gone well.

My first question was "Have you detected any surveillance since you first met with Ivan?"

"I did not," he answered "but I thought there was going to be. I was very careful not to do anything out of the ordinary."

After his initial, personal contact with Ivan, DG said he left the embassy and drove directly to Sukhumvit Road, DG had taken the usual route back to his apartment, picking up his fast food burgers along the way. He also checked his official distribution at the office on his way home. His wife had worked until 2200 and had returned home by taxi. They had dinner, watched TV until 2300, and then retired for the night.

DG stated that on Friday, he had once again visited his office to check his official distribution. On the way home, he had driven past the intersection of Sukhumvit and Soi 49, where he readily observed the tape signal. He knew then that I'd seen his signal.

And today - the distance from his apartment to the Windsor was long enough, and his walk from the Windsor parking lot into and through the lobby area allowed him to watch for surveillance. Had he noticed anything even remotely suspicious, he would not have come to the room, but would have had coffee and returned home.

We poured coffee and "toasted"; then I asked him about the contacts. He talked first about his phone call to Ivan.

On Wednesday, after picking up the sheet music at the music store, DG checked the bulletin board and discovered Ivan's business card. Since there were three copies of the card, he simply took one and then waited to use the pay phone located next to the exit. After about 2 minutes, he dialed the number listed as "office" on the card. It was not a direct line to Ivan, but rather a designated English language number to the embassy switch. He identified himself relayed his brief cover story to the operator, and was put on hold. After approximately one minute, a voice answered, identifying himself only as "Romanyev". After explaining who he was once more and outlining his basic cover story, DG was given an appointment to meet with Romanyev at 1300 hours the next day. Romanyev provided simple directions to the embassy.

DG said he was hardly able to fall asleep Wednesday night, rising early on Thursday. Anxious, he left early, and was happy that road construction slowed him down, and he was able to time his arrival and to enter the embassy compound just before 1300 hours. He relayed the story of the security challenge at the gate of the embassy, and the escort inside. I opened my briefcase and showed the photos of DG driving into the embassy compound, entering the consular section offices. I also showed those photos of the guards checking out his car while he was inside, and of his departure. The photos had been blown up and cropped to prevent triangulation, which could allow pinpointing of our surveillance location.

DG was impressed and shocked. "How did you get these great photos?" he asked. I only smiled, and he went on with his story. He said that once inside, he was required to show his ID card, and they had kept the card while he was visiting. He had been escorted to a waiting room adjacent to the lobby, which was equipped with surveillance cameras. Within a few minutes, a gentleman entered the room and identified himself as Ivan Romanyev, Vice Cultural Attaché. He invited DG into his office, saying "Now, what can I do for you, young man?" DG said this statement caught him off guard, as he had assumed they were approximately the same age.

DG started, "Well, Mr. Romanyev," and was immediately interrupted by Romanyev.

"Please, please call me Ivan." Smiling, Ivan was very personable.

He followed his cover story. Ivan poured a soft drink for DG, and they engaged in casual conversation while DG continued to explain his simple dilemma. Before offering any kind of assistance, Ivan asked a few questions of DG:

"How did you learn of me?"

DG opened the envelope containing the purchased sheet music which he had carried in, and had surrendered for examination at the guard post and again at the front desk.

"I bought this at the bookstore," DG told him, "and took one of your business cards from the store's bulletin board." Then as an apparent afterthought "I called you from the phone right there in the store." DG said he was totally unprepared for Ivan's excellent English.

The ensuing conversation involved a description of DG's job position, and his outside employment at the King's Palace. Ivan asked specific questions about the outside job, the days he works, and of DG's desire to be a full-time entertainer.

DG was sufficiently observant to provide detailed answers to my questions. At my request, he drew a floor plan of the portions of the embassy he had observed, to include Ivan's office. He described the interior of Ivan's office as gloomy, and stated that Ivan did not seem very organized. There were no curtains, just blinds on the windows, and Ivan had not decorated the office with pictures or Russian travel posters as DG had somehow expected. Documents and personal papers were scattered on his desk, and on a small table located under his office window sill. A single book shelf was centered on the table, and was used to hold a few bottles of foreign whiskey. Both his safes on one side of the office were opened. An opened padlock hung on the hasp of each of the safes which were equipped with locking bars. A third filing cabinet was located on the opposite side of the doorway. The blinds had been adjusted to deflect the sunlight, but DG could still see the guard house and the guards roaming around outside.

Ivan had not provided him with any sheet music at this meeting, but was obliging and courteous. He offered to loan DG any and all sheet music from his personal Bangkok collection for copying, and to obtain even more from his home in Russia if DG was still in need or even interested.

When DG told him he didn't want to 'bother' him, Ivan was insistent, saying "It's no bother at all, it's my job." Ivan was happy and even appeared flattered that a foreigner could be interested in the Russian classics. Ivan admitted his own expertise in the reed instruments, and this discussion went on for over a half hour, while they each described their respective lives and musical studies. DG was of the impression he was being tested. He was.

DG did not deviate from his simple cover.

He described his departure, saying that at 1540 hours, he had departed Ivan's office and walked with Ivan to the front desk to retrieve his ID. Before returning it to him, they asked for his driver's license. He handed it over to them, and after making Xerox copies, handed both his identifications back to him.

He shook hands with Ivan who said "I will be calling you in a day or two, my new friend".

At 1548, DG walked to his car and moments later was waved through the gate. After departing the Russian embassy grounds, DG drove east and directly to Sukhumvit Road, where he turned north.

Contact had been successfully initiated. DG did not have to consider arranging for recontact, as Ivan had taken care of that for him. I told DG that although it may appear that Ivan swallowed his cover story, DG should not be complacent, and should expect that Ivan and his office will likely check him out much further. I told him he could expect a call from Ivan early the following week.

We spent another hour in the meeting, eating the cheeseburgers and discussing my expectations for him over the next few weeks. I passed on Leon's guidance as to how he should react to Ivan's predictably clumsy attempts to befriend him. I cautioned him several times that it was about 99 percent likely he will be surveilled following his next meeting. He should not attempt to lose surveillance. DG Should drive as directly as possible from one location to the next, and should always have a logical reason for any diversion or stop. I cautioned him against taking any provocative action, but added that if he could identify the car or persons following him, it would be appreciated. I told him not to take even the slightest chance of letting anyone know that he had detected the surveillance. No eye to eye contact with members of any surveillance team.

"Actually," I told him, "Russian surveillance techniques are very similar to those of our own. Their operatives are very thorough, particularly during the early stages of an operation; however, once their Case Officers reach a certain point, they tend to become over confident, and begin to trust their contacts and recruited agents. At that point, their surveillance practices become shamefully lax and slipshod. It normally requires genuine trauma to shock them out of their apathy."

We went over some of the previous training before calling the meeting to a close, and DG departed at 1630 hours. He informed me that he would be at work the entire next week, but could make himself available at Ivan's request. I told him that he need not always be immediately available, as it might appear unusual to Ivan. I would expect his STU call as soon as he received a call from Ivan. He would comply.

At 1015 hours Monday morning, DG called Mike's STU and asked for "Dale". Mike keyed the STU as he called me to the phone. DG said he'd received a call at 2100 hours on Sunday night, and that "Eric" (meaning Ivan) wanted him to come to the office at his earliest convenience. Again DG had set up the meeting for Thursday – this time for 1500 hours.

Our prearranged meeting had been scheduled for Wednesday providing Ivan called before then, and we agreed to keep with that schedule. Before hanging up, I reminded DG of our last discussion. I would call him again Wednesday morning with a brevity code for the room number.

That afternoon, Dan G, another member of our office made reservations for Tuesday and Wednesday. Dan picked up the key to room 521 Tuesday afternoon, and stocked the refrigerator with a variety of soft drinks. Early Wednesday, I called DG on the STU and gave him the room number by brevity code. I again purchased lunches for DG and myself, placed those lunches and notes for the meeting in my briefcase and this time drove to the Windsor. I parked in the parking lot at 1030 hours. This meeting would not take long, as it was simply another dispatch meeting, to prepare DG for his encounter with Ivan. I also wanted to reinforce DG's confidence and encourage him that we were there for him.

I entered the Windsor through the rear lobby entrance, and walked to the vending machines and purchased a newspaper. Observing nothing out of the ordinary, I took the elevators to the fifth floor, paying in advance for the pot of coffee for room 521.

Note: Now, imagine if you can our small office of eight Case Officers. Our Russian target personalities alone numbered 23, including Russian embassy, consulate and trade mission. Each US Case Officer has approximately two personal meetings a week, all of which must go through the same security precautions, and require assistance not only from their fellow case officers, but also coordination for foot, vehicular and technical surveillance support, through the CI operations office.

Early in this writing I explained also that every phase of every contact must be documented by reports and supported with cover documentation. That means that every phase of a clandestine operation requires literally hundreds of pages of Case Officer-authored documents. Suffice it to say that the routine paperwork alone can be overwhelming.

As operations progress, advance coordination requests are submitted for envisioned technical assistance such as wiretapping, investigative monitoring and eavesdropping activities. Not only does each activity require coordination through local operations officers, but often must go through the headquarters before any new phase can be initiated. Monthly intelligence funding reports and expenditure requests are also submitted, outlining all expenses incurred or anticipated in the conduct of operations.

Periodic source status reports are required, and Case Officers are called upon regularly to attend budget and operational meetings. "Frustration" is a mild word to describe the unremitting administrative burdens which CI operatives must be prepared to endure.

One might think "I never saw James Bond writing reports!"

How very, very true.

As planned, the meeting was relatively brief. DG was excited and ready for his next contact with Ivan. We reviewed previous training and I stressed again the importance of maintaining his simple cover story.

Per Leon's guidance, I told DG that he could expect to see Ivan at the Kings Palace sometime in the near future. I suggested DG be prepared to entertain him a little when he shows up.

We made arrangements to get together Saturday afternoon, for debriefing of his contact with Ivan, and then terminated our meeting at 1530. DG departed the Windsor. We had gone over every point at least twice. I did not leave the room until 1730 hours, allowing plenty of time for DG to accomplish his surveillance detection.

When I finally left the hotel, I conducted my own surveillance detection, shopping in the lobby and then along the street shops, before picking up my car in the parking lot. I then took a circuitous route back to my own apartment, stopping to pick up two rattan bar stools I had ordered a day earlier. No surveillance was detected, and I felt comfortable turning into my parking lot and carrying the two stools to my virtually empty apartment.

Friday Morning, I observed DG's signal on the designated window. The signal was only two to three inches long, indicative of a very quick touch. This more discreet mark led me to believe that he was not as nervous or anxious as he had been when he placed the first one. I reminded myself to rotate signal locations.

CHAPTER 19.
THE ART OF DECEPTION.

A brevity code given over the STU set up our meeting at the prearranged site. To my surprise however, the debriefing was of a greater significance than I had expected. When DG arrived at the personal meeting site, he was noticeably more anxious than usual. We quickly discussed our mutual cover for being together and made arrangements to use the Windsor Hotel for our next meeting. Then I asked "Well, how did it go".

"Wow," he exclaimed, "everything you said would happen – DID! - and more!"

"That's great!" I replied, trying to sound calm. "So what happened?"

"First," DG said, "He gave me these." He handed me a thick envelope. I handed it back to him, smiling "OK, open it."

DG opened the envelope, and carefully emptied the contents on the desk. There were several complete sets of various Russian operas, sheet music, and two audio tapes – which, according to DG, were copied "from Ivan's personal collection."

Even I was surprised.

DG went on to explain that Ivan was very friendly this time. When he arrived at the embassy gate, the guards appeared to be expecting his arrival. They waved him on through, and once inside the embassy, he did not have to sign in at the front desk. The receptionist recognized him and took note of his arrival. The receptionist directed him down the hallway toward Ivan's office. He was not required to surrender his ID. DG thought it might have been because Ivan was waiting for him at the entrance into his office.

Once inside the office, they had talked casually for awhile, then Ivan took the sheet music from his briefcase, handed it to DG, saying "This is for you, my new friend."

DG was so excited he almost didn't notice the other documents in the briefcase. Also, Ivan was so quick to close the briefcase that DG was still not one hundred percent sure of what he thought he had seen.

"Well," I asked "Don't keep me in suspense. Just what did you think you saw?"

"I'm afraid you'll think I'm being paranoid or something," he began.

I assured him that I hadn't even considered that possibility.

DG then went on to say "I'm sure I saw a US passport, and" he hesitated, "I think I saw a set of credentials – like yours."

"Like mine?" I asked. "What makes you so sure?" Even I couldn't contain my excitement.

"Don't misunderstand," DG started. "I didn't stare at anything. After all, I was too busy looking at the sheet music and Ivan closed his briefcase right away." Then he went on to describe the contents.

"Things were scattered around in the briefcase. There was a sandwich in a Ziplok, a flask, a passport case with the US seal embossed on it, and there was another black case with gold seal that I thought read

'US Department of War'". DG further said "It looked identical to your credential case." He then added "Except it looked brand new."

"Do you think he saw you notice them?" I asked.

Without hesitation, DG again said "No, Ivan barely opened his briefcase. Of course I watched him remove the envelope, but as soon as I saw the contents, I turned, focusing my full attention to the sheet music. He didn't seem nervous. He closed the briefcase and put it back under his desk."

"You did well." I told him. "And, we'll definitely come back to that discussion later."

I allowed DG to tell me of the entire meeting in his own words, uninterrupted. As DG described his contact, it became obvious that Ivan was taking the bait. DG pointed out that Ivan was not so business-like during this visit, and actually seemed genuinely warm. He gave his small gift to DG, and reminded him that he would have more sheet music for him the next time they meet. Ivan went on to say that he had already "called Moscow", and more music was on its way by diplomatic pouch. Ivan told him the next package would include some of the "more popular music being played in Russia today." It was as though he was now baiting DG.

DG was very happy with the music he already had, and the news of more to come. Ivan told him he would call him again, as soon as the next package arrived. Ivan even suggested that they get together for a "jam session", and on this occasion, DG invited him to come to the King's Palace. There, he could introduce Ivan to the drummer, the piano-player and the guitarist, all of whom are Thai nationals.

During the meeting, Ivan even briefly played his trumpet for DG, demonstrating his own musical talent. When Ivan played part of the classic *"When the Saints go Marching In"*, DG asked if Ivan had ever been to New Orleans. Ivan replied that he had not, but hoped to some day.

"You never know." Ivan pondered, "Maybe I'll be posted back in the US someday."

"By the time our meeting ended," DG said, "I believe he was 100 percent convinced that I am a legitimate musician. He also promised to come to the Kings Palace to watch my performance – just like you and Leon said he would."

After taking a break and consuming our lunches, I returned to the subject of the possible detection of American credentials and passport.

Once again I asked DG to describe to the best of his ability, the circumstances surrounding his observation. DG explained that Ivan was anxious to give him the sheet music, and took the briefcase from beneath his desk. When he opened the briefcase, it looked as messy as his desk, and while he fumbled inside for the envelope, DG caught a glimpse of what appeared to be the credential and passport cases. The credential case was not opened, and DG did not observe its contents. When asked, DG stated that he also had not seen a badge. But then he had not taken time to look for one.

He saw the edge of a plain, passport-type document emerging from the passport case, and noticed that it appeared to be one of the old light-blue/gray American passports, but of course DG saw only a small portion of the cover and the US seal. I cautioned DG never to mention his observation to Ivan.

DG was positive, again restating that Ivan did not see him observing the contents of the briefcase. DG had looked away immediately, and looked back toward Ivan only when Ivan spoke. They went through the sheet music one by one, and it was then that Ivan again picked up his trumpet and played a few notes from each of the charts.

I asked "Was he any good?"

"Not bad," he replied, "But I wasn't all that impressed." Then he smiled, saying "I'm much better."

I'm sure he was.

I began preparing DG for his next meeting with Ivan. Again, I told him that he should keep his eyes open for surveillance, and reminded him once more not to take any evasive action. If he is enroute to meet with me, he should abort that plan, go on to do some personal shopping, visit a tourist attraction, or do something else that any surveillant would find boring. He should then return to his office or home in a routine manner.

"Always," I instructed, "have a legitimate, non-operational reason for any of your movements. At each of our meetings, we will always go over our mutual cover for being together and talking. Then, before we get into discussion of our operation, we will make the next meeting arrangements and plan a follow-up/emergency meeting in the event we are interrupted or must abort for security reasons such as detection of surveillance of any kind."

Before departing the meeting site, I instructed DG to be extremely cautious when carrying anything Ivan gives him. I talked of double enveloping or exchanging the envelopes used for items such as documents or sheet music. Pointing out the Russian Embassy seal in the upper left-hand corner of the envelope he had brought with him to the hotel, I said that if DG was being followed and/or photographed, it could come back to haunt him if he were questioned by Ivan as to why he carried that particular envelope into the Windsor Hotel.

His response: "Duuh?!"

Further, I explained the Russians have excellent, concealable listening devices for recording conversations, and tracking devices for following someone. If Ivan ever gives him any gift whatsoever, it should be wrapped and placed in a metal container, such as a coffee can. I also stated that I would personally take any larger gift items to my office and let our technical services personnel inspect them before DG tries to use them.

Ivan, the American?

On Monday morning, back at the office, I briefed Mike and Leon. They were impressed with DG's observation skills. On one hand, Leon was hoping that DG was not so paranoid that he was "seeing things," while Mike was concerned as to the probability of Ivan testing DG. I opined that DG understandably was a little paranoid, but I felt that he had handled the sighting like a professional.

"The very idea," Leon said, "that a Russian spy who speaks perfect English, conducts himself like an American, has lived most of his adult life in the United States, could be in possession of a US passport AND possibly credentials that at the very least appear to be authentic – it's astounding!" He went on to say "It would not be impossible for him to have walked off with someone's passport from one of his trips aboard ship, but the possibility of possessing credentials that may support his operational activities - is frightful."

Leon went to the control safe and took out our credentials. His case, like mine, was identified with the War Department seal, while both Frank's and Mike's displayed the Intelligence and Security Command (INSCOM) seal. The War Department seal had been used for those with the older black and white CIC credentials; while the INSCOM covers were issued to newer agents. Leon had opted to keep his old case. I joked with him saying "Your case looks brand new; you must not have used it much." He punched my shoulder.

Dick was talking. "The worst case scenario goes something like this: With a good set of professionally counterfeited credentials, Ivan could successfully identify himself as a CI investigator, even to unwitting Americans. With the US passport, he could walk into US facilities such as the Windsor Hotel, The Chao Phraya Hotel where he probably could register and perhaps even use the facilities. He may be able to fake Temporary Duty or military-on-leave-type travel orders, and use his identification to ease his movements within the US community. He could enter US facilities such as the army Finance

Office – just to make his face known, or to become recognizable at American facilities – to build his cover as an American.

An official-looking US passport and easily-obtained, US Military ID card which could pass a cursory inspection by non-government employees at some facilities may not be difficult to counterfeit. (With a valid US driver's License, one may obtain an International Drivers' License (IDL) at any AAA Office in the US.) "Flash items" such as an IDL would serve to further verify his identification and status.

Ivan's perfect English language, combined with his mannerisms and dress habits would provide the icing on the cake.

Leon even agreed that "A young American soldier who is not familiar with official CI credentials could easily be tricked into cooperating fully with any "Ivan" he should encounter."

Using my own credentials, I pointed out the phrase *"All US persons are enjoined to cooperate with the bearer of these credentials"*, and added my two cents worth: "Ivan would need only to explain that he needed "confidential cooperation". Any soldier would cooperate and probably report it to no-one, just to be accommodating."

Leon and Mike agreed, and the conversation ended in silence.

Before we left Leon's office, we confirmed an afternoon meeting with all the Case Officers and with Dick F as well.

While I prepared reports, Mike briefed those case officers in our office, and invited them to attend the afternoon meeting in the conference room. He called Parky and asked if he could make it as well.

I also contacted Frank to notify him of the afternoon meeting. He would be there.

At 1330 hours that afternoon, we convened in Leon's office. I began by briefly outlining the progress on this relatively new operation and by explaining the observations of DG, and a very exciting set of opinions followed. It was finally agreed that we would wait until after the next encounter, and observe Ivan's performance before recommending any specific action. In the meantime, Dick's office would begin planning for counter-surveillance support of DG's activities, and would only need a "go-ahead" from Leon.

Back in our own office, Frank walked to my desk saying "Man, I am jell-us. It's because of y'all that ah'm in this business. I've waited all this time to get somethin' sexy goin', but nothin' really good seems to fall into place. Now here y'all are, only a few months on the job and y'all's project turns out to be great!

I wasn't sure what to say, then Frank came back with his Texas drawl, saying "Ah'm just kiddin' ah'm as proud as I can be fer y'all. One thing we know fer sure is that those Russian assholes out there are really comin' after us. It's like we're matchin' wits and winnin'!"

That evening, Frank and I had our usual sandwich at the Trolley. It was "Trolley sandwich of choice and all the beer you could drink – 1700-1900 hours." That meant one for me, and three for Frank. Thai beer comes in liter bottles. Tuesday, I drove to the office, and noted there was no signal from DG.

"That's good." I found myself thinking, *"I can work on the Alex Project!"*

I spent the entire next day finalizing my approach plan to meet with Bill Tanner. It was simple. I would call and interview him regarding one of his co-workers, and come up with an excuse for a follow-up meeting. The follow-up would not occur at the Patana School or Vic's #3 Restaurant for lunch; but I would have to find another more secure location.

Although I preferred using the Windsor and Chao Phraya Hotels due to the level of security they provide, recent developments were now forcing me to avoid US installations and move out into the economy.

I began the selection process of potential meeting sites by going over the list of clubs and hotels, and eliminating those known to be used by the Russians.

Next, I looked through the telephone book with "Pechnoi" our local liaison office translator. He stated truthfully that there are many hotels in Bangkok which are quite secure. This, he explained was because there were hundreds, maybe thousands of visitors to Bangkok every year who come for the single purpose of conducting discreet, personal, encounters with call girls (and boys), and wish to keep those activities private.

I explained to Pechnoi that I was unmarried and had my own apartment. I was in search of locations where one could expect privacy for the purpose of conducting business meetings. Pechnoi was embarrassed by his own initial assumption. He then went on to say that there were 'business hotels', often used for a single day, where people could meet privately to discuss legitimate business matters.

Now, we're getting somewhere.

I spent that afternoon getting acquainted with Pechnoi – a valuable asset. We drove around, locating small hotels which offered adequate privacy and could be used for personal meetings. I would select one of the business hotels, and run a test meeting with Frank to insure there were no unexpected interruptions or signs of interference.

We located a small, family-owned, private business hotel called "River Bend", which was actually located at the end of Soi 2, adjacent to the "klong" (canal) where one can take a riverboat (klong-boat) to the main Bangkok City Market.

The owner allowed us to look over the private rooms. They were kept neat and clean. Each had its private entrance and private garage which took up the first floor. The steps leading to the second floor hotel rooms were located in the rear of the garage. It was worth a try, so I decided to rent it for two nights, at $30.00 a night. The owner gave me one single key which opened both the garage, and the door into the apartment. The very small deck on the second floor faced the solid brick wall of an adjacent apartment complex.

Unlike larger hotels, there were no security cameras. The residence across the street was shielded by a high wall. No windows were visible. The second-floor room was furnished with a single bed and a desk/table with three chairs. A small kitchen area had a two-burner gas hotplate, an electric coffee pot, a small refrigerator, and a toaster oven. The single cupboard held coffee mugs, rice bowls, and a serving of four plates and saucers. Plastic ware, paper towels and napkins were in the drawers of the small bar which separated the kitchen from the rest of the room. Two bottles of Thai beer came with the room, and would be replaced daily. The table radio would suffice for sound cover. A tiny 'closet' with ample space for a thin man to turn around, housed the bathroom, with a sink, a toilet and a very small combination shower/tub.

This would suffice.

When we returned to the office, I learned that I had received local approval, which meant the contact with Bill Tanner was a 'go'.

Tanner's office had 21 personnel, and only one - Sergeant Jones - was currently undergoing his periodic Background Investigation. I would interview Tanner regarding Jones. When I called, Tanner was not surprised since he was aware SGT Jones was undergoing his BI. He invited me to come over at my convenience – early morning or late afternoon. I assumed that was his normal work schedule, allowing for the tennis lunch hour.

On Wednesday afternoon, having confirmed an appointment with Bill, I went to his office to conduct the normal interview regarding Jones. Bill recognized me immediately from the short encounter at Patana. The interview went well, and he recommended Jones for continued assignment to the position of trust. We discussed the Patana School and the Rugby Club. Bill said he could never get scheduled on short notice at the MACTHAI tennis courts, but could almost always play tennis at Patana. Tanner seemed to have time to talk, so I took advantage and asked about his wife and children, and how they were adjusting to life in Bangkok. His only complaint was that the American School was not challenging enough for his children. It was his way of bragging on his kids' level of intelligence. His sons, Timothy and Thomas were born ten months apart, and were as similar as twin lion cubs. At this time of year, they are both the same age for two months, and constantly fight like the same twin cubs - all in play. The rest of each year, Timothy is one year older, and plays the older-brother role. Timothy will soon be 11.

I maneuvered the conversation back to tennis, asking if there were many competitive players at the club. Tanner said there weren't many American players, but there were some excellent players from other countries. He mentioned a tennis player from France, and a second from Russia, both of whom he thought would be interesting challenges. They usually played with each other, two or three times a week; and he had seen them watching him play occasionally. He had not met either of them.

Bill, a relatively new Captain, would not be looking for a promotion for a few more years. He had been in Bangkok for nearly two years, and had learned his way around quite well. He enjoyed the local customs of the Thai people, and had already submitted the paperwork for a 12-month extension of his tour of duty. I made a mental note to see if we could influence his request for extension if the project went well.

I mentioned that I was certainly a new comer to Bangkok, and was looking foreword to visiting the ancient city located 38 miles to the North. Bill too had not yet been to the ancient city, and I invited him to go along, and make a day of it. We were beginning to hit it off, and as we talked I could see that our relationship was forming well. He had an excellent sense of humor. I trusted him already.

It was set. We would spend Saturday 'bumming around'. I would pick him up in the Chokchai building parking lot, and after breakfast at the International Market, we would then drive to the Ancient City.

Thursday that week was time for writing my reports and submitting requests for expediting my proposals, concepts and Oplans. Our other Case Officers were all working steadily on their respective projects. Leon endorsed all of my requests, and local approvals would be received within days. I initiated an operational reports file for Bill.

Friday morning, I ran into Dick F. in the hallway. He was also anxious to get his surveillance team started. "They need practice badly," he stated.

"I understand," I said, "When I was doing that, years ago, I got involved in every possible opportunity for surveillance, just to keep in practice."

We talked for awhile, and once Dick learned of my previous experience at Fort Holabird and with CAST, he asked if his US team could practice with me during any of my upcoming personal meetings. He needed a 'rabbit'.

I agreed to this proposal and told him that I would have certain stipulations. 1) that only US personnel be utilized; 2) that they abort their practice surveillance on me if they should detect any surveillance activity conducted by anyone else; 3) That they accept my signal to break off, if I should detect any such activity. (Their breaking off prematurely would be the signal to me that I was under surveillance. And they could continue discreet activity to determine the identity of our adversary.)

Dick readily agreed, and we discussed it immediately with Leon and Parky. We authored the joint proposal, and it was signed by Parky that afternoon. The surveillance would take place the very next day. It would be initiated at my apartment complex at 0615, and would last until I returned to that location expected to be around 1500-1530 hours. They would not be told that I was meeting with someone else, and this unexpected action would cause them to double their efforts, as I would be driving Bill back to his office where he would pick up his own car and go shopping before he went home.

At 0630 hours on Saturday, I departed my apartment. Walking through the apartment complex, I saw Thai members of the apartment complex workforce, setting up the restaurant, the gift shops and sweeping the area. I did not see the two Asian-American CI agents that work for Dick F, but was sure they would be involved in this surveillance. I did however observe five Caucasian surveillants sitting in the lobby area, reading newspapers and drinking coffee. I walked into the garage, where I saw one of our unit sedans, and a sixth Caucasian sitting behind the wheel, trying to be discreet. Two of the CI agents from the lobby had followed me into the garage. I avoided eye-to-eye contact with any of them. Their reactions were by the book. None of the surveillants whom I had spotted followed immediately behind me as I drove from the parking lot.

Since it was still early, both pedestrian and vehicular traffic was at a minimum. I spotted the remainder of the surveillance team almost immediately, and by the time I drove past the Chokchai building, I had singled out two sedans and the eight surveillants. Of course I was already acquainted with them, and one of the two sedans was the one I'd driven on a single occasion when I first arrived in Bangkok.

The two Asian-Americans had been sitting at the corner of Sukhumvit Road and Soi 52, and as I turned right, they followed me at a comfortable distance, keeping one car between us at all times. As I passed the Chokchai Building, I signaled a left turn by the "China Garden" restaurant, and then turned left on Soi 21 heading toward the parking lot. The AA guys drove on past, as did the car they had used as a blind. The second surveillance sedan, the one I had seen in my apartment parking lot, turned left behind me. I easily located a parking space near the pedestrian overpass, and as I exited my car, the surveillants were parking near the vehicular exit. *"Good maneuver,"* I thought.

Ignoring the surveillants, I walked across the overpass, into the building. I saw DG's mark on the window. This small signal inspired me even more. I would not rest until I was able to talk to him on Monday morning.

Just as I entered the main building, I saw Bill entering the elevator. I rushed, caught the button and startled him as I entered. We took the elevator up one floor, walked across the hallway and caught the opposing elevator back down to the parking lot level.

What I had not realized was that by making these few moves, I had apparently ditched the team for awhile. As Bill and I reached the ground level, I noticed the opposing elevator door closing. The team was now on its way up, and had no idea we were already on our way out. I felt a little bad, because I didn't want to ruin their practice this early. It was an honest move though, and something they could expect during an actual surveillance.

Bill seemed happy that we were going to have some time together, saying "It's great to get out with someone who can carry on a good conversation." I knew he wasn't as happy as I. We drove slowly to the International Market, parked on a side street, and walked slowly into the restaurant area, where one of the best smorgas-boards in Asia was on display over the steam tanks. Every conceivable European and Asian breakfast dish was offered. I chose the turkey rice gruel, French toast and a small plate of fruit. Bill followed suit.

While we were having breakfast, the surveillance team arrived. They looked somewhat disturbed. They had no way of knowing that the ditching was an accident. Likely, they had called Dick who told them where they could pick us up. They drank iced tea and had toast while we finished our breakfasts. The two Asian-American guys were apparently sitting in the cars, awaiting our departure. The team did not stand out, as at this time on Saturday morning the majority of the customers were early-rising Americans.

"There's a typhoon coming," Bill mentioned, "have you ever been here for one?"

"Not yet," I answered, "When is it due to hit?"

"Wednesday." He replied, and he then went into a briefing on what to expect. "The shocking thing to me" he said, "is how many snakes the typhoon brings out." He explained that when the floods come, Sukhumvit Road becomes submerged in about two feet of water, and snakes can be seen swimming up and down the road. He went on to say that "the snakes float in from the klongs, and come up out of the drains, searching for a place to 'land'."

"I'll do my very best to avoid walking around." I promised. "I dislike snakes of any kind."

We dumped our trays in the refuse basket and started to leave the restaurant at 0730 hours. The surveillance team was hurriedly dumping their trays, and moving toward the restaurant exit as well, when I suggested we pick up a cold six pack of *Closter's'* beer to take along. Bill agreed, and this gave the team enough time to get back to their cars. I'd made up for the ditching accident already. Driving north on Sukhumvit road with the surveillance team in tow, we followed the signs to the 'Ancient City'.

The trip was enjoyable, and we arrived at the Ancient city in less than an hour. The sun was already beating down, the temperature at near 95 degrees, and the humidity was rising rapidly. Stepping out of my air conditioned car, the initial shock of humidity seemed to be even worse. Bill and I simultaneously reached for a cold beer. We opened the bottles and carried them with us as we strolled through the city.

I began the new conversation by asking Bill if he had ever considered a career in the Intelligence field.

"No," he answered, "but I've always thought it would be challenging."

He went on to say "Almost everyone in my Thai language class at DLI was an Intel type."

I agreed that it can be challenging. "The expectation of challenge is extremely appropriate in Asia." and continued, saying "Even the Russians seem to enjoy operating in such places as Bangkok."

I was trying not only to perk his interest but to bait him into asking more questions. It worked.

"Are they keeping you guys busy?" he asked.

"Well," I answered, "Do you remember the SAEDA brief you received from our guys?"

"Of course", he answered "After every one of your SAEDA briefs, my troops line up to report foreign contacts and to ask how they can get into the "spy" business." He went on suggesting. "The selection process must be pretty stiff."

"Every time we complete a series of those briefings, our business picks up." I began, "we have to follow up on every lead. Since we are so short-handed, it's time consuming. Actually, we're always on the lookout for 'A Few Good Men'". I quoted the popular Marine Corps slogan.

"Maybe, when I can't play tennis anymore, I'll give it a try." He joked.

"Don't wait that long, Bill." I cautioned him. "We don't need a bunch of old guys coming into the business. Do you have any idea how hard it is to teach old dogs?" We laughed, and I continued, saying "If you're really interested, I can drop some information by your office; you can look it over and decide for yourself. Take your time."

"If it's no bother, I'll go along with that idea." He responded.

He was interested.

Relaxed, we talked casually, discussing everything except Military Intelligence for the rest of the morning, stopping one time back at the car to retrieve two of the last four bottles of cold beer. I watched the surveillance team scramble into their sedans as we reached my car, and then relax when we only removed the beers. We walked for some time before returning to the car for the return trip. The surveillance team stayed with us, exchanging positions and trying to overhear the gist of our conversations. Occasionally they would break away to take up rotating positions; but they managed to keep their eyes on us. To me, they were obvious, but Bill paid no attention to them. After all, there were many Americans in the area.

We had seen all of the Ancient City, and Bill commented that he was happy he'd not brought his family to see this sight. We decided that it would eventually become a successful tourist trap. It would probably be cleaned up, and would even be made accessible from the river. Tourists would be able to take 'klong' boats to the site.

By 1230 hours, we departed the city and drove toward Bangkok. Enroute, we decided to have lunch at a roadside snack bar. When we pulled into the parking lot, I noted that the sign read: "Roadside Snack Bear".

With no restrictions, I would have asked for his cooperation during this meeting, but because my proposals had not yet been finally approved, I had no choice but to be patient.

After lunch, I drove Bill back to the Chokchai parking lot, stopping behind the car he had identified as his own. I watched the surveillance teams preparing for the follow-on, shook hands with Bill and then parked in the lot. Bill drove away, honking his horn as he departed the lot. I then walked into the Chokchai building and went to my office.

Dick was in his office, and when he asked, I explained what had happened on the elevators. He laughed. Half of his surveillance team had returned to the office already while the AA Team had continued following Bill Tanner. Dick invited me give a performance critique to those who had already returned.

I started with the elevator incident, explaining that the maneuver had been unintentional and was not meant to be devious. I explained that when I jumped into the elevator, I was surprised to meet with the person with whom I had made an appointment. It was also natural to then return to the first floor and depart without warning.

They agreed. I cautioned them to keep their eyes open for hostile surveillance of their own activities, and not to react with panic when their subject is on the move. Patience, I explained is one of the most important virtues of a successful surveillance. After the critique, I supposed Bill was probably already home, and the second half of the team would be on their way back to the office by now. "They did quite well," I told Dick, "we were never totally without surveillance. When Bill T and I returned to the parking lot following the elevator ordeal, other portions of the team were already in place. Sensing the absence of the 'lost' group, they had picked up the slack and followed us."

I returned to my office and drafted the report on today's activities. There would be no need for me to place a signal for DG, and his signal would be removed with the Sunday window cleaning. I would simply call him first thing Monday Morning on his supervisor's STU. We would work around the typhoon.

I spent Sunday stocking up on supplies and beginning preparations for typhoon Iris.

By Monday the weather was cooling down. My 14-day, 24-hour ship's clock and barometer from my hold baggage had somehow made it past "importation inspection". Perhaps the thieves had no idea what the two items actually were. I had mounted them to an outside wall, wound the clock, and calibrated the barometer, which had dropped from just over 30 inches to 28.8 inches of mercury in less than 24 hours. I'm not a weatherman, but I think that may be an indication that a storm's acomin'. My old citizen-band antique German - *Loewe-Upta Komet* - desk-top shortwave radio, a lone survivor of the 'hold baggage bewailing' had new batteries and had been set on an English weather station.

There was no contact with DG. Common sense would prevail; he would wait for my call on the next available duty day. I would bet that Ivan was also postponing his activities.

A bag of ice cubes filled two-thirds of my mini-fridge freezer. I had accumulated two 5-gallon jugs of drinking water, four 12-pack cases of C-rations, a six pack of aerosol/gas cans and tested my new gas hot plate. My first-aid kit was stocked, and the medics had provided me with extra water purification tablets, just in case. I'd stocked ample batteries to get me through one or five typhoons.

After receiving my fifty percent reimbursement from Uncle Sam, I had replaced my old stereo set with a combination tuner, turntable, cassette-player, amplifier and set of 4 small patio speakers. It would do for now.

My L-shaped apartment was situated on the 2nd floor corner of the building, with the kitchen, bar-dining area and living rooms facing northeast, across Sukhumvit Rd. The foyer and bath were located at the inside of the "L", dividing the living room from the bedroom which faced the inside of the complex. A fairly large balcony extended 10 feet out from the bedroom, across a veranda area, overlooking the pool. I found it relaxing to sit on my patio in the evenings, listen to my favorite piano concertos and sip a little JWB or Chivas Regal on the pebbles. Two of the four speakers had been mounted on my patio walls, under the eave, and I kept the volume turned low enough so as not to disturb my neighbors.

Strong to gentle breezes brought gusts of wind and misty rain into the streets of Bangkok, and shop proprietors were already beginning to batten down for the typhoon. Schools were scheduling closures, as were official and non-official offices. Our office had already put out the word that only extremely critical personnel were required to be present during the storm, which was now scheduled to hit Bangkok Tuesday evening. Although I considered myself crucial, the command did not consider Case Officers to be critical for maintaining the office during a typhoon. OK with me.

At first, I decided to pop some corn and watch a little TV while the electricity was still on, so I began working on the "jiffy-pop". I turned on my new, compact Panasonic pop-up TV, and found that the three TV stations had already signed off for the duration of the typhoon. *"Perhaps,"* I thought, *"I should take this typhoon a little more seriously."*

I went to the patio and sat, nibbling on my pop corn and drinking Chivas. Down at the pool, a group of young bikini-clad sweet things from the bar across the street were jumping around in the all-to-chili air; in and out of the pool, wrapping and unwrapping their towels, laughing and trying to catch the eyes of anyone daring to sit outside and watch. It worked – I sat outside and watched. Once they looked my direction, I even toasted them. How magnificent they were. But alas, as the winds and rain picked up, dropping the temperature well below the comfort zone, the gals darted back into the complex, not to be seen again.

I remained seated on the patio, listening to one of my favorite versions of "Moonlight". This particular recording of Ludwig van Beethoven's piano sonata was originally recorded in 1937, under the direction of Lothar Mendez, and performed by the famous pianist Paderewski. It was released in 1938, and my mother had obtained the record that same year. I had listened to it all my life.

The old record had been badly scratched over the years, and I had often kicked myself for not copying it on tape while it was still scratch-free. Now, I wondered once more why I'd not taken the time to do so. Who knows, perhaps one day, we'll be able to buy all the classics on a recording system that will be read by laser beams instead of needles, and can thus avoid being scratched even by the drunkest, and clumsiest of fools among us.

The record finished and I listened to the turntable arm retract and snap into place. I was too lazy or too buzzed to change records, so I sat under the awning, warm, dry and snug, listening to the sounds of the increasing wind and watched as small pellets of rain began skydiving under the awning to dance on the patio floor.

When it was time to go inside, I retracted the awning, picked up the chairs and table, folded them, and placed them inside the bedroom. I unplugged the speakers from the patio wall and brought them inside also. I noticed that it was conspicuously darker than when I'd gone onto the veranda. I instinctively flicked the switch – the electricity had already gone off. I walked to the living room window pulled the drapes aside and looked out over Sukhumvit. By this time, the winds were beginning to blow much harder and sheets of rain were washing the windows in rhythmical fashion. A few sparking power lines could be seen writhing and dancing in the street. Obviously, the storm was not yet of typhoon strength, but the rain and wind had increased greatly over the past few hours and some damage could be seen in the making.

I listened to the Loewe-Upta, telling those of us with batteries that typhoon Iris had visited Singapore the day before and was now moving due North. Iris was currently destroying the beaches of Song-kia and the Ranot sand dunes. It would be paying its respects to Phet Buri and Bangkok within the next 12 hours.

A knock at the door startled me. I was not expecting anyone. As I looked through the wide-angle peep hole, I saw Frank standing outside, dripping wet. I opened the door.

Gesturing for him to come inside, I said "Frank, what the hell are you doing out in this god-forsaken weather?!"

"We need ta git "typhoonized", he joked. "Ah just thought y'all needed some company."

When I asked about his family, he responded only that they could take care of themselves. "Besides", he continued, "this is yer first typhoon!"

I reminded him that I had already gone through two monsoon seasons in Viet Nam and had spent years living in 'Typhoon Alley', both in Okinawa and in Taiwan. Ignoring my response, Frank plopped himself on one of the papasan chairs and opened a beer. My plans to quietly sit out the typhoon had come to an end.

Frank and I sat and watched the storm trespass on our environment until we both fell asleep in the papasan chairs sometime around 0200 hours. About half his case was gone. Something reminded me of "Bop".

During the night, heavy rains had fallen along Thailand's south, and unimpeded storm waves had washed the beaches of Sadahip, as the Typhoon moved toward Bangkok. Occasionally, bright blue bolts of lightning and instantaneous claps of thunder demanded our immediate attention. Concurrently, the apartment had cooled to about 60 degrees. I awakened to total soundlessness at 0715 hours when the typhoon was directly overhead. Although it was fairly light, darkness surrounded the city of Bangkok. We were in the eye. The winds had temporarily slowed to a gentle breeze with an occasional gust, and the rain had temporarily ceased. I walked around the apartment, inspecting windows and doors for leakage. Fortunately, I had suffered no glass breakage. I set about perking some coffee on the gas hot plate, and by the time the coffee was ready, Frank had risen, and was also looking out over the road.

"The worst is yet to come," he observed.

"Could be," I remarked, "at least we're halfway through."

"Y'ain't seen nuthin' yet," Frank warned. "Once the klongs are full, Sukhumvit Road becomes Klong number one!"

"It's OK," I responded, accepting his warning, "People occasionally need a little distress or surprise to waken them from their laziness. Everyone's a little too complacent nowadays."

I spent a few minutes frying up some hash browns, sausage and eggs, and attempting to toast bread over the gas hotplate, while we talked through a list of "Remember-whens", discussing our related backgrounds over the last 15 years.

After breakfast, I chucked the paper plates and plastic spoons into the garbage can and while inspecting the apartment once more, noticed a slight seepage on the windowsill of the bedroom. Twisting a few towels, I placed them on the sill and brought in an empty bucket for periodic wringing out. Frank told some good jokes.

By 0900, the typhoon was back in full force. Through the static sounds of the Loewe-Upta, we learned that the Iris had again reached sustained winds of 115, with gusts to 125 mph. Enough, already.

Frank began attacking the beer again, and I was convinced that his case would be gone in two hours.

The second half of the typhoon passed much quicker, and the winds had rotated the direction of their high-speed onslaught almost 180 degrees. The typhoon was moving inland. I wondered how the ancient city was fairing, and then decided that the winds would blow through the structures, the water level from the nearby river would rise, and bleeding dogs would swim. In normal fashion, my mind wandered – then wondered how fast the germs of the extremely contagious infectious dermitae could spread during a typhoon. I then banished those thoughts from my caring lobe, and mentally transferred them into the apathetic lobe. I really didn't want to know the answer.

By early evening Iris was subsiding. Sounds were emitting from my neighbors' apartments, and the complex was coming back to life. By 1730, life inside the complex seemed almost normal but still without electricity. Outside was a different story. The flooding was in full force, and people could be seen wading through waist-deep, flowing water on the road. As I had been told, occasionally a snake could be seen swimming along as well.

I wondered aloud, "why are they not biting the pedestrians?"

Frank responded, saying "The snakes want to stay alive too." It made sense.

The most appalling site was that of policemen using bamboo poles with small hooks, to pick up snakes and deposit them in the public mailboxes.

Frank also explained this phenomenon. "The cobras" he said "can be sold for a good profit, and some of the snakes, particularly the vipers are cooked into soups and sold to believers for brain food, for sexual stimuli, or to enhance rehabilitation. Not all mailboxes are used for the snakes." He went on to explain, "Those in use bear temporary, Thai-language signs designating them as 'snake boxes'."

I decided I would use the Military Post Offices for my personal mailing, and would learn enough Thai language to be able to recognize the labeled boxes. I had heard enough about snakes.

The static-ridden weather report was describing the flooded roads, estimating drainage in 6 to 8 hours and dryness within 48. The Sukhumvit "klong" was flowing fast, and may be drivable in 12 hours. We had a very late lunch, and after noticing that there were still a few beers in the cooler, Frank decided to stay through another night.

The next morning before going to the office, I took a picture of the clock and barometer for my personal history records, showing the current reading (30) at nearly 1000 hours, and the low point as I had recorded the night before (28.8).

Frank left without breakfast, probably because he felt a little guilty for leaving his wife and children home during the typhoon.

"Thanks for the hospitality, Bud." As usual, he displayed no visible after effects from the beer.

Back in the office on Wednesday, I learned that the Chokchai building and the MACTHAI compounds were equipped with ample generator power carrying enough amps to service lights, plugs, and pumps to remove basement water. When I entered the building, the musty smell of non-air conditioned, damp drywall, plaster, wood, and an occasional dead rat that may have floated from one of the elevator shaft vents, filled my sinuses. Cleanup was underway. Others awaiting the single, working elevator were telling their individual stories and describing their varied horror tales of, and heroic methods they had employed to cope with Typhoon Iris, or "Irit", if they were Thai.

Parky came in Joking "What are you guys doing here? It's Wednesday – haven't you heard? We're going to have a typhoon!" We laughed at his clumsy attempt at humor.

I called DG on the STU and he told me of the call he'd received from Ivan just days earlier telling him that he had received a small package from Vladivostok with a 'surprise' for DG. In view of the pending typhoon, DG had not made an appointment. They agreed that he would call sometime the day after the typhoon. That would be today.

Later in the day, when DG got around to calling Ivan, he sat through a Russian-language announcement; then a Thai language announcement; and finally the English language recording announced that the embassy had suffered water damage, and regretfully, business would not be conducted normally until the following Monday morning. An emergency number was given for contact. DG wrote the number down and passed it to me, but decided rightfully that he would not call Ivan until Monday.

Back in my own office, the Chinese-speaking custodial crew was busy wiping everything down. A cup of tea had been poured in my cup, and covered with a clear glass lid. As I stood looking down at the cup, a cute little Chinese lady approached and said "Jasmine."

I responded, holding out my hand "Hi, Jasmine, I'm Irit," I joked."No, no!" she responded, "Tea is jasmine." She shook hands anyway.

I acted dumb, "Oh, oh, thank you very much." She laughed and I then spoke to her in Chinese, saying "If this is Jasmine, then what's your name?"

She was shocked, and at first didn't know how to respond. She stared at me for a full 15 seconds and finally spoke in Chinese. We talked for a minute, until her supervisor ushered her away. Her name was "Lan".

Normally, we did not have custodial personnel in our office, but on rare occasions – like after a typhoon – escorted custodians were allowed to accomplish the initial cleanup, and maintenance personnel were also guided around to examine damage. I never saw the Chinese maid at our office again.

The rest of the lazy week was taken up with paperwork, writing and updating lead development reports and other administrative matters. Leon and I talked shop while playing bumper pool at least once a day. During that week, the maintenance personnel had gotten around to cleaning all the windows and thus removing DG's fading crayon mark from the signal location.

Saturday, with nothing better to do, I came to the office. I noticed a new signal from DG. Apparently he'd had another telephone contact with Ivan. I turned on the TV in the main office, and learned that over night one of the local anti-government factions had staged a small riot, involving opposing bus companies. Apparently one of the city transit bus companies was owned by the Minister of Transportation who was under investigation for embezzling, misappropriation of government materiel, for misuse of power and conflict of interest. The opposing, privately-owned bus company had taken the law into their own hands. The result was turmoil in the streets. Some innocent passengers and other bystanders had actually been shot.

There were shades of corruption, shades of war, and shades of Viet Nam. I turned the TV off.

The office radio was on the local English station, and the results from the Typhoon were coming in. In Bangkok, nearly 100 persons were feared dead or reported missing, and another 4 members of the Thai Telephone and Telegraph union were killed in one violent swoop when a power line dropped onto a telephone line on which they were working. Altogether, 6 had died during the Bus war. I turned the radio off. The office was silent without the turmoil and sounds of war.

With everything being postponed another week, I spent Sunday writing to and calling Betty. Trying to sound encouraging, we discussed our wedding plans, but she informed me that Chiang Kai-shek had fallen ill, and was hospitalized. He had been diagnosed with failing kidney function. Should he pass on, there would be an extended period of mourning during which there could be no celebrations of any kind. She feared that his illness could affect some of our plans. I assured her that it would not.

Monday, I called DG's STU. He had made an appointment to see Ivan Tuesday afternoon at 1500 hours. Unless DG needed to ask questions, we did not have to arrange a briefing. He had no questions. I told him not to leave any signal until it was perfectly convenient, adding that he should not make a special trip back to the office just for that purpose. DG stated that he would plan on picking up some snacks and returning home following his meeting with Ivan.

This gave me time to arrange for surveillance, and I set up a briefing for Dick's team. The team would cautiously initiate surveillance at DG's home, and follow him to the vicinity of Ivan's office. The next phase would be when DG departs the Russian Embassy, and the purpose - to detect hostile surveillance. They would follow DG as long as possible for verification purposes, and drop off before he reached home. While it would be interesting to know just how long a hostile team would stay in place, it was not worth taking any chances at this time.

Debriefing of DG occurred at the River Bend Hotel, in a different room of my choosing. DG arrived carrying an envelope, and what appeared to be a 5 pound rectangular coffee can. Once we were seated and partaking of our soft drinks, DG told his story.

With Tuesday afternoon off, DG had gone home for lunch with his wife. At 1315 hours he departed his home, and drove directly toward the Russian Embassy. Enroute, he had been delayed by the activity of a picketing bus riot group who had blocked the street. Eventually, he was waved on through the crowd along with other vehicles, and was able to make his way to the Embassy. He drove into the compound, stopping only momentarily to show ID at the front gate, and then drove directly to the parking area and parked. He chose a space in sight of the front gate. As he walked toward the front entrance, one of the guards called to him. As he approached the guard post, he was confronted and apparently asked for his identification again. He presented his ID, and was ushered to the front entrance. Our 'fixed' surveillance was in place filming the outside activity.

Once inside, he was immediately met by Ivan who took him to his office. A one-liter bottle of Russian Stolichnaya Vodka *Ohranj* was sitting on Ivan's desk. It had been opened, and a single red pepper was floating two inches above the bottom of the bottle. As soon as they were seated, Ivan reached under his desk. This time, he brought out an envelope for DG, and a box, measuring about 24X10X10 inches. He asked DG to open it. He did. Inside was an elegant, black leatherette case, containing a highly polished, beautiful Russian trumpet. DG estimated the total value at well over $400.00.

While DG was admiring the trumpet, Ivan went to his table and picked up two crystal glasses, and poured an ounce of the *Stolichnaya* for them both. Proposing a toast, Ivan said "Please. A toast to us; to our friendship!"

At first DG considered protesting by saying he rarely drinks when driving, but when he realized it could possibly insult Ivan, he stood, smiled and graciously accepted the drink.

"This," Ivan proudly stated "is to you!" He continued "It is rare that we can make friends with someone who is so talented, and so broad-minded as to appreciate and study the music that is so dear to our hearts. You DG are such a man. This is a small token of my appreciation for this rare opportunity to be your friend."

DG stated that he was truly embarrassed, and could not find words to express his appreciation. Finally, he was able to blurt out "This is too much Ivan," and then "How could I ever thank you for such an expensive gift."

"Oh, my young friend," Ivan patted him on the shoulder, "We don't worry about that between friends. It is my pleasure; your friendship is my honor, your "thank You" is my reward."

Ivan was really pouring it on, and DG was playing his role perfectly. Ivan drank the vodka an ounce at a time, while DG nursed each shot, sip by sip.

As they went through the sheet music, DG selected one piece with which he had some familiarity, and at Ivan's insistence, wiped of the mouthpiece and played about halfway through the music. Ivan was visibly impressed, saying "I can't wait to see you in concert – In Moscow! I'll tell all my family and acquaintances 'This is my friend from America – and he has come here to play our own music for us'."

DG stated that again, he was truly embarrassed. As he opened the coffee can to show me the contents, he said he had taken the trumpet home and played it. He couldn't find anything to indicate there was anything 'planted' inside it. "It plays so smooth." He commented. "I've never played a trumpet this nice before."

I could see that DG admired the trumpet. He removed the case and trumpet from the can. My paranoia would not allow me to speak, fearing the remote possibility that there could be a concealed listening device contained in the case. DG then opened the case, displaying the interior. It was professionally made, with hand-stitched seams, and completely lined with royal blue felt. The trumpet was as DG had described - absolutely beautiful. DG carefully placed the case and trumpet back into the metal container and closed the lid tightly.

"I'll take it to the office, have them check it out; we'll photograph it and prepare a proper receipt. It will be yours to keep. You will have it back in 24 hours. Now", I said, "you can surely expect that Ivan will go to hear you play at the King's Palace."

"Anything else?" I asked.

"Oh, yes!" DG exclaimed, "I'd almost forgotten. I think I was 'tailed' from the Russian Embassy compound."

I was not exactly surprised, just pleased. I had feared that the 'gift' would have DG so excited he would forget to be tail conscious. "Tell me about it."

He described his trip home following the meeting. He had driven out of the parking lot, and as he glimpsed into his rearview mirror, he noticed a car pulling into the lane behind him. When he turned the corner, another car pulled into the same lane behind the first car. DG then turned into a small alley and stopped at a store to pick up some snacks. Car #1 followed him into the lane, passed by and parked about 50 meters further into the lane. Car #2 apparently moved along, up Sukhumvit road. The #1 surveillant remained in his car. DG stated that he shopped for a few minutes, bought a few items, and paid no particular attention to #1. When he departed the shop, he heard #1 start his car. As DG drove from the area and turned left, back onto Sukhumvit Rd, he did not see #1 following, but he noticed #2 pull in behind him from a parking space along the road. They had changed places. The #2 car was now directly behind him. He did not notice when they broke off, but stated that as far as he could tell, they were nowhere near him when he turned into the parking lot of his apartment complex.

DG stated that he had then noticed an unfamiliar car leaving his parking lot as he was maneuvering for a place inside. He had never seen that car before. DG added that there are only eight apartments inside that small complex, and he is familiar with all the occupants and their cars.

"You handled it perfectly," I told him. "No panic; no provocative movements; no eye-to-eye; no glaring at them in the mirror".

DG was able to describe the two Datsun Bluebirds, and hadn't been able to catch any of their license plates. The car leaving the parking lot was a fairly new, gray, 4-door Isuzu Prince. DG could not describe the drivers, as he had intentionally avoided looking in their direction.

"You did great." I told him.

The two Datsun surveillance cars matched the descriptions of Russian Embassy-owned vehicles we had on file at the office. This list was maintained by the "Other Agency", obtained through their own surveillance efforts, and was provided to Dick's office on a regular basis.

We then spent an additional hour nibbling on snacks and sodas. I asked him "So, how was the Vodka?"

"Even that was good," he responded. "I don't drink often, but I found it tasty. It tasted like orange juice!"

"That's the "Ohranj", I told him; "but what about the hot pepper?""

"I'm not sure what that was for," he answered, "but I could taste that too. The vodka was already strong enough though – didn't need the pepper."

Before calling the meeting to an end, I discussed the probability that Ivan would soon be asking for some small favor. "It doesn't matter what he asks for, classified or unclassified" I instructed, "it must first be approved by our office. Don't worry about the time crunch, I can request approval by STU, and you can pass it as soon as I receive approval. If it's a highly classified item though, it will take some time – and may have to be sanitized or even fabricated for passing. That takes time."

He understood and of course, agreed.

Wednesday, back at the office, I opened the coffee can. Everyone looked it over – the case was of more interest to the tech guys than the trumpet - and almost immediately it was determined that there were no concealed devices within. We prepared a receipt and attached photos for accounting purposes. DG would be happy. I personally took the elevator to the 4th floor and passed the boxed, gift-wrapped trumpet and case back to DG. He agreed to tell no-one of the origin of the acquisition. It would be explained as a "gift from home."

Moments later, Dick came into our office, carrying a sheet of paper. It was the updated list of Russian vehicles. He pointed out that during the previous week, two new cars had been purchased for their fleet – one was a Gray, 4-door Isuzu Prince, and the second was a dark blue, 4-door Isuzu Bellet'.

"Great!" I almost yelled, "This means they were awaiting DG's return home. They had him all the way."

"We've never been able to finesse one this far." Dick stated positively. "I'm proud that I'm part of it."

So was I.

Tonight might be DG's first opportunity to entertain Ivan during his show.

Two members of the surveillance team were in attendance, and Frank and I sat at a table on the main floor. At first sighting of Ivan, the signal was to extinguish the small candle on our table, and move it to the edge of the table top. If the candles had not yet been lit, and if Ivan should walk in, we would light ours. The rest would be up to the surveillance team, and Frank and I could depart at will.

Following introduction, DG came out on stage and began going through his repertoire, beginning with the famous Jimmy Dorsey version of "*So Rare*". I was surprised DG even knew that particular piece of music which was originally composed by the famous Christopher Popa, but he played it well. As I enjoyed the music, I wondered if DG could see me. I decided that he probably could not, particularly with such bright stage lighting. Also, on this occasion, we were deep enough into the crowd that it was not likely.

Out of the blue, Frank said "Bingo". Ivan had entered the club, and was looking for a seat. My back was to the entrance, so Frank kept me informed. He stopped talking, and placed a small sauce dish on top of the candle holder, snuffing the candle. Frank then moved it close to the edge of our table.

Ivan was seated at the table directly beside us facing Frank - and my back. I glanced into the balcony in time to see the team putting out their candle as well. They had seen our signal and of course had noticed Ivan sitting just a few feet away. Glancing around, I noticed several other candles had been extinguished in the club as well, but we were only concerned with the signals to and from our Team.

We finished our initial drinks and ordered two more. I could not see Ivan, but was sure it was him when the waitress took his drink order. "Tovar's on the rocks". He ordered.

DG had eased into Aker Bilk's version of *"Stranger on the Shore"*. He could make the saxophone talk.

It was common for DG to roam around a little during his intermission, greeting new customers and welcoming the regulars. The stage lights dimmed simultaneously with the lights in the main floor brightening. He spotted Ivan and moved toward his table. DG almost stopped dead in his tracks when he saw me sitting next to Ivan. He then ignored Frank and me, and casually walked past our table to greet Ivan.

Ivan stood, shook DG's hand vigorously, saying "Splendid, splendid. You are really very good!"

Near the end of his 15-minute intermission, and after acknowledging several other 'regulars', DG walked back on stage and played an abbreviated selection from *"Blue Mountain"*, obviously for Ivan. When he had finished, he bowed to the applause, and acknowledged Ivan in the audience with a gesture. "For my special friend from Russia," he announced. A few members of the audience turned, temporarily focusing on Ivan. Ivan raised his glass and smiled. He was soaking it all in.

Before taking requests, DG played a few stanzas from *"Zorba"*, and the entire audience including Ivan began clapping to the music.

This was our cue to exit, so Frank and I departed the King's Palace, and walked to the Chao Phraya for dinner. Following the meal, we drove back, and on the way, discussed the Ivan project. Frank said that he had read the entire file in our office. He was impressed.

"I'm surprised y'all didn't give up after all those years." He reminded me just how long it had been since I first identified Ivan, saying "All that started while I was still stationed in Pacifica, 10 years ago."

Politely refusing my invitation to stop by for just one more drink, Frank dropped me off near the intersection of Sukhumvit and Soi 52. I was confident there was no surveillance on me. There was no need. I watched as Frank drove north, and there also appeared to be no surveillance on him. I walked into my apartment complex.

The next morning at the office, I retrieved the surveillance report from Dick's office, and went over the details. Following his performance, DG was approached by Ivan for a few minutes of casual conversation. This led to the introduction of Ivan to the members of DG's local band. DG departed the KPC and drove directly home. No surveillance was detected. The two Datsun Bluebirds used previously by the Russians remained parked in the Embassy parking lot throughout the night. Other vehicles arriving and departing at the embassy were all identified as personal vehicles or staff vehicles belonging to the embassy.

During my subsequent discussion with Leon that afternoon, he laid out precisely what was to be expected of Ivan. Leon had not been wrong thus far.

"DG," he stated, "can expect that Ivan will soon ask a small favor of him. Make sure it's approved and well documented. We can't afford to leave any holes in this one." Leon went on, "Also, DG can expect extensive surveillance over the next few weeks, and it will continue well past the day that Ivan asks him for the first "favor".

I assured him that I'd already briefed DG. He was aware of the red-tape involved in the processing of passable material, and was prepared to delay passing anything to Ivan long enough for approval. I was also confident that DG would handle surveillance well, and would not draw any undue attention.

Little did we know the extent to which such trivial, inconvenient delays can effect an operation.

Following Friday's performance at the King's Palace, DG was surveilled back to his home, and his debriefing revealed the exact same MO as during the previous surveillance. This was becoming their ritual.

Ivan was in the club again, and our AA team from the surveillance team was seated closer to the stage, just three tables away from Ivan.

Brandishing his new trumpet, DG gave a special performance for his Russian friend in the audience. To the surprise of the surveillance team, three additional Russian friends of Ivan arrived, were seated at his table. They seemed to enjoy the performance as much as Ivan.

They were also photographed. The team's photographic technique was excellent. Although the camera was but a small 8mm device, it was concealed within a cigarette lighter. With Ivan and friends sitting so close to the well-lit stage, available light was ample and would provide for ID-card quality photos.

During his performance, DG announced that one of the local TV stations had contracted for a live performance at the King's Palace, and that he would be seen in a one-hour special on TV, at a later date. The filming would take place over a week, and would include excerpts from three performances. "So, please," DG urged, "come often; fill up the club, and enjoy the live performance. Maybe you will be on TV too."

Saturday morning, when I arrived at the office, I saw DG's signal. Not surprisingly, Ivan had again contacted him. When I got to my office, I retrieved the STU key and called DG's office on the chance he might be in. He was. Ivan had called him late at night at his home. They had talked for 35 minutes. Ivan was again complimentary of DG's performance, and invited him to come to the Embassy to meet with him again. DG agreed, saying he could be there on Tuesday, if there were no changes in his schedule. He explained that he was in the midst of rewriting the personnel portion of the MACTHAI contingency plans, and was going to be quite busy. We had contrived this excuse as a possible future reason to delay passing anything to Ivan, if needed.

I told DG that I had received a list of pre-approved items which can be passed to his 'friend' with local approval, adding that he could expect Ivan's initial request to appear innocuous at best. DG was anxious to make the meeting. We would meet again on Sunday, after DG attended Chapel services with his wife.

Per Leon's suggestion, I felt this was a good time to bring up the idea of briefing DG's wife, Irene.

"I think," DG responded, "that's not a bad idea. By now, she's probably wondering where I am half the time. It's normal, don't you think?"

"Absolutely." I replied. "But I think it's probably better if you brief her. When the time comes, I'll give you some guidance as to what can be said." I continued "Leon has volunteered to brief her or to sit in if it would make you feel more comfortable."

DG felt he could handle it, and was flattered that Leon would be willing to be there for him. We temporarily shelved the subject.

CHAPTER 20.
SUNDAY MORNING SURPRISE.

On Sunday morning, I decided to forego my usual, brief visit to the Buddhist temple, and attended the morning Chapel services at MACTHAI. DG and his wife were in attendance, and I sat through the services, a few seats behind them. We did not make contact at the Chapel, and there would be another 90 minute break before DG and I were scheduled to meet at 1300 hours. I casually observed as DG and his wife drove from the compound, and as I was about to exit, noticed a gray, 4-door Isuzu pulling into the lane behind them. I yielded to the Isuzu, and I also eased into the same lane of traffic. A Datsun Bluebird fell in behind me. I knew that DG was under surveillance, and although I probably was not, decided to turn in another direction. When I did, I noted immediately that both cars continued on the route with DG. No-one followed me.

My only hope was that he too would notice the tail, and would act appropriately. Convinced that I was not under surveillance at this moment, I drove directly to the Chokchai building, knowing it would be normal for me to go to my office on a Sunday. I took two well-known short-cuts, parked and walked into my office. I called DG's home number and left an innocent message. "DG, this is Dale, Sorry, I can't get to the picnic. I have to work." I hung up.

I was hoping that when he took his wife home he would check his messages before going on to meet with me. If DG remains under surveillance, It wouldn't look good if he went to our ICP and waited,

273

then went to the alternate ICP one hour later just to have no-one show up again.

I placed the key in the STU and awaited a call.

Minutes seemed to drag by. At 1230 hours, I received a call on the STU. It was DG, asking for "Dale". I keyed and we talked. DG informed me that he had in fact detected the tail, and as a result, had driven straight home. When he pulled into his parking lot, he also noticed one of the same Datsuns that had tailed him earlier parked near the exit. The driver had crunched down in the driver's seat as DG drove by, and while DG and his wife were getting out of his car, DG saw that Datsun drive out of the parking lot. When he entered his apartment, he listened to my message, he was sure I had also detected the surveillance, and since he had already told his wife that he must attend a meeting with some of his staff at his office, he left in time to get to his office by 1300 hours.

On the STU, I was able to give him the pointers I had planned to pass at our meeting. Personal, one-on-one briefings are much more appropriate, and are used under normal circumstances. The surveillance activity had rendered this a special occasion, and we would have to do without the usual physical pat on the back.

I tried to convince him that the surveillance was routine, and to me it was only a strong verification that our friend Ivan was seriously interested in furthering their relationship.

DG stated that from his apartment to the Sunday services, he had detected no surveillance, and in view of that fact I wondered how they knew his destination. Had they actually picked him up at his residence and followed him to MACTHAI undetected, or had they picked him up outside the MACTHAI compound? Had they planted a tracking device in his car? We must assume the worst case scenario, and this would mean that we had to step up our security still another notch.

I told DG that in view of everything that has transpired; he should go on to meet with Ivan on Tuesday, adding that he could expect these "routine" activities to continue. Once again I reiterated that he should conduct himself normally. The STU would be our primary means of direct communication, leading up to our meetings. Using the STU we could make our arrangements directly, with no fear of any misunderstanding. Fearing that they would be watching his every move, I ended the conversation with "No signals for the time being." I could feel the urgency and hear the excitement in DG's voice.

In recent years, we'd always had the STU option, but the reasons I had introduced the use of signals were three-fold: 1) I wanted DG to feel the need for a serious element of clandestinity in our relationship, 2) through this hands-on training he would become accustomed to taking instructions from me, and responding with minimal guidance, and 3) with pre-arranged signals already in mind, they are easy to fall back on if the need should arise. On the other hand, although STUs were considered secure, I've never completely trusted any electronic means of communication.

Tuesday came and went, and I was beginning to wonder if DG had met with Ivan at all. Then, at 1115 hours on Wednesday morning, Mike answered the STU, and keyed, while motioning for me to take the call.

After recognizing my "Hello", DG said "Wow, those guys are really getting sloppy." He went on to explain that one of the cars had actually followed him into the Russian Embassy parking lot.

He went on to say "Once he realized what he had done, he rushed on past me and parked in the parking lot around behind the Embassy."

"Which car was it?" I asked.

"The Prince," he recalled.

"You may never see that car again," I joked.

DG told me that he feared he had also been followed into the Chokchai Building. He explained that three men he believed to be Russian were probably in the Chokchai Restaurant on the 23rd floor – as we speak. DG does not speak or understand Russian, but they had followed him from the parking lot, across the pedestrian overpass, to the elevator. He had listened to them, laughing and making gestures as though they were hungry. They continued on the elevator after DG had gotten off.

Having ascertained that DG would be in his office the rest of the day, I told him I would get back to him after lunch to arrange a get-together. We hung up. I dialed Dick's number to leave a message, but he was not at his desk, so I immediately walked into his office and told him of this development. It was his choice if he wanted surveillance coverage of the suspect Russians' activities. Dick had two new men assigned to his surveillance team, and decided to give them some practice, and a free lunch. They would only attempt to verify the identities of the three. We briefed them and showed the set of 'other agency' photos we had on file.

Not wanting DG to prepare reports for me and then have to go through the procedures of discreetly passing the reports by one or two-way pass, or through the use of a dead- drop, I opted for another personal meeting. During previous meetings, we had already arranged two-digit brevity codes for five initial contact sites, and another five meeting sites which had been cased and were considered secure. Although the sites were on US soil, we would go through the usual security procedures – just in case. I needed only a few minutes to talk to DG about this last encounter with Ivan. Calling him on the STU again, I used the codes to set up our meeting in the snack-bar at the MACTHAI compound.

I arrived first and walked through the line, selecting a coke, hamburger and fries. I chose a table near the rear. I sat against the back wall and watched DG arrive. He was not followed. One soldier in uniform and apparently his wife were seated in a booth along the outside wall. I moved the salt, pepper, to one side of the table, indicating that all appeared secure. When DG walked away from the cashier with his tray, he glanced in my direction, observed the signal, and then walked toward my table. "Hey," he greeted me, "is it OK to sit with you?"

"Certainly." I gestured for him to sit, and he did.

After ascertaining that the meeting with Ivan had gone as expected, DG hesitated and asked "Do you mind if I ask something?"

"Of course not, please."

"Aren't you guys finished with my BI yet?" He went on "I actually thought that when you did the subject interview, it would be over, but apparently not."

The light bulb floating over my head had just been turned on. "What's going on?" I asked.

"Well, you know – whenever you have a BI, your friends always tell you that they were interviewed, and how they recommended you for participation in the next moon-shot."

"Yes?" I urged him to continue.

"Well, some of my guys have now been contacted twice. That is, another of your guys called, made appointments, and have interviewed them.....again," He paused; another pause... "..at the Windsor." .... DG trailed off with "Oh, shit…!"

He had reached the same shocking realization as I, and his floating light-bulb had also been lit.

Whispering, DG leaned close, asking "It's those fake credentials, isn't it? He's using them isn't he?"

"It sounds like it," I agreed. I glanced around – there was no change in the clientele.

We both sat in silence for a moment while our minds ran over the implications.

Note: If in fact Ivan was conducting this activity himself, then I had a few questions; beginning with:

Why? For what good reason would he want to take the chance of exposing himself to any Americans during this phase of his operation? He must be very confident.

My mind was racing.

Perhaps the impersonation operation had already started before DG had walked into his office. If that's the case, Ivan is probably trying to establish himself at US facilities in order to build his cover. He's testing the system – to determine if he can actually use the credentials in a US environment. As the single, native English-speaking operative, he would be the first to try this new approach. This of course leads to that even more interesting scenario. Leon was right. There is a good possibility that as a recognized (but bogus) US 'Intelligence Agent', he could "recruit" an American to cooperate with him; train the American and convince him to visit the Russian Embassy; and allow a Russian to recruit him? Then Ivan could even orchestrate the passing of sensitive, highly classified materials to the Russians...... Wow!

At first I tried to second-guess the information... perhaps I was being paranoid. "No." I coached myself, "the evidence is here and the scenario is unfolding before our eyes".

My mind was still racing – *"What a fascinating idea!! Why didn't WE ever think of that?"* I asked myself.

"Great deception." I found myself talking aloud.

Our next step should probably be to talk with one or both of the soldiers who had been "re-interviewed"; next would be to ascertain if in fact it was Ivan; then we would need to determine the apparent authenticity of his credentials. What do they look like? Did he just flash them, or did he allow the soldiers to examine them closely?

I was getting ahead of the game. I needed to talk with Mike, Leon and Dick, and let them work on this.

"Of the two who have been re-contacted, which would you trust the most?" I asked DG.

"Either. They're both good men; conscientious, loyal, and good friends." He anxiously responded. "Do you want to talk with them?" DG volunteered to make the introductions.

"No, not right now," I warned him. "We needn't raise any flags at this time. Neither you nor I should be directly involved. I'll let the CI guys do their job." I went on to say "We do need to let others know about this possibility, that's for sure; and that's also the job of the CI Agents.

We discussed his meeting with Ivan, and following the discussion, I called both Mike and Leon. Mike was not home, so I drove to Leon's home, only about a mile from my apartment. He opened the door.

"What a pleasant surprise! Come in, come in. Take a load off. Can I get you something?" He was carrying a glass with ice, and what appeared to be Scotch. It looked good.

"What ever you're having," I suggested.

"Seidle", Leon beckoned his wife, "It's Don. Bring us some more Apple juice."

I thought, *"Apple juice is OK too."* I was thirsty.

Seidle entered in 60 seconds, carrying our drinks. Grateful for something to quench my thirst, I tilted my glass to the two of them and gulped. It was Scotch!

I choked. Leon laughed. Seidle returned to the kitchen.

We sat privately for a few minutes, while I provided the headlines for Leon. He listened intently, and then remarked "This is fascinating!" He picked up his phone and dialed Dick's memorized number.

I could not hear Dick, but Leon's portion of the conversation was:

"Dick, Leon." Leon started. "I gotta talk to you tomorrow first thing." He went on: "Well, cancel it! This is more important." Pause..."No, you gotta cancel it, believe me this is more important. It's operational - Don B's project!" Moments later he hung up. "0745 tomorrow morning in Dick's office." "Get you another one?"

He twisted my arm. "Sure Leon, thanks. But this is the last - I have to drive." I smiled.

"Seidle!"

That night, sleep was bad. My dream was interrupted regularly with short bursts of consciousness.

My clown was sitting in front of the only door in the cinder-block constructed room, smiling in my direction. He held an AK-47 across his lap. Ivan was standing across the table from me, wearing a Nazi uniform of High Colonel rank and holding a swagger stick. A single light glowed overhead. On the table, his credentials identified him as "KGB Special Agent" and were embossed with a Star and wreath encircling a hammer and cycle. My eyes focused on his face, and then on the wall behind him where photographs of Richard Nixon and Brezhnev were hanging. He was lecturing me: "We, under the leadership of the Honorable Mr. Leonid Brezhnev, have now assumed control. Our great leader is a rigid Stalinist with hard-line ethics.

Mr. Brezhnev's goal is to remake the USSR, formulating the strongest political superpower in the world."

I awoke momentarily, glanced at my clock. 0113.

My dry tongue stuck to the roof of my mouth. *I closed my eyes and listened to Ivan continue his lecture. I had no choice; I was now bound to the wooden chair. My clown looked on, smiling.*

"Our military is richly funded, and the authoritative influence of Brezhnev can be felt in the attitudes of the population. When Brezhnev is gone, he will leave behind an empire of the world's strongest military. We have just begun!

I awoke again. 0555! "Wow," I said to myself, "it took Ivan nearly five hours to make those last three statements." I spoke aloud, responding to Ivan's claims. "You forgot to mention that Russia is suffering from the world's weakest population morale. Russia will be an empty shell of a superpower with crumbling financial, social/political sectors, and so-on, Ivan," I predicted. I was rapidly forgetting Ivan's comments. I rinsed my mouth.

Now I was awake. I brushed, shaved, showered and shampooed. Exiting from the shower, I glanced outside as I turned on the radio. "….clear and mild with temperatures in the 90s and humidity around 90 percent." The announcer went on "And in the south, those of you lucky enough to be combing the beaches for collectable sea shells can expect a gentle, cooling breeze from the east, as it begins to escort our new friend Typhoon Jacob into our area. Still a tropical storm, the name Jacob has been designated, and he is expected to reach Typhoon strength sometime tonight, and arrive in less than 48 hours……." I turned him off, and decided I would walk to work today.

I arrived at the office at 0700 hours, and briefed Mike. When Leon arrived, Parky was with him, swelling with pride. "What's this I hear? You getting in pretty deep there Don."

"I can handle it – I hope," I responded, "but only with your guidance of course, Parky."

We all walked into Dick's office at 0740 hours. Although Leon spoke first, he said only "I'll let Don tell you what's happening."

I spent the next 30 minutes spelling out what happened and gave my hopes and opinions for the next steps to be taken. We were all in agreement that we must first interview the two men who had unwittingly been contacted – possibly by Ivan.

Later that morning, both SGT Bresnehan and CPL Tiley were interviewed separately, with Leon and I observing the interviews through one-way mirror/glass. They gave precisely the same story.

During the previous week, they had been contacted by an individual who identified himself as Special Agent "Jay Johnson" from the Bangkok Field Office. Bresnehan had met him early Monday afternoon and after giving Tiley's name as a character reference, Tiley was interviewed late Wednesday morning. Both had met him during lunch, and at the Windsor Hotel. When they met, he had identified himself with credentials, and asked routine BI questions about DG. He reminded them to keep the interview and the nature of the questions confidential. They both recommended DG for continued assignment to a position of trust. 'S/A Johnson' informed them that he would get back in touch with them if needed.

They had trusted him. He spoke perfect English, and conducted the interview professionally. Each interview lasted 15 to 20 minutes. The special agent had picked up the tab for their respective lunches.

Several photographs of Ivan were shown to both Bresnehan and Tiley, and they positively identified the photo of Ivan as 'Jay Johnson'. Both stated however that the photo on his credentials had been taken when Ivan was younger. His hair was now slightly longer, and he had a thin moustache.

True, current credentials were also shown to both subjects for close examination, and they were unable to say with certainty that they were not the same as the 'Jay Johnson' credentials. Bresnehan thought the format for the credentials was basically the same. He opined that without first hand knowledge, anyone would have accepted Jay Johnson and the credentials as legitimate. S/A Johnson had allowed them to hold and examine his credentials as long as they wanted.

Dick made it a point to remind our new interviewees that the subject of this discussion should be kept SECRET, and that they should not discuss this conversation with anyone whatsoever. It was believed serious enough to give them debriefing statements to sign.

After the interviews, Leon, Mike and I sat with Dick and discussed the situation.

Somewhere along the line, Ivan or someone in the Russian Security Services had seen US MI credentials close enough and long enough to draft a facsimile. A badge had not been displayed, and DG had not recalled seeing a badge in Ivan's briefcase.

Dick was already drafting the incorporation of Badge and Credential recognition into SAEDA briefings, and on instructing all briefed personnel that from this point on, while overseas they can expect that a badge will always be included when credentials are used to verify official status. This information would also be passed to the American personnel in charge of security at various overseas installations and government offices. Briefings to the "other agency" as well as to the Military Police and other intelligence and security agencies in Asia were also scheduled. It was also important to give wide distribution of the suspected Soviet espionage MO.

This interim measure might allow US officials to identify someone trying to enter our installations, and even more important, we may have an opportunity to identify the methods of operation used by adversaries to obtain information. Badges and credentials must bear the same serial number.

We decided to keep both Bresnehan and Tiley in mind for follow-up dangle operations.

Most importantly, it could allow us to cautiously develop more operations designed to expose the Russian efforts. In all likeliness DG's alertness had just led us into a gold mine.

In any case, it would be self-defeating to bring our discovery to the attention of our enemies at this time. Confrontation is not the answer. The ultimate goal of an Offensive operation such as this is to obtain and document as much information as possible on the enemy's requirements, their intentions, their Modus Operandi, and their activities. We had spent too much time and effort on Ivan to tip our hands this early.

The next two meetings between DG and Ivan went as expected. Through the utilization of codes, we were able to arrange and carry out debriefings in a secure manner. Then, the expected finally happened. On Tuesday, just 16 days after the revelation of the Special Agent Jay Johnson episode, Ivan popped his first request.

"You know," he started with DG, "I've come to think of you as a brother. The brother I never had. Unlike others, you came to me. You came to the right place when you needed some assistance, and I fell in love with your musical talents. You are very, very good, you know. I expect someday you will in fact visit my country, listen to our music and enjoy our culture and history first hand."

"I certainly hope so," DG responded.

"I wonder," Ivan pondered "if I could ask a small favor of you."

"Of course," DG responded without hesitation. "Just ask."

"From time to time, our office does business with foreign entities here in Bangkok," Ivan began, "and it is always nice to have up-to-date references and contact numbers. Oh, yes, we are able to maintain a good list of contacts through business dealings and such, but I have often thought it would be good to have some – how do you say – Line and Block charts and a US Government telephone directory......You know, the current publishing."

DG had already seen the list of items for which he would be able to obtain permission to pass without delay, and it included US Government telephone directories; but line and block charts had not yet been specifically addressed.

"I'm sure there wouldn't be much of a problem helping you out," DG stated, and then went on to say "We have brand new telephone books in our offices – after all, we are the ones who provide the information to the US Government Printing Office for those books." But, he explained truthfully, "Line and Block charts are another story. Ours are only updated once a year, in October – and the new ones will be out in a month or so. Can you wait that long?"

"Sure," Ivan stated happily – "but can you get me the telephone book right away?"

"I'll see how fast I can do it," DG responded confidently, "I owe you Ivan. It's true, we have become friends."

"Although I have asked for something which is not considered 'sensitive'," Ivan cautioned, "there is probably no need to tell anyone about this. After all, I'm Russian, and you know how people are....."

"That doesn't bother me," DG responded. "We're friends."

The dye had been cast. The question had been popped. The dibble inserted, and the seed planted. The hand had been dealt.

Without a formal recruitment, and based on a personal relationship, Ivan had co-opted DG as an unwitting source. Their professional relationship had now begun.

During the debriefing, I told DG that he could expect more requests coming from Ivan – gradually increasing in both frequency and sensitivity. I warned him not to be startled if Ivan begins to pressure him a little. DG was anxious to move into the next phase.

Leon was happy with the results, saying "I told you so, didn't I?" "Everything's going according to plan, isn't it?" He was fishing for a compliment – I gave it to him.

"Yes, Leon; I certainly couldn't have gotten this far without your professional expertise and guidance." I went on. "We're very lucky to have you in charge." Leon smiled to himself. It's true. Every one, even the boss, needs an occasional pat on the back. It's called 'recognition'.

The request for release was approved without hesitation. Parky decided that Line and Block charts fell into the category of telephone directories, and DG was allowed to pass the current charts to Ivan, along with the book. As an operational incentive, DG was also given the US embassy directories and Line and Block charts to pass along as well.

Occasionally over the next two weeks, Ivan visited the Kings Palace to watch DG perform. Our surveillance/counter-surveillance activities observed that the Russian surveillance of DG was now decreasing, as the Russians broadened the scope of their surveillance focus to other subjects. DG and I continued our training meetings, and after waiting for a reasonable period, on Wednesday, DG called Ivan and informed him that he had fulfilled his request. Ivan appeared happy, and they arranged a meeting for Saturday. Ivan then asked DG if he had ever been to the Elephant grounds.

Since DG had not, he so stated, and Ivan asked if he could pick him up and take him to see the performance, stating "It will be good for you to do something different; to relax."

DG had hesitated only momentarily and then stated that he would be happy to accompany Ivan. Before hanging up, DG gave Ivan his local address and driving directions from the Russian Embassy to his apartment. Not that Ivan needed the information.

I discussed the idea with Leon and Dick, stating that I thought Ivan's plan might be a decoy, designed to draw our own surveillance team out of hiding. Dick agreed, and asked if it was absolutely imperative that a complete team accompany DG and Ivan. We all agreed it was not worth taking any chances, and Dick said he would let his AA team make the trip; arriving at the Elephant grounds before DG and Ivan, and also departing in advance of their departure. I stated that I would have a telephone session with DG before Saturday, adding that in all likeliness, Ivan would also have a team in place at the Elephant grounds.

Friday morning, I noticed DG's new signal on a light pole at the intersection of Soi 49 and Sukhumvit. This new site had been chosen as a temporary alternate, since DG often stopped for donuts at the Soi 49 pastry shop on his way to work. After arriving at the office, I called him on the STU. Ivan had arranged to pick up DG at 0900 hours. DG wrapped his documents in a birthday gift package, and scotch-taped an envelope with a birthday card on top. He planned to pass the package to Ivan sometime during the drive. I cautioned DG not to appear 'tail conscious, to relax, and try to enjoy the trip."

"You know," DG laughed, "I'll bet elephant shit really stinks in this hot, humid weather!"

"I know, but we really appreciate your dedication. It's for God and our country." I chided jokingly.

At Sunday's debriefing, DG stated that Ivan had arrived at DG's apartment on schedule. He was introduced to DG's wife, who invited him in for coffee. Surprisingly, he accepted, and she poured fresh coffee and provided cake doughnuts for them. Ivan recognized the "Blue Mountain" coffee immediately, and complimented her selection. Ivan was quite talkative, carrying the conversation; and was also very complimentary of DG's music, saying "You know your husband is a fantastic musician – and a very good singer. He is bound for fame."

Irene responded humbly, saying "He's no Elvis, but he'll do."

They talked casually for about 15 minutes when Ivan stated that he was sorry to be taking her husband away for an entire day on the weekend; and Irene responded both tactfully and jokingly, saying that it's good to have him out of the house once in a while.

They bade farewell with Ivan saying how honored he was to finally meet DG's wife, and that he hoped to see her again. Her response "Likewise, I'm sure."

As they walked to Ivan's car, Ivan complimented DG, saying "Your wife is very charming. You are a lucky man."

DG acknowledged the compliment with a blushing "Thank You." and as they walked to Ivan's car, handed the 'birthday package' to him saying "And this is for you."

"May I open it?" Ivan asked anxiously as they were getting into his car.

"By all means," DG answered. "Let's see if it's what you wanted."

They sat in Ivan's Toyopet for 5 minutes while Ivan went over the documents. "Wow," he exclaimed, "It's even more than I could have hoped for. This line and block chart is two years newer than the one we obtained from your embassy."

Ivan neatly folded the documents back into the gift box, and before they departed the parking lot, placed them in the trunk, inside still another box.

They drove westerly, out of Bangkok, on the main highway to Nakhon

Pathom. The Samphran Elephant Ground and Zoo is just past the Rose Garden and Don Wai Floating Market.

They arrived at the park at 1145 hours. During weekend schedules, the first show is the Crocodile Wrestling Show, beginning at 1245 p.m. While waiting, they wandered around to see what else was on the agenda. When they arrived at the entrance, Ivan retrieved two advance-purchased adult tickets from his vest pocket and presented them, and their wrists were stamped with an entrance marking. Before entering, DG and Ivan had their pictures taken with a pair of tiger cubs that were born at the park. They were allowed to use their own cameras, and took turns taking pictures of each other with the cubs as well.

Nearby, a half dozen young elephants were chained to long metal stakes which were screwed into the ground, and each of these calves was attended by a "keeper" who apparently took care of its every need. DG noticed that one thirsty elephant, too impatient to wait for its trainer, used its trunk to open a faucet for a drink of water. Once finished, the elephant turned off the tap.

The 20 minute crocodile show was very similar to the one in show at the St Louis Zoo. The audience gasped with shrieks of horror at all the right times while the wrestler strained trying to "control" the virtually toothless, ageing crock.

After that show, they wandered around some more, looking at the crocodiles in the pens and admiring the orchids in full bloom. Ivan carefully examined the potted orchids, and selected one for purchase, saying he would pick it up on the way out.

The next two hours was spent listening to a history lecture of the relationship between the Thai people and their elephants, watching the elephants move and skid gigantic mahogany logs, and perform their acts. Guided by their trainers, the elephants played soccer. DG described one the older elephants, named "Reynaldo", who would bow graciously each time he scored a goal, and how the crowd cheered enthusiastically.

They watched the elephants perform in battle dress, carrying their brightly costumed Thai and Burmese keeper/trainers into battle. During this episode, the losing pair would have their camouflage screen set afire, and the elephant would then extinguish the fire by spraying river water on the flames with his trunk.

Afternoon found the temperatures beginning to drop slightly, as the Typhoon Jacob was beginning it's approach. Although still a long ways off, the peripheral winds were escorting a gentle breeze to portions of the outlying areas.

As they exited the grounds, Ivan stopped by the orchid shop and picked up the potted orchid. He requested it be placed in a box for carrying, and then selected a gift card on which he wrote:

Dear Irene, - Meeting you was a pleasure. Thank you for your splendid hospitality. He signed it: *Truly, Ivan.*

Ivan affixed the card to the flower pot and handed it to DG, smiling. "Please give this small token to your wife." He said.

Surprised, DG said "Thank you, Ivan. You are so kind."

On the way back to DG's apartment, Ivan stopped and insisted they snack on some fresh pineapple snacks and cake at a roadside stand. They topped off their snack with a generous serving of the famous Chokchai milk iced cream. Ivan returned by a different route, circling north, along a rarely traveled side road and coming back on Sukhumvit Road.

Before dropping DG off, Ivan said he'd never had a better time in Thailand.

Tentative arrangements were made to meet in another week, and Ivan said "Keep an eye out for me at the King's Palace." He then dropped DG off inside the apartment complex parking lot, politely turning down DG's offer for a drink, saying he wanted to be home before the Typhoon arrives.

I was convinced that the circular route Ivan had taken back into Bangkok was just an opportunity to conduct surveillance detection DG estimated that it took an additional 20 minutes to return by that route.

The next morning, I returned to the office to write my reports, and was nearly through by 1100 hours, when Leon walked into my area. He whispered "Don, come here a moment."

I obeyed, and followed him into the recreation area.

Leon had set up the balls on the bumper pool table. He handed me a cue saying "I'm going to kick your butt! I've been practicing. I'll start."

With his first shot, I was surprised to see the first two balls drop, and the cue-ball was perfectly aligned to put in the next two sequential shots.

Leon grinned "So, what do you think of that, my friend?"

"Wow," I answered. "You **have** been practicing." Leon sunk the next two balls, and was aligned for the fourth shot. He missed, as the ball bounced off the pegs.

Leon liked to move the cue-ball ever so slightly with the tip of the cue each time he took a shot, but I'd gotten used to the habit, and let him get away with it. He won the game, and was so excited he excused himself to the men's room to relieve his bladder.

In his absence, I began to set up the next game, when I noticed four small tick marks of blue chalk along the rails. One strategically placed on each side of the table. My suspicion was right, Leon was cheating.

Smiling to myself, I gently erased each of the chalk marks and replaced them with another mark, just about one inch away. When Leon returned, I had the table set up, and said "OK, Leon, you won – you can start again." Grinning, Leon happily grabbed his cue, aligned the cue ball - with one of my new marks, and made his first shot. He missed.

"What happened?" he yelled. "That's not right, let me shoot it again."

I did.

This time, Leon aligned the cue ball on the opposite side, in line with my second new chalk mark. He missed again.

At first he was angry with himself – then he took a close look at my new marks. Realizing that something was awry, he asked me suspiciously "Did you do something to the table?"

"Oh, no," I responded, "I just cleaned it off a little. You know, there were a bunch of chalk marks all along the edges!"

"You son-of-a-gun," Leon retorted, grinning. "You knew all along. OK, ok, I owe you lunch."

At 1130 hours we walked next door to the China Garden restaurant, and partook of their delicious buffet lunch – at Leon's expense. To the best of my knowledge, he never cheated at bumper pool again – at least not by using chalk marks.

After completing my report, I passed it to Mike and on to Leon, and we sat down for a brief discussion trying to anticipate what Ivan may ask for next.

Surprisingly, at the next meeting with DG, Ivan did not ask for anything, but instead talked casually with DG about his plans for a follow-on assignment when he leaves Bangkok.

Ivan openly admitted to DG that in addition to residing in San Francisco, he had lived in the Washington DC area where his father had also served as a diplomat. He thought it would be nice if DG were assigned to the Washington area, because Ivan felt that his own chances of going to DC from Bangkok were pretty good.

DG stated that he was still considering getting out of the military following his next reassignment. DG was trying to be truthful in saying that he was also considering staying overseas until that hitch is up. He did say however, that if the US and Thailand decide to discontinue their joint US Military Assistance/Advisory effort, he could rotate earlier; then immediately said that he had no indications of how that decision was going to go.

Ivan did not take the bait. Although he had previously expressed some interest in the status of MACTHAI, he pretended not to follow DG's lead on the subject, opting instead to talk about DG's personal plans.

"Actually," he stated, "With the amount of time you have already dedicated, don't you think it would be wise to go ahead and complete your twenty years."

DG responded, saying "That would be my second choice, provided I am also gainfully employed as a musician. That way, it would be an easy transition for me when I finally retire."

"That's good thinking," Ivan complimented him. He then went on to say "The Washington area would probably be a good place to continue either career, don't you think?"

"You're probably right," DG commented. "It's certainly worth thinking about." Not knowing why Ivan was fishing, DG went on to say "I've got to start thinking about it, otherwise someone else will decide for me."

"Well," Ivan responded, "whatever you decide, let's promise to keep in touch. OK my friend?"

They shook hands, agreeing that where ever DG might go, they would keep in touch with each other. Ivan lapsed into a long one-way discussion of his life and times when he lived in San Francisco and Washington DC. Ivan distinctly mentioned Golden Gate Park in San Francisco, and how his family would often picnic there. He recalled the early morning bagpipe player standing on a fog-shrouded knoll in the park. "He appeared to be a messenger from heaven standing in the clouds," Ivan remarked, and described how much he enjoyed that music. He was proud to have been born in America, stating that only because of his father's dedication to Russia, had he decided to select Russia as his country of citizenship.

From the way DG described this meeting, I knew there must be some reason Ivan was trying to convince him to attempt reassignment to Washington DC following completion of his overseas tour. During this meeting there were no requests on the part of Ivan.

When I discussed the meeting with Leon, and the obvious lack of tasking, Leon opined that Ivan was probably going through his paperwork and updating biographical information on DG. "Appearing to open up is a good elicitation technique. It gives the interviewee a feeling of familiarity."

Then referring to the elicitation for biographical information, Leon went on to say "After all, the Russians have the same bureaucratical red-tape to follow as we do. Patience is a virtue my friend"

Typhoon Jacob came bearing down on Bangkok that same week, following almost the same pattern as did "Irit". We were still in the early months of the monsoon season, and the usual rumors that 1974 would be 'the worst typhoon season on record" were beginning to emerge based on data from those two storms.

DG continued regular meetings which became routine, as Ivan insisted they meet every other Thursday. Their relationship resulted in only bits and pieces of production insofar as our reporting was concerned. Sporadic surveillance of his travels revealed no indication whatsoever of any increase in Surveillance activity by the Russians. I provided DG with a list of desired bio-data we could use on Ivan, and their "personal" relationship continued over the next two months with DG providing most of that needed information. We had now documented Ivan's personal tastes for wine, food, women, and music; his hobbies and languages. Ivan had begun studying the Thai language, and was not shy in speaking the language, practicing at every opportunity.

Two of their meetings were mobile, and on these occasions, Ivan had arranged to openly pick up DG on the street in front of the Chokchai building and drive to the local *Wat Arun* "Temple of the Dawn" Buddhist temple in Bangkok's Chinatown. Ivan conducted their meeting while strolling through the park, giving the impression that no secrecy was involved with their relationship.

On both those occasions, Leon felt it was logical to assume that a fixed KGB surveillance had been set up to observe and possibly photograph the two, at the pick-up point and/or during their stroll through Wat Arun Park. DG made it a habit of carrying a small 35mm camera with him at all times when their meetings were conducted in public.

Near the end of September, Ivan asked DG if it would be possible for him to entertain at an embassy party, where foreign dignitaries and other guests would be in attendance. DG would check with his wife; and after notifying me, our office immediately approved the participation. At our expense, DG was fitted with a conservative Tuxedo for the black-tie event. Although our office encouraged Irene to accompany him to the event, she chose to work on that evening, and was not able to attend.

The local television station *(iTV (Thailand)* , that had already filmed three entire evenings of DG at the King's Palace, also covered the embassy event, focusing much of their attention on the American who plays Russian and popular American music. The human interest story was picked up by many of the local radio stations as well, and DG was able to put together an album entitled "American in Russia", which was placed on the shelves in selected music stores. DG had become a local novelty

The operation was going smoothly, and there was little doubt that DG would soon become a 'household name' at the Russian embassy. Oddly enough, Ivan's name was never mentioned in any local media programs or publications regarding DG. The only remote mention of any embassy association on the part of DG was in the beginning of the TV program wherein it was stated that he had obtained sheet music from the Russian Embassy to prepare for his performances.

In the meantime, approvals had been received, not only to continue to meet with Bill Tanner, but to brief him on the ongoing, overall project (without specifics), to obtain his cooperation and to coordinate with Colonel Wilson as well. The receipt of such a rapid response was likely attributed to Leon's request for expeditious handling, and in part to the pending departure of Col Wilson.

I called Bill and arranged a meeting, asking if his office had a place where we could speak in private. Since his immediate supervisor, Major Smith was currently on leave, Bill suggested we use Smith's office, where he was temporarily hanging his hat. I descended immediately, entered his office and was beckoned into the private digs of Major Smith.

Bill had already prepared coffee, and we sat and talked casually for a few minutes while I passed the rather bulky folder I had prepared for his application to transfer to the Military Intelligence field. He thumbed through the documents and regulations I had assembled, saying "This is a lot of reading – and a lot of preparation."

I cut to the quick, saying "Actually, Bill I've been giving our discussion a lot of thought." And continued "You may have an opportunity to get involved in the 'nitty-gritty' without actually being part of the MI bunch. Are you interested?"

"Let's hear it." He answered without hesitation.

Without being the specific, I spent the next few minutes explaining the type of operations in which we would like to become involved, explaining as I had before that Russian operatives in the Bangkok area are extremely active.

"Sounds like that SAEDA briefing you guys give us every year."

"Precisely," I said, reacting to his comment,. "Let me brief you. I first need to tell you what I have in mind." And, I went on to explain how I could use his assistance. I further explained that there would be no publicity, thus no glory in performing this small task for us, but added immediately that if he agrees, we may be able to influence his request for an extension of his tour in Bangkok.

Bill would be asked to allow us to help him arrange an initial contact with a suspect KGB operative, for the purpose of playing tennis. I did not provide a name at that time. The results of that first contact would determine the next steps, the follow-on contacts, and the possible, eventual "dangle".

Bill was immediately and obviously delighted, saying that he'd always wanted to do something like this. He wondered however if his Commander would have to be briefed and expressed concern that Col Wilson would probably not go along with the utilization of any of his personnel. I admitted that Colonel Wilson's approval would definitely be a requirement for Bill's involvement. Of course, I did not mention that our office was already acquainted with Colonel Wilson, or that we had dealt with him before.

DONALD BRADSHAW

We shook hands, and while reminding Bill of the 'secrecy' of this meeting, I told him I would be in touch - soon.

Now, it was time to deal with Colonel Wilson again. Since Leon and Wilson were friends, I decided I should take him along again.

Back at the office, I sat with Leon while we war-gamed our approach. He recommended we handle it as we had with DG's briefing, and I agreed. It was important that Col Wilson be in the right frame of mind though, otherwise we could be setting ourselves up for failure. We discussed the situation with Parky, and he suggested that we ask our own Commander (Col W) to make the appointment this time. He explained that it was not at all difficult to obtain approval to use one of Col Wilson's enlisted men, but to obtain permission to use one of his most accomplished young officers whose father and grandfather were both retired military, and of General rank - just might be a different story.

We all agreed. Parky walked into the commander's office directly behind his own, and stated "Sir, Leon, Mike and Case Officer Don B are here to brief you and ask for some help."

"By all means, Parky," we heard the Colonel say, "Bring them on in."

We entered, and began briefing the Colonel on the plan. About two minutes into the brief, the Colonel raised his hand, causing us to pause, and said "Actually, I've been keeping an eye on your projects. Leon, your office is conducting the only real spying we have going at this time. And you, young man - he was gesturing to me - are doing a great job."

"Thank you, sir. I have good mentors."

"You do," he agreed, "and, you also have a good imagination." He went on "I've read your proposals, and think you have some great ideas here. You know of course that Colonel Wilson keeps a tight reign

298

on his personnel, and doesn't like to lose anyone, not even temporarily. If you're going to try to use this guy – what's his name – "

"Captain Bill Tanner," I answered.

"Yes, yes, Tanner. Well, you know, Colonel Wilson just might not go along with it. Do you have another lead you can fall back on? Maybe some enlisted guy?"

I answered that Bill Tanner was the only person I had in mind.

"Then, I would suggest you use those exact words when you brief Wilson," the Colonel said, "and, what ever you decide, don't let Wilson know that you've already asked Tanner. Go over this with Tanner first too, so he won't drop the dime on you."

"You had good luck last time you talked with Wilson," the commander continued, "It must have been the timing – believe me you caught him in a good mood. I'll set up the meeting with Wilson; then we can all hope that he's in a good mood when you walk back into his office."

Before leaving his office, the commander asked if he could speak to me alone. Leon and Mike walked out and the Col said. "So what's this I hear about you wanting to marry a foreign national?"

"Yes Sir," I answered. "I submitted the paperwork from Ft Bragg, and I assume it's in the mill by now."

"Actually," the Colonel continued, "I got the news from COL Vallese in Taiwan." "He's retired now, but I'm sure you know that already. He speaks quite highly of you."

"He's a great guy," I joined in, "a leader's leader."

"Well put." He answered. "Well, if you talk to him, always pass my regards. In the meantime, if you need any support with the marriage application, just let me know."

"Thank you, Sir," I replied. I meant it.

Back in my office, I used the STU to call Bill's office. We made an appointment for a quick meeting, and had lunch at the China Garden that afternoon at 1300 hours. Over lunch, I explained the situation and obtained his promise that he would not relinquish the confidentiality the two of us had already established if he should happen to talk to Col Wilson before the operation is formalized.

After updating the SLDR on Bill's project and submitting it, I went through the rituals with Frank, arranging for a rental for my formal recruitment and initial training session with Bill Tanner. The meeting would take place in 10 days.

Since Frank was also beginning to realize success with the operation he had developed, we discussed the feasibility of renting a safe-house/ safe-site for future meetings with our recruited sources. From the standpoint of expending confidential funds, it seemed justifiable, but other considerations, such as security, convenience, maintenance, cover, frequency/necessity, etc always seem to have a direct bearing on the coordination and implementation of safe house plans.

A safe-site would always be available, for regular use by any of our Case Officers, and on short notice. Someone in our office would have to be responsible for maintaining the site, and we would have to be certain that the safe-site would not be abused, or used for anything other than operational purposes, or in any way that could draw undue attention to our activities.

We also decided that this would be a good time to request additional administrative support, in the form of an experienced Intel type who could carry out the functions of a safe-site keeper. We would begin drafting up the proposal.

This was a good example of the growing administrative burdens which occur whenever operations begin to reach an acceptable degree of success. The more you do, the more you are expected to do.

Finally, at 1530 hours, when I thought I'd be able to leave early, I caught the elevator down to the 2nd floor, and began walking across into the parking lot. I glanced at the old signal spot and noticed a white mark – obviously left by DG. A signal with a white crayon mark was to be used only when there was some urgency. I went to my car, opened the trunk and picked up a small box. I walked back into the building and to my office, where I used the STU to call DG's office. His supervisor was not in, and he answered the STU. He was relieved, saying he'd left the signal this morning at 1000 hours, after Ivan had called him urging a get together at their earliest convenience – hopefully this afternoon. He had called Ivan back and asked if he could come by after work, indicating that he was also very busy. Ivan OK'd that arrangement, and stated he would wait for DG across the street from the main gate of the Russian Embassy. DG had agreed to this short-notice arrangement. Every time he had called my office, the line was tied up. This was an unusual arrangement. We would have very little time to set up surveillance.

We had originally set up calls to my office for "Dale", on either an open line or by STU, we had modified this plan as the situation became more sensitive. Also, because of the paranoia built into these type operations, I had arranged for DG to contact me through my office STU, only from his own office STU. Signals were now only an alternate means of contact. Using a white crayon for this instance was justified.

I asked if he could go on to the meeting with Ivan as usual. DG felt no urgency, other than getting in touch with me. He had done that.

I assured him that our 'people' would be near by. DG would leave his office at 1715, and arrive at the RE at around 1745 hours – in the middle of rush hour.

I immediately contacted Dick, who called in his team, consisting of the two AA guys and the two new arrivals. Photos of the initial contact would be arranged with a phone call, as soon as that particular surveillance was in place. Since the pickup would be across the street from the embassy gate, DG would be going southwest – away from Sukhumvit Rd, and we would arrange pickup in that direction. No problem.

Surveillance was in place and during the debrief, DG informed me that by the time he arrived, Ivan was waiting. He was carrying a small valise, and according to DG's sketch-map, I deduced that Ivan was standing within about ten feet of our fixed surveillance. DG pulled up to the curb and Ivan got into the passenger seat, directing DG to make a U-turn in the truncated entrance of the embassy driveway. DG did as directed, as Ivan said, "We need to go back in the other direction and south on Sukhumvit Rd."

The new surveillance team was parked in a traffic-blocked lane, unable to commit in either direction, but the AA team had been facing the other way. With Bangkok's rush hour traffic moving along at a good pace, half of the surveillance was immediately lost.

Obviously, my assumptions had been wrong. Dick received a call from the AA team almost immediately. I was confident DG was alert enough to remember the routes taken.

DG did as Ivan instructed, and casually asked "Are we going over to Wat Arun?"

"Not this time", Ivan answered, "we're going over by Lumpini Park."

At Ivan's directions, they drove to the intersection of Wireless Road, across from Soi Nana. There they turned right, driving southwest, across Rama IV, onto Sathorn-tai. They drove past the German and French embassies, then west on Silom, turning into the Unico Grand Sathorn Hotel at 59 Silom Road.

They entered the hotel parking lot, and parked in a guest slot. Ivan explained that he had rented the hotel room for some family 'guests' who were going to be in Bangkok over the weekend and through

Tuesday night. In order to avoid a weekend-rush, his office had rented the room, beginning on Thursday; and since he had the room for these two additional nights, he would use it, as it would give them some privacy for their meeting. "You did tell Irene that you would be home late, did you not?"

"Of course", DG replied "But not too late, I hope."

"Absolutely," Ivan said encouragingly. "We'll be through in an hour or so. I hope you have time for dinner though. The food here is amazing." They parked in the guest parking, and walked inside.

According to the surveillance report, the new Team had observed Ivan pick up the room key on arrival. He presented his credit card and signed. It appeared he had made reservations by phone and was just checking in. (This was very sloppy agent handler MO). Ivan's receipt was placed in slot #1104. The team took a table in the bar area next to the lobby, and decided to sit it out. As a cover for their presence, they had carried a folder of insurance documents, which they opened on their table. From that position, they could see the elevator. One-way, indirect contact was made with the AA team, through Dick's office by pay phone. The AA team arrived about 25 minutes later and took up a separate position to observe the main entrance to the hotel. From this location it would be easy to rotate places after a reasonable period of time. Signals would be used for communication.

CHAPTER 21.
AN UNEXPECTED PARTICIPANT?

During my follow-on debriefing with DG, I confirmed that they had used room 1104. Ivan checked the fridge and brought out two chilled Vodka miniatures, a tray of ice and a near frozen bottle of orange juice. He retrieved glasses from the counter and poured drinks for himself and DG. He turned the music up to cover their conversation and proposed a toast.

"To my new friend and to his wonderful music."

"Toast," DG responded smiling. They sat at a table overlooking the courtyard.

Their conversation began with a casual exchange of amenities, and for the first few minutes, DG noticed Ivan checking his watch several times, and occasionally staring into the courtyard as though he were looking for something or someone. Then, after one final glance into the courtyard below, Ivan closed the curtains and as though on cue, their operational discussion began with Ivan asking "a favor. – or two."

Ivan reminded DG that they were already nearing the 1 October publishing date for new US Government Line and Block charts, saying that he needed current ones, as soon as possible.

DG told him truthfully that he had already received the new charts, but this meeting was arranged in such a hurry that he'd had no chance to wrap them. They were still in the original packaging on his desk. DG apologized, and asked if he could bring them "next time".

"Of course," Ivan answered, and seemed relieved.

Now, Ivan went on with his "surprise request", saying he had one additional small favor to ask. He explained that he had read a newspaper article regarding a planned US/Thai, Joint military exercise that is scheduled to occur during the months of January and February, 1975. DG was surprised that Ivan already knew dates, because that information had just been released to the press today.

Trying not to show his surprise, DG asked from which newspapers Ivan had read the article. Ivan responded that he had read an article on US/Thai military cooperation wherein a one-line mention was made of "an upcoming, US/Thai joint military exercise, early in 1975". "I'm quite sure I read it in a *Stars and Stripes* newspaper, printed in Japan", Ivan guessed, "and perhaps in the *Bangkok Post* as well."

"Oh, well, no wonder," DG responded. "The Stars and Stripes often does that."

DG had seen the S&S article as well, and leaned closer to Ivan saying "It is true though, the joint exercise is coming."

Ivan continued, saying "Everyone seems to be reporting on it, so I thought it was a big deal".

"It might be that," DG responded, "but I'll check on it and bring you up to date."

DG noticed Ivan's surprise that DG seemed so cooperative – but then, what did DG have to fear? After all, they were simply two friends talking about something in the paper.

"Your offer was perfect timing," I told DG.

Ivan continued, saying "With Viet Nam winding down, it appears that Russia may now get involved with Viet Nam. (He was leading DG – who appeared to have no specific interest.) Ivan went on, "Perhaps we all should have taken a lesson from Dien Bien Phu". Ivan was referring to the French-Indochina battle of 1954. He continued. "Between you and me, DG, I don't believe that Russia should become involved in Viet Nam either."

DG agreed, and then returned to the subject at hand, stating that he had of course seen some official correspondence on the planned joint exercise, and that proposals were just now beginning to come across his desk. He reminded Ivan that it would be his job to allocate personnel in support of the exercise, for a six week period, beginning in January 1975, – once the final plans are approved. This was DG's attempt to delay handing over any documents until approved by my office.

I told DG that I would get something approved for turnover, and DG agreed to provide me with a list of draft proposals and their dispositions to reference in my own request. In the meantime, my advice was to stall in passing any information whatsoever to Ivan, and let the hierarchy decide the next move.

"We will get permission to pass the new Line and Block charts immediately" I encouraged, "but insofar as the joint exercise is concerned, it is likely that you will be allowed to pass only the most recently disapproved or rejected proposal that was based on the same dates in January and February. Once the US government is ready to release the entire plan to the press, it should be a matter of routine to allow passage of that information to Ivan."

DG understood, and told me confidentially "There are plans in the mill that will likely be approved in the next two weeks, and some have already been discarded."

"Perfect!" I was pleased. And if we can beat the press releases by even a few days, Ivan should be happy.

DG went on to describe the meeting with Ivan, saying that they had taken dinner at the Hotel, during which Ivan told DG he would be bringing his entire family to see the show at the Kings Palace on Monday. After dinner, DG had driven Ivan back to the Russian embassy to pick up Ivan's car. Ivan confirmed their next meeting for the following Thursday afternoon, but avoided any further operational discussion.

DG and I terminated our meeting and departed separately.

Our surveillance teams had been active, following DG back to the Russian Embassy and then breaking off as he turned onto Sukhumvit Rd to move in the direction of his home.

Ivan was not followed by our teams from the embassy, and as far as anyone could tell, the Russians had not followed DG.

Back in the office on Friday, Leon gave me verbal approval to allow DG to pass the items he had already promised to Ivan. I called DG to inform him that he could make the next meeting and pass the charts; then told him that he could "mention" that the "plans are in the mill". In the meantime, I would work on approval for passing those plans. I again encouraged DG that we would make it look good, and that he could expect his friend to be very happy.

Friday afternoon I called Bill and arranged a Monday afternoon meeting with him. I would pick him up in the Chokchai parking lot at 1100 hours. The plan was to stop and pick up a snack along the road, and go to the 'River Bend' Hotel.

The thought of an entire weekend with no meetings, no reports, no requests, just the possibility of another small typhoon, was perfect. How relaxing.

By noon Saturday, I was becoming bored with watching the Thai weather reports. The typhoon was stirring around, but was no immediate threat to the local area. Departing Malaysia, Typhoon

Kate had turned northeast, heading toward Phnom Penh and was expected to break up as it headed inland. This brought some winds into Bangkok, and had lowered the temperature and humidity into my comfort zone.

Back on the deck, I poured a rare double of Rock-&-Rye into a glass of crushed pebbles, and was sipping away listening to a recently obtained tape of *"Jesus Christ Superstar"*. While the subject matter was not necessary my first choice, I found the music tasteful, and the Rye even more so. So much more so, that after a second shot, I drifted into a semi-conscious dream – and my clown returned.

This time, I was trying to call Betty from a telephone booth somewhere in China. I kept dialing the operator and asking for Betty by name.

"Chen, Chang-ping", I repeated over and over, but the operator was responding in a dialect with which was totally unfamiliar.

Perched on a small Cushman motor scooter just feet away was my friend, the clown. His painted face sardonically fixed in a wide, tooth-filled grin. He seemed to be enjoying my frustration while he mimicked my actions, pretending to hold a phone to his ear, and mouthing silent communication. When I opened the telephone booth door to yell at him, he had disappeared. When I closed the door, he was there again. Open – gone; close – returned.

I awoke, trembling with anger. The deck was dark, the pool area empty, and the odor of garlic and hot pepper spices being stirred in peanut oil was beginning to drift upward from the restaurant below and permeate the air. Blending with the obvious aroma of Oxtail, simultaneously brewing in a licorice spiced sauce, the stew was one of their specialties; and it was beckoning to me. I walked back into my room, secured the door, and changed into a pair of beige, hemp trousers and a 'Chiang-mai' pullover shirt, and descended into the lobby area of the complex. Immediately on entering, I felt a sense of dé-jà vu. Sitting on the circular bench in the center of the lobby area, reading a newspaper was one of the two members of the AA team. In the corner, not far from the Exit was a member of the "new team". Two inside meant there were probably two more in sedans - outside.

They were working. I ignored them, and walked into our Maidee Court Restaurant, sat and ordered my Oxtail stew with the side salad and fresh, hot French bread.

Out of habit, I had sat facing the opened glass windows that separate the restaurant from the lobby area, and of course also facing the surveillance activity. I couldn't allow myself to continue ignoring them after all. I sipped the spicy, Oxen-flavored broth slowly, occasionally tearing a piece of hard-crust French bread and dunking it into the broth. It was delicious as usual.

Suddenly, I caught one of the surveillants turning toward the lobby counter, and looked just in time to see three men in suits descending from the second floor into the lobby area. I easily recognized them as the three who had accompanied Ivan to the King's Palace when Frank and I had also visited a few weeks earlier. They resembled a Chicago Mafioso trio from the 1930's.

As they started past the counter, they were confronted by the Thai receptionist, who offered help. The three began speaking all at once, demanding a room, overlooking Sukhumvit Road. "I am sorry," she replied "This is not hotel, it is apartment."

"Are there any apartments available – for a few days?" The noisiest one asked.

"No, sir, I'm sorry sir." She replied. She pointed toward the sign over the counter and read it to the visitors: "We cannot rent our apartments for periods shorter than three months."

The surveillance team was watching – as was everyone else within earshot. Not once were the Russians asked of their business at the apartment complex, who they were visiting, or how they'd gotten inside the residential area without escort.

In anticipation of the Russians departure, the team members had moved into the street and were walking in the direction of their cars.

The Russians stared blankly at each other (for some reason I thought of my clown), and then the noisy one who seemed to be in charge said in a voice much louder than it needed to be "Then I suppose we must take our business elsewhere."

The Mafioso marched in unison from the lobby and entered their car which was illegally parked just outside the entrance to the complex. The puzzled receptionist watched them drive away. The surveillance team allowed another car to drive past, and then entered the street, continuing on their surveillance.

My adrenaline was flowing – I wanted to be a part of the excitement. Alas, I returned my attention to the now warm oxtail stew.

It must be consumed while hot.

Belligerent, condescending, intimidating, and antagonistic are four words commonly and accurately used to describe the attitude of many Eastern Europeans when they are caught making a mistake, doing something socially unacceptable, or when they are just trying to cover their actions. I decided they had probably been snooping around, and had accidentally descended the wrong staircase, ending up in the lobby, where they were bound to be challenged. The Lobby, like the restaurant was open to the public, but signs posted in the lobby area directed unescorted visitors to call their hosts from the lobby courtesy phone. The resident host could then come to the lobby and escort them to the apartments. Residents were allowed routine access and passage by virtue of personal recognition. At any rate, for the time being, I would not be concerned. I would find out Monday what the surveillance teams were up to.

The rest of Saturday fizzled. I retreated to my room, began watching Thai TV, and after another two-shot Rye on crushed pebbles, fell asleep, sprawled across my most comfortable papa-san chair, where I remained quietly through the rest of the night.

CHAPTER 22.
BOND, JAMES BOND.

Sunday was beautiful. Although the humidity had risen again, the sky was clear; and typhoon Kate had blown into the jungles of Cambodia, where she died of natural causes. As the first customer, I had an early, 0600 'American breakfast' at the restaurant, and walked into the street at 0630 hours. Shop owners were un-battening their hatches, and beckoning to passers by, inviting them to be the 'first customer'. I walked along the street, wandering without purpose toward the Chokchai building, and was surprised to notice that the traffic had been blocked off for an entire three-block strip on Sukhumvit Road. Happy that I'd not driven, I walked inside the area, and noticed that the filming of the famous "007" movie - "The *Man with the Golden Gun*" was in progress. The open area of the first floor of the Chokchai building had been temporarily converted into an automobile showroom, and was filled with exotic sports cars, and a sign in both Thai and English advertised that they were all for sale. I entered the building in time to notice that a camera had been positioned on the pedestrian overpass, and the operator was practicing his movements back and forth alongside the glass windows, awaiting the "ACTION!" signal from a director.

As the camera moved back to the street entrance, the director halted him and gave him instructions that as soon as Roger (the new James Bond) Moore entered the building at the ground floor, the camera man was to begin moving the camera along the walkway to pan downward, across the showroom.

James Bond was to "borrow" a red sports car and crash out onto the street, going immediately to the right - in the wrong direction and against traffic - toward the river. The Thai police would then chase him to the river, and he would make his famous broken-down bridge flight across the river and escape. Of course.

As I watched, I realized that DG had left a signal on the window for me. I suddenly realized that if all went well, the camera would pick up the mark, and my agent's signal would live in obscure infamy as part of the famous James Bond movie.

It worked perfectly.

Not knowing when the signal was placed, I entered the building and went to my office. I retrieved the STU key from the safe, inserted it and called DG's office. DG himself answered the call, and explained immediately that he had come to work on Sunday, hoping I would check the signal site. He continued, saying that Ivan had called him at home to confirm their appointment for Thursday. He had asked if DG would have the items he had asked for, and DG had answered that he would have the charts for sure, but could not guarantee that he could yet provide any substantive information on the "other matter." (Meaning the planned training exercise).

DG had continued, saying to Ivan "I'm expecting some kind of agreement this coming week, and I will surely let you know, as soon I am notified."

""That's great." Ivan had replied – "then, I'll see you Thursday afternoon." As an afterthought, before hanging up, Ivan said "Oh, I almost forgot, I'll see you Monday at the Palace." He apologized for interrupting DG's weekend, and explained that he was just sitting at home reading the newspaper when the thought crossed his mind to call DG.

"It's absolutely no bother," DG replied. DG correctly thought it strange that Ivan would call him on his home phone, just to 'confirm their appointment.'

I agreed, warning DG again to be very cautious about what he says over his phone, or anywhere in his apartment for that matter. DG was planning on leaving his office immediately, so I spent a few minutes writing notes for my report. I would arrange for a discreet sweep of DG's apartment, and his car if deemed necessary. His wife should also be cautioned, but DG would be capable of handling that. I then waited another 90 minutes before locking up and leaving.

The sports cars had been removed from the now vacant first floor, sale signs had been removed, and there was no indication that two hours earlier the Chokchai building had been the sight for the filming of James Bond's famous crash-away scene from "the *Golden Gun*". There were no souvenirs. The windows had been cleaned. Pedestrians on the street were as oblivious to the filming activity as they were to the activities of my operation.

Walking back to my apartment, I tried to tie the two incidents together - The Russians in my complex, and the phone call to DG). Were they testing a new electronic surveillance system?

I returned to my apartment complex, and found a note from Frank had been slipped under my door. It read "Come on over, if you have time. BYOB" – it was signed: "Frank". 'BYOB' meant that this was an urgent request.

I immediately took the remaining 6-pack of Bud from my fridge, walked out and across the walkway into the covered lot and put the nearly-frozen six pack in my car. I then descended to the main floor and walked two doors down to a Chokchai Market where I picked up two cold, 1-liter bottles of *Amarit* (Thai lager) for Frank.

The 10 minute drive was quick, and on arrival I noticed that there were several other cars parked in the driveway and along the road outside the wrought-iron gate and stone fence surrounding Frank's rental. Nearly everyone from our entire section was present, and Frank had fired up his Bar-B-Q. Everyone hailed as I entered, and I handed an *Amarit* to Frank and placed the rest of the brews in one of his ice chests.

"I thought you'd be checking into the hotel today," I said.

"Ah'll get to the hotel this evenin'." Frank took me aside immediately and told me that this short-notice soirée had been arranged to discuss a situation.

"Ah know you've been busy," Frank continued, saying "this came up late Friday."

Apparently, one of our recruited American sources had visited his Russian Agent Handler at the Russian Trade Mission. While he waited in the lobby area, he had overheard two trade mission employees discussing eavesdropping activities; then, when he entered his handler's office, he noticed a classified, Russian-language bulletin on the desk, entitled "Surveillance of Americans". He saw only the cover page of the 3 or 4-page document which the handler removed immediately and placed in a filing cabinet. He was positive the Russians were setting up a program for monitoring the telephones and apartments of Americans.

The source, Sergeant First Class Kolinsky, was quite certain his Russian handler had not seen him glance at the document. His handler had no knowledge of Kolinsky's Russian Language abilities. Kolinsky was born of Polish immigrants, who had migrated to the US as children of immigrant families, in the 1920's. Kolinsky was born in 1938, in New York, and at his father's insistence had studied both Polish and Russian. His Russian was considered fluent.

With limited resources, Dick had set up two-man teams at various complexes where some of our Case Officers and sources reside, and had actually had some grunt-luck at my complex.

I told Frank of my observations Saturday, and of my contact with DG just that morning. "Hot Damn!" Frank exclaimed, "I can't wait till Leon hears this." He glanced around and caught Leon's eye. "Hey, Leon – Get over here."

Leon sauntered over, mumbling something about privacy. Dick was walking through the gate to the party, and joined us.

I told of my observations on Saturday, and Dick said that his team had seen me at the restaurant. "But," he opined "I don't think you are necessarily their target. There are a lot of Americans living in your complex, and most of them have pretty high security clearances. It could be any one of them."

"..Or all of us." I grinned; my paranoia showing through.

Dick went on to say "Now as for your friend the musician - that information might be pretty important. It sounds like Ivan just might be setting up to eavesdrop from his home. Be sure you don't call the musician from your home for any operational purpose." He further instructed "Our STUs are not traceable."

I assured him I would never even consider it, and explained that DG and I had established plausible brevity codes.

"Unfortunately, we already know the Russians have that capability." Dick responded, "My primary concern is at locations where there is a telephone switchboard. A single recruitment could literally give them unlimited access to all the phones in the entire apartment complex; and that type access could greatly enhance their information collection efforts. All they need is a recorder."

Dick was on a roll. "We believe that most of the Russian tech support guys have been identified; and my teams will be working every day for the next few weeks to try and identify their activities. We arranged this little get-together to get the word out for you guys to brief your agents. I've prepared several packets with photos and an assessment of what we believe we're up against. You'll have them tomorrow morning." Dick turned to me. "The three guys at your apartment Don, they were their tech support staff." Dick then asked "As for your musician guy Don, what's your take? Do you think they've also tagged his car?"

"I believe so," I answered. "Remember two weeks ago on a Sunday? DG was surveilled by the Russians who apparently picked him up at the MACTHAI compound. They had to have some way of knowing he was there. And remember, they didn't follow him there – they picked him up there." I said again.

As a post script, I said "They do have access to his car every time he visits his handler – Ivan. But he parks in the front of the embassy, in full view of the main gate and our fixed surveillance. On the other hand, they also know where he lives, and are familiar with the comings-and-goings in his parking lot. It wouldn't be difficult."

That evening, Frank made the reservation at River Bend for 5 days, allowing enough time to run a tech sweep. He would have the room to himself daily until the sweep was conducted.

Monday in the office, I looked over the folder from Dick containing photos and a brief description of the three Russians who had visited my apartment complex, along with seven other photos of their technical support team who were considered "operatives". I copied the photos onto one page, and folded it into the concealment slot in my briefcase.

I would brief both DG and Bill. I called DG on the STU, and asked him to take a good look at Ivan's friends attending his show at the King's Palace, alerting him that we would have other items to discuss at our next meeting, now scheduled for Tuesday evening. I asked him if he could discreetly brief his wife today on the possibility of their home, telephone and car being monitored, so she wouldn't slip up.

"Where, how?" he asked.

I suggested he write a note telling her that they were not to discuss anything we had talked about, or to have any discussion regarding Ivan – while talking on the telephone, while at home, or whenever they are in their car. I further suggested he downplay the subject by including that while there is some concern that Americans were being monitored, this is a routine concern and is briefed to all US Forces personnel on assignment overseas. No need to frighten her in any way.

I further suggested he hand her the note and give her the "hush-sign" as soon as he gets home. "I'm positive", I said "Irene is quick enough to get the idea."

I added, "Don't forget to flush the note after it has been read."

"Absolutely", he agreed. "I've already told her not to mention Ivan to anyone, or to talk about him unless I start the conversation. She has never asked for an explanation"

Changing the direction of our conversation, DG went on to say that he had worked up two new pieces for the show that evening, and was planning to play them when Ivan and his guests arrive.

"You're getting good." I complimented him, "maybe you should consider doing this for a living."

We hung up. I briefed Mike and Leon, and finished my reports covering the past three days.

On the STU again, I called Bill, informing him that we would have to postpone our meeting for a few days, and tentative arrangements were made for Thursday.

This would give me plenty of time to have my car checked out. Talking to Dick, he said he could have it swept on Tuesday, tomorrow morning. At least my car would be clean. I would arrange for surveillance support for the Tuesday meeting with DG.

With the enemy's technical surveillance capability growing daily, our job was becoming more and more difficult. We were now confident the Russians were going all out. They had the capability to fabricate acceptable versions of our identification cards, credentials and probably badges as well; they were targeting American residences', telephones and automobiles; likely they were planning the use of wiretapping, listening devices, photographic eavesdropping, and more surveillance activity with the assistance of tracking devices. They were forcing us to operate on the defensive in order to counter them and the only choice we had to accomplish our mission was to improve our own detection and counter-surveillance methods.

I had received DG's signal, and had called him on the STU. Our meeting was a go for Tuesday afternoon. I confirmed the 'safety signal' we would use.

Frank passed the hotel room key to me on Tuesday morning, saying "Y'all have a good one, my friend. The fridge is stocked. "

By noon Tuesday, My car was deemed clean for the time being. After conducting my own surveillance detection for approximately 15 minutes I drove into the parking lot, and after observing DG's safety signal, picked him up. He was carrying a dark green, medium-size, Heavy-duty, metal *Samsonite* suitcase, which he placed in the trunk. Although it was already dark by 1930 hours, the parking lot was well lit. We drove out of the Chokchai lot, turning first south, then west, then south again toward the River Bend. The drive that would normally take 30-45 minutes in relatively heavy traffic would now incorporate even more provocative surveillance detection stops and moves, taking an additional 15 minutes. Dick's surveillance followed us for a substantial period and then broke off. That early termination of the surveillance was their safety signal, meaning no surveillance detected.

I felt it was safe to talk so we discussed the item he had brought. He described it as an Austrian-made Saxophone. Apparently, Ivan's family from Russia had brought it to Bangkok with them and Ivan had given it to him on Monday evening during an intermission. During the show, DG openly expressed his gratitude to Ivan.

DG then took the Saxophone home where he disassembled it to the extent that he could. He reassembled and played it. DG felt it was not equipped with any bugging or tracking device; but I told him that I would still have the tech guys look at it the next morning, and would return it to him – before lunchtime – to keep.

Convinced we were not being followed, we entered the River Bend parking area.

With each hotel unit having a separate, covered parking garage, and with Dick's guys having conducted not only a sweep of my car, but also of the hotel room, I felt quite secure.

Inside the room, I immediately turned on the new radio I had brought with me, and placed the hotel radio inside the closet. We carried on casual conversation while I checked out the room. It appeared that nothing had been touched since Frank left it a few hours earlier.

The training session lasted two hours, including my explanation of the theory that his car and possibly his home and home telephone were under surveillance.

I continued. "We now have reason to believe that any foreigner who is in regular contact with any of the diplomatic personnel of the Russian Embassy or members of the Russian Trade Mission is probably a target for wiretapping and eavesdropping activities. My primary concern is for you and your family, and we want to insure that you are cautious in what you do and say at all times. We have every reason to believe the Russians are escalating their activities along those lines." I then asked "By the way, how did Irene take the note?

"No problem at all," DG answered, "She's quick, and smart. She caught on right away. She took the note, read it, turned it over and wrote 'let's take a walk this evening'. Later we went shopping and talked. I tore the note to shreds and flushed it like you said."

"That's great. Hopefully we can find a way to neutralize their attempts in such a way as to cause them to discontinue these efforts. But we'll have to stay alert and try to keep a constant eye on their actions. You've been very helpful in your observations DG, keep up the good work."

"How are you guys planning on getting the word out to the American community?" he asked.

"We'll incorporate it all into our new SAEDA briefings." I said, "That will give everyone a pretty clear idea what's going on."

"By the way," I asked, "did Ivan introduce you to any of his friends?

"Yes, I made it a point to approach his table during the third intermission. He introduced me to all of them, including his mother."

I was prepared for that possibility, and took out an old picture of Ivan with his mother in San Francisco. DG positively identified her, saying only "She's much, much older now, of course. Her hair is completely white.

Two others were introduced as cousins, and another elderly lady was introduced as Ivan's Aunt Ivana, his mother's sister. DG opined that Ivan may have been Ivana's namesake.

When I took out the ten photos of the Russian technicians, DG immediately recognized the other two attendees from the King's Palace.

"These two, right here!" DG was excited as he pointed out two of the technicians. "These are the two that Ivan introduced as his cousins."

"Are you positive?" I asked.

"Absolutely positive," DG responded. These must be pretty new pictures. They look exactly the same!"

I tick-marked the two and refolded the photos back into my briefcase.

"You are great!" I told DG. "You have absolutely no idea how much you are helping."

We arranged the next meeting for one week. Fortunately, both DG and I had access to the STU and would communicate without fear of compromise in that mode. DG will continue to use a designated mark signaling any contact with Ivan. DG would use his car in the normal manner, going to and from work, for personal running around and for traveling to and from the Russian Embassy. Our system was pat. We talked for a few more minutes on how he could further brief his wife. What he could and could not say.

On the way back to the Chokchai building, I took my time, insuring that no special attention was given us. There seemed to be no surveillance of my car. Enroute, I noticed the Asian team following us part way. And again, there was no signal from them indicating surveillance. Sukhumvit road was extremely busy by 2045 hours, and I dropped DG off in front of the Chokchai, since we were stalled in traffic at that point. I watched as he entered the building to walk past the elevators and toward the parking lot on the opposite side. Anyone in the parking lot would assume that he had left work late, and was going home.

Traffic began to move again, so I moved along Sukhumvit for another block, then turned left, and right again, taking an alternate route to the Windsor hotel, for dinner before going back to my apartment.

I forced myself to partake of the dinner which was the Tuesday night special. Roast beef had been overcooked by reheating far too many times between 1700 and 2100 hours; the baked potato, which likewise had been reheated several times; and the green beans were dried and shriveled. After I passed the 'so-hungry-I'll-eat-anything' stage, I pushed the plate aside and ordered a cherry pie ala-mode for my desert. Unfortunately, the meal had already ruined my appetite, and after consuming about one half, I pushed the pie aside also, paid my bill and walked into the club. I sat and ordered a double J W Bop, and watched the Filipino Band play while one of their members did his best to gyrate through a set of Elvis impersonations. The show was equally as bad as the meal - The perfect combination. Even the double J W had not helped.

"Thang-ya, thang-ya vera mush." The singer called out to me as he made a twisting jerk, knelt on one knee and pointed toward the ceiling. I exited into the lobby.

Back in my apartment, I wasn't at all sleepy, so I took the hottest possible shower, poured another J W Bop, pulled a book from the shelf which I had not yet read. *The Man in the Mirror,* by Frederick Ayer, Jr. would be my partner for the night.

When I awoke at 0545, the book was opened to Page 13 chapter two. I had somehow forgotten chapter one. Fred went temporarily back on the shelf.

On Wednesday, I was in the office at 0645 and made a pot of coffee. Putting in the prescribed amount of coffee for the 25-cup maker, I poured in 15 cups of water. I added the requisite teaspoon of salt to soften the bitterness. That should be about right. The aroma of the percolating coffee filled the office, but attracted no-one. By 0745, even Frank had not yet arrived. I walked through the office, opening blinds and peering out over Sukhumvit road. Traffic was slower than usual for a Wednesday morning. Pouring a cup of black coffee, I decided to forego the usual cream and sugar, and returned to my desk to proof my reports before turning them in.

Voila! On my desk was a note from Frank, reminding me that Wednesday was the unit picnic/Holiday.

Of course it was – two weeks before Columbus Day. Why wouldn't I have known that?

Somehow, Frank had known I'd come to work. He also wrote that his draft proposal for the safe-site rental was in a folder in the top drawer of his safe, and was available for my perusal. We had long since exchanged safe combinations for security and CYA reasons.

I finished inhaling the first cup of coffee, poured a second, and opened Frank's safe extracting the safe-site document. I xeroxed a copy and began making notes. It was an excellent proposal, and should get plenty of attention with the current situation being as it is. Leon had promised his endorsement. I then returned both documents to his safe and poured a third and last cup of coffee. The first two cups had done their job, and the third provided the needed reinforcement. Now in this cup I had used the requisite amount of both cream and sugar.

I spent the next three hours final-proofing my reports and adding my remarks in an attempt to influence Mike and Leon's comments. I made an extra copy of the DG debrief for Dick's file on Russian eavesdropping activity.

After emptying the remaining coffee and rinsing the pot, I was through, and by noon with nothing else on my agenda, decided to lock up and visit the unit picnic.

Spies and more spies.

Adjacent to the MACTHAI administrative area – but still inside the compound - was a small park with several picnic tables a small baseball diamond and a tennis court. Walking along the chain-link fence to the compound entrance I could see the party was going strong and the Col W was giving his annual picnic speech, complimenting all for a job well done. As the Colonel finished his spiel, I found our office's table and sat at the end where Leon, Mike and Frank were discussing solutions to the world's problems. Frank handed me a beer and Tom Mc directed me toward the hamburgers and hotdogs burning on the grill. The four of us decided quickly that world politicians are all the same, and then lined up for our shot at some potato salad and meat product goodies.

Dave Atherton was mixing puns and telling jokes at the fourth floor's table as we passed by. At Dick's table, everybody was listening to Rick S talk of his exploits on the FTX committee at Fort Holabird. The two AA team members were watching through the chain-link fence, and I turned to see what had caught their attention.

Alongside the main road leading past the compound was a locked gate which is used for emergency vehicle entrance only, in case of fire, disaster or other emergency situations requiring immediate access. Standing in the gateway were two Thai Military Policemen, apparently challenging an individual who had been taking pictures from that virtually unobstructed vantage point. One of the MPs had the man's camera, and was removing the film canister. He then stripped the film from the canister and returned the empty camera to the individual, motioning for him to go elsewhere. The individual walked very quickly across the street to his Isuzu Bellet, and drove away.

The AA team went to Dick's table immediately to explain that the Isuzu was one of the surveillance vehicles from the Russian embassy.

Dick walked to the Colonel's table and talked for a few moments, then went from table to table passing the word. Our office began the exodus first, departing the compound one at a time until it seemed only Frank and I remained.

Frank spoke, saying "Well damn! I guess that kinda firms it all up." We walked to the Bar-b-que and filled our plates, then moved inside the snack-bar to finish our picnic.

"We could have used the Field House to begin with", I said with perfect 20/20 hindsight. "It's air conditioned too."

The AA team followed us inside, carrying their lunches. Frank called to them "Was that a positive ID?"

"For sure," one of them answered, "It was one of them."

Looking out over the party area, we watched as the picnic slowly came apart. The admin section, led by Chu-chu the Thai receptionist was putting away the last remnants of the picnic goodies and wiping down the tables.

Dave Atherton, was a young and single son of missionary parents. Diligently frugal and not one to waste, Dave had stuffed his briefcase with unclaimed, overcooked hamburgers and hot dogs fresh off the grill. He stared momentarily at the soda dispenser and, I decided, he chose not to put a coke in the briefcase. He then sat alone at the table for a few moments, feeding the last of the table scraps to the pigeons before stepping over the bench to stand up. Upon doing so, I realized that Dave had somehow clamped his tie in his briefcase, and by standing had pulled the briefcase off the table. It hung from his neck, swinging like a pendulum. Dave looked around quickly, sat back down and removed the tip of his tie. Of course by this time, everyone in the snack-bar had not only noticed, but had been discussing Dave's comedic actions.

Moments later, strolling into the snack-bar, Dave walked to our table, where he was greeted by Frank. "Well, hello there Mr. Atherton – what're you doin' wearin' a tie to this shindig anyway?"

Dave's face turned beet red. His revealing smile, told us he realized we had all seen his performance. He chose to ignore Frank's question and the indirect reference to the tie incident, sat and engaged us all in a half hour of full entertainment, filled with comedic animation and accented with a seemingly unending list of puns. It was worth waiting for, and was just the beginning of my lifelong relationship with David. Now, Dave lives just twenty minutes from my door.

The next day, Thursday would be busy. DG would be meeting with Ivan, and I would meet with Bill to finally formalize the recruitment and begin his training cycle.

CHAPTER 23.
CAPTAIN T. ON BOARD.

I picked up Bill Tanner at the Chokchai, and we drove out of the lot. Before turning south, we stopped to pick up some fried bananas from the dry-leprosy saleslady who peddled on the street. From there, we drove to the Pizza Inn, where I picked up the vegetarian pizza which Pechnoi had called to order for me. We then drove back to Sukhumvit and drove circuitously to the River Bend, parked and went inside. I placed my radio on the table, turned it on, and we began.

"Wow," Bill exclaimed, "we're getting pretty hush-hush already." He was referring to the circuitous route and twists and turns we'd taken to get to the hotel as well as the use of the radio to drown the conversation.

I spent about thirty minutes explaining the basics of Offensive Counterintelligence Operations, while Bill hung on every word. I then asked "You've not changed your mind yet have you?"

"Absolutely not!" he replied, "This is what I've been waiting for. I'm glad to see you guys are really involved, doing things like this."

I explained how 'dangle operations' work, adding that my intention was to have him make contact with Alex Topov. I gave a brief biographic outline of Alex, his activities and MO, and showed him a few photos. Recognizing Alex immediately, Bill said he had watched him play tennis at The Patana School and at the Bangkok Sportsman's Club.

"I was impressed." He said, "He's very good. I don't have to beat him, do I?"

"That's not necessary yet," I said, then joked "Maybe eventually you can knock his socks off."

I also explained that we had not formally coordinated with Col Wilson to approach one of his people, but would be doing so in a couple of days. Bill already understood clearly that he was not to spill our confidentiality.

Bill was excited to get started, and after going over the use of the STU and explaining our meeting arrangements, we ate the pizza and drank two of Frank's *Amarits*.

I spent another full 30 minutes explaining some of the known facts regarding the level of Russian surveillance activities to Bill, adding that a formal classified briefing would be presented at the next SAEDA brief as a hypothetical situation. I assured him there was nothing hypothetical about the situation here in Bangkok. He was awed, but not surprised.

Before departing the hotel room, we shook hands in agreement, and I allowed him to look over the security agreement which I had already filled out. Although he was willing to sign it then and there, I told him that we would formalize the written agreement once Col Wilson gives his blessings.

The trip from the meeting was uneventful, and by the time we returned to the Chokchai building the rush hour was in progress. I was able to drop Bill off in the same manner as I had with DG following that last meeting. He melted into the pedestrian crowd, heading for the front entrance of the building.

DG would be meeting with Ivan, and I wondered how his meeting was going.

An unexpected delay.

On Friday, when I arrived at the office, I passed by and saw DG's signal. There was no sign of urgency in the signal, and I was confident all had gone smoothly.

Inside my office, I keyed the STU and gave him a quick call. His meeting had lasted about one hour, and all had gone well. DG was anxious to tell me that this morning his office distribution included a message for his commander that the latest joint exercise proposals had been approved and would be implemented with very few changes. The exercise would begin on 17 January and run through 28 Feb 1975. The classification was SECRET.

I asked him when the article would be released to the press. DG responded that it was not likely to happen before mid November. He explained that the US and allied units involved would need time to arrange troop deployments in January, and there were the Holidays to consider.

His next meeting with Ivan was scheduled in 6 days; however, during yesterday's meeting Ivan had given DG an emergency contact number for setting up meetings, and had arranged a place for them to make initial contact, should that signal be employed.

I told him I'd get back with instructions for passing information to Ivan, and he could test the new contact number. We hung up and I returned to my cubicle to find a note indicating that the commander wanted to see me in his office that morning at 1100 hours.

Mike was already in our office, and we discussed the status of the Ivan project. When Leon arrived the three of us drafted up a proposal for DG to pass the Information to Ivan in two weeks at the scheduled meeting. I suggested we allow a few days before testing the contact system Ivan had arranged.

At 1100, Mike accompanied me to the commander's office, and it turned out that the Colonel had received a notice from the Headquarters Admin section regarding my request to marry Betty. It seems that somewhere along the line, they had lost her Statement of Personal History, and there could be some delay in completing her background investigation.

To me, a loss seemed highly improbable, as I personally knew that multiple copies of her SPH are included with lead sheets accompanying every portion of the BI. It seemed more likely that someone was intentionally trying to delay the process. However, since I had made four additional, original copies of the SPH, I told Col W that I would simply forward another set to HQ. It was not worth making an issue.

I thanked Col W for the heads up, and before leaving his office, we gave the draft request to Parky. The proposal was messaged to Headquarters that afternoon. We could expect a response within a day or two – or not.

I talked with DG over the STU again. I was able to finalize a report regarding the telephonic contacts.

Betty's SPH was mailed that afternoon.

On Monday, our Colonel called to let us know he'd been in touch with Col Wilson, and he had stated we could call his secretary any time this week for an appointment. After talking with Leon, I called and arranged to meet Wilson on Wednesday Morning.

Leon and I planned the meeting with Colonel Wilson 0930 hours; to be followed by lunch at the Patana School - Vic's #3 restaurant. His secretary had told us that Col Wilson has no appointments before 0830 because he runs the five miles from his home to work, and needs an hour to shower and look over his correspondence and suspense files every morning. We spent Tuesday afternoon war-gaming our approach.

Tuesday night I was sleeping soundly when my friend, the clown visited me again.

I had heard a 'crunch'. The next sound was that of someone picking the lock to my apartment, and in ten seconds my clown entered. Apparently unaware of my presence, he walked directly to my bar, where he poured himself a drink of my best Wild Turkey *bourbon – straight, without pebbles. He sat on the barstool grinning at himself in the mirror behind the bar.*

I spoke "Hey there, clown."

He spun around grinning, "Yup," he responded, sounding much like Mickey's dog-friend Goofy. Was this the first time I'd heard him speak?

"You're wasting my bourbon!" I complained. "You can't drink, you're just a dream!"

"Nope, not wastin'," Goofy's voice replied. "Just drinkin'."

He began to fade. "No!" I yelled. "I have to talk to you."

He gulped the last two ounces of the drink as though he had to finish the glass before disappearing completely. Laughing again, he said "bye-bye."

I must have dreamed of my clown at least a thousand times, and this was the first time he'd spoken. Now I was waking up. A bright, silent flash of light filled the living room and lit up the bedroom.

Half asleep, I blinked my eyes, slowly allowing my surroundings to come into focus; and then woke suddenly, sitting up in bed. Had I imagined someone coming through the door? Had someone actually manipulated my lock and come inside? Blinking my eyes, I could still see the bright light image inside my eyelids. I was fumbling for the lamp switch while my eyes were struggling to come into focus in the darkness. I knocked something off the stand. Finally I found the lamp cord, and was feeling for the inline switch. The clock radio displayed 0414 hours.

"Ah, there it is." I turned on the night light. Now, spots still lingered, floating in front of my eyes. I sat still momentarily, then slowly got out of bed and moved to the floor-to-ceiling bookshelf which serves as a divider between the bedroom and living room. Quietly removing the two books that covered my view window into the bar area, I was able to see that there was absolutely no movement. The apartment was silent. I could observe the entire living room from this location. I stood motionless, controlling my breathing for a full minute, searching back and forth. No movement.

I replaced the two books and moved quietly into the living room, staying close to the wall that would lead me past the main entrance and into the kitchen and nook area. I stopped at the kitchen entrance and listened intently. No sound. Peering inside, I searched counterclockwise – sink, cabinet, table, and the door which would open into the hallway.

The glow of light under the hallway door revealed a shadow moving quietly and quickly away.

'I've had had a visitor.' I whispered to myself.

Moving to the door I opened it quickly, looking out just in time to see someone – a male – darting around the corner at the end of the hall, toward the stairwell. I began to run after him, and then realized I had not dressed. I was wearing only my Jockey shorts. In my virtual Sunday suit, I opened the hallway closet. That lock had been forced, and I realized that the large propane tank which fed the hot water pipes in the bath was gone. The flexible line that led through the wall had been cut.

So I'd heard the lock being forced and probably the valves being closed. Quick, convenient and almost…silent.

Back inside, with all the lights now on, I looked around the kitchen, further discovering that someone had also taken the propane tank from beneath the sink. The thief, or thieves, had actually come inside, removed that tank first, and then moved back to the hallway closet to take the large tank.

Now, had my clown actually spoken to me? Or had someone walked into the bedroom to sadistically let me know they'd been there. "Bye-bye", I imagined the voice again. The hair on the back of my neck was standing.

The flash of light! "What the hell was that?" I was asking myself. Faded images of the flash still lingered.

I looked at the clock/radio. It was now 0425. Only eleven minutes had passed. I picked up my phone and dialed the front desk. I was not expecting an answer, since the operator on duty usually locks the front door at around 0200 hours, and then sleeps behind the counter. The phone rang incessantly.

The words "Inside job" immediately came to mind.

0430 hours – not a good time to go back to sleep; but on the other hand, it's too early to stay awake. I pulled Fred Ayer Jr. from the shelf again, to reread the first chapter. The one I'd forgotten.

Fifteen minutes of reading and another hour of sleep later, I awoke with a jerk. Fred Ayer was again displaying page 13, 'Chapter Two', which began with a background description of the character Karl Friedrich von Tetlow. Had this whole episode been a dream? Back on the shelf again, Fred.

The shower lasted only about two and a half minutes, as the unheated water became increasingly cold and the realization of the dream became increasingly clear. After the quickest shower of my life, I masochistically tormented myself by shaving with equally cold water. I pulled my small electric cup coil from the cabinet and dropped it in a cup of water. When I plugged it in, I half expected it wouldn't work on the 220 volt electricity in Bangkok. It worked great – taking only a few seconds to boil. As soon as the steam began to emit from the cup, I unplugged it and made an unpleasant, insalubrious cup of instant coffee.

"Now, let's see – is it one or two teaspoons of instant coffee – I looked at the jar, discovering the label was in the Thai Language. I settled for one Tablespoon. I added sugar and milk, covered it and let it steep while I dressed in a suit for my visit to Col Wilson's office. The Thai-tailored, light beige hemp suit somehow reminded me of the first suit I'd ever owned – the hemp-cloth seersucker suit from Sears Roebuck, my mother had bought for me when we still lived in Michigan.

I drank a half cup of the coffee before I realized it should have been 'one teaspoon'.

Before going to work, I stopped by the complex office, where I got in line to voice my complaint. Sinh, the office manager, and son of the owner, took my complaint. He asked me how full the tanks were, and I gave him the receipts for payment which were one week old.

"My father," he said, "will take care of it, and you will have new tanks by this afternoon when you return, too."

We discussed locks for the hallway tanks, and decided to lock the doors with an extra lock to help prevent future thefts. The locks would only be a delay factor, and not necessarily a deterrent.

I chose to let Sinh and his father handle the thefts, and before leaving, gave him the precise time of the theft at my apartment for their report to the Police.

On the way to work, I saw Leon walking along the street, so I pulled over.

"Hi Sailor, going my way?" I asked jokingly. Leon got into my car, but he wasn't laughing.

"I was robbed last night!" he stated immediately. He stared at me as though it was my fault.

He went on "They stole my propane tanks and my car battery, right there in the carport. My dog slept!" he complained.

After relating my story to Leon, he felt much better. "You're a friend of old man Maidee, aren't you?" he asked.

"Yes, he and I are friends. He owns both my apartment complex and Maidee Court where you live," I told him, "but his name is Pranat – not Maidee".

"It doesn't matter what his name is," Leon retorted, "could you just give him a call, and tell him what happened at my house."

"Sure Leon," I volunteered. "I'll call him this morning."

Leon did not say another word until we got to the office. Once inside, I called Sinh and told him of Leon's predicament. He responded immediately saying it would be taken care of "right away, too". He asked for the spelling of Leon's name for his police report.

Apparently the gas thieves were quite active at many of the complexes and homes throughout Bangkok, as the information was already on the English news.

When Frank arrived, he had his own story to tell of the gas thieves.

Frank's dog had quietly awakened him at 0330 hours, nudging him awake, and moving toward the patio. Frank had picked up his baseball bat on the way out, and encountered a thief noisily attempting to cut the stainless chain he had anchored around his tank and through an eye-bolt buried in the cement carport floor.

Completely nude, Frank had screamed "AAaaiieeee!" at the top of his lungs as he ran full-speed toward the would-be thief, holding the bat over his head with both hands.

According to Frank, "That skinny little bastard didn't know up from down, and ran into my back yard and the stone wall fence instead of out the gate and into the alley."

Frank laughed as he went on, saying "Well, the top of my wall has the shards of a thousand Heineken beer bottles embedded in the cement, and that little bastard jumped up, cut himself up bad, and came screamin' back down."

"I picked him up and threw him toward the gate. You know that little bastard didn't even try the gate. I guess seein' me nekked was just too much fer him."

I couldn't have agreed more. "A lot of blood?" I asked, still trying to delete the vision from my mind.

"Oh, Hell yes." Frank went on, "Ah just let him get away. It was funny just watchin' him climb over the wrought-iron gate, and make it to the three-wheeler truck his podnah was drivin'. Ah got the license number and called the MPs. They came over with a Thai cop and took my statement. Ah just hope they let me know the case disposition. Aughta be interestin'."

Leon and I departed the office at 0900 hours, and drove directly to MACTHAI to meet with Colonel Wilson. Enroute, we discussed the possibility that Col Wilson had also been robbed of gas the night before, and how that could have a direct bearing on his decision as to whether or not he would cooperate and allow us to use Bill for our operation. It was too late to postpone our appointment now, so we decided to wing it.

We waited only 3 minutes for the call into Colonel Wilson's office, and in that period, his secretary prepared coffee (real coffee that is), tea and cinnamon rolls.

I entered first with Leon on my tail – and in military fashion - saluted. Col Wilson returned my salute, saying "Have a seat boys." He was grinning, "What's this I hear about all you guys getting robbed last night?" he asked half-laughing.

Leon immediately went into his rant, retelling and embellishing the story as he went along.

"How about you, sir," I asked. "Did you get hit?"

"No," the Colonel answered. "I learned my lesson the first week I was here." I got hit, and then my old hand-ball buddy 'Frank' told me to wrap my gas tank with stainless chain and lock it with an S & T combination padlock. The chain runs through an eye bolt anchored in the garage floor. The noise a thief would have to make just to get through that chain would wake the devil. I haven't been hit since."

I knew that!.

Leon and I stared blankly at each other. I realized it was very likely his old handball buddy 'Frank' was probably OUR Frank. We'd had an 'in' with the Colonel all along.

"So what's up Leon? You guys want to use another one of my guys? Can't do the job yourself eh?"

Leon ignored the comment. I simply said "Yes-sir. We don't have a good enough tennis player to get to the Russian we want."

The Colonel's eyes lit up. "You're not talking about Bill Tanner are you?" He was no longer smiling.

I continued. "You see, Sir, Captain Tanner is the only person who's qualified to help us with this operation. He has the proper security clearances, plays pro-level tennis, he's got the smarts to work and make decisions on his own…"

"I know, I know," the Colonel interrupted. "He's one of the best officers I've ever had; comes from a line of good officers - just like DG is one of the best NCOs I ever had. Why is it you guys always want the best…" He looked embarrassed. "That's a dumb question, isn't it?" he asked, now grinning.

Neither of us had the urge to respond positively to the expletive; one would find it difficult to argue that particular point.

"Well, Hell!" the Colonel went on, "I'm getting short anyway. I'm leaving right after the exercise. But I guess you guys already know that."

We both nodded.

"Go ahead," the Colonel acquiesced. "Take my best man. Your mission is just as important as mine – maybe more."

He seemed dejected at the thought of leaving, and Leon detected it too. We joked with him for awhile and enjoyed the cinnamon rolls and Ban-me-thuot coffee. The Colonel smiled when I said "We'll miss you Sir, and we'll miss your cooperative attitude. It's difficult nowadays to come across a Commander who understands the overall mission – and isn't just concerned with his own career."

Colonel Wilson stood and removed the body bag from his wall. "You see this? You'd understand Sarge,". He was addressing me. Moving his pen set and writing pad aside, he displayed the body bag on his desk, exposing his name, rank and serial number. Slowly caressing the body bag as though it was made from the finest of linen, Colonel Wilson looked up at us. His eyes were filled with genuine tears.

His voice was breaking. "I plan to be buried in this when the time comes. The greatest sacrifice a man can ever make is to give his life for his country – bar none." He was serious. His voice still shaking as he hung the body bag on the brass hooks; he stared at it for a moment, saluted it and said "Colonel Wilson Reporting for Duty, SIR!" He sat back down.

Clearing his voice, he continued, "Now, gentlemen, let me see that security statement. Tell me if you can, exactly what will Bill Tanner be up to after I'm gone from here?"

As he signed the prepared 'permission' documents, I explained that we would be asking Captain Tanner for one to two days a week at most – to play tennis with the suspected Russian KGB agent and hopefully, under controlled conditions he will gradually establish a personal relationship with the Russian, hoping the Russian will take the next step and begin asking small favors of him. We hoped that Bill would eventually be able to verify our theory that Alex Topov was in fact a KGB agent, that Alex would eventually co-opt Bill to provide data to him, and that Captain Tanner would then be able to keep us informed of Russian interests in US military operations and contingency plans. I did not tell him that we had already gained Bill's cooperation. I'd said enough. The Colonel was being cooperative, and that was all I could ask of him. A third request for another body probably would not meet with the same resigned acceptance.

As we shook hands, Colonel Wilson asked, "So how did our musician work out – I read the Thai papers, you know."

"He was an excellent choice." I answered. "And he's moving right along."

The Colonel smiled.

We departed the Colonels office and drove to the Vic's #3 for lunch. On this occasion, I was reluctant to choose the catfish fillet 'special of the day', but on Leon's recommendation did so.

Again, lunch was unbelievable. The waiter arrived and happily took our order, saying the meal would be served momentarily. A chilled consommé was served in a double crystal bowl, over a crushed ice bottom. The whipped asparagus cream with just a hint of chives and rosemary touched my taste buds and then melted.

The appetizers consisted of a tempura batter fried, stuffed mushroom delicacy, the likes of which I'd never before partaken. The sweet rice and lightly-spiced stuffing was absolutely delectable.

The main meal was beautiful and equally as tasteful.

The catfish fillets had been properly peeled and marinated. Seasoned with salt, black pepper and hot pepper sauce, they were placed in the fridge for about an hour.

Separately, a sauce combining strawberry preserves with a drop of vinegar, soy sauce, a seafood cocktail sauce, touch of powdered garlic and just a dab of wasabi paste was stirred while simmering over low heat.

A breading of cornmeal and flour was also prepared. When the catfish was removed from the fridge, the marinade was not poured but rather patted well onto slightly damp filets'. It was then dredged in the cornmeal mixture, with a generous but delicate coating on all sides.

When chopsticks create bubbles in the olive oil in an iron skillet over medium-high heat, the catfish is gently placed inside and sautéed until it turns evenly golden brown. Drained once more on paper towels, the catfish was then wrapped in pita to maintain heat, and served with a side of about 1/3rd cup of the strawberry sauce. The garnish consisted of more sliced strawberries sprinkled lightly with a little ground cilantro.

A small saucer of plum sauce was served aside.

Leon unwrapped his filets as though it was a religious formality. Using his fork, he folded the pita and put it aside. He later dipped the pita in the onion-based plum sauce, and washed it down with a sip of his favorite, semi-sweet, slightly chilled *Rose'*.

And desert was yet to come. We opted for the famous Vic's chocolate mousse and a small titanium-plated cup of Cuban coffee.

Leon hardly spoke a word during the meal. Obviously, he'd partaken of this selection before. He spoke in Greek to the waiter, arranging to pay for the meal. It was the language I had not previously recognized. We departed at 1330 hours, and drove back to the office.

As we walked into the office, both of us saw DG's crayon mark. This one was an indication that he'd had telephonic contact with Ivan. That would probably be good news.

Inside the office, I checked my messages, and Mike confirmed that permission for DG to pass the information regarding the joint exercise had arrived. It would be released to the press in about two months. I keyed the STU and called DG. He had indeed received a message from Ivan confirming their meeting the next day. They could meet in Ivan's office between 1530 and 1600.

DG would call him back and inform him that he had "some good news", meaning that he had information to pass. DG was not to tell him of the press release date. We were well ahead of schedule.

After making the call to Ivan, DG called me back with the gist of their conversation. "Ivan was very happy," DG said.

"Great job!" I complimented him.

I compiled a report of the meeting with Col Wilson, including the proposal to formally recruit Bill Tanner; and drafted another report covering the phone calls to and from DG, including the list of information DG would pass to Ivan. I would have a few days break before meeting with Bill and beginning the training phase of the Alex operation.

Frank and I went over the final request to obtain a permanent safe-site, before he passed it to Mike and Leon for their comments. I had already attached Dick's comments regarding regular surveillance and tech sweeps of the selected site.

Administrivia was complete. At 1530 I took advantage of being through for the day, and went home. On arrival at the complex, I walked through the restaurant, into the lobby area and began to ascend the stairs.

Suddenly, I was confronted and challenged by the entire new complex staff from the lobby. They were asking my name and demanding identification. For a moment, I thought my old friend Mr. Pranat had sold the complex. There was not a recognizable face in the crowd. Sinh then entered the lobby and shooed them away, speaking Chinese he told them I was OK, and to always remember my face. Sinh explained that following the gas theft incident most of the staff had been replaced. I realize that the Chinese way of dealing with incompetence is to eliminate the problem. He also informed me that his father had hired two new "undercover agents," to roam the complex and watch for thieves. They would occupy the studio apartment adjacent to my suite.

He said that as though somehow it would make me feel better.

"How about Mr. Leon's problem?" I enquired.

"That's no problem too," Sinh responded. "He got a new battery too!" he was proud to announce. "Aannd", Sinh concluded, "Since his lock was broken too, Papa gave him a new lock for his front gate too."

Everything was "too". "He'll be happy too" I told him.

Back in my room, I called the post office and arranged a long distance call to Betty for 1730 hours. I then caught a cab to Chinatown. With a little more than an hour to kill, I shopped in the Chinatown area, picking up a few souvenirs and a poster to hang in the nook. At 1730 hours, I was dialing the number in Taiwan, and in moments, Papa answered the phone. He immediately and anxiously told me that Chiang Kai-Shek was now hospitalized. The prognoses were not good. He had suffered from kidney failure. Many people, he said were worried about the probability that the mainland would attack Taiwan if Chiang Kai-Shek dies. Neither of us actually believed the mainland would attack Taiwan; but then I had never thought CKS would ever die. He was the Generalissimo!

I could hear Betty's voice in the background, and Papa surrendered the telephone to her. We spent a few minutes telling each other how much we cared for each other and missed being together, and she asked again if CKS were to pass on, can we still get married on schedule. "There will be no celebrations of any kind until 30 days after CKS passes. Can you stay that long, Don?"

"Of course," I said. "That's been the plan all along."

"That's wonderful!" she responded. She had been studying the Chinese horoscope calendar book, and had settled on April 25 for our actual wedding day. Keeping with Chinese tradition, Betty was also studying the arts of one-stroke painting and cooking, in preparation for marriage.

I did not tell her of the loss of her paperwork, rather that I would be there as soon as needed. Papa had already drafted the invitations, and was expecting about 12 to 14 tables of guests at the first reception. He could now make tentative reservations at the Guo-ting restaurant on Nan King East Road in Taipei.

We talked for another 30 minutes before hanging up. Somehow, just talking to her seemed to build my spirits. I still had 5 more months to process the rest of the paperwork, complete the BI and take five weeks leave in TW. The first thought on my mind was who would handle my projects while I was gone. Undoubtedly, Frank was the first candidate on my list.

The first phases of the Ivan project are now complete. 1) DG had been selected and recruited, 2) trained, 3) dispatched, and had been successful in establishing a relationship with our target KGB personality). Phase IV was the tasking by Ivan. It had begun with seemingly innocuous requests for telephone books and US government organizational charts – then graduated to information regarding the upcoming joint field exercise. By this time, we were acutely aware of Ivan's MO. He would use a contrived personal relationship and friendship to manipulate DG. The sheet music, the horns; even the *Ohranj* vodka were all part of his plan to attain DG's 'unwitting' cooperation.

If all goes well, this operation will continue long enough to help us understand the intricacies of the Russian MO involved in spying on US Forces in Bangkok. If all goes perfect, we will be able to turn the tables, and eventually recruit Ivan as a double agent.

Enter - Murphy.

Russian doctrine dictates that their espionage operations be treated as long-range. However, we have come to know better. Murphy's Law almost always rules. Once we have realized the type of information Ivan is after, who he is targeting, and his MO is known, then somewhere along the line, Murphy takes control. Almost without fail, in the normal progression of circumstances: 1) Ivan will be transferred, or 2) DG will be transferred, and Ivan would be forced to arrange an introduction to a new agent handler convenient to DG's new duty station, or 3) Upon the inevitable reassignment of either of them, Ivan and DG will arrange to maintain contact. Almost without exception, under Murphy's Law, operations are not allowed to continue at their point of origin.

At any rate, for USI to maintain good control, the ideal arrangement would be for Ivan to be reassigned to another location where US Forces are stationed, concurrent with reassignment of DG nearby. Their relationship would continue, and eventually Ivan's activities would provide irrefutable evidence that he has been spying – with no plausible deniability. When the proper motivation is determined, he will be approached by the appropriate "other agency". With a little coercion, by revealing evidence such as photographs, edited surveillance reports, and excerpts from Contact Reports describing his clandestine activities; and then applying the appropriate ideological pressure, Ivan could be recruited - and effectively doubled as an agent working for the US. A little duress goes a long way.

It is true. We do not like to use the word 'assassination' – but would rather employ an acceptable form of 'termination' to finalize the accomplishment of our mission. Likewise, the word "blackmail" is not within our vocabulary, and we would much rather use the term "acceptable level of persuasion" when and if such an occasion should arise. In the end, and contrary to popular belief, killing of the enemy is not always the preferred action. If he is of value, he may be "redirected". Only as a last resort is he "terminated with prejudice". Again, these are the ideal follow-on, but obviously there are millions of scenarios to the contrary.

Wednesday evening was very quiet on the street. Back at my apartment however, the sounds associated with a poolside party, the splashing of water and the consumption of too much Amarit were disturbing my solitude. The off-key singing of "*Happy Birthday*" rang out as the lasses from the bar next door entertained their guests. I tried to listen to my own music, and decided that I was better off trying to tolerate the sounds emitting from poolside than to participate in a battle of the boom boxes. Moreover, my small stereo unit was designed for private enjoyment and not competition.

For a full half hour, I put up with the music, but when the live Filipino band arrived, I turned off the patio speakers, exited back inside my apartment. I closed the windows and drapes, and turned my air conditioning fan on high. The poolside sounds were almost muted. Now it is my own time and place. I selected a 60-minute cassette of Leon Redbone, and set the volume just high enough to drown the faint remaining sounds from outside. I shall enjoy the sounds of the 1940s, while absorbing a refreshing sip of J W BOP. And perhaps a second.

By around 2030, the pool sounds had faded, Redbone had sung his final tune (*Marie*), and following a fourth "sip" I decided to retire early for the evening.

The hot shower must have temporarily washed the remnants of my clown from my dream-controlling memory lobes, for I slept without phantasm through the night, waking at 0445 hours. My mouth was dry, my stomach churned with hunger, I arose and made the mistake of looking in the mirror. Another hot shower was in order.

On the way to the office, stomach still churning, I parked illegally in front of the *Bakery Shoppe* and purchased a tray of assorted Danish for the office. Landlord Pranat was inside sitting at a small table, gnawing on a cinnamon roll, sipping tea and carrying on a Chinese language conversation with two young men. From the gist of the conversation, I assumed they were our two new "undercover agents" Sinh had referred to the previous day - my new next door neighbors.

"I will say just one more time," the old man was clearly explaining, "there will be no guns on these premises." They seemed to understand.

On arrival at the office I kept telling myself that this was DG's day to pass the coveted information to Ivan. I was hoping that Ivan had not already picked up the information over the grapevine. At this stage of the game, it is not nice to provide him with information which he already has.

I put out two trays of pastry – one in our office, and one in the community space to share with Dick's shop.

I could wait no longer. I keyed the STU and called DG. He was more than prepared. He had placed the approved information in a plastic, translucent envelope, covered on both sides with sheet music. He would carry it into the office for Ivan. With Ivan knowing DG was going to be there at 1530, I was one hundred percent convinced he would meet DG in the lobby area and escort him inside. The 'see-through' envelope would provide for flash material, keeping with DG's cover as a musician meeting with the Cultural Attaché. According to DG's description, the material consisted of a three-page message, outlining the acceptance of the joint proposal for the conduct of allied forces combat field training exercise. The message listed the countries of South Korea, Japan, Taiwan, The Philippines, Thailand and the US as participants, and established the specified period of 17 Jan through 28 February. The official-looking message seemed authentic and complete, but had been edited to omit certain specifics which would obviously have raised the classification. Although much less sensitive, the classification stamped on the document was "SECRET". DG would keep a copy for me.

DG was prepared to answer any question Ivan may ask. Should Ivan ask for detailed statistical information beyond that which was provided in the 'message', DG had been instructed to respond by saying:

"I'm sorry, Ivan, I just don't have access to that type information." And then tease him a little with "At least not yet." He should also display some reluctance to remove such information from the office, saying it was against regulations.

I typed up the first half of my report, covering the last two telephone calls.

Parky called me to his office later in the morning, to inform me that Mr. Gary Sandell from Taiwan was being transferred to Thailand, and was scheduled to arrive on 1 December. Could I be his sponsor?

"Of course, it would be my pleasure," I volunteered.

Parky asked a few questions regarding Gary's background, and informed me that Gary had been tentatively selected for assignment as the US Embassy liaison for our Detachment. I recommended him highly for the job. Gary was a professional in every way. I was convinced he would do a good job.

I did not tell Parky that I had been corresponding with Gary, who had already informed me that he was planning to quit working for the Defense Department. He had become interested in Washington State politics, and would be moving in that direction as soon as he could fulfill his current obligation. He was in the process of purchasing a 160 acre parcel of land in Western Washington and was planning on settling there.

He had been promoted to GS-12, and would not accept another promotion which would increase his current commitment.

Ivan, the character.

It was 1400 hours when Ivan sat back down at his desk. This had not been his best day. The staff had waited a full 20 minutes in the conference room for Ambassador Yuri Antakolsky to arrive. When he finally walked in, he was not alone. He was accompanied by the Security Chief, Vladimir Sokolov, and a new female employee who was carrying a black, eel-skin attaché case. From her appearance Ivan initially assumed her to be an administrator from headquarters. They sat around the conference table, with the Ambassador seated at one end. Sokolov was to his right, and the unknown woman sat at his left.

With routine administrative matters out of the way, the Wednesday morning staff meeting with the Ambassador had been aimed primarily at the 'US Intelligence' Country Team. The Ambassador was apparently showing off.

"You Intelligence guys," The Ambassador complained, "don't show me much. You run around all over Bangkok; some of you spent the entire summer down south at the beaches. You've been visiting night clubs, strip joints, sneaking into US clubs, spending our money like it was water. What do you have to account for it? You, Alex," pointing his finger at Alex Topov, "all you do every day is play tennis and eat. Have you any idea the cost of maintaining our membership at the Bangkok Sportsman's Club? By now, you must have met a dozen promising leads among the Americans who go to the Club or to Patana School. Have none of them been worth your efforts?"

"Not really," Alex complained, "They either have no access to information or no long-range potential at all!" He went on "It was your idea Yuri that all our leads show promise for long-range operations; was it not? Besides, Americans don't play tennis for shit!"

The Ambassador hated being addressed as "Yuri", but chose not to make an issue with Alex. Instead, he would simply turn the screw a little deeper.

He acknowledged Alex's comments with a grunt, saying "Is tennis the only thing you understand, Topov? Have you no other talents – maybe something not quite so expensive?"

Not waiting for an answer, he then turned his attention to Ivan. "What about that American Soldier friend of yours? Can he do anything other than play your horn?" He laughed at his own suggestive joke.

The room burst into laughter at the remark, and Ivan felt himself getting uncomfortably hot.

Angry, Ivan yelled back at the Ambassador. "He can, and he does!"

That comment brought more laughter from the group. Alex nudged Ivan. Winking he said "Are you going to share?"

Even more laughter erupted.

"Actually," Ivan proudly retorted, "He is providing me with the information we've been trying to get regarding the American joint training exercise early next year." He hesitated, "I'm meeting him here today. There will be even more very soon."

Ivan wanted to sing "na-na-na-na nyah-nyah" but wasn't sure the Ambassador would appreciate the attempt to further humorize his staff meeting. He also wanted to point out that he had paid for the "horns" from his own personal account, and then thought it better not to put more pressure on his friend Alex.

The Ambassador then turned his attention to the new staff-member, still patiently sitting on his left.

Enter: Alexandra Dombrovsky.

"Gentlemen, you've probably been wondering about this young lady on my left..." All eyes met with the wife of the new Consular Representative Peter Dombrovsky. "Alexandra, these gentlemen are the Bangkok members of our Intelligence Bureau, American Intelligence country team – Gentlemen, please meet Mrs. Alexandra Dombrovsky. She is assigned to us from Gorky Street where she has acted as a courier and as a funds custodian. Her husband transferred to Bangkok last month. She now joins him at our location where she will eventually be employed as an agent handler. She was trained in Moscow, and has had some experience. Please cooperate with her. For the next two months, she will be seated at our front desk. She may occasionally act as a receptionist, but for the time being, her main duties are to become familiar with the conduct of our collection activities. We are hoping to incorporate her into various phases of our ongoing operations."

The team members looked at each other blankly for a moment. Finally, Ivan stood and greeted the new member "How do you do? I am Romanyev. Please call me 'Ivan'."

"Oooh, so diss iss you." She smiled, causing the hair on the back of

Ivan's neck to stand at attention. *"Her English teacher must have been from East Germany!"* He thought.

The introduction was over. The pep talk was over. The Ambassador and Sokolov began their exit, as one by one the rest of the team approached Alexandra, introducing themselves and trying their best to engage her in small talk.

Her reputation had preceded her assignment. Alexandra AKA Alexandra Voronin, had married Peter Dombrovsky six years earlier during the last two years of his assignment to Gdansk. Being of Polish ancestry, and speaking the language fluently, Peter had done well in that assignment, and there remains good rumor that he will return to Poland after a few years, to serve in Warsaw as the Ambassador. The same unsubstantiated rumors place credit for his rapid rise in the Diplomatic Corps with the 'special qualifications' and persuasive techniques of his loving Alexandra Voronin. Talk of her loose moral character was rampant in the confines of the embassy before Dombrovsky signed in. She had followed him to Bangkok within the month.

Initially, Ivan had chosen not to pay attention to the gossip. But now, seeing her in person, the rumors seemed more believable. She wore entirely too much makeup, perhaps in an attempt to cover her age; and too few articles of clothing. Her appearance resembled that of an American hooker. The part in her bleached blond hair revealed a good half-inch of dark roots. Close up, she appeared to be at least 45 years old, and that would be a full ten years older than Dombrovsky himself. All this made it difficult for Ivan to visualize her as an Ambassadress in any situation. He decided that she would not be involved in any of his operations – unless he is ordered otherwise. Not to worry though, Ivan had overheard her speaking English at the front desk. Her accent was heavy and her grammar and pronunciation were atrocious. He thought *"She would have to provide some service other than that of an agent handler."*

Her name and a 15-year old photo had made the Thai press within days after her arrival, as she had been involved in two automobile accidents almost immediately. The Thai government, in accordance with accepted reciprocal protocol practice had issued her a gratis driver's license based on her previous driving experience. This is considered normal for Embassy employees and the family members of diplomats. It is most difficult however to drive on the left hand side when you've not been exposed to that method before. Both of her accidents had occurred when exiting to the left from the inside lane of a traffic circle – the same traffic circle, the same turn, and just two days apart.

Ivan politely excused himself and walked back into his own office. *"Why,"* he asked himself *"do so many Russian women refuse to shave their legs?"* he shuddered. He also decided *"She no longer even slightly resembles the photograph used in the newspapers"*.

Now, seated at his desk, he groaned. His surroundings were bleak to say the least. All the gray metal furniture was of Thai manufacture, and obviously contracted to the lowest bidder. His double-pedestal desk was covered with a matching gray, vinyl top, which had already been stained with coffee and red wine, and had been burned by fallen cigarette butts from his predecessor's ashtray. From where he sat, to the right, two gray filing cabinets stood side-by-side in the corner, next to the single, barred window. Opened, 3-combination padlocks hung from brackets which had been welded to the two safes for security purposes. The door to his office opened inward at the center of the east wall, and to the left of the door was another filing cabinet. All this was surrounded by four light-gray, painted cement walls. No personal photographs, no travel posters, or decorations of any kind had ever been hung. Nothing could tie this office to Ivan Romanyev. Sunlight pouring through the single window was not ample for room lighting, requiring the four overhead fluorescent fixtures to be switched on constantly.

As he rotated in his desk chair, the squeaking was loud enough to activate the voice-motion activated camera mounted directly overhead.

On his left was a five shelf book cabinet, filled with his favorite books. The top shelf, dedicated mostly to espionage, was stacked with English-language books including a burgundy-colored Webster's New World Dictionary, 1965 edition; a well-read copy of *The Penkovsky Papers* by Penkovsky himself, and prefaced with remarks by Frank Gibney. Ivan enjoyed reading Gibney. And next to the Penkovsky book, stood another of his favorites - the Gibney-Deriabin co-authored *The Secret World.*

As a young man, Ivan had admired the stories his father had told him about the Russian Secret Police, but he held a particular admiration for former police officer Peter Deriabin who had fled from behind the Iron Curtain nearly 20 years ago.

A shelf-section belonging to his book cabinet had been removed and placed on a small metal table to display his rather limited collection of foreign liquors and wines. It also held three bottles of his favorite *Ohranj* Vodka. Six washed glasses had been placed rim-down on a white napkin spread on the table, and a Thai ice bucket resembling a Monk's 'beggar's bowl', was sweating condensation onto the cotton cloth napkin. Ivan walked to the table, picked up one of the glasses and examined it. Holding it like a monocular, he closed one eye and peered at the camera mounted directly over his desk. Through the bottom of the glass, he could see the distorted glow of the red light, indicating that someone was still monitoring his office. "Oh, yes, I see you too," he murmured. He then filled the glass with ice and placed a new bottle of *Ohranj* in the ice bucket, in anticipation of DG's arrival.

Returning to his desk, Ivan called the galley and ordered a tray of pumpernickel and 'the usual' pickled cucumbers to be in his office at 1520 precisely. He sat and leaned back, looking straight up at the camera. The red recording light was still on. Ivan sat directly below the camera, out of sight. "Why," he asked, almost out loud, "would they want to watch us in our own offices? Perhaps," he defended, "they are only testing the system".

He hadn't visited the embassy security office or barely spoken to the Security Officer since Sokolov initially walked through when he arrived in Bangkok. They were collocated with the Internal Affairs office in the center of the building. No windows; just a single door on each side of their room. Once during a weekly staff meeting he had challenged the necessity of the cameras. It was for their own safety they were told.

Ivan had never liked his office. It reminded him too much of the basement office in the old stone building on Gorky Street in Moscow. As a youth, it seemed that every time his father returned to Moscow for short temporary-duty periods of reindoctrination, it was within the confines of the cold, dark basement of SMERSH, the Counterintelligence School where his father had worked. He always returned to the training facility – either to attend a series of seminars or to provide training to the various American Information country teams from around the world.

On rare occasions when KGB operatives - their 'street men' - were allowed to visit the modern, well-furnished, KGB headquarters less than a mile from SMERSH just across from Dzerzhinsky Square, it was for the sole purpose of receiving some award or decoration – or for being reprimanded or disciplined. Ivan had attended ceremonies for his father on three occasions. The first was when his father was promoted to the rank of Full Colonel.

The Order of Lenin

The second and third were when his father was presented with the *Order of Lenin* for his outstanding service to the motherland, and the *Order of the Red Banner of Labour* for exceptional working achievements.

The Order of the Red Banner of Labour

Yesterday, Ivan had received a notice that during his next 'routine visit' to Moscow, he should stop at the Kremlin and receive his father's posthumous award of the *Order for Service to the Motherland*. His father would be one of the first to receive this brand new medal. This new medal, to be created and dated 28 October 1974 is the first Military awards medal created after the end of World War II.

Order for Service to the Motherland

Suddenly, a knock at the door awakened Ivan from his day-dream. Startled, he jumped up as a voice called out reminding him that he had ordered the chasers from the galley. Glancing at his watch, Ivan noted it was nearly 1520 hours. Ivan had been in deep thought and had not realized time had raced by so quickly.

DG arrived at the Russian Embassy at 1520 hours. He was recognized by the guards, and allowed entry without challenge. He parked in the same visitors' slot, and walked inside. Ivan was not waiting in the lobby area as expected. At the front desk, DG was greeted by a new receptionist who asked for his identification and the purpose of his visit. Her nametag read "ALEXANDRA" in English. Her makeup was so white, it caused her ghostly face to appear a full three shades lighter than her neck, and the contrast with her bright red lipstick made her look old. DG noticed her extended fingernails, painted to match the lipstick. *"Obviously,"* he thought, *"with such elongated nails, she's not a typist."* Her walk was an indication that she was not accustomed to wearing high heels. The afternoon sun shone brightly through the barred window on the west side of the embassy reception office. The bright light was not kind to her pock-marked face.

He explained he was there to see Mr. Romanyev.

She then asked to examine the envelope. DG was not prepared for the request, but obediently placed it on the counter. She picked it up, examined both sides of the envelope observing only sheet music through the translucent plastic, and then handed it back to him.

"Oh," she commented "you are DAT American." DG retrieved the envelope just as Ivan announced his arrival.

"Good afternoon, DG," a smiling Ivan called to him. "You're a little early. It's wonderful to see you again." He approached, reaching to shake hands.

As he passed the front of the counter, Ivan remarked "This is my American friend," He seemed to be bragging to the receptionist. Glancing over her shoulder, Ivan looked at the security monitor and took note that it was on, and that it was still focused on his office. Ivan had left his radio on just to use up the film in the camera.

"Good to see you too, Ivan." DG responded.

Ivan had no idea how relieved DG was to see him walk in. DG wasn't sure how he would have reacted if the receptionist had opened the envelope. They walked into Ivan's office.

Inside, DG immediately handed the envelope to Ivan. Ivan thanked him and placed the article on his desk, as though he was not anxious to examine the contents. He offered vodka, and this time, DG accepted without hesitation. Somehow, he felt he needed a drink.

"I see you have a new receptionist," DG started.

"Oh yes," Ivan stated. He glanced upward. A faint rewinding sound was emitting from the camera. At least temporarily it was not recording. "You'd better be careful," he warned half-jokingly, "She may jump on you." He left interpretation open to DG.

"Sorry I asked," DG responded. He politely stifled an urge to vomit. "But thanks for the warning anyway."

"I see we have the same first impressions, DG." Ivan smiled. "That's a good sign."

The light on the camera lit up as though prompted. Since it was now recording, Ivan decided to change the direction of the conversation.

"How's Irene?" Ivan asked while measuring two generous doubles of chilled *Ohranj* into each of their glasses.

"She's doing fine," DG responded. He told Ivan truthfully that Irene's dance troupe would be going to Japan for a two-week tour in November, but would be back in time for Thanksgiving.

"Wonderful!" Ivan remarked, handing the drink to DG and simultaneously lifting his own. "*Na Zdorovie*! To health!" Ivan exclaimed, "Or better yet, '*Vashe Zdorovie!* To your health".

"To health!" DG responded.

"Nu." Ivan took a deep breath; then tilting his head back inhaled his entire 2-ounce shot.

He ritualistically passed the tray of pumpernickel and pickled cucumber to DG, taking a piece of bread and the smallest slice of pickle for himself. Ivan breathed out loudly, producing a sound just short of a full whistle. He then ceremoniously smelled his slice of black bread. "Some people" he said, "like to smell their sleeves, but that is optional." He then ate his chaser consciously and quickly.

While Ivan poured himself another double, DG did his best to imitate Ivan's ritual. Sipping his drink, and then eating the chaser.

"You did very well." Ivan remarked – "Now, repeat after me: *'Khorosho poshla'!* That means "it went down well!"

"Khorosho poshla!" DG mimicked.

"Excellent!" Ivan complimented him.

They were now seated on either side of the small table.

"Hey, I've an idea; let's do something together while Irene's out of town. You know, just the two of us." Ivan suggested.

"I'm game for that." DG answered.

"Good, I'll make some reservations or something. It'll be my treat," Ivan said as he stood and walked to his desk. He opened the envelope. "Hey, this was a unique idea DG, the clear envelope and all." Leaving the sheet music in the envelope, he pulled the three-page document from inside and opened it on his desk. He read it quickly. "This is fantastic, my friend! This time, you've really proven yourself. Tell me, will there be more instructions to come?" Ivan's trained eyes noticed immediately that DG had cut the overall classification markings from each page; but had left individual paragraph markings of 'S/NF' intact. It was classified Secret, with no foreign dissemination.

"Of course," DG answered. "You know, there's always an increase in the amount of correspondence relating to these military exercises – right up to the end. There are daily planning documents, status reports, synopses, conclusions and recommendations….."

Ivan smiled, but did not task DG for any of the reports at that time. The suggestion had been planted. Instead, he changed the conversation to a more casual tone, asking DG about his plans for Christmas vacation. Would he be going back to "Oregon?"

Immediately, DG knew Ivan had slipped up. Perhaps he was too excited or maybe just not paying attention. DG had never told him of his family home in Hillsboro, just outside Portland, or that he had ever lived in Oregon at all.

"I don't think so," DG answered, giving no indication whatsoever that he'd picked up on Ivan's mistake. "I'm due for rotation late next year, and I'll visit home at that time."

"I understand," Ivan answered, "I hate transfers!" he went on. "It seems that every time I start getting comfortable, it's time to go elsewhere."

"Oh!" DG was trying to sound disappointed, "Are you expecting to leave too?"

"Leaving is for certain." Ivan answered.

"Where will you go?" DG was still trying to sound innocent, and hoped he wasn't asking too many questions. He decided to continue on this line of discussion, after all, it was Ivan who had raised the subject.

"Oh, there are many possibilities." Ivan answered. Surprisingly, he continued talking. "I'd like to go to San Francisco in the United States, but they're talking of sending me to Beijing for my next assignment. We don't have many Chinese linguists any more."

"Your English is so perfect!" DG remarked; "It would seem logical to assign you to the US." DG went on, "Is your Chinese as good as your English?"

Without hesitation Ivan replied "My Chinese is OK, but certainly not as good as my American English. Don't forget, I was born, raised and educated mostly in the US. I'm practically an American!"

Ivan glanced at the camera. It was still recording. He wished he could see back through the lens to the monitor, and in that way ascertain who was now watching their meeting. Was it Sokolov; Internal Affairs; or The Ambassador? Or was it Ms Dombrovsky? That last thought caused him to shudder visibly.

"But," Ivan concluded "There's always D.C. There are tons of positions in DC that I could fill. I've still got a few months to decide. You never know, just maybe we could both be assigned to the same location – different jobs, of course. Wouldn't that be great?"

DG could not disagree. "That would definitely be great." He took another sip of his drink as Ivan downed his second double.

"Have you decided to stick out the 20 years?" Ivan asked casually. He was pouring himself a third.

"I've really been thinking about it," DG answered. "As you know, I'm past the point of no return. A six year reenlistment would put me near 18 years. And then, there's the music career to consider." DG pondered, "This assignment to Bangkok is no longer considered a 'combat tour', since we've discontinued logistical support to the phase-out in Vietnam; so I probably won't have the assignment of choice when I go back to the states. I'll do my best to get the assignment I want of course."

"You're a good man, DG." Ivan encouraged. "You'll likely get what you want. But don't wait too long, you know what John Lennon said – '*life is what happens when you are busy making other plans.*' How true that is." Ivan continued his philosophical chatter, saying "My father always told me 'Son, make your own decisions. That way, if you make a mistake, you need not explain it to anyone. It was your decision to make, right or wrong, and you still learned something from it. But never' " he continued, 'allow anyone to take away your piece of history…your right of choice."

"That's pretty deep", DG responded, "but very true." DG was still trying to put the three statements together in a meaningful dialogue.

The conversation had come full circle, and Ivan returned to the three-page document that DG had carried to him. "Did you have any problems taking this from your office?" Ivan asked, "I noticed it's classified."

"Not really," DG replied, "I wouldn't have been allowed to copy it if the classification had been any higher. That may have presented a problem. I wouldn't even have been able to bring it to you with a higher classification."

"Are you allowed to make copies yourself?" Ivan asked.

"Oh, no," DG replied, "We have to give it to the distribution center with a written request. They provide authorization, make copies and do our distribution."

"If you are going to have problems reproducing those copies, or when time is of the essence, I have a small tool I could give you that could perhaps make things easier." Ivan mentioned cautiously. "It's very convenient – all you have to do is roll it over the document and 'voila' it's copied." Ivan said "Of course, you would need to use it in private."

"That sounds like some kind of toy." DG smiled.

"Actually, it is a toy." Ivan said, trying to downplay the importance of a 'rollover'. "I've played with it many times. I use it whenever I want to copy anything. It's good for newspaper articles, photographs, and even documents. It's made in Russia. Tell you what, I'll bring it along when we have our outing, and we can play with it."

"OK," DG answered casually.

Ivan thought it was probably time to change the subject again, but was happy with himself for casually mentioning the rollover and suggesting there would be an exchange of more information. He had planted another seed.

"So, how is that alto saxophone? Isn't that the smoothest you've ever played?" Ivan was changing the subject.

"Yes, Thank You so much Ivan. That was a wonderful gift." DG went on "Next time you show up at the King's Palace, I'll play that *'Stranger on the Shore'* piece you've always liked, and I'll use the Sax you gave me, of course."

"I'd enjoy that." Ivan responded, glancing at his watch. "You know, my family and friends were very, very impressed at your last performance. It was flawless."

"I do my best," DG said, "And I'm learning something new every week. And by the way Ivan, it was nice meeting your family."

"You know, if you are ever lucky enough to travel to Moscow, you'll always have a place to stay with my family", Ivan offered without warning. "If you intend to make the international scene, you must practice every day," Ivan coached, "Practice makes you perfect." Then, still guiding the conversation slightly, Ivan glanced at his watch and said "You know, DG, we still have time for another shot."

"I shouldn't," DG smiled. Then noticing he had but a sip left, continued saying tactfully "Well, since you're twisting my arm. The Orange Vodka is delicious, but it's strong too!"

Footnote: Particularly ingenious was the East German/Soviet rollover camera, disguised as a notebook. The espionage agent would regularly carry a real notebook to work, and use it often. Then, when it came time to make copies of documents, the agent would bring the rollover camera notebook, which was identical in appearance to the real notebook. In order to photograph a document, the agent would run the opened edge of the notebook carefully across the documents to be copied. Inside were wheels that both activated the light and propelled the film which was hidden, along with a battery-powered light source, inside the notebook. Two, three-second passes over one page would photograph the entire page. One roll of film would copy more than 80, 8"X10" pages of information, to include photos. The photo action was continuous, and did not require winding the film.

Ivan poured himself another two-ounce shot, and added a measured ounce to DG's drink. They lifted their glasses. "To us!" Ivan said loud enough for the monitor to pick up the toast.

"To us," DG responded, "Salud!" They emptied their glasses.

Ivan retrieved another piece of sheet music from his desk, and placed it in DG's plastic envelope. Handing the packet to DG, he said "Here are some more sheets and a little something for your efforts, DG. Please give my regards to your charming wife. Now, don't forget our plans for a night out."

"I'm looking foreword to it," DG smiled. They shook hands.

Tentative meeting arrangements were made for Thursday, the following week. "Perhaps around 1600," Ivan suggested.

"I think I can manage that." DG nodded, adding "I can always take off early if needed."

"In that case," Ivan further suggested, "Let's have a meal – an early dinner perhaps."

"It works for me," DG responded.

"Done," Ivan agreed.

Ivan insisted he would drive. He would confirm their meeting arrangements by phone.

Back in the lobby area, Ivan directed DG back past the front of the reception counter, so he could observe the monitor. It was off. "So, I'll give you a call early next week." Ivan stated, trying to sound casual.

As DG departed the Embassy, Ivan walked back into the hallway. On the way to his office, he was wondering when the monitor had been turned off. *"Perhaps"* he thought again *"I'm just being paranoid."* Back inside, he poured another double shot and sat in the squeaking chair behind his desk. Before closing his eyes, Ivan reminded himself to call 'maintenance' and have them oil the wheels. "The squeaky wheel gets the oil." He pondered aloud.

DG recognized one of the Isuzu surveillance cars depart the embassy behind him, and follow him back to Sukhumvit Road. DG turned left, as did the Isuzu; but when DG reached the Chokchai building, he signaled a right turn and the Isuzu passed him on the left continuing North. DG walked from the parking lot into the building. Confident he was no longer being followed, he cautiously administered the dark crayon mark as he walked by the designated window. Alone, back inside his office, he looked into the plastic envelope, located the sheet music, and found another smaller envelope folded inside.

He sat alone inside his cubicle, and decided to open the envelope. Following my previous instructions, DG was careful not to touch the contents. He could clearly see that it contained 5 crisp one-hundred dollar bills.

Friday morning I went to the office as usual, and noted DG's signal on the window. Keying the STU I called him at 0900 hours, and we discussed his meeting with Ivan. He further informed me of the five hundred dollar compensation. He was aware that he must bring the money to the next meeting. He would of course be allowed to keep it, and would be cautioned against showing any indication of his newly acquired 'wealth'. I told him that a small gift to Ivan – perhaps a bottle of Cognac, purchased from the Class Six Store at MACTHAI would be appropriate.

We talked long enough to set up our meeting for Monday afternoon. After hanging up, I began the draft of the report on DG's meeting with Ivan, and then checked our incentive cabinet. In stock, we had one remaining bottle of Hennessy's Very Superior Old Pale (VSOP) which I selected for DG to pass. It was a special-design bottle in a gift box, marked US$78.90. That would be a good gift for DG to pass, expressing his gratitude for a $500 bonus. Ivan would pay much more through the open market for the same bottle.

At my desk, I found a note from Dick. I called him and he asked that I meet with him in the mutual area. When I walked into the pool room, Dick was waiting alone, holding a manila folder. He informed me that while DG was parked at the Russian embassy, two of the Russian surveillance techs had paid a visit to his car. Our fixed surveillance had filmed the activity. The movie film was being developed, and he had brought some still shots of the activity. Opening the folder, he showed photos of two previously identified Russian tech specialists, opening the passenger side of DG's car and leaving the area within a minute with a small unidentified item.

"Hopefully," Dick continued, "the movie film will show more. Our guys had set it up with a tripod and a good telephoto-lens for the shoot. It should be very clear." Dick went on "The movie show will be ready this afternoon."

We were both happy with this discovery.

I arranged the hotel room through Frank, who seemed happy to have an opportunity to use it for Sunday night. He would as a matter of routine, pass me the key Monday and I would give it back to him Tuesday Morning. On Sunday afternoon, Case Officer John would be using the rented safe-site for a meeting with Russian Linguist Sergeant First Class Kolinsky. They were to be gone by 1600 and Frank would spend the night in the room.

At 1615 hours, Dick called me to his office. He had set up the projector, and was excited to show the accomplishments of the fixed surveillance activity. The movie began with the two identified tech reps walking out of the main door of the embassy. They began their activities by examining all the vehicles in the first parking lane with a mirror fastened to the end of a 3-4 foot handle. They looked quickly under the rocker panels of each car, until they approached DG's car. From that point, the examination became more than just cursory.

It was much more thorough. It seemed they had located something under the left, rear door. One of the reps placed a piece of cardboard on the ground, knelt and apparently replaced a battery inside an unidentified device. Next, the other rep sat in the passenger seat and reached under the glove compartment. He removed a small article, and replaced it with a similar article. They then wiped off the door handles and surfaces they may have touched. Once they finished with DG's car, both of them looked at their watches and walked around his car one more time. This film confirmed the probable existence of both a tracking device and a concealed recorder.

Once it appeared they were confident everything else was clean, they walked to the guard shack and talked to the guards for approximately one minute. As they walked back toward the embassy, Dick stopped the film several times, backed up and stopped again. The item in one of the tech reps' right hand was an audio cassette. This was the item exchanged under the dash.

When DG departed the parking lot some time later, he was waved through the gate with no delay, and as soon as he had cleared the area, one of the gate guards picked up his field phone and made a quick call. We decided they were calling the tech reps, and that they would be continuing their monitoring activities.

"These guys have really stepped up their surveillance of your guy now." Dick was saying. "They have his car tagged for surveillance; they have him being recorded-probably by a voice activated recorder; and likely have his apartment and home phone tapped as well."

"Good," I responded. "At least we know what they're doing."

I reminded Dick of the DG and Ivan meeting which took place at the UNICO Grand Sathorn Hotel near Lumpini Park. We recalled that Ivan had been watching for something in the garden area when the meeting began, and that he finally closed the blind and began operational discussion. Putting two and two together, we decided it was likely on that occasion when devices were first placed in DG's car. DG had driven Ivan to the hotel, and Ivan had kept DG busy for several hours while they held their meeting and had dinner.

"I'm absolutely sure your guy briefed his wife, and everything is OK there," Dick started, "but the point I'm making here is that they are capable of conducting the same efforts against any of us. We have to step up our countermeasures and prevent them from having access to us. Don, it would be self-defeating to neutralize those efforts insofar as our recruited assets are concerned – it would only tip off the Russians. Not only would they know that we are aware of what they're up to, but would wonder how, when and where we made the discovery. It could be dangerous for DG. You're going to have to tell him to continue to work with this knowledge we have."

Saturday morning, I slept until 0800 hours. After going through the rituals, I descended to the main floor, planning to walk to the International Market for my usual weekend breakfast. As I walked toward the exit, I was almost mowed down by the three-man Mafioso team barging into my apartment complex. I slowed my pace, turned and began looking over some local tour brochures in a caddy near the door. Initially, it appeared that there was no-one to greet them, as Mr. Lin, the new receptionist was seated behind the counter. Just as the Russians approached the front desk, however, Lin stood, appearing instantly in front of them, as though by magic.

Lin, I might interject, is a young Thai gentleman who always dresses in a suit and tie. By the fit of his dress, it could be easily ascertained that he was not born with the physical attributes he now exhibited. His physique was one which requires a daily ritual of strenuous exercise, involving quick movement, thrusts, spin-kicking and, I would guess - board-breaking. The primary, secondary and third knuckles of each hand were calloused with the telltale marks of one who has used them well. He was a very proud of the level and degree he held in T'ai Ch'uan Tao. A man of any size would be intimidated by Lin.

Lin was my friend!

His English was impeccable. "Can I help you gentlemen?" He asked.

Surprised at Lin's sudden appearance, the Mafioso leader sputtered, turned pale and then responded by inquiring about the hours of operation for the adjacent restaurant.

Mr. Lin smiled and said "As it is posted on the glass door entrance, our restaurant is open to the public from six o'clock AM until 12 O'clock midnight, every day." He went on "The bar remains open on Friday and Saturday nights until two o'clock AM the next mornings."

I departed the complex and walked onto the street. It was obvious to me that the three had not discussed their cover, their ruse or reason for the visit, and were just snooping around again. Walking slowly, I noticed that within 30 seconds, the threesome hurriedly departed the complex and entered their sedan. Again, it had been illegally parked in front. They sped away moving northward. I watched until they were out of sight. They may never return. Thank you, Mr. Lin.

After a rather quick breakfast at the Pastry Shop, I returned to the complex and talked momentarily with Mr. Lin, asking him of the strange actions of the Russians. He informed me that they had asked about the restaurant hours, about renting again, and when he explained that there were no rentals available for short-term use, they departed in a huff.

"Maybe," Lin joked, "they are looking for a room to share....with each other." He smiled.

I laughed politely. "Déjà vu", I said aloud, and then explained to Lin that the same group had visited several weeks before for the same reasons. I suggested he talk to Sinh, and to the rest of the staff, and that they keep a lookout for these men in the future.

There was no doubt in my mind that if they found the lobby area unguarded they would have taken the stairs up to the residential level.

"Perhaps," I thought *"it might even be a good idea to find out where they would go."* I would discuss it with Dick.

I returned to my room and decided to catch up on my reading – just a little. By the time I finished reading the *Bangkok Post*, Rain was falling quite heavily. I decided to postpone a planned visit to the tailor shop, and instead poured myself a short Rye. I sat under the patio awning and opened *The Man in the Mirror* to page 13. Ah yes, Karl Friedrich von Tetlow.

The book became increasingly interesting as I read, but my concentration level was drooping by noon. Another Rye wouldn't do much to bring me back to life, so I decided a little exercise routine and a shower might just be what the doctor ordered. Before stepping into the shower, I put a pot of coffee on the plate, hoping that caffeine would also augment the desired level of stimuli.

By 1330, the rain had ceased, the patio was dry, and the traffic on Sukhumvit was picking up. I could always continue reading The *Man in the Mirror,* but it seemed like a waste of a good afternoon. I opened windows and the patio doors, allowing a breeze to pass through the apartment. Looking around, I realized that the parquet floors had not been waxed since I moved in. The kitchen and bath floors would not require so much attention, so over the next three hours I completed the task on the rest of the apartment to include a light coat of wax on the rattan furnishings as well. I was pleased with the results, but my knees and arms ached from the kneeling and polishing. That small chore had taken up the rest of the afternoon. The stimulus had worked. I called Frank to invite him to partake of a bowl of goulash at Vic's #3, but he was bound to a family commitment. I drove to Vic's and self-served a large Goulash, and a Heineken Beer. Following the overindulgence, I returned to my apartment and by 2100, found myself yearning for comfort and a good night's sleep. Following a 20-minute warm shower, I sunk into the down of my mattress. I fell asleep thinking of my upcoming meeting with Bill Tanner.

At night I could clearly see the running lights of the small Cessna, as it passed along the runway in front of me. The frowning clown couldn't seem to get it off the ground. The engine was running at a very high RPM, the prop buzzing, and the clown was waving at me. With my briefcase in my left hand, and a Mamiya-16 spy-cam in my right, I began to run toward the plane. He picked up speed, moving ahead; and then, when I stopped running, he slowed.

"You forgot your camera!" I yelled, waving the camera in the air..

Now grinning, the clown brought the plane to a halt. I ran, holding the Mamiya 16 in front of me. The vision of the clown in the plane morphed into a large poster, and the camera had suddenly changed into a 'rollover'. From the far side of the camera, the copy was extending outward, showing the clown's face, smiling sardonically. Holding a spyglass, he looked back toward my poster and then accelerated quickly, moving away. He gradually lifted off, and disappeared into the clouds.

The camera ceased to exist, and the poster melted in my hands. Furious at my quixotic charge at the windmill, I woke in a cold sweat.

So much for a good night's sleep.

Sunday was even less eventful than Saturday.

Early Monday afternoon, I executed a rolling pick up of DG at the exit to the Chokchai parking lot, and we took a circuitous route toward the River Bend Hotel. Enroute, I once again rehashed our mutual covers for being together, and having determined that we were not followed, we parked in the covered parking and walked up into the room. With the sounds of my radio covering our conversations, he talked about his meeting.

I was somewhat amazed at how soon Ivan had surfaced the subject of a roll-over camera. It seemed a little premature, but then perhaps we did not yet know the extent of information Ivan was planning to get from DG. This was another subject for Leon.

I complimented DG for guiding the conversation into Ivan's possible impending transfer; telling him how important it is to remain current with Ivan's biographical data. Again, we discussed methods of elicitation, and I gave him suggestions for getting back into that same conversation when they go out for their night on the town. I cautioned DG not to drink to the extent that he could lose control of the meeting or of himself during that upcoming event. DG had no idea what Ivan had in mind, and we decided we should sit down and war-game with Leon the possibilities and ramifications of such a meeting.

DG stated that he felt he had detected sincere, but mixed emotions on the part of Ivan. "At one point," DG stated, "I actually thought he was planning on asking for the periodic reports on the planning and implementation phases of the training exercise. But he didn't. Instead, he changed the subject!" Even DG was surprised.

"That's interesting," I pondered. "Perhaps he's having second thoughts. By now, he knows you have your hands on the information. He's on the brink… Why would he hesitate? Yet he did bring up the subject of the rollover."

"Oh, yes," DG started, "I almost forgot. He also knew I was from Oregon. He actually mentioned it in our conversation." DG had been surprised.

"Did you acknowledge his mistake?" I asked immediately.

"Oh, no," DG responded; "I acted as though I didn't even notice."

"Good!" I replied, "That only means he's doing his homework. Obviously, he's had you checked out with the help of their US offices. They don't have to do the legwork themselves; they can simply hire a private detective to do their checking. It's quite easy."

"Is that legal?" DG asked, somewhat astonished.

"Yup," I said. "It's not only legal, but common practice."

DG provided me with a list of the types of messages he expected would cross his desk over the next few weeks. I would use this for an advance request for approval of passage material. It would be ideal to have a pre-approved list on hand.

DG handed me the money envelope, and I removed the money from inside. Being extremely cautious not to disturb any prints on the contents, I counted the money and noticed that although crisp, the serial numbers were not in sequence. Also included in the envelope was a hand-written note which read *"For your efforts"*, It was signed simply *"Ivan"*.

I then carefully scooped his original money into a separate envelope inside my own briefcase, along with the small envelope and the hand-written note. I would discreetly return the cash to him the following morning at the latest.

We discussed the partial surveillance the day before. DG followed up saying he was positive the surveillance was only part way, and no one followed him home. He had recognized the only two cars in his apartment complex parking lot as belonging to fellow American tenants.

I allowed DG to go through some still shots of the Russian tech reps working on his car. He was not surprised of the activity, but was impressed with the clarity and detail of the photos. This left little doubt as to the intentions of the Soviets. I cautioned him again as to the probability that his apartment and home phone were both being tapped.

Just as we were preparing to terminate the conversation, DG mentioned the new employee – Alexandra. His description of her was very thorough, and I told him that we had not yet received any information on her, but I would inquire and attempt to obtain a photo for his verification.

Casual conversation, the consumption of hamburgers and fries, and training continued until 1545 hours, when we decided to terminate. DG was scheduled to perform at the King's Palace that evening.

Tuesday morning, I arrived at the office by 0630 hours, and prepared the first round of coffee. I decided that my recipe was better than the weak, tea-colored coffee most of the others would make. "If they want it weak," I thought out loud, "They can water it down." I put a teapot of hot water on the hotplate.

Frank was next to arrive and we set about solving a few problems of the planet. Gradually, the rest of the office began drifting in.

Mike stopped and interrupted our conversation asking for an update.

"Ivan has started paying DG." I answered.

"Wow, that's great!" Mike remarked, and then said "so where's the cash?" I went to my desk, opened my briefcase and took out the envelope. "He also surfaced the idea of a 'rollover', to speed things up." I mentioned.

"That's double great!" Mike responded. "When's the training session?"

"Before TK-Day," I answered, handing the envelope to Mike.

"Let's get this to the tech guys," Mike suggested, "so you can give it back to DG right away." And then "What's he going to do with it?"

"Already talked with him. He'll buy Ivan a bottle of Cognac and use the rest for home."

"Good thinking." Mike agreed "Check the cabinet and see what we have to give him. We have to let Ivan know that giving is a two-way street." He smiled. I didn't bother to tell Mike I'd already taken the bottle of *Hennessy* for DG to pass.

Mike accompanied me to the 4th floor tech office, which consisted of four men, four desks and four safes in one large cubicle. Jack Bohannan took the envelope and examined the contents. The crisp money had no prints. It had been wiped thoroughly before being placed in the envelope. The note also was print-free. Specialist Kulani lifted one thumbprint from the envelope which was matched with those on file in Ivan's dossier. One other print was assumed to be DG's. I would verify with his personal dossier in my safe within a few minutes.

I placed the money in the envelope and put Ivan's note along with the original envelope in the Ivan project file. Back in my office, I made up a receipt for DG to sign for the money. I checked the lifted print with those on file for DG. It was his.

I examined and 'brushed' everything I would give to DG for passage, to insure that no telltale signs from our office remained – no prints.

After calling to make sure DG was in his office, I placed a package of gift wrap, the Cognac package, a class-six store shopping bag and the cash envelope in an unmarked bag, and delivered them to him. His office was virtually empty, so we sat for a few minutes while I reminded him again to be discreet in spending the five hundred dollars. He would deposit the cash into his personal account that afternoon, along with his accumulated salary from the King's Palace. At my request he signed a receipt for the money.

In passing the bottle of *Hennessy* to DG, I drew his attention to the duty free seal on the bottle before placing it in a shopping bag from the MACTHAI Class Six Store. "Be sure," I instructed, "to let Ivan know where you 'bought' it."

When I stepped back into the elevator, Dick was on his way to our floor.

"I got something for you from the "The Quakers," he mumbled, meaning the 'other agency.' "Did you request some info?"

"Not yet," I replied. "Let's hope they're reading my mind."

They were.

CHAPTER 24.
THE VORONIN/DOMBROVSKY FILE.

We arrived at our floor, punched the combination and entered the offices. I followed Dick into his office, and he handed me an envelope marked "1357". I opened it to find a dossier entitled *Alexandra Dombrovsky, nee: Voronin.*

Trying to read over my shoulder, Dick finally said "Sit down! Let's go through it here."

Dick had as much interest in the identification of this new operative as I, and we went over the file synopses together. I opined that the so-called passport photo was at least 15-years old – according to DG's description of her.

Alexandra Dombrovsky was born as 'Alexandria' Voronin on September 30, 1932 in the village Corjova, Dubăsari district of the Moldavian Russia. Her father, Alexander T. Voronin, was an elite member of the CPSU Central Committee, in charge of both the Secret Political Directorate of the KGB and the 6th Special Section for Censorship.

At the age of seven, Alexandra entered Dubăsari elementary school where she remained for four full years. At eleven, she went on to High School, called "middle High School" in Moscow, where she remained for 6 more years while her father was assigned there. By seventeen, she had finished public school and was immediately accepted to study at the undergraduate level. After 5 more years, at age 22, Alexandra was Allowed to begin studies at the Moscow institute of Foreign Languages. She resided with her parents while studying English at that academy for two years. From there, she moved to the KGB- sponsored Leningrad Institute of Foreign Studies to study Polish for two more years. It was in Leningrad where she first met middle High School student Peter Dombrovsky. He was but 16 years old. She was 24. Peter, considered a genius among his peers and within the school faculty, was young and naïve. He was a willing and very compatible tutor.

As though she was waiting for Peter to complete his studies, she remained in the Leningrad office of the Ministry as an accountant while Peter, who had graduated from MHS a full three years early, attended the Language academy in Leningrad. Peter stayed on as a foreign language professor until she urged him to move into the political arena in the Foreign Service, with an eye on the Diplomatic Corps.

As a result of his political orientation and standing with well-known officials within the Ministries, her father, Alexander was able to orchestrate Alexandra's education and orientation into the Internal Affairs Bureau, and in 1959 at age 27, she laterally transferred into the First Intelligence Bureau of the Ministry of State Security.

At her request and with her father's recommendation, Peter was also transferred to Moscow and ultimately assigned to State Security. Both Alexandra and Peter attended various country programs, focusing primarily on the European theater, and in 1965 Peter was assigned to Gdansk. She immediately insisted on joining him and against her father's will, traveled to Gdansk on a non-diplomatic passport. In 1966, she and Peter were married at the consulate; she was granted diplomatic status, and remained with Peter for the duration of his tour.

After returning to Moscow for his periodic reindoctrination, Peter was asked to accept assignment to Bangkok, and in return was promised a more lucrative reassignment to Poland in the future. Several weeks later, following an abbreviated attendance at the SMERSH Counterintelligence School, Alexandra was transferred to Bangkok.

Also contained within the dossier was a copy of the Bangkok Post article regarding her automobile accidents at the traffic circle, along with photographs - which were only a few years more current than the 'passport photo'.

Without knowing of her pending official assignment to the American Team, 'the Quakers' had no immediate plans to select her as a target.

However, 'Alexandra, **our paths will cross again'**.

Back in my office, I finalized my report on the DG meeting, and checked my calendar. I realized I'd not finalized my next appointment with Bill. When I called his office, he was not available. He would return the next morning. I left no message.

On Wednesday I received a STU call from DG. His friend had called to tell him he would be at the King's Palace again that evening. DG would acknowledge him again. Their next meeting was planned for Thursday. DG said he didn't have much in the way of passage material - only an acknowledgement of the previous message regarding the upcoming joint exercise. I told him he already had approval to pass that message to his friend.

"Is there anything new on the message?" I asked.

"Yes, it has the complete list of organizations involved, in the actual exercise. But, he went on, "they're only listed as 'addressees' for dissemination of the message, and not as participants."

I would get back to him.

I talked with Mike who stated it was OK to pass the message, "but be sure to tell DG that he should not verify the addressees as 'participants'. Let Ivan make those assumptions. If DG is asked, he may say he's not sure."

Next on the agenda, I talked with Dick to see if he wanted to set up any surveillance at the King's Palace. He did, and was anxious to get his teams back into the habit of participating.

"I'll use two teams and signals," he suggested immediately. "No close surveillance. Nowadays, I think they're too tail conscious, and might pick us up."

I agreed.

Before calling DG back, I discussed the situation with Frank. He also wanted to go to the King's Palace and watch DG perform again, put in his two-bits worth and of course write up the surveillance report.

"My treat." Frank insisted. "It'll be your early birthday present from Uncle Sam." he joked, knowing full-well he would be reimbursed for participating. We both laughed.

"How'd you know my birthday is coming up?" I asked.

"Ah know everthang." Frank drawled. "All ya ever gotta do is ask."

I called DG on the STU, telling him it was OK to pass the message as he had before, explaining the caveat. He understood. I also told him to take the exact same route from his Wednesday performance as he had previously established. This would facilitate our team in setting up fixed positions for our surveillance.

I made reservations for two at the King's Palace for Wednesday night. Reservations were difficult, and I had to accept balcony seats. The operator however promised me that the seats were situated along the front of the balcony. Our view would be unobstructed.

We arrived and stood in line for tables just a few feet behind Ivan. Once inside, Ivan walked through the front, past the maître d', and into the dining room. Frank and I ascended to the balcony.

Frank recognized the wine servant and ordered "*Amarit* and a Scotch on pebbles" The waiter stared blankly at Frank.

"Crushed ice!" Frank blurted out, "you know, small rocks – PEBBLES!"

"Ooohh," the waiter laughed, "small rocks – pebbles – OK, dass fine." He smiled.

We sat at Table number M-7, which was idyllically situated between two large marble pillars, giving us an almost private dining area. Drinks were delivered immediately.

The band was tuning up, as Frank and I looked over the audience. It was extremely crowded for a weeknight. Ivan was seated at his usual table. The adjacent table to Ivan's left was empty.

"He must have made reservations well in advance," I remarked.

"Well," Frank responded, "Just maybe he's got some pull. After all, he did call the 'headliner' directly and let him know he'd be here, right?"

Just as the lights were lowered, DG walked out on the stage, and the audience applauded longer and louder than ever before. The Master of Ceremonies gave the usual introduction, and DG began with his opening routine version of *Yakkety Sax*.

Gesturing toward Ivan, Frank murmured "This aughta be interestin'."

A group of five more guests were being guided to the table next to Ivan. They consisted of two members of the 'Mafioso', two ladies and one more unidentified man. I assumed the unidentified ladies to be Ivan's mother and Alexandra and more than likely the other, younger male was Peter Dombrovsky. One of the Mafioso members sat at Ivan's table with Ivan and his 'mother'. Frank was right; this was 'interestin'.

"Welcome, welcome," DG was saying. Welcome to all of you, and a special welcome indeed to my good friend Ivan and his Friends from Russia." The audience continued to cheer. The timing almost gave the appearance that the applause was for Ivan.

Ivan raised his glass. ***"Na Zdorovie*! To health!"** toasting DG loudly, Ivan grinned. Most heads turned to look in Ivan's direction, and he seemed to love the recognition.

DG exchanged his saxophone for his guitar, and sitting alone on stage, sang a solo impersonation of Art Garfunkle's *'Bridge over Troubled Water'*. Then, as promised, DG followed with the alto saxophone rendition of *Stranger on the Shore*. To this, Ivan and his group started the ovation, calling "Bravo, Bravo". Even Frank and I joined the chant.

DG bowed and blushed as a few effeminate screams emitted from the audience.

Before taking his first break, DG played his own version of several other popular songs of the time. Finally, as the evening's performances were drawing to an end, and DG filled a few requests from the audience, Ivan's mother approached the stage with a large bouquet of flowers that had been delivered to her table. She presented them to DG. She spoke to him for a moment and DG kissed her hand. Blushing, she then returned to her table. I wondered if she had any idea as to the professional relationship between her son and DG. As a final performance, DG played a portion of the lone horn solo of *Blue Mountain* – obviously for Ivan and his friends. The performance was followed with an extended ovation – prompted by the Romanyev table.

At a table for two near the left end of the stage sat the AA team. One was seated, facing Ivan directly. His lighter/camera was placed on the table, and I assumed it was poised and focused on Ivan and the Mafiosi.

Coincidentally, as Frank and I descended the stairway, Ivan and his entourage were exiting the main dining room. Ivan and his mother spoke in English while the others conversed in their native language. One thing is for certain, they were in agreement about the performance.

We left the KP parking lot before DG, and resisted any temptation to search for the Datsuns or Isuzu sedans. The AA team was out of sight; I knew they would already be in position to discreetly observe surveillance.

"OK, Birthday Boy," Frank declared, "what's your pleasure?"

We stopped at a Chokchai Kiosk for two of the world's best hamburgers and ate them in Frank's car before heading home. On the way, Frank joked about the coincidence of my being born on Halloween, and making a career of being a 'spook'.

Thursday, my birthday was a free day, but I couldn't resist the temptation. I stopped by the office and made an early STU call to DG. Frank and the surveillance team had already given their own joint opinions of DG's performance the night before.

DG confirmed that the lady who presented him with flowers was in fact Ivan's mother, and the other woman was the new 'receptionist'. DG had written down his conversation with Ivan's mother. DG commented that her English was superb; then he read: *"You make me homesick for San Francisco – I absolutely love your music. Please make some recordings for our family- your music really takes us back..... I'll be returning to Russia shortly, and will never forget this moment."*

DG admitted he had kissed her hand.

"Your pleasure," I joked.

Before leaving the office, I spoke with Mike and Leon regarding DG's upcoming meeting with Ivan. I volunteered to meet with DG that afternoon, but Leon spoke up. "No need. Let's not take any chances with their surveillance. I'm confident DG can wing this one." Then as an afterthought, Leon instructed me to remind DG by STU that he should bring up the subject of his wife's upcoming trip to Japan, and "let Ivan follow up with final plans for their night out." Leon explained that this would allow planning time for Dick's surveillance team.

I did. He would.

Following the talk with DG, I took a taxi directly to the Post office and scheduled my call to Betty. The appointment was for 1345 hours. Not only was this my birthday - it was also the birthday of President Chiang Kai-shek. Many Thai Chinese were calling relatives on this Taiwan national holiday. I did not realize that this would be the last celebrated birthday of the President's lifetime.

With a few hours to waste, I spent some time having lunch at the King's Palace, and while there sat in the main dining room. I couldn't help but notice that Ivan's table was designated as a 'permanent' reservation for every Wednesday night, with a small placard bearing the 'R' for reservation, over an embossed ornamental 'D' for "Diplomat". Beneath the designation were the words *"each Wednesday evening"*, and the name "ROMANYEV".

At 1330 hours I departed the King's Palace and caught a samlar taxi, instructing the driver to take me to the international post office. He drove North on Rama IV Road, then turned southeast on Surawong to Patpong I Road where I told him to stop. As I was getting out of the Taxi, I noticed Frank walking North on Patpong I. With him was SGT Bresnehan who had been interviewed during the enquiry regarding the faux background investigation conducted by Ivan. I assumed Frank was working, but could not avoid passing face to face. I displayed our mutually agreed safety signal.

"Well, hello there, Podnuh," Frank called to me. "What're you doin' in Patpong?" It was a leading question. In late afternoons, the Patpong district begins its transformation into one of the most famous 'red-light' districts in Bangkok – perhaps in the world. Frank understood when I mentioned I was going to the IPO to call Betty.

"You remember SGT Bresnehan, Don't you?" Frank queried.

"Of course." I shook Bresnehan's hand. It seemed a lifetime since his interview with Ivan.

"Yeah," Bresnehan stated. "I remember you too. You're one of the guys there when Corporal Tiley and I were interviewed."

I acknowledged his remark with a nod. Of course I assumed Frank was vetting him for possible use as a 'walk-in' or dangle.

I looked at my watch. "I gotta run guys, or I'll be late for the call. Catch ya later."

Frank winked. "I gotta head back to the office anyway."

They caught my 'samlar' and taxied away. I couldn't help but notice as the little samlar struggled back into the traffic that the shocks on Frank's side were compressed to the max. The little samlar leaned noticeably.

I made a mental note to have Frank brief me on his operation. *'It's going to drive me nuts until I know what it's all about.'* I told myself.

The conversation with Betty was calming as we continued formulating wedding plans. "The President," she said, "is not getting better." She was seriously concerned.

"Don't worry Sweetheart." I encouraged. "It's not going to change our plans."

After about 30 minutes of conversation involving wedding pictures, invitations and menu, we hung up. I missed her very much, and I was even getting excited about the menu.

Before leaving the IPO, I made a quick call to Bill Tanner at his office.

"I've been expecting your call there, Pal," he acknowledged my voice.

"I called yesterday, but you were out," I started.

"I thought that was you," he explained. "The secretary said someone had called, and left no message."

"I was hoping we could get together again – maybe this weekend." I suggested.

"So was I," he sounded anxious, "And as a matter of fact, I put my name on the list for the finals competition starting next week at the Club. I thought you might want to come by and watch me kick ass – or get my ass kicked."

I knew immediately that this meant he had signed up to play against Alex Topov, but wouldn't allow myself to ask over this insecure communication. "Let's meet Saturday for breakfast, if that's convenient." I suggested.

"Sure, same time, same place OK?"

"Absolutely," I responded. I then changed the subject, asking about his family.

He informed me "I've got 10 free days, as my family will be in Korea, shopping over the TK Day holiday."

"Good, that will provide us with some good opportunities to get together." We talked casually for two more minutes before hanging up.

Although it was my off day, instead of returning home, I taxied to the Chokchai Building and entered the office. I took the time to check my mailbox for messages and type up a draft of the telephonic contact with Bill Tanner.

Walking back toward the coffee pot, I saw Frank in the office typing. I told him of the planned meet with Bill on Saturday Morning. Frank said he had already reserved a room at the River Bend, and it would be available all day Saturday. Case Officer Dave F would be using it on Sunday and again on Monday. The tech guys were planning to sweep it on Friday afternoon. We could pass the key around at the office. It would be placed in the top, right hand drawer of Frank's desk.

"When you have a chance," Frank requested, "would you give me a quick assessment of our new Case Officer Roger F? Ah got a feelin' he might be a good candidate to run our safe-site. He's single, nerdy, and not the type to tote a favorite 'pu-ying' back to his hooch. Since he drinks nothin' but Orange *Nehi*, he has no interest in bar-hoppin' or even gettin' involved in COLE; and he's checkin' out a penthouse apartment with a back-door entrance to a studio rental. A two-fer, so to speak"

"No problem. I'll take him to a get-acquainted lunch on Monday – if he's free."

I asked him about his meeting with Bresnehan.

"Ah knew you'd ask." Frank grinned. "Ah'm workin' him up for an operation. He's gonna be makin' friends with the Thai owner of the Caltex station, where all the Russian vehicles are serviced. Get the picture?"

"Yeah, yeah!" I replied without hesitation. "Turn about's fair play. What's he got going for him?"

"Bresnehan's a master mechanic in his real life. Before he joined the army, he worked in Indianapolis at the '500' track, and had quite a reputation. He's also a graduate of Shelby's school in LA. He really knows his stuff. He's also an audio/visual hobbyist, and used to mount those small TV cameras in the Indy cars. He spends a lot of time over at the Auto Hobby shop. Ya never know he might be able to turn my old Oldsmobile piece of shit into a 'screamin' piece o' shit!'" he laughed. "And then again, maybe not. That ol' car is probably a lost cause." He grinned.

"So, besides placing devices onto their cars......" I started.

"The neat thing is," Frank interrupted, "Bresnehan can equip any device with a remote-activated release. We can 'eject' it any time we want - in a parking lot, along the road, when the car is moving or at a standstill. Kinda like the black box on an airplane. All we have to do is retrieve it, and then snap a new one in place next time we have access to the car."

"They do tune-ups every six months," he continued, "and give their cars a diagnostics every six months as well. So their cars are in the shop at least once every three months. Most of their employees also service their POVs and gas up at the same Caltex near their embassy."

Frank went on. "Bresnehan's wife is Thai, and he's been thinkin' of locatin' employment on the economy and getting' out of the military 'right here in River City!'".

Changing the subject, Frank commented "Ah almost forgot to tell ya Don, there's a message from 'The Quakers' in your safe. Dick dropped it by earlier today."

I opened my safe and took out the secret message, marked 1357-1. It read: *"Per your rfi, the following additional information on Alexandra Dombrovsky: SUBJECT has been assigned to the RE Intelligence Collection Office as a potential Agent Handler. She will be attached to the American Information country team, where she will be working with our mutual targets. Our agency has no specific activity in mind for this target at this time. We will forward all personal data regarding both DOMBROVSKY's to your office, and are prepared to coordinate OI on request."*

"Did you see this?" I asked Frank. Not waiting for a response, I went on to complain that "the 'Quakers' are always willing to pass on something useless to us, without our even asking. But if she was a worthwhile target, we'd have to pay hell to get OI!"

"Yup," Frank agreed. "That's the one of the bennies of being in charge."

"I think we ought to go for it Frank. Let's come up with a real sexy dangle on this – assuming she's worth it, of course. Let's request her husband's dossier and see what type of access he has too."

"Great idea," Frank was already rolling paper into his typewriter. "I'll write up the request. We Might as well request OI on both of them."

After an hour or war-gaming the request, it was ready for Mike's comments and Leon's approval. Mike and Leon were in a closed-door session in Leon's office, so we would pass it through them first thing tomorrow morning.

At 1620 hours, traffic was light as Frank and I departed the office from the front entrance, going to the Trolley for a quick beer. DG's signal was still on the window from last night's contact, and as we walked toward the sidewalk, I noticed DG standing at curbside. He was waving, and a familiar Toyopet was slowing to pick him up. As the Toyopet slowed, DG slipped a translucent envelope into the shopping bag he was carrying.

As they pulled away from the curb, Frank warned "Hold up – there comes two more!" Traffic was moving, so we allowed Ivan's convoy to pass on by.

Ivan made a quick turn into the Chokchai parking lot as Frank and I crossed the street. From the doorway of the Trolley, we watched as Ivan made his U-turn and came back out just in time to see his C/S team going inside. Recognizing the common error, we both laughed at their antics. "Dumb shits!" Frank commented excitedly.

Two hours earlier, Ivan had been sitting at his desk. On his light-gray, painted cement walls were two new travel posters, framed in dark-bronzed aluminum frames. From his perch, Ivan was directly facing the one of San Francisco's Golden Gate Bridge. The second, a poster of Varshavskoye Chaussee crossing the Moskva River, was hung on the wall behind his desk, and would be clearly noticeable from the entrance to his office. Ivan guessed that the second poster photo had been taken from the roof garden of the Balchug Hotel, looking northward into Red Square.

Although he had never been one to 'decorate' his office, Ivan had to admit the travel posters seemed a little more appealing to the eye than blank walls. Ivan's greatest joy in this transformation was in the thought that the camera mounted over his desk would be continuously directed at and focused on the Golden Gate, and anyone monitoring would be obliged to always gaze at that image on their screen. He had also purchased a travel poster of the Eiffel Tower, and another of Big Ben in London. When they return from the framers, they would be hung on the opposing walls on either side of these two.

It was already past 1430 hours, and DG would soon be waiting outside the Chokchai. Ivan hoped DG would have some information for him, but he had not pushed the issue at their last meeting. *"Sometimes"*, he thought *"It's better to plant the seed than to ask directly for something. Besides, DG was smarter than average. He'll deliver."* he thought confidently. *"Patience is a virtue."*

Ivan walked to his table and looked over the glasses. He immediately picked up one, noticing lipstick marks on the rim. He was angry at the thought. Only one person came to mind instantly as the culprit – only one person in the entire embassy wears that ugly bright red shade of lipstick. Most of the female employees of the embassy wore only a little makeup, and their lipstick was barely a subdued pink. It was conservative and appealing. Alexandra was the only person who dared to cover her entire face with a façade of clashing red and white. She reminded him of a clown. Yes... a clown.

Ivan picked up his phone and called the galley. Without exchanging amenities, he blurted out "You need to exchange my drinking glasses for clean ones immediately!" He hung up.

Ivan stood at the doorway staring at his watch. In less than 45 seconds, the maid turned the corner into the hallway carrying a rack of clean glasses, and broke into a half-run when she saw Ivan waiting. "This is totally unacceptable." Ivan started, as she placed clean glasses on the tray.

"I am so sorry, Sir," the maid responded apologetically, moving the monk's-bowl ice bucket to the new tray.

"Imagine," Ivan exclaimed, "If I should give this glass to someone important. Imagine the embarrassment. How could this have been overlooked?"

"I'm so very, very sorry," she repeated. "I'll see to it – it doesn't happen again. I shall personally take care of it."

Ivan looked at her closely, deciding that it was not her shade of lipstick on the glass. "See that you do…" He ordered. Then somewhat ashamed of his outburst, Ivan added "….please." The redness in her cheeks began to fade.

As she walked from Ivan's office, she turned slightly and said "Your hors d'oeuvres' will be on time at precisely 1730." She turned and walked away.

Watching her as she hurried down the hallway, Ivan vaguely recalled that the maid had been hired for her linguistic abilities. She spoke French, German, English and Thai with native fluency. He had also noted also that her Russian language abilities were more than just passable. She appeared Eurasian, and her natural hair color was a shade darker than blond. Her eyes were dark blue. She was petite in build and her posture erect. For a moment before she disappeared around the corner, Ivan thought of how she would look in a bikini. *"Such a talent!"* he thought. With her out of sight, he was able to control his thoughts; but he did wonder if he had called the galley and then waited at the door, just to see her come running. He shook his head, trying to shake her image loose, and walked to the table to pour his first single shot of the day. *Ohranj,* over two ice cubes. *"I'm starting this habit earlier every day!"* he thought. *"It's only a little past 1430!"*

Turning toward the camera, Ivan lifted his glass "Salute'." he said aloud. The camera was not on.

Ivan returned to his desk, sat and began looking over the opened file folder on his desk. The outside was marked with a SECRET marking, along with a caveat designating the file as 'eyes only', which meant it was to be released only to those whose names were on the attached list and that special precautions should be taken to preclude observation by anyone whose name appears within the context of the dossier itself. Inside, it was entitled 'Alexandra Voronin/Dombrovsky'. The file was being passed to the agent handlers with whom she would undoubtedly be working in the near future, for their perusal. Looking at the list of names affixed to the cover, Ivan observed that The Ambassador, the Security Officer, Alex Topov, Sergei Zuyev, and two members of Internal Affairs had already initialed the list. Ivan smiled as he looked at the markings. Both Alex and Sergei had signed with a large minus mark (-). He would follow their established pattern.

The first portion of the file pertained to Dombrovsky himself. He was described as a meek man of above average intellect. Dombrovsky had always graduated early in every phase of his formal education, and in the top of his class, whether the course of study be elementary or advanced, military or government. Dombrovsky had an instinctive grasp for attention to detail. He was an 'Honorary' Colonel in the reserve Officer's Corp, and had attended the Candidates school just before coming to Bangkok. He had been awarded a Majority on graduation, and the honorary rank when assigned to his current position. He was truly on a fast track to success.

"Wow!" Ivan pondered. *"To see such a young man being awarded the rank of Colonel – albeit 'honorary'. Father would turn over in his grave."*

From page three, the file was completely devoted to Alexandra. Covering various levels of her education, it became obvious why she had waited to marry Dombrovsky. He was naturally gifted, and a virtual sponge when it came to retention of information. On the other hand, her grade average would be somewhere around a 2 or 3 on any American Academic scale. She was mediocre at best. Her language proficiency scores were extremely low. Ivan was not surprised.

Aside from her father's letters of recommendation, the file contained numerous recommendations from her list of supervisors and superior officers throughout her career. Most were filled with 'glitter litter', and as Ivan read the file, he became aware of a pattern. Her superiors had been anxious to get rid of her. Not one had requested she be retained in her current position. From each of her assignments, she was being promoted outward. Every superior officer felt she had attributes which would be better suited for assignment to the KGB. In her favor, she was described as a 'leader', and as a 'controller'.

Alex did not like her already. Reading her dossier made him wonder how his own file had looked when he was first assigned to Bangkok, and how the other members of the American team had affixed their signatures.

He placed his minus mark after his name and slid the file through the 'out' slot in the wall. The Ambassador had arranged these 'in' and 'out' slots in the wall for easing distribution of sensitive information between his own office and those of key personnel. *"They were convenient for distribution,"* Ivan thought, *"but far too convenient for eavesdropping as well."* Every office around the perimeter had a 'direct deposit' slot into the Internal Affairs office. They controlled distribution. Glancing up at the camera, Ivan realized it had been turned on. On his desk was the empty glass, and Ivan decided that he would not pleasure himself with a refill until later, when he returned with DG. It was 1510. He had already called DG's office number and informed him that he would be passing by the main entrance to the Chokchai building between 1615 and 1630 hours. DG would wait at the curb.

This would be an important meeting for evaluating DG. The American Team would review the reports and decide if DG was worth keeping. If he was to be terminated, Ivan would begin making plans for transfer and the team would continue to work as usual. It would be a clean break. If, as Ivan expected, the rest of the team members approved the project, it would be designated 'long-range'. The budget for the operation would be increased, and Ivan would have to rewrite his operational plan. Ivan was so confident, he had already planned a trip away from Bangkok for DG, during which he would do his best to solidify their affiliation, and hopefully develop a situation or two which would secure their relationship. "Blackmail" is not a word Ivan likes to apply, but it is very effective, and the hierarchy normally considers it to be most appropriate. There must be a basis however to justify resorting to the use of blackmail.

It was nearing 1545 now, and time for Ivan to walk out through the reception room and into the parking lot. Out of sight of the camera, he carried the used glass into the washroom, where he rinsed it thoroughly and dried it with a cotton towel. He replaced the glass on the table and glanced around the office one more time.

Ivan hated to enter the reception area when Dombrovsky's wife was at the front. She always tried to make chitchat in English. But, he understood that she was to familiarize with the comings and goings of the American sources, so he would put up with it for the time being.

Ivan walked slowly into the reception area. As he turned toward the front entrance, he glanced at the monitor. The screen read 'REWIND'. This meant that someone had monitored his departure. They would rewind the tape and then push the 'Record' button when he returns with DG. He glanced at Alexandra who was busy taking fist-sized bites of what appeared to be a sausage sandwich, and gulping suds from a liter bottle of Thai soda. Ivan was sure he could smell the bratwurst from 15 feet away. Fortunately, her mouth was too full to talk. She looked in his direction and waved her sandwich at him.

Ivan descended the front steps, walked into the parking lot, and turned toward his car. The Toyopet had been washed and parked back in its space. Ivan assumed the listening device was in place. He started the engine and drove from the lot at 1552. As he passed the security shack, Ivan glanced in his rearview mirror to notice one Nissan and one Isuzu following him through the gate. Once on Sukhumvit Road, they backed off to allow the requisite 2 to 3 car distance. His counter-surveillance team already knew the precise route Ivan would take. Ivan could not have noticed the AA team cautiously following well behind all three of them.

Moving northwest, he was passing the Chokchai building at 1610 hours, so Ivan continued for four more minutes, before stopping to have his car gassed up. His counter surveillance team took up positions to follow him back south, and the American team passed unnoticed, continuing north. By the time he paid for his gas, Ivan retraced his route and saw DG standing at curbside waiting for him, envelope and shopping bag in hand. DG recognized Ivan's car and waved 'innocently'. Ivan slowed to a near stop, then DG opened the door and jumped inside.

Ivan accelerated away, asking "So where would you like to take dinner today?"

"It's your choice," DG stated. "I have the rest of the day off, but I'm not really all that hungry." He was placing his 'gifts' in the back seat.

"Great!" Ivan remarked, "I'm not so hungry either, but what say we go to the International Market?"

"Sounds good to me," DG responded. "They've got a good smorgasbord there."

DG had responded just in time for Ivan to make an unsignaled turn into the Chokchai lot in order to execute a turn-around. As they exited the lot, Ivan observed his counter-surveillance teams as they were both turning into the lot, reacting to his most provocative move.

"How clumsy!" Ivan thought, rolling his eyes.

"It's THEM!" DG thought, as he looked away.

There was no American surveillance following in and out of the parking area. With the green light, Ivan drove directly across Sukhumvit road and into the an alley which took them southwest to the intersection of Withayu Road, where Ivan took another turn northerly, circling back to Sukhumvit Road. DG was temporarily lost, but Ivan drove confidently, and apparently fully aware of the route he was taking. When he reached Sukhumvit, Ivan again turned right and drove directly to the parking area near International Market. DG handed the envelope and shopping bag to Ivan as they were exiting the car, and the smiling Ivan placed them in the box inside the trunk.

Once Inside the market, they lined up at the smorgasbord food line and walked through, selecting their respective lunches and drinks. Ivan chose the crispy deep fried catfish, spicy pilaf, a mixed salad and a small half-pint of chilled Sweet Sake; while DG selected a chicken pot pie, the same salad and a *Fosters (Light)* beer. They were seated at a table near the entrance to the market area. While they ate Ivan managed to keep the conversation personal, jumping from subject to subject and finally landing on DG's musical career. "Your performance was simply marvelous last night," he started. "My Mom may not wash her hand for a week!"

DG blushed. "That was my first bouquet."

"How about the screamers – were they your first too?" Ivan joked.

"Yup," DG answered. "I'll bet my face was red."

"It was." Ivan stated truthfully. "Tell me, does Irene ever attend your performances?"

"She was there for the grand opening, but I do all my practicing at home, and I think she kinda gets tired of hearing me play. My neighbors don't seem to mind though. I go for the 'easy listening' stuff – so there's not much to dislike."

"Me, too." Ivan agreed. "Mom's right you know, your music makes us homesick for San Francisco. Mother and Father used to go to the 'Hungry Eye', where there were lots of folk singers." He mentioned the famed 'Kingston Trio'. "Those were happy sounds." Ivan reminisced that when they returned to Russia, his parents had shipped literally hundreds of records, and that his mother had often played them when they entertained guests who had also resided in the US. "Now that she's here in Bangkok temporarily, she's busy replacing all her old worn-out records with pirated tapes."

They joked and told stories for a full hour before Ivan suggested they go to the embassy and "talk" for awhile. DG agreed, saying he was ready for some air conditioning. The market area was hot.

Forty minutes later, they arrived at the RE gate. Ivan was waved through and he parked in his designated slot. He retrieved the items from the trunk and they entered through the main door.

Alexandra was still seated behind the counter reading files. She greeted them loudly. "Hallo, you, Sir."

DG responded first, saying "Yes, Ma'am. Hello to you." He looked at Ivan.

"Hello, Alexandra. I spoke to you earlier, but you were occupied." He smiled.

Alexandra' eyes crossed for a short moment while she tried to decipher the word 'occupied'. Then she responded, "Occupied, oh yes, I wass bissy".

Ivan couldn't help but smile again. Had he opened his mouth to speak again, he would unquestionably have burst into laughter. He and DG turned toward the hallway as Alexandra pouted as though she felt she was being ignored. Ivan glanced at the monitor. An enlarged picture of the Golden Gate Bridge was now being projected on the screen. He smiled again to himself. Whoever was operating the camera had zoomed in on the travel poster.

As they walked along the windowed hallway, Ivan noticed the technicians moving toward his car, so he picked up his pace, draped his arm over DG's shoulder and ushered him toward the office. Ivan was happy he'd not discussed anything operational during the drive. Now he was looking forward to the excuse for refilling his glass.

As they entered the office, the maid coordinated her arrival. She darted ahead of them to hold the door. She placed the hors d'oeuvres' on the table and turned two crystal glasses upright on the linen cloth. "There you are gentlemen." she said politely, smiling in DG's direction. She then curtsied slightly and departed.

"Wow, " DG said approvingly, "Why isn't <u>she</u> the new receptionist?

"I agree, DG" Ivan was laughing. "We seem to have the same idea. You have excellent taste," he continued as though he was also complimenting himself.

Ivan placed the gifts on his desk, saying "So how's everything at home; and how is Irene doing?"

"She's always fine," DG answered. "She's leaving with her troupe on the 10th of November. Her performance in Tokyo will begin on 11 November and run through the 22nd - Monday through Friday. Then, she'll have one free weekend to go shopping in Tokyo before she has to fly back." DG had given Irene's complete schedule in one neat paragraph. Ivan looked at the items on his desk and decided to open the shopping bag first. It contained the neatly-wrapped bottle of Hennessy's VSOP. As he unwrapped the package, Ivan appeared overwhelmed.

"DG, you needn't have done this." He was impressed.

"I just wanted you to know how much I appreciated your generosity," DG replied. "Besides," he said, "I bought it from the Class-Six store. That's much more reasonable than buying it from outside."

Ivan removed the bottle from the box and neatly placed it on top of the liquor shelf, above the rest of his collection. "This is entirely too much, but it would be an insult not to accept such a gracious and generous gift." He joked. "It's just beautiful, DG. Thank you again, so very much. Shall we open it?" Ivan offered.

"Oh no, please," DG said without hesitation. "Let's keep it for a special occasion."

"Good! And I agree." Ivan responded happily. "Then, how about some *"Ohranj"*, he suggested.

"It works for me!"

Ivan poured their two glasses, and then turned; glancing at the camera's glowing recording light.

"Toast!" Ivan said loudly. He wanted to be sure his voice was recording.

"Na Zdorovie!" DG responded. "Now, let's see – 'Khorosho poshla!" DG continued. "How's that?"

"That was great – Perfect! Now remember those phrases for your trip to Moscow when you go there to play." Ivan encouraged him.

"I'm afraid I'll have to learn a lot more," DG predicted. "I truly would like to be able to do that tour some day."

"Don't worry, your music is excellent. That will get you through." He went on "You know what the famous American musician Louie Armstrong once said? 'Music is the international language of love.', and he was so right"

Ivan sat at his desk and looked at the document. "Wow, DG, you've done it again." He complimented. "And all these organizations; are they participating in the exercise?"

"They are all involved one way or another," DG confirmed, but whether they are going to be actively involved in the exercise, I really don't know. Many of them, I'm sure are just administrative support groups. For example," he pointed at one, "This is a personnel group and their responsibility is only in coordinating personnel actions and insuring the participants are paid."

"This unit here," DG was pointing to the medical readiness company, "is a medical unit-on-call. They are required only to stand by in case of some emergency. They can arrange helicopter medical evacuation, and that sort of thing."

"That's just fine, DG," Ivan spoke out. "I'm sure the Stars and Stripes will eventually print the whole story. This is certainly newsworthy, and that's all I needed."

Then Ivan continued, trying to disguise his excitement by sounding casual.

"Is there any organization – such as a news organization – that will be monitoring the exercise, and reporting it to the press?"

"Of course," DG responded. Then pointing to the top of the distribution list, he went on to say "Right there on top is the "Armed Forces Radio and Television Network. Logic tells me that they will be the reporting agency."

"Of course they will." Ivan responded.

Just as Ivan was about to ask about Intelligence organizations involved, he noticed that all three – Army, Navy and Air Force Intelligence organizations were listed in the distribution paragraph. No need to ask; no need to question the obvious. To do so might just make DG more sensitive.

Ivan put the documents into an empty folder, opened his desk drawer and took out two more pieces of sheet music and placed them in the envelope along with another small envelope. But before passing it back to DG, Ivan changed the subject.

"Now about our trip… Can you take a few days off work?"

"I can take three weekdays in conjunction with a weekend of my choice." DG replied. "My boss likes me, and has been urging me to take some time off before the holidays and the upcoming exercise.

Once it begins, most of my office will be busy providing support to the exercise, and time off will be difficult." DG realized that their 'night out' had just been upgraded to a trip.

"That's fantastic!" Ivan seemed happy. "I've been making some enquiry, and have been thinking of going on a road trip up country for a couple of days. If you would like, we can travel up to Lop Buri, stay on the highway to Nakhon Sawan, and go all the way to Lampang and Chiang-Mai. I hear it's beautiful up there almost any time of year. Chiang-Mai is in the mountains. It's a bit cooler than Bangkok, and I hear the fishing is great."

"Wow," DG was surprised. "Isn't that a long way to go?"

"It's less than 400 miles one way," Ivan answered. "Not such a long trip; perhaps the same distance as San Francisco to L.A. The roads are good, and I'll have one of our embassy sedans." Ivan then brought up DG's second employment, saying "Will it be a problem at the King's Palace?"

DG noticed that Ivan used 'miles' instead of 'kilometers', or 'klicks'.

"There's no problem with the King's Palace, DG answered, "My contract is such that I can take vacation on my own schedule. They only request a few days notice in order to arrange for another band." He went on, "It sounds like a very unique opportunity, but you know, I'll have to clear the travel with my boss, and call in every couple of days while I'm gone."

Sensing a slight hesitance on DG's part, Ivan explained "Don't forget, as I promised, this trip is on me. I've been planning a trip anyway, and taking you along is certainly no burden. We'll call it a Christmas gift. It's a chance for both of us to get away for a few days. I for one will not miss the Bangkok traffic." He went on, "It's no problem getting hotel reservations and such. As you know, I have a little pull." He smiled adding "We're just a couple of guys taking a road trip."

"I can give you a tentative 'OK'," DG stated truthfully. "But if something should come up; for example if my wife's trip is cancelled or some emergency should arise, I'd have to call it off, you understand."

"Of course I understand," Ivan replied immediately. "It's the same for me. But for now, let's go ahead and make the plans." Ivan gestured toward the hors d'oeuvres'.

Then in a confidential and rather reflective tone, Ivan went on to say "You know, being a foreigner and raised in the US, I sometimes find it rather difficult to make friends. Meeting with you occasionally is the highlight of my week. You and I have so much in common, it just seems so natural for us to be friends, and whenever possible to do things together. It would be a shame to let this opportunity pass us by."

"I couldn't agree more," DG said.

Ivan was already standing and pouring another pair of drinks. "How do you like the posters?" he asked, casually changing the subject.

"I noticed them right away," DG answered. Then, gesturing to the poster of the Varshavskoye overpass, he asked "Where was this one taken?"

Ivan handed the drink to DG, and then explained the Russian poster, pointing out a portion of Red Square in the background.

"You know this one of course," Ivan turned, pointing to the Golden Gate Bridge poster. "When I was but a boy, my parents took me to the very spot from where this photograph was taken. We would travel across the bridge from the Presidio, and then take the exit to Sausalito. Instead of going into Sausalito though, we would often turn left and go through the one-way tunnel toward the military bases out there on the small peninsula of Point Bonita. The beaches were open to the public, and we could picnic there. I have wonderful memories of those times."

Note: Coincidentally, the famous photo of the Golden Gate Bridge was taken from the crest of the mountain in Marin County, across from the Fire Control Area Main Gate, for "A" Battery. This was the very site at Fort Barry California where I was assigned as a Military Policeman, fifteen years earlier.

To Ivan, the entire conversation was meant to appear on camera as though he were confiding his true feelings to DG, in an attempt to gain his confidence and trust. As far as he could tell, it was working.

"You really do miss those days, don't you Ivan?" DG asked.

"As I have said many times, 'I'm practically an American'." Ivan responded casually.

"You've never mentioned your Dad." DG said, "Does he work in the diplomatic field too?"

Ivan looked DG over with a quick calculating glance. Deciding again that his initial evaluation of DG as a naïve young boy was accurate, he answered, saying "Father was a dedicated, career diplomat who died much too young. He was but 54 years old, and had not yet finished his career, when that terrible disease took his life. Father never complained, but our doctors had said his lungs must have been giving him much pain. He had quit the smoking habit many years earlier, but cancer has a way of coming back to haunt you. Father had suffered from pulmonary problems for decades. He coughed incessantly. Whenever he returned to Russia his condition seemed to worsen."

"I'm sorry." DG said with all the compassion he could muster. "I had no idea, and didn't mean to invade your private memories."

"Actually, it's good to talk about it some times," Ivan responded. "I miss my father, and so does my mother, for sure."

Ivan raised his glass, and they toasted in silence.

It was a convenient time to change the direction of the conversation, and Ivan spoke again.

"Mother was really impressed with your music. In two weeks she'll be returning to Moscow – just in time for the winter weather." he stated frankly.

"I told her I'd put some music on tape for her, and I can get it to you by next week – maybe even before she leaves." DG suggested, hoping to set the exact date and time for their next meet.

"I hope it's no trouble..." Ivan started.

"None at all", DG answered ". As a matter of fact, I've already made several tapes with the band; all I would need to do is consolidate and update. I could easily put 60 minutes of the show on the tape, and throw in another studio-recorded tape."

Ivan was already replenishing their drinks. Gesturing for DG to take a seat at the table, Ivan continued the conversation. "Wonderful! So, can we plan our trip for 13 November then?"

"That works." DG answered. "And if we can meet again in a week, I'll give you the tape for your Mother."

"Wonderful!" Ivan sat down beside the table.

Ivan noticed the tape had stopped, and was not yet being rewound. That meant they were changing the tape. Seconds later, the red light came back on. Since Ivan did not want this meeting to end so abruptly, he continued talking casually with DG for another 45 minutes. Gradually, DG's drinking became sips, but Ivan continued to drink each glass in one or two quick gulps.

The ensuing conversation was totally of a non-operational nature, and they talked of their respective childhood periods. DG's life story had been simple. He was born in Portland Oregon, and had grown up on the Miles family farm. His marriage was ideally decided to his childhood sweetheart. He joined the military, and eventually worked in the personnel division and travel branches, finally being assigned to MACTHAI.

Ivan's childhood memories differed from DG. He envied DG for his American heritage, and at one point said "As an American you have the world at your beckoning, and you still have a bright future, full of choices and decisions that will expose you to an entirely new world at every turn; a life of excitement and intrigue. For me, my epitaph has been written. I followed my father's guide and walked in his shoes. I have but one choice in life, and that is to continue in the same direction. That is unfortunate – but," he paused, "it is also …acceptable."

Ivan glanced up to notice the red light was still on. As the two talked of their dissimilar cultures, Ivan stated that "at least fate has brought us together, and I'm happy for that." He then began changing the subject again, suggesting "Let's bring some toys along on the trip. "I'll bring plenty of cameras so we can take some memorable pictures. What do you think DG, should we bring a couple of horns?"

Before DG had a chance to respond, Ivan thought that when the ambassador hears this recording, surely, he'll make another joke about playing with each other's horns. He decided to negate the suggestion, and said "Well, maybe not. I wouldn't want to carry them around in the car for those days, and certainly we wouldn't want to leave them in our hotel rooms."

"You're probably right," DG agreed, adding "but I do like the camera idea."

"Good, then it's settled. I'll even bring along that toy I told you about. You know - the 'rollover camera'."

"Great!"

"Na Zdorovie." They toasted again in unison.

Ivan drove as they departed the embassy complex at 1930 hours. His driving was not impaired by the amount of *Orhanj* he had consumed.

"The entire conversation had lasted more than three hours," DG thought, *"and virtually nothing had been accomplished."*

Ivan's feelings were exactly the opposite. Confident of the pending long-range approval, he thought *"How good this meeting went. We're moving along smoothly now."*

On the way back to the Chokchai building, Ivan continued their conversation. He knew the voice-activated recorder was recording their conversation, and wanted to make it sound good. The 15 minute drive involved a discussion of their favorite music, their ideological beliefs, and even religion.

"It's almost uncanny?" Ivan was commenting. "We were born into such very different societies, but when it gets right down to the nitty-gritty, we can be so philosophically similar. I can tell," Ivan continued, "that you are a man of principle – as am I. We can't help it; we were just raised that way."

"How true," DG responded. "That's the way I feel too." But DG was only being acquiescent, because deep down, he knew that the ideology which shaped their separate personalities must be very, very different in so many ways; but alike because Ivan had grown up in the 'US of A'.

As they approached the Chokchai building, DG said "Actually, you can let me off on this side of the road. I really don't mind walking across the street."

"I must turn around anyway," Ivan protested, "I might as well turn around at the light and drop you off at curbside."

Ivan drove the few yards up the street, and turned around at the next light. He drove back and turned on his flashers as he stopped in the traffic for DG.

Reaching into the back seat, DG retrieved his envelope and then stepped out onto the sidewalk. "See you next week," he said smiling. "Thanks for everything."

"I'll give you a call for sure." Ivan answered and waved.

Ivan reached into the glove compartment, located the switch and turned off the recorder. When he arrived at the embassy, he retrieved the tape from the device and walked back inside through the side entrance, bypassing the reception desk. He listened to the tape one time, and then rewound it.

"Perfect!" he complimented himself.

Ivan sat at his desk and began typing his new proposal for utilization of DG as a long-range agent. He sat and stared at the blank wall to his left, daydreaming of his awards ceremony and the recognition he could receive for the successful recruitment of an asset with such potential as DG. He shook his head to rid the image, and went back to typing. He would brief the embassy staff and his co-workers on the project Saturday morning. A knock at the office door shocked Ivan from his semi-trance. The distribution lady was delivering his package – the framed Eiffel Tower and the Big Ben Posters had arrived.

"Sports are my life." Bill Tanner was saying. The three of us, Bill, my friend the clown and I were seated at an outdoor dining table

along the waterfront in South Beach, Miami. Grinning from ear to ear, the clown was enjoying the bikini-clad wonders strolling along the walkway, moving gracefully from table to table and chatting with customers.

Suddenly, the scene magically changed. We three were back in Bangkok, seated at the International Market. An aroma of coffee filled the air; and the smell of fresh Danish pastry filled my senses with a flavor of sugar and cinnamon.

"You hungry?" I asked the clown. He nodded gleefully.

"Help your self then." I offered. The clown picked up the plate and placed it on the table in front of him. I watched as he devoured the cinnamon rolls. I wanted to express my anger at his greed; I wanted to choke this creature with my bare hands.

Then I awoke. Everything came back in a flash. It was Saturday. I had awakened at 0430 and put on a pot of coffee before showering. The shower was quick and refreshing; and as I stepped out, I could hear the coffee maker beginning to percolate. My small refrigerator was filled with a bottle of wine, a liter of Chokchai milk, a package of Chokchai butter, and a package of four cinnamon rolls I had purchased from the nearby *Pastry Shoppe*. The bottom shelf held one tub of pre-whipped cream. Unable to ignore the cinnamon rolls, I removed one from the package and placed it in the warming oven. I set it on two minutes and pushed the *'start'* button. I also removed the tub of whipped cream. I then set about crushing the three small trays of ice. Placing the pebbles in a one-quart Zip-loc, I put them back into the freezer, along with three trays of fresh, filtered water. I then returned to the bedroom and lay on my bed. Awaiting the final perking sounds from Mister Coffee, I had fallen asleep. The aroma of coffee and the warming cinnamon roll had influenced my dream.

Now, awake and alert, in two minutes I managed to dress in casual khakis, my favorite white cotton pullover 'Chiang-mai' shirt and tan sneakers. Finger-combing damp hair, I sat and poured the first cup of sludge, and added a dollop of whipped cream. *"Cream and sugar in one neat scoop."* I justified the indulgence. The cinnamon roll had dried while I slept, so I sacrificed the sweetened crumbs to the balcony birds.

Although it was early November, the forecast was calling for a hot, humid afternoon, with both temperature and humidity in the high eighties. If I timed everything properly, Bill and I could conduct this pre-contact briefing and be having a beer somewhere along the way back by the time it really warms up.

The *Bangkok Post* made its surreptitious entry under my door at 0530 hours. I immediately picked it up, turned to the local sports page schedules and located the amateur tennis schedules for the international Sportsman's Club. There it was, with two matches scheduled for William Tanner, USA; and two matches scheduled for Alex Topov, USSR. The winners of these two, along with another set of winners would be lined up for several sets in the semi-finals and subsequent winners would move into the finals.

According to sports editor Bob Marley's article, he had been watching both the Russian and American contenders. He wrote that they were professional-level tennis players, and the final match, expected to be between the two of them, would be filmed for presentation on a local - yet unidentified TV channel. The *Post* displayed photos of both men. Bill was shown with both feet off the ground, serving; and Alex was depicted executing what appeared to be a difficult return. Neither photo was necessarily complimentary. Their listed physical attributes and numerical standings were almost identical.

Dispatch!

I could not have been more prepared for the meeting, and at 0600 departed the complex, driving my Corona. All of our operatives' cars had been swept for tracking/listening devices this past week, and the temporary safe-site at the River Bend Hotel had been swept again, yesterday. Driving south on Sukhumvit Road, I stopped long enough to retrieve the room key from Frank's desk at the office, and then continued toward the International Market to meet with Bill. I had offered my travel plan to Dick for his team to practice, and was confident they would be in attendance. They were.

As I approached the parking lot, I observed the unit surveillance vehicles in place. One was on the street covering the exit and able to commit a follow-on in either direction. The other was in the lot, awaiting our arrival. At this point, the team would not know which car Bill and I would take after breakfast, but I noticed they had alerted as expected when I entered the lot. I selected a parking slot near the exit and walking into the market area, saw the surveillance team maneuvering into a better position. Bill was just now parking in the slot they had vacated.

I was still hungry for cinnamon rolls, and stood in line staring spellbound at the oversized, fresh, calorie-filled cinnamon, sugar and heavily buttered, rolled pastry in front of me. They seemed hypnotic.

"You're not really thinking of eating something like that, are you now?" Bill's voice interrupted the air.

"No, not me." I lied, hesitatingly.

"Well, I am!" Bill remarked, grinning widely. "I'm going to need the energy." He joked.

"Actually, I was thinking about it." I admitted. "But, I've a package of cinnamon rolls ageing in my fridge. When they're just about right, then I'll indulge. For now, I think I'll do some Danish and milk. After all, they're just as bad." I grinned.

We shook hands, then both opted for the continental breakfast - croissant, O J, a bowl of fresh fruit, and of course, another cup of coffee. I immediately recognized the delicious flavor of brewing coffee as either *Blue Mountain* or *Ban Me Thuot.* Both are popular in Bangkok.

We picked a table convenient to both the windows and the exit, and seated ourselves. In line, each of our identified surveillance AA team members picked up a bowl of fruit, coffee and an extra bag of selected doughnuts, and found seats along the front wall. Although they were seated together, I knew they would depart separately and carry their donuts to separate vehicles for snacks along the way, or for their respective team partners.

Bill was excited and talked constantly for the first 10 minutes about everything but the project. He was being careful not to broach that subject. Suddenly, he seemed to realize he had been doing all the talking and said "Hey, it's your turn. How have things being going?"

"Great! I'm doing my best to gear up for the holidays." I answered. How about your family – are they excited about the Korea trip?"

"Oh, yeah. I'm glad I'm not tagging along though," he stated. "They need this break." He was eating as fast as he was talking. He described his family and said again that they were finally adjusting to life in Bangkok. Tim and Thomas, both chips off the old block were happily engaged in the early stages of a martial arts fantasy. His wife Amy, a devoted mother and partner, lives for their occasional family outings.

I had successfully avoided personal conversation about myself. The AA team members had finished their light breakfasts, and were meandering through the market toward the exit, 'window shopping' along the way.

After breakfast, it was time to leave, and as we walked out of the market toward my car, I observed the teams taking up their positions. I made a mental note to talk to Dick about their tendency to stare at their targets. It is more natural for the surveillants to be standing and facing each other. One operative may also be facing the targets, and the second can then cue on his actions. Patience is a virtue.

As we drove from the parking lot, traffic was picking up, and the team was forced into the third and sixth vehicle positions behind my car. We drove circuitously, and the second, position #6 car lost us enroute. The first car (position # 3) remained on our tail at a safe distance. I assumed that Dick had instructed them to try the surveillance without radios, and due to that suggestion the second car did not immediately recover his position.

Before we reached the River Bend, the second car was back in line, and they were using their transceivers. When they broke off, we parked as usual in the covered stall. We entered and turned on the radio to cover our conversations.

I began by first going over our mutual covers, and congratulated Bill on the tournament selection. He provided me with details, and said he had been watching Alex Topov play. He was complimentary, saying "Alex is an exceptional player. He's quick, accurate, and gets into the 'zone' almost immediately. He rarely loses."

"Good," I remarked, "I've heard he's a real pro, but I've also heard you are better. It's not necessary you beat him. Just try to be good enough to establish some mutual respect. He's competitive, and will likely try to recruit you as a tennis partner first. His interest in you as an intelligence asset will develop once you've established a regular routine and have gotten to know each other." I was quoting from Leon's brief.

Before going any further, I handed him the security and privacy statements to sign, which he read carefully.

"Damn Don, you mean I can't tell anyone about this?" He Joked.

He signed without hesitation. The recruitment was formal.

I talked to him about his role in the upcoming joint exercises, and he explained that he had originally planned to be in the field with the troops, but he said, Colonel Wilson had asked him personally to accompany the staff, and avail himself at headquarters during the exercise period. "What can I do?" he asked. "He's my boss, and he'll likely be the one who approves or disapproves my request for overseas extension."

I was impressed with the Colonel's action, and hoped it was because he wanted Bill's involvement with USI to be successful and didn't want to interfere with our plans.

"Maybe he likes you..." I suggested.

"Fat chance," was Bill's grinning response. "He doesn't 'like' anybody."

The primary purpose of this meeting was to formalize the recruitment, build his confidence and prepare him for the initial contact with Alex. I began by outlining some basic security procedures and stressing our mutual covers. Bill had his own private STU, which would be our primary source of communication. He was already confident, and had an excellent idea as to exactly what would be expected of him.

I introduced the use of signals, at a convenient location to both of us in the event he needed to reach me, or if I needed to talk with him. Although his signals would also be a crayon mark, he practiced with chalk in the hotel room.

Chalk is much easier to remove.

I restated our expectations.

"I realize how anxious you are Bill to make this thing work. But please don't expect overnight success. *Patience is a virtue* - behave normally. Please don't beat him so bad he won't want to meet you again."

416

I complimented him by saying his natural cover of playing tennis is one of the assets that makes him perfect for this initial contact and for follow-up meetings with Alex. "Concentrate on the game, make it good, friendly competition, and let Alex make the next move. Win or lose, he'll probably want to play against you again. He enjoys good competition."

I cautioned him to make sure he doesn't show his hand. He should not appear over-anxious.

"You should act just a little 'stand-offish'. That is, don't avail yourself to Alex too easily, but also don't hold off too much either. Be reserved, and be a little evasive when it comes to commitment. He'll come after you. Let him.

"A beer after the match would be normal and probably expected." I brought out the outline I'd put together on Alex, and Bill and I went over those points of which I wanted him to be aware.

"Expect occasional surveillance" I told him, "both friendly and unfriendly. If you detect surveillance, don't over-react; simply go about your routine duties in a normal manner. Under no circumstances should you attempt to evade surveillance. If you are on your way to a meeting with me, abort that idea, and go shopping for something you need, then go back home or to your office. If you are coming from a meeting with Alex, don't bother with our signals. Wait until you are alone before you do anything operational which could tip them off, then call me as early as possible when you are back in your office – on the STU."

"During the course of the two of you becoming acquainted, casual exchange of your respective biographical data is expected. For the time being, stick to the unclassified job description when discussing your duties. Topov will be seeking some type of motivational or control factors in your personality. We won't make it easy for him." We practiced a cover story for Bill to use, and I cautioned him to keep it as simple and as true as possible.

Bill was acutely aware of the concept. This meeting had established his common sense.

"Begin with a casual acquaintance. Eliminations for the final match will occur on Monday and Tuesday, and the five-game final matches are expected to begin on Thursday. I'm fully confident it will be you versus Alex, and I'll expect a STU call from you sometime near the end of next week. You, my friend, are ready."

On the way back, we first drove 20 minutes further out Sukhumvit, stopping at a beer stall where we drained one ice cold beer before turning back toward the International Market. 10 minutes before arriving at the IM, we passed both of the counter-surveillance team vehicles. None of the surveillants were in sight, but I knew they had taken up position to conduct surveillance detection.

That same day:

Saturday at The Royal Bangkok Sports Club.

"I've seen that guy play tennis", Alex was thinking of his American competition as he showered after going through the six phases on the Yamashita Brand 'Bull-Trainer'. Fifteen minutes each of straining legs, arms, upper-torso, neck, bi and triceps, and another fifteen kilometers at fast pace on the 20 degree elevated Roto-Track had exhausted him. The shower felt refreshing and he was pumped.

Stepping out and catching a glimpse of himself in the full-length mirror caused him to halt and step back to take another look. He was proud of his physique. Posing, he admired his body even more as he flexed, and counted once more the lower-torso ab-lines across his stomach. Over the past few years, he had lost the lower two, and blamed it on the Thai beer he had come to appreciate.

"Ah well," he sighed. "I'm no longer twenty-nine." (He had turned 37 just a month earlier). "But I'm still the best." He bragged to the image in the mirror. Nodding, the image agreed and flexed back at him.

Glancing around to insure he was alone, Alex almost ran into the dressing area. He quickly punched his private guest number into the combination, opened his locker and took out his treasured Mexican-made, black leather cowboy hat, trimmed with a band of silver Pesos. Naked, except for the hat he'd placed on his head, he ran back to the mirror. Grinning, he tilted the hat, and said in a deep voice "Well ... howdy Ma'am".

Now, he wished he'd also purchased the matching black leather boots. *"I wonder if I can find a black, leather jock strap..."* he thought as he grinned to himself.

Having experienced his cheap thrill for the day, Alex returned to the dressing area. He dressed in casual slacks, deck shoes and burgundy jacket bearing the International Sportsman's Club emblem, for his trolling at the American Club on Soi 39 later this evening. He would make a quick stop at the embassy to check his mailbox for messages, and pick up some cash to spend at the club.

As he walked through the lobby area toward the exit, Alex paused to read the new Club History page posted on the bulletin board, which included two new photos of the club. He thought *"The pictures look much better than the old, black and white, life-sized monarchial portraits that used to hang here."* He sat while he read the article.

Still seated in the lobby, Alex recalled his most recent confrontation with his Ambassador. Late Thursday afternoon at Antakolsky's request, they had sat together in front of the security monitor in the Ambassador's office to watch the clandestine meeting between Ivan Romanyev and the American Soldier unfold. It was while watching this meeting that Antakolsky had said:

"You see what can be done? See how Ivan is manipulating this poor simple-minded American soldier? He just passed another *'SECRET'* document to Ivan. Ivan has that dumb turd eating from his hand. This is what you need to be doing! Watch, watch!" Antakolsky ordered, "It's like watching a good movie!"

They sat in near silence watching the two-hour tape. 'Yuri' watched the entire episode with a smile on his face. At one point, Alex started to speak, only to be halted by the Ambassador raising his hand in a signal of silence. Alex had to admit he was impressed with Ivan's smooth approach and how well it must be working. He envied Ivan's English fluency, and his natural ability to control the situation. *"Except for his love of 'Ohranj',"* Alex thought *"Ivan seems so... American!"*

Finally, the meeting was over, and the Ambassador turned to Alex. "Yes, Mr. Topov. You were saying..."

"I can do that – that's just simple shit. Besides," Alex continued, "this project just fell into Ivan's lap. The guy was a walk-in! You'll see, Yuri. I'm still the best."

This time, the person facing Alex was not nodding in agreement. Instead, the red-faced Ambassador stared at Alex. He would never get used to subordinates addressing him by his first name.

Moments later, on his way to the embassy, Alex complained to himself. *"Why do we have to account for every penny we spend? Our budget is clear, and the expenses we have are legitimate; but the Ambassador acts as though we are taking money from his personal funds. He acts as though he's running the operations himself, counting our expenses, disapproving anything he doubts is reasonably justifiable."*

Alex drove through the embassy gate, grimacing as he noticed immediately that the Ambassador's sedan was parked in slot #1. That meant he may have to see him inside. He wanted to avoid more confrontation, but the side entrances were secured on weekends, and he would have to pass by the Ambassador's office located directly behind the reception desk.

Alex parked in his designated #13 slot and got out of his car. The Tech guys were already approaching his vehicle with their long-handled mirrors in hand. Alex grunted to them as they spoke. He didn't like the tech guys either, but their duties were a necessity.

He entered the embassy and as he walked past the new receptionist he noticed the door to the Ambassador's office was opened.

"Oh, Goot day to you, Mr. Topoff." She spoke to Alex.

Again, Alex grunted and walked toward the hallway. *"Why does she have to speak English?"* he wondered. *"She pronounces my name 'Top-off' as though she's filling her gas tank. She's Russian for Christ's Sake!"*

"Suh, you fuhgot to sign the registuh!" She almost yelled.

"Wow!" Alex thought, *"Why does she have to talk so loudly? It's as though she were announcing my arrival! That shrill voice could wake the dead – AND the 'Ambassador!"*

Without immediately responding to her, Alex executed a U-turn and returned to the reception area. He walked to the register and noticed that no-one, not even the Ambassador had signed in.

"The Ambassador also forgot to sign in, Alexandra." He complained, while signing his name.

"He duss not haff to sign in Suh," she smiled. "He's the **Ambassaduh!"**

Anxious to correct her, Alex blurted out antagonistically "Everyone signs in on the weekends. It's the rule!"

He turned to walk into the hallway, and noticed the Ambassador standing in his path, smiling. He stopped abruptly.

"Well done, Topov. Well done." The Ambassador spoke. "So what are you doing for your country today, hmm? Spending more money at the sports clubs, I suppose." He went on, "You know of course, everyone else is out there working. Everyone who is someone is out there practicing their surveillance techniques today!" He went on. "You know also that you were conspicuous by your absence at 0800 hours this morning. You were supposed to be in the meeting with Ivan Romanyev and the rest of your team. Its evaluation time for his project with the American soldier. You know – the successful project...?"

Alex did not respond directly to that remark, and instead said only "I'm doing what's right, and I'd like you to know Yuri, I've got several meetings planned with an American Army Captain over the next few weeks...... He's a tennis player!" He was trying to impress upon the Ambassador that his approach plan was working.

Alex turned and walked into the corridor as the red-faced Ambassador called after him. "I hope he's worth the money, Topov!"

As Alex walked into his office, he spoke under his breath. Quietly he promised himself, *"I'll make this into the best operation yet!"* Then he said aloud "You'll see Yuri." He closed the door.

Removing his cowboy hat, he flung it toward the peg alongside the others in his collection. It landed with perfection on its designated peg.

Alex inhaled slowly, taking in a deep breath. He held it while he counted 10 seconds, and then let it escape through pursed lips. It was part of the relaxation procedures he went through daily, to rid his mind of the confrontational atmosphere at the embassy. "Why," he asked himself, "does this man not like me?" He shook his head. He looked into the mirror facing his desk, ran his fingers through his 'prematurely' thinning blond hair and asked aloud "After all, what's not to like?" The mirror image seemed to agree with him. He then looked at the camera overhead – it was on. Anger turned his face red again.

He glanced around his office. The décor was truly American. His furniture was a combination of hand-carved, maple-stained, early American and Southwest Indian. It more resembled a bar room in an American Western movie than an embassy office. The purpose of this pro-American style was to impress his American sources – of which he currently had none. *"Someday,"* he thought, *"I'll show these guys. All this careful planning will pay off."*

He walked to his concealed, wall-mounted bar, opened the front doors and selected a bottle of *"Jack Daniels"*. From his antique designed, ice-box refrigerator, he took out a tray of cubes and placed two cowboy-boot-shaped cubes in a tumbler and then filled it with JD. He dumped the rest of the ice cubes loosely in a plastic ice bucket in the freezer, refilled the tray and placed it back inside the freezer compartment also.

"This will help." He murmured, as he sat behind his desk. He rolled his chair back to the wall, and placed his head on the pad between the set of long-horns hanging on the wall. To anyone walking into his office, it should appear that the horns were protruding from his head. It had always made Ivan Romanyev laugh, but no-one else had ever noticed.

He gulped half his JD, and closed his eyes momentarily – phase two of his relaxation procedure was now beginning to kick in.

He listened to his heart beat and counted the rate. 66 was acceptable. Now he could get on with his business.

Glancing at his desk, He noticed a pink-colored note. He snatched it up immediately, and noticed the bottom line – "Thank you, Desafred." He recognized the pen-name. He then read the English contents.

"Hey there, Cowboy," the note started, *"I have placed my source's operational file in your filing cabinet. It contains copies of all my proposals, and the reports from my meetings. Please give me your honest appraisal of how this is going. I trust your opinion.*

Keep in mind that he will be transferring (as will I) in a few months. I'm hoping that this one has long-range potential, and that he will be assigned somewhere in the US where he and I can continue our operational relationship.

After you've given your appraisal, please pass it through the other members of our operational staff for their opinions as well. I'm hoping that your first opinion will influence a positive opinion from the rest. I verbally briefed the rest of our team this morning.

Thank You, Desafred.

"Good God," Alex commented aloud, "Ivan even writes good English!" He then smiled at the word "*Desafred*". It was a code for "destroy after reading" they had long since established. He wadded the note and placed it in his 'Gene Autry' ashtray, picked up his 'Roy Rogers' *Zippo* lighter and lit the note. When the note had burned entirely, Alex stirred and divided the ashes into two small piles, dumping half in each of his two trash cans. For a single moment he wondered how anyone could put the faces of Gene and Roy on ashtrays and lighters, when they never smoked. It's almost sacrilegious.

Since he had already seen the 'good movie' in the Ambassador's office, and was aware of the extent of cooperation Ivan was receiving from the American soldier. Without even looking at the file, Alex sat and wrote a lengthy, complimentary recommendation for Ivan's project to be upgraded to 'Long Range'.

"I hope" he thought, *"that he'll remember this when it's my turn."*

He went to the safe, opened it and found the file from Ivan. Another note on pink paper was attached. It read: "*I noticed Friday afternoon that your safe was opened, and you were not present. If at 1530 you had already left, then it was probably an accident. You should be more careful my friend. Desafred.*" He didn't have to sign it, Alex knew Ivan had written the note – and had locked his safe for him.

He destroyed the pink note and placed his letter of recommendation inside the file folder.

Spies without Borders.

Sunday was a fair-weather day. The signs of autumn were in the air. Temperatures were not expected to exceed 85° F, and a cool, but gentle morning breeze was drifting southward at about 40 KPH. On the patio, I'd already poured my ritualistic first coffee, and had managed to dunk half a dry cinnamon roll in my cup before realizing that it was so desiccated, it was drinking my coffee for me. I then burned my thumb and forefinger retrieving the roll; and plopped it on the saucer. In the time it took for me to walk back inside for a fork, my local raven friend had landed on the wooden patio table and was busy eating the coffee-soaked roll.

"Scat!" I shrieked as though I was yelling at the neighbor's cat. Before departing, the defying raven squawked, picked up the remaining dry portion of the roll and flew away.

"He must have wanted it more than I did." I took the saucer of crumbs and coffee and dumped them into the bougainvillea bed, and went back inside. Here at least I could have some required coffee without interruption. Switching the speakers to *'interior'* the sounds of Steve and Eydie's *"Our Love is Here to Stay"* came at me over AFRTS.

"It's OK for Sunday music." I supposed, but something else was missing.

"Maybe some 'Irish' was what the doctor ordered." I spoke to myself aloud.

"Irish music?" I asked myself bewilderedly.

"No, not Irish music." I replied. I poured two ounces of Irish whiskey into a tall glass cup and filled it to 80 percent with the freshly percolated coffee. I then placed a dollop of whipped cream on top and watched as the sweet cream began leaking its way toward the bottom.

I took a long sip. "Yup, that filled the order. Good idea, Doc."

Halfway through 'breakfast' I was trying to decide what I should do when the phone rang. It was Frank.

"Hey there old friend," he started, "What're ya up to doin' today?"

"I had no plans at all. It's a beautiful day. You guys up to anything special?" I asked.

"Well, Ah'm thawin' out some ribs. You feel like comin' over and floatin' a few beers?"

"Sounds good to me. What can I bring?" I was serious.

"Bring yerseff!" Frank ordered. Then, "Anythin's OK. Come over about Noon. We'll make an afternoon of it. Next weeks gonna be busy. This isn't really a party", Frank added, "It'll only be us. It's a family thang."

I checked the fridge for beer – there was plenty.

After 'breakfast', I decided to walk to the bakery/deli down the street and look over their menu for something to take to Frank's. I walked out of the apartment. The only two cars on a virtually empty street were a limousine parked across the way with the motor running. A few meters in front of the limousine a small gray 4-door Isuzu Prince......

I stopped myself from taking a second look, turned right and walked toward the deli. As I moved toward the first truncated entrance – to James S. Lee Tailor Shop - I noticed that the Isuzu had started up and was slowly moving in the same direction as I.

Stepping inside the tailor shop, I watched from behind the painted sign on the front window as the slow-moving Isuzu moved up the street. I was unable to identify the license, but would make note of the car and two passengers. The salesman was alert and curious, so I purchased a needed dress shirt, and a tie that would match my light gray business suit. I had satisfied his curiosity, so I walked out in 10 minutes. The Isuzu was not to be seen, but I immediately recognized one of the Russian Embassy's Datsun Bluebirds parked across the street, 20 yards ahead. Again, two men were seated in the front, and a blond woman was looking out the rear window. She ducked down when she saw me walking in their direction.

"What a pro!" I said to myself facetiously.

After I casually walked 15 seconds past the point, parallel to the Datsun's location, it started up. I walked to the deli, and noticed the car stopped idling as soon as I turned into the doorway

"I wonder where they learned their technique." I already knew the answer.

As soon as I tasted a sample of the fresh potato salad with bacon bits, chopped celery and a few lean chunks of smoked ham, and the required amount of ground black pepper, I made my selection; and also purchased a package of smoked Muenster for myself. I carried a two-liter package of potato salad and the cheese back to keep chilled in my fridge. I first cleared out the remaining two cinnamon rolls, walked onto my patio and broke them into pieces to place on the feeder. Within seconds, my local flock of fearless gold-finch was feasting on the pieces while my favorite raven soared overhead.

After hanging the new shirt and tie in the closet, I called frank, and told him "I picked up some great potato salad; and also picked up some cheese."

'Picked up cheese' meant that I had 'detected surveillance.'

There was a very brief pause.

"You always do more than you have to," Frank grumbled. "Well, bring it all out, and we'll see what we can do with it."

I knew he would decide to go on with our plans; after all, we had made those plans over an insecure line. To cancel would be tipping our hand. It could be fun.

There was no reason at this point to involve anyone else in this venture. It would only expose them to unneeded attention. My only concern was that the Mafioso or perhaps Alexandra, if they in fact were members of the surveillance, would recognize Frank and me from the King's Palace, and make some remote connection with DG. We would be careful.

I packed the beer, cheese and potato salad in my back pack and walked slowly to my car. I casually drove almost directly to Franks place, arriving at 1230 hours. I drove through the opened gate and parked next to Frank's Olds inside his carport. Frank waved and secured the gate behind me. We walked through his house and onto the patio in back where his Bar-B-Q was already fired up. The ribs were still thawing in the overhead oven and Frank's stereo was blaring some God-awful version of Hank Williams' *'Hey, Good-lookin'.* The singer's accent bore a striking resemblance to that of the Filipino "Elvis" at the Windsor Hotel.

"Where did you come across that music?" I asked.

"…'member that Philippine Band down at the Windsor? Well, it's their tape." Frank bragged. "Cost me 15 Baht."

My guess was right. "And well worth it!" I spoke quietly, "75 cents!"

Frank tossed some ribs on the grill, and they began to sizzle immediately as the thawing ice dripped into the coals and caused black steam to rise from the briquettes. We sat on his fiber-plastic yard lounges and Frank opened one of the *Amarits*. I found the bucket of pebbles, filled my glass about half way and poured it full of JWB. It was great.

"Where's the cheese?" Frank asked.

"I left it on the street about two blocks back. It's pretty ripe, I'm sure it'll find its own way here eventually." He knew I was joking, and opened the plastic seal on the Muenster which I had decided to sacrifice for the sake of this soiree.

"Whattya think brought this all up?"

"We've given them no reason to follow us," I began. "It's my guess that it's just a random follow, with no specific target in mind," I answered. "Just practice."

"That's my first guess too," Frank agreed. "Maybe they're goin' through an elimination process, while lookin' for real targets." He went on. "Think we should take 'em fer a joy ride?"

"We probably shouldn't, but I know we will," I opined. "Then again, a drive around the block wouldn't hurt anything. We can go pick up the paper and some more beer...... maybe even stop at the American Club for a quick performance by the *'Lonesome Cowboys Quartet'*." Or, as far as I was concerned, they could sit in their cars and sweat while Frank and I enjoyed a few cold beers.

I spent a few minutes describing the cars, and passengers to Frank.

We sat facing the road and enjoyed the warm sun while partaking of our favorite beverages. Suddenly, without warning, the Datsun Bluebird drove past Frank's wrought-iron gate. The driver and passengers were staring straight ahead.

"That does it!" Frank started, speaking quietly, "We just gotta take 'em for a ride."

"I'm sure they'll all drive by to see what we're up to," I responded, "and then we'll take off to our left, and watch them scramble to get back in line. We don't even have to try hard."

Leon's home was located about one km further down, toward the end of the same lane. It was a dead end, so eventually the Russian Embassy cars would have to return.

"It'll be fun!" Frank replied, "But let's demolish some of them ribs and taters first."

Frank's wife had dutifully turned the rubs a few times while we were talking, so I followed his lead along the table and through the BBQ line, heaping the taters, peas and roasted corn on my plate, before selecting a well-done half-slab to gnaw on. By this time, they even had me saying "taters".

"How can you eat charcoal like that?" Frank queried. "For me, I like meat cooked about 35 seconds over a dim flashlight. Blood's good fer yer heart." The oversized 'Piltdown Man' picked up a full slab of ribs that had barely thawed on the grill, and dropped them onto his platter.

Allan and Jessica, Frank's teenaged son and daughter grabbed a hamburger and hot-dog each. Filling the buns with the required condiments, they piled on the oven roasted fries.

While I sat with Frank and his family, within another 20 minutes a second Datsun with only a driver, and the gray Isuzu also drove past Frank's gate to the right.

"What?!" frank whispered, "no foot surveillance?"

Then, moments later, just as Frank had walked under the shade of the patio cover to pick out another pair of beers from the cooler, a Caucasian couple came strolling casually along the sidewalk, moving in the same direction as the cars. They were dressed in 'Aloha' shirts, white slacks and matching pairs of sneakers. These were the missing passengers from the second Datsun.

"Your prayers have been answered." I murmured. Neither of us made eye contact with them, and likewise, they appeared to be paying no attention to us. Both were carrying bulky 35mm Nikon Cameras. *'Obnoxious'* was the first thought to enter my mind.

Glancing over their attire and demeanor, "These are not pros," I breathed. Frank agreed.

Frank's children were playing 'catch' near the front of the gate, and traffic was picking up along this narrow lane. We still had not seen any of the RE cars depart, and the 'couple' continued strolling down the road. The Limousine did not come down this lane.

Without warning one of the children threw the ball a little too high. It missed the catchers' mitt and bounced once before hitting the fence and rolling into the street. As Allen ran toward the gate, Frank called out.

"I'll get it!" He turned to me grinning. "Never let it be said that I let my kids play in the street." He opened the gate and walked across the sidewalk to the curb where the softball was waiting. As he knelt to pick up the ball, he turned a half circle looking over the surveillance situation.

He tossed the ball to Allen and walked back inside, closing the gate behind.

Sitting back down he said "Here's the situation. All three cars are parked likes 'ducks in a row', and the lovin' couple just got back inside the second Datsun. The cars're all facin' away from us. Around the curve, 50 yards ahead of them the street comes to a dead end just past Leon's place. Ah'm sure they don't even know it – yet." He grinned.

"Great," I responded. It's almost time to go on a beer run."

"Yup!" Frank agreed. "Ya gonna drive that little car of yers?"

"Sure!" I replied, "They've already seen it, parked right here in your yard."

We exited Frank's front garden through the gate, turned immediately left, and drove toward Sukhumvit Road. We recognized none of the male participants who were jumping back into their cars, but Alexandra was unmistakable. Even at a distance of nearly a block away, her dark roots were obvious. The first car drove out into the traffic just as Frank and I turned left, going northwest on Sukhumvit.

10 minutes later, Frank suggested. "The Caltex up ahead on the left has a 'quick stop'. We can pick up our needs, and wait for them to catch up."

We arrived at the Caltex at the intersection of Sukhumvit and Soi 94. Turning in, I glanced to the rear. The two Datsuns and the Isuzu were not yet in sight. Frank got out and went into the store while I watched the road. Two minutes later, sliding into the passenger seat, Frank handed me the *Bangkok Post*. He opened an *Amarit* and we sat.

And we sat.

Another 15 minutes passed before the Isuzu drove by, moving noticeably slower than the rest of the traffic. The passenger was talking into a large, black 'brick'.

We sat for a few more minutes, until the rest of the RE cars had also passed the Caltex. We then exited the station onto Soi #94 by turning left with the traffic. At the first access road, we turned left again and headed southerly, back toward Frank's house.

Almost accidentally, we had lost them completely... again. Eventually, after a few more turns, we arrived back at Frank's and parked back inside his carport. All was quiet for the remainder of the afternoon, until nearly 1700, just as we were starting to clear the picnic table. Frank and I watched from under the covered portion of the patio while one of the Russian Embassy Datsuns drove by slowly. From the back seat, through the rear window, a third member of the party took a photo of Frank's gate as they passed by. About 150 feet up the street, the sedan executed a turn-around in someone's driveway, and drove back out of the area. They were not seen again. The limousine had never reappeared.

We discussed the activity for a short time, and decided it was impossible to determine how and why this activity had been initiated. We hoped it was just a random training activity. Due to the short duration between Frank's call and the time I departed the complex, there was only a very remote possibility that one of our telephones was being monitored, and that the surveillance had been initiated by virtue of Frank's call to me. Since the surveillance activity started at my apartment complex, we both felt it likely that we were simply random subjects.

Figuring the odds and the lack of expertise on the part of the surveillants, we decided finally that it was a training day for new members of their security or surveillance team. They were obviously inexperienced, and the Russian teams seemed always in need of training. Frank and I were positive of the identification of Alexandra in the back seat, and humorized that she probably felt more comfortable in the back seat anyway. We joked that she may even have been in charge of the training – after all, she had just graduated from SMERSH.

It was also common practice for their surveillance teams to pick a subject – a random, unwitting subject - and follow their activities for a day, just to hone their surveillance procedures and test their performance. It was even more likely that my apartment complex - where many Americans reside - had been randomly selected, and that I was the first to walk out of the front door of the complex once they were set up for a training exercise. More than likely, Frank's phone call was immaterial to the surveillance.

We had been good 'rabbits'. We did nothing out of the ordinary, were not obviously provocative in our actions, and had gone about accomplishing routine tasks. Unless we were specifically targeted, there would be no recurrence of the surveillance.

We decided to write a joint report for Dick and brief him the next morning. I would pay particular attention returning to my complex, and make an effort to detect any follow-on or stationary monitoring of my return.

By 1800 hours, Frank was beginning to snooze in the warmth of the afternoon sun, and I decided it was time to break out. I thanked Frank and his wife for the hospitality, said 'goodbye' to his kids, picked up my back pack and started to walk away.

"I wrapped some ribs, taters and corn in this foil package for ya 'D'," Frank's wife called out. "If I keep 'em, Frank'll just eat 'em." She grinned.

"Your hospitality is absolutely unforgettable." I placed the package in the pack, walked back to my car and drove directly back toward my apartment complex. As I drove, I saw no sign of any 'RE' vehicles. I continued down the street to the Chokchai shop and purchased two liters of Chokchai milk, and then returned home by going around the block and coming to the rear entrance of the parking lot. No RE vehicles were among the few parked cars in the lot, and all bore the residential windshield tag indicating they were 'authorized' parking.

I had long ago replaced my Thai home telephone instrument (bearing the brand name *'Feng-yeh' – made in China)* with a similar-looking US-made phone purchased from the exchange. The wiring was precisely the same, and according to the description on the label, the amperage, wattage and related specifications were identical. Using the American-made phone though gave a stronger signal, preventing all the in-line static and scratching that was so common on the Chinese-made telephones.

For me, the most important advantage of the US-made phone was that it would allow me to attach a bug-detector by simply removing the original mouthpiece and screwing the new mouthpiece/detector in place. Once the receiver is lifted from the base, any attempts to tap into my phone are immediately detected, and the slightest change in resistance on the line will activate a light on the mouthpiece. A recording device attached anywhere along the line would cause the same signal when turned on. Likewise, a nosey telephone operator listening to my private conversation would also be detected. I had attached the device to my phone soon after moving into the apartment, and had never seen it light up.

When I returned to my apartment, I checked my telephone to be sure it was working. I called the Post Office regarding the availability of open time to call Taiwan. Instead of hanging up the receiver, I placed a bone-handled dagger on the receiver buttons, unscrewed the mouthpiece/detector and checked the battery and bulb in the device. The battery was slightly down, so I retrieved a new one from the fridge door shelf and replaced it. I tested the activation by removing the receiver and then lifting my *Decotel,* Cigar Box phone receiver in the bar area. The light glowed brightly. The bulb was now much brighter.

I turned on some of my favorite music, and then gave my apartment a once-over for any new clandestine listening devices that may have been emplaced. I found none, but made a mental note to ask Dick to arrange another professional sweep. Maybe I was being paranoid, but better safe......

With nothing better to do, I took a walk down Sukhumvit to my office, and walked by DG's signal for having made his meeting with Ivan. I entered the building, went to my office and wrote up the drafts for my meeting with Bill and of the detected surveillance. I put the latter in Frank's safe as my input.

At 2005 hours, after taking care of those small matters, I took a 15-minute walk to the Windsor Hotel where I partook of the evening dessert special and listened to Frank's Filipino Band. I decided that if I had to always be part of the controlled audience, I would likely never return to the Windsor Hotel. *"There must be better entertainment than this in Bangkok."*

There is, of course.

Monday, I awoke early, and went through my ritual. I was not hungry, so I passed up breakfast, and walked out of the complex at 0650. The office was cold, as someone had apparently left the Central aircon blowing all weekend, so I began making coffee while everyone drifted in. Within a few minutes we were all engaged in telling our weekend stories while waiting for the Mr. Coffee to finish his bubbling serenade.

Dick had an early morning meeting with the US Embassy security office and when he returned at noon, Frank and I had finalized the report for him. Briefing took another 20 minutes. Dick's line of questions was aimed primarily at our initial observations, and conclusions. He agreed that the incident had likely been a planned training vehicle for the RE's new security team members, and related to us that there had been a noted increase in reports from military personnel regarding the spotting of suspect surveillance. He dug into his files and came up with a recent memo from the 'other agency', which indicated an increase in technical staff at the Russian Embassy. Newly assigned personnel had just arrived from Moscow, and according to sources reporting from that location, the Russians were beefing up their monitoring capabilities worldwide, with an emphasis on surveillance and surveillance detection. The training sessions were to be expected.

As for Alexandra's involvement, in light of her academic reputation, we all decided that she was probably in dire need of honing her surveillance detection proficiency as well.

A copy of the memo had been circulated 'FYI' to operational members of the unit, but had not yet reached our case officers.

I had almost forgotten my luncheon appointment with Roger F, and when I returned to my office, he was waiting for me at my desk. We'd not had time to chat since his arrival, and I found him refreshing to talk with.

The Safe-site keeper.

Roger was born in Menlo Park, California, and had lived there through High School. He attended Junior College in Palo Alto, and a few months later left home to join the army.

He confided that he had been raised by his aunt and uncle, as both his parents had died in a car crash along the coast highway #1, between Valley Ford and Bodega Bay, on their way to a picnic. Eight year-old Roger, who had been dozing in the back seat, survived the head-on, but never survived the trauma and psychological aftereffects of such a sudden and dramatic change in his life. Both his parents died instantly.

As a result, Roger admitted, "I crawled into a shell, and never really crawled back out."

Roger finally reached his maximum growth to 5 feet nine inches at age 23. He suffered continuing health problems, eventually outgrowing childhood asthma, and a vicious bout with acne. During each of his summer vacations through High School, Roger underwent weeks injections and skin grafts treatments to cover scarring from the acne problems, and even for several months following completion of an AA degree at the Junior College in Palo Alto, he continued the treatments.

To this day, Roger does his best to avoid direct sunlight, using heavy sunburn protection; and he has never become accustomed to riding in the back seats. He found surveillance training very difficult at the Intelligence School.

When I asked Roger if he was married or had a girlfriend, he responded, saying "I've never had time for women in my life."

As our lunch progressed, I learned that Roger had always feared rejection. His self consciousness over the acne and ensuing problems, along with his physical inabilities to become involved in sports, had disallowed any attempts at female companionship.

His favorite hobby was photography, and Roger invited me to visit his penthouse apartment once he gets settled, and look over his collection of storm photos. He was proud to say that he always sets up a darkroom for developing his film, and prints all his own photos. His rooftop penthouse would be a perfect place to continue his hobby.

Roger enjoyed his privacy, and called himself a modern-day hermit.

When I asked him if he had ever thought of maintaining a safe site, he lit up like a Christmas tree. "I've actually dreamed of such a wonderful opportunity!"

"This guy," I thought, *"is probably the perfect safe site keeper."*

We talked for a few minutes about the possibility, and then departed the Chinese restaurant and walked back to the office.

"I don't think I've ever been invited to lunch by any of my co-workers," Roger remarked. "Thank You. I really enjoyed the chance to talk."

"So did I." I answered, and then thought I was happy he'd been so candid. He had provided me a good insight into his most suitable personality for the position Frank and I had in mind.

By 1330 hours, I'd spoken with DG regarding his meeting with Ivan. It was obvious that he was somewhat disappointed in his own actions at the meeting, but I was able to explain that the majority of his meetings will be routine and boring. Now is the time to continue the contacts, keep Ivan happy, help Ivan build his reputation, become aware of the tasking and requirements from his higher headquarters, and most of all – make no mistakes.

We granted approval for him to take the trip with Ivan, and I set up a predeparture meeting for Tuesday afternoon. The plan was to prep him for the trip he was about to take. I asked him the amount of payment, and he said that it was another $500.00. We would routinely exchange the money at the Tuesday meeting. We hung up, and I walked into Dick's office to give him a heads up for the long-distance surveillance opportunity coming up.

Tuesday was a change of routine for the meeting with DG. Frank had made reservations at the River Bend, and I drove DG to that location, using my best SD techniques. I had no reason to believe we were being watched, and also no reason to think the Russians were aware of our temporary Safe-site. I found myself more alert than normal, however as we drove the circuitous route, and watched more closely than usual for parked sedans here and there. No surveillance was detected, but that fact did not ease my paranoia. The meeting was conducted routinely, although I made a special effort to make him aware that the expected increase in surveillance activities had begun.

DG explained again his perception of Ivan's attitude. "He actually seemed anxious to be transferred," DG stated. "But he gave no specific reason for any impending transfer."

"I believe he's trying to set you up for the coincidence – remember, when you are transferred he will try his best to be transferred nearby, or at least to a location wherein an occasional trip to meet with you would not seem so unusual." I went on to explain "Remember, he hasn't actually recruited you. He has your cooperation, and has gained that thru establishing what he believes to be a mutual trusting relationship. Once you've transferred, he may not show up at your new location for a year, or possibly longer."

Thanksgiving and Christmas 1974 came and went, as Betty and I moved closer to our long-awaited wedding day. In the meantime, the word from our headquarters was filled with unconfirmed rumors that our organization might withdraw from Bangkok. I was making plans for transferring my projects. The 'other agency' had decided - the Ivan project would be returned to their control, and the Alex project would be transferred locally. I was allowed to brief the projects, and make the case officer selection, knowing full well that my selection would only be a suggestion, and the respective case officers could and probably would be changed before too long.

Ivan had taken his 'trip' with DG, ending up in Beautiful Chiang-mai, where they took many pictures, and caught many fish. All the fish were thrown back into the streams and ponds virtually unharmed.

The trip actually became a training session for DG. He not only learned the intricate functions of the rollover camera, but Ivan spent a full day teaching him how to macro-film and develop microdot messages, transfer the 'dots' to a video tape and then photo display them on a TV screen. Dick's surveillance team followed the entire trip and managed to record not only portions of the outdoor training sessions, but portions of the picnic table-top rollover camera training as well. I was proud of the techniques employed by the AA team. Disguised as local national maintenance, they were able to seat themselves within earshot of Ivan's training sessions.

Now, my primary goal was to get the marriage over, take my expected reassignment, and get back onto the streets at my earliest opportunity. I was happy with my successes during this phase of my career; with one single regret: That I would not likely be involved in the final episodes of my ongoing projects.

Not necessarily so.

The Trip to Taiwan went off without a hitch, and although the first few days were filled with making wedding arrangements, I was forced to extend my leave for an additional 10 days due to the passing of the Generalissimo. The 'Gimo' was gone.

On April 25, 1975, Betty and I were allowed to participate in a civil ceremony on schedule at the American Embassy in Taipei, with LTC Blaise H. Vallese in attendance as my best man. We were also allowed to make plans for the Chinese celebration; however, the majority of our marriage-related activity was postponed for the mourning period. In the meantime, the airwaves were filled with solemn Christian music. Even DG's music would have been disallowed for the mourning period. There would be no 'cheerful' celebrations in Taiwan during those 30 days.

During the 'extra' time, Betty and I traveled North and South, visiting our friends and relatives and seeing sights. Much activity in Taiwan was at a standstill, making travel and lodging arrangements much easier than usual. We did our best to evade any activities resembling cheerfulness or delight. Although we were legally married on 25 April, our celebrations took place on 10 and 12 May. As far as Mama and Papa Chen were concerned, Betty and I even slept separately during the waiting period.

Having more than one wedding day is an ideal situation for any married man – should I miss our anniversary for any reason, I have a two week window in which to make it up.

Col Val and I were able to set down several times during the waiting period while in Taiwan, and we spent a few hours together, simply reminiscing the 'good-old-days'. I learned much of Val's background, and my respect for him grew even more over that period:

A short tribute to Col Val.

Following two years at Providence College, Blaise H. Vallese was inducted into the army in February 1943, when I was less than two years old. He took his basic training at Fort Devans, Massachusetts, and advanced individual training at Camp Edwards Maine and Camp Gordon Johnson, Florida.

After completing his training, in May 1943, as a member of the 4th Engineer Special Brigade, (Army Amphibians), at Camp Stoneman, Pittsburgh California, Val boarded the USS Extavia, and headed for the South Pacific (Milne Bay – located at the southern tip of New Guinea); Finschafe, Madang, and Wake Island, where he was involved in staging operations.

With nineteen months in the army, in September 1944 Val was involved in the invasion of Morotai Island, located halfway between the islands of Borneo and New Guinea, approximately 300 miles S/SE of the Island of Mindanao in the Philippines. It was the first strike north of the equator. He landed with the 33rd Division - Golden Cross.

By November and December 1944, Val was preparing for the invasion of Luzon, the Philippines, Manus Island (Admiralty) and Bougainville, just north of the line between the Solomons and New Guinea.

On the night of 5 January, 1945, Val's unit landing boats were aboard the Australian *APA Westphalia*, which took a kamikaze strike in the fantail. Nonetheless, the invasion of Luzon began the next morning, as they landed in Lingayen Gulf, located on the west side of Luzon, and about 125 miles north of Manila.

From there, they moved in and began staging operations north of Manila for the invasion of Japan.

An Abrupt Changing of events occurred on 6 August when the Atomic Bomb was dropped on Hiroshima Japan, and 75,000 people were killed instantly. A second blast on Nagasaki killed another 40,000 three days later. On 14 August 1945, Japan agreed to surrender, and on 2 September, the formal ceremony was held aboard the USS Missouri, just a little over two weeks after accepting the Allies terms. The ceremonies, less than half an hour long, took place while the Missouri was anchored with other US and British ships in Tokyo Bay.

By Mid September 1945, the Occupation of Japan was underway, and Val was stationed in Wakayama, 45 miles S/SW of Osaka, Japan.

On 31 December 1945, Val returned to the US - Fort Lewis Washington, and from there traveled to Fort Devans Massachusetts where he was honorably discharged on 16 January 1946. He was just three weeks shy of having completed his first three years of service to his country. During that year, on 6 March 1946, he married his lovely Leona, and returned to college to complete his educational endeavors. He majored in Sociology, with a minor in education at the Rhode Island College of Education, and by 1949 Val was qualified to teach.

Then, on 10 February 1950, Val was offered and accepted a direct commission as an Infantry second lieutenant in the Officer Reserve Corp, under the provisions of an Army regulation which extended commissions to qualified WWII non-commissioned officers with college degrees. In May 1951, he was called to active duty, with the 47th Infantry Regiment of the 9th Infantry Division at Fort Dix New Jersey. His specialty - Grenade Instructor.

In that same year, Val was assigned to the Language Qualification Unit of the 1013th Army Unit, First US Army, and Fort Devans Massachusetts where he served as a classroom instructor. There he taught basic non-technical military subjects to non-English-speaking alien enlistees who were serving the US Army under the Lodge-Philbrick Act.

He was promoted to First Lieutenant on 27 Feb 52, and later that spring was selected as a member of a special observation group to participate in an atomic device detonation with troops deployed 100 meters from Ground Zero; Operation Desert Rock, Yucca Flats Nevada.

In May 1954, Val was assigned to Monterey California where he attended the Chinese Mandarin Course. During that one-year tour, Val became acquainted with many of the same instructors I had the pleasure to encounter – ten years later. Our careers were just beginning to merge.

Val's follow-on assignment to Korea was as the Commanding Officer of the Boat Detachment, 8157th Army Unit, and Combined Command Reconnaissance Activities Far East. Therein, he was involved in unilateral operations wherein they dispatched sources across the 38th parallel. One special operation was bilaterally conducted with Chinese Nationalist intelligence services from Taiwan, the Republic of China.

In September 1955, Val attended the Company Officer's Course at Ft Benning, GA; was assigned to the Infantry School as an instructor, and in March 1956 was promoted to the rank of Captain. He served in such positions as a member of the General Staff under General Thomas Hickey and as Protocol Officer, Visitor's Bureau, at the Headquarters, Third US Army, Ft McPherson, Georgia. He finished the 1950's by integrating into the Regular Army in March 1958, attending the Intelligence School at Fort Holabird, Maryland (Field Operations Intelligence Training), and was assigned to the 45th Military Intelligence Company, Second US Army. From September 1959 to June 1960, Val attended the Infantry Advanced Course at Fort Benning, Georgia.

His career began to merge even deeper into the intelligence field, as he was assigned to the 163rd Southeast Task Force in Verona Italy. Here, he was assigned such duties as the Targeting Officer for Yugoslavia operations and Battalion Liaison Officer, Udine, northeast Italy. He was employed at the Italian Intelligence-operated interrogation center at that location, and was involved in the debriefing and exploitation of Yugoslavian refugees (among others). Of interest, Val proudly pointed out that during this tour he was involved in the official mapping of all major highways in the country as part of an Italian/US joint effort. This activity was tantamount to the world-wide digitalization programs of today.

In 1962 He was promoted to Major, and in December he accepted a branch transfer from Infantry to USAINTS, the new Branch established on 1 Jan 1963. Our careers were drawing even closer, as I had arrived at Fort Holabird in the fall of 1962 to begin Counterintelligence training.

His subsequent assignment to Miami Florida from 1963 to 1966, provided him with more bona fides, and led him to attend the C&GS College at Fort Leavenworth, Kansas. While I was still in Okinawa, Val was assigned to Viet Nam in June 1966, to the Field Activities Branch of the Operations Division (J-2), MACV where he performed as the project officer for Operation Shamrock – an operation eventually deemed unsuccessful – which was organized to attempt recruitment of Khmer Kampuchea Krom (KKK) Communists for turn-around operations. He departed Vietnam in May 1967 – I arrived in December that same year.

Val was assigned to the Caribbean Admission Center, Opa-Locka, Florida. His new unit fell under OPCON of 'the other agency', and participated in joint-service debriefings of "fence-jumpers" airlifted from Guantanamo Base, Cuba.

In 1970, on his way to Taiwan, Val stopped at Monterey California where he was placed into a Chinese Mandarin refresher course to prepare for his follow-on reassignment. We would finally meet.

The differences between a combat veteran and those who have not experienced war other than through reading books are astronomical:

Like the formative years of childhood, war has a way of molding and solidifying the personality of youth - of the young people of our world. The experiences, the sounds and tastes of survival, the sights of disaster, catastrophe and death; the fears, the action, the relief experienced following close combat encounter; the camaraderie and lifetime ties - they are all part of the psychological development that make mankind tick, and provide the survival and social instincts needed to survive this tumultuous world, particularly through the tender periods of life. Prayers are paramount throughout war, and in the end, tears are also requisite to recovery and rehabilitation,.

Frank the Philosopher said: "Life is a bitch!"

The Surprise.

July 1976, San Francisco.

"This is James Gaylord from Virginia, calling for Don Bradshaw." The voice at the other end said.

"This is Bradshaw," I answered. "What can I do for you?"

"Mr. Bradshaw, I'm going to be in San Francisco for a couple of weeks beginning July 16th. I was wondering if it would be possible to get together for some discussion."

"That would be possible, yes. But would you mind telling me what it's about?"

"Can we "push"? Gaylord asked

Surprised, I balked momentarily.

"I'll have to get the key." I stammered anxiously, "Can I call you back?"

He gave me the number.

I retrieved the key from the main safe, keyed the STU and called the number.

When Gaylord answered I said "Now we can push."

Within seconds the line was secure the window displayed the destination as "US-GOVT-VA-TS".

Gaylord continued our conversation. "Don, you there?" His voice was slightly distorted from the scrambling.

"Yes," I confirmed.

Your Bangkok project, #1357 was transferred to me when you got married last year, and I've been running it since. You know your project has made some absolutely outstanding advances, and we are preparing to bring the target personality on board. Our agency was wondering if you would like to be involved. That is, would you consider availing yourself to conduct the recruitment?

There was another short pause while I absorbed the shock.

"Are you still there, Don?" Gaylord asked again.

"Js, I'vestlhairr." I sputtered. "I mean - yes, I'm still here."

"We're planning on 'popping the question' there in San Francisco, and in going through our files realized that you are now assigned there. We also know that you will be leaving the first of next year for your follow-on reassignment to Japanese Language training and on to Japan, since your wife's background investigation was completed......"

"You know, Mr. Gaylord," I interrupted. "It would be a dream-come-true to be involved in the final disposition of this case. As you know, I followed the personality for over a decade, and was of course instrumental in the army's initial ACE/OFCO portions of this operation. The only problem I can foresee is that my involvement would require coordination through my headquarters and with my commander and operations officers here at the Presidio. You would also need the cooperation of my local boss, Major Vissey here at the Detachment."

"We realize that, and have already taken care of the coordination at those levels. I just wanted personally to discuss this with you before I talk to your Major there at the Detachment." He went on, "It would require perhaps ten days of your time – one week for briefing on the case and prep for the meeting, and then the actual recruitment, which we believe can be accomplished in three to five days."

"Of course, I want to be involved." I was at a loss for words. "When would you like to speak with Major Vissey?"

"Right now would be fine, he's expecting our call. If you can transfer this call that will be OK, otherwise, I'll call him as soon as we hang up."

We hung up, and a moment later, I heard Major V's STU ringing in the next room.

In 10 minutes, the Major walked to my desk, grinning from ear to ear.

I stood.

"He'll call back as soon as he makes the arrangements through his headquarters." The Major informed, "And we'll cut the temporary duty orders here."

"This is unbelievable," I responded. "I wonder how this decision came about."

"This is how it happened." Major V was saying, "About a month ago, Col S over at Group Headquarters received a call from the "other agency". They wanted to present you with an award for your involvement in initiating this operation, which was transferred to their agency some time after you left Bangkok. In there discussions with Col S and Col Y, one of their guys asked if we thought you'd like to do the recruitment. The handwriting was becoming clear. Y now says that asking for you was the sole reason for their call. Of course, you'll receive an award too," And then he added "maybe even a promotion." Major V then added "I've been keeping this a secret now for weeks. It's very rare that any of these type operations ever come this far, you know."

"Wow, that's just around the corner! Today's Thursday, July 1st."

When my orders were received three days later, they read that my TDY would begin on Saturday, 17 July, and would be for 12 days, thru 28 July. That gave me nearly two weeks to accomplish the task. Strangely, the duty assignment was to take place at the Federal Reserve Bank Building in San Francisco.

The safesites.

The marble pillars of the Federal Reserve Bank Building at 310 Battery Street towered majestically about 25 feet above the steps. It was an attractive structure; the type that should be maintained forever. When I arrived at the building on Saturday, the Main door appeared locked. When I tried the door, it confirmed my suspicion. I peeked inside, and noted all the lights were turned off. *"Surely,"* I thought, *"there's a guard in there somewhere watching me."*

As I descended the steps back to the sidewalk, an individual approached me asking if I was "Mr. Bradshaw.". When I informed him that I was, he asked me to follow him to the side of the building. Walking along the building, he introduced himself as an associate of Mr. Gaylord. Then using two keys, he unlocked both the latch and the deadbolt of the heavy, solid oak door and ushered me inside. We walked into an office in the rear of the building, where he turned on the lights, and adjusted the heating back to 72 degrees. The office had one single window, located high over a large wooden desk. The window had been sealed and was secured from the inside. The office suite seemed to be situated along the entire rear end of the building. He then took out his credentials, which identified him as Mr. Steven Gant, a "Special Investigator" for the FBI.

"And you're Gaylord's 'associate'?" I asked.

"Not exactly," he admitted. "We arranged this office for the 'other agency'. I just met Gaylord yesterday, when they told me he will be using it for the next two weeks."

"That makes sense," was my response. "I believe I may be working out of this office for a few days as well."

When he asked for my identification, I presented my credentials.

While Steven Gant made coffee and set the thermostat back to 'auto', he explained that Mr. Gaylord would be in around 1030 hours, as he had to pick up someone at the airport. The heat kicked on, and we sat awaiting the coffee.

"I just walked to the building when I saw you park," he explained. "I assumed it was you. Nobody informed me until yesterday that your guys would be involved in this too. Gaylord told me you would be the first to arrive."

I knew he was fishing. It was obvious he had no idea what was going on.

"So, what are you guys going to use the site for?" he finally asked.

"Sorry," I answered, "I don't know the details either." I lied.

As Gant talked, I realized he was a contractor investigator for the

FBI. He was not an accredited "Agent". His experience included a Shore Patrol background for three years in the Navy, and 20 years in the San Francisco Police Department. Following his police years, he had worked as a guard for a private investigative agency for two years, and then applied for his current job as an FBI contractor. His principle duties were maintaining clearance rosters, requesting Special Background updates for the local FBI Special Agents, and also included maintaining this safe site.

Gant was not accustomed to a steady physical exercise regimen. His stomach now drooped over his belt line, and he walked with the tired stoop of a much older man. I would have guessed his age as an old 59, give or take a few.

Trying one more time to get me to talk about Project Ivan, he admitted he was very curious as to what was now going on.

"I'll know more after I'm briefed." was my answer. That included no promises to brief him any further.

"I'll be here every day to let you guys in," He hinted. "So if you need anything, just let me know."

"Thanks," I said seriously, thinking *"some donuts would be nice."*

At 1045 hours, there was a knock at the wooden door. Gant jumped up immediately and almost ran to open the door. "It's Gaylord." He informed. I stood. But the first person through the door was DG.

DG dropped his luggage immediately, approached me and embraced me as though I was the long-time Godfather whom he'd not seen in decades.

"Hey there my friend," I was almost speechless. "Long time, no see! I wasn't expecting to see you here." I intentionally did not use his name.

"Likewise," was his response. "What a pleasure!" As we shook hands again, I could see he was as excited as I at this chance to meet again.

"I see you two know each other," Gaylord had walked in and was introducing himself. We exchanged business cards. "Call me 'Jim'" Gaylord announced, and we began our first-name basis. He was as polite in person as he was on the phone.

Gaylord turned to Gant and said, "OK, my friend, I'll take care of everything from here on. We'll be in touch with you on the 28th, and I'll let you know when your guys can have it back. I expect we'll be through here on the 27th, and these two will move out after the 28th." He asked for and accepted the door keys from Gant.

Gant was obviously disappointed, but responded, saying "Sure, Top. If anything goes wrong with any of the equipment or facilities, call this number. He gave each of us a business card bearing the name of *APEX Maintenance and Property Management*, and several telephone numbers to call for 24/7 services. He then departed the safe site.

Jim immediately collected Gant's Business cards, saying "It's just not smart for everyone to be carrying the same card – it ties us all together. Bad OPSEC."

Gaylord presented a lasting impression. Physically fit, he was energetic and possessed an innate ability to make one believe they had been long time friends from the start. His smile was contagious, and I often found myself smiling back, even when I didn't understand why. I could tell that an unspoken mutual respect existed between us. One could not accurately estimate his age, as with a full head of prematurely gray hair, quick wit, clean-cut appearance, he could be 38. I guessed him to be pushing 55.

While Gaylord set about unpacking some communications equipment, DG and I unpacked our bags.

"So tell me DG, what's been going on since we saw each other last year." It seemed to have been a lifetime.

DG explained that following the turnover to the 'other agency' he had continued meeting and passing approved and sanitized information to Ivan. He described his continued involvement, saying that after the 1975 joint training exercises, the 'other agency' had continued to provide him with fabricated information to pass, but DG had only remained in Thailand thru late 1975. DG had accepted an orchestrated transfer to the Washington DC area where he worked in the Pentagon as a personnel 'paper pusher' in the Travel and Transportation Branch. Apparently this was to Ivan's liking.

DG was allowed to continue corresponding with Ivan, and not at all surprising, Ivan was transferred to the Soviet Mission in DC three months later. They met, and immediately reestablished their professional relationship.

Over the past eight to nine months, Ivan had provided DG more detailed training, involving signals, the use of dead drops, and one and two-way passes. In order for DG to write lengthy, detailed reports, DG was taught to use different secret writing methods to camouflage his reports within the text of a seemingly innocuous letter, document or even a term paper. DG was also taught to develop secret writing messages from Ivan, in order to receive his tasking instructions.

DG organized a small back-up group band called 'The Immortals', and once they had worked up a few numbers by studying copies of DG's recordings, they began making appearances at Military Clubs in the Virginia/Maryland area. DG was too busy to sign any permanent bookings.

The long-range, Ivan operation deserved even more communication training, and Ivan spent time teaching DG the basics of OWVL, the utilization of 'burst transmissions' to receive instructions by virtue of a short wave radio. The transmission, generally 10-25 seconds long, was recorded and played back at a much slower speed. It consisted of a series of numbers, and the code was translated directly into the Roman alphabet.

Ivan had once again taken DG on a road trip. This time, they traveled to Florida, and enroute, Ivan provided him a lump payment of US$15,000, and presented him with cameras as gifts. In turn, DG agreed to use the cameras for photographing target personalities and facilities. One of the cameras was a German Minox kit, complete with filters, remote controls and a micro-telescopic lens.

"Your project," Gaylord interrupted, "really hit the big time." He turned to me. "This guy Ivan really knows his stuff. Apparently he's as good a teacher as DG is a student."

"It's almost ironic," DG stated, "How similar their methods are to US methods. I'm so involved now; I can't imagine my life continuing without being involved in espionage in some way."

"Welcome to the Club!" I complimented him.

"Ah, but I get first shot at him," Gaylord chimed in grinning. DG winked at me.

Gaylord presented each of us with keys to the safe site, and informed us that there were five rooms to this particular unit. As we walked through, Gaylord introduced us to the facility. The ceilings were approximately 16 feet high, and there were no windows near floor level. In all, there were two small bedrooms, an adequate living room with a well-stocked bar and entertainment center, the den, where we had spent our morning and a combination kitchen and nook area. The freezer/fridge had enough stocked food to satisfy a survivor squad for a month, and the shelves were filled with miniature bottles of Scotch, bourbon, gin and vodka. On the bottom shelf was a bottle of *Ohranj* Vodka, with a note affixed. *"DG – we understand you've always liked this!* " It was signed by Gaylord. A cooler chest beside the fridge contained at least a half-case of chilling Budweiser; and an extra half-bag of ice cubes filled one shelf of the freezer. In the corner behind the fridge was a closet/pantry which was stocked with canned foods a variety of freeze-dried snacks, and a complete shelf of *'Jiffy-Pop'*.

There was no access into the Bank area, and the only entrance to the safe site was through the large Oak door. Each of the two bedrooms and the kitchen/nook area had a pair of narrow, barred windows situated about 10 feet above the floor, which were sufficient only to observe the weather and to provide minimal lighting during the day.

"These will be your quarters for the next few days, and the actual recruitment will take place at our Treasure Island site." Gaylord explained. Looking at me Gaylord said "You'll need to rent a car. Your old T-Bird is a little too easily recognized. There's ample parking inside the gated area behind the bank. The gate key is the same cut as the door deadbolt key." The rest of the day was spent in casual discussion, and Gaylord began his exit at 1500 hours.

"I'll check in around 0900 hours, Monday." Gaylord was addressing me. "I'll bring in the case file. I'd like you to go through it and bring yourself up to date. I'm sure you'll have plenty of questions."

I agreed, and we shook hands again as he departed.

I turned to face DG. "This is amazing," I exclaimed. "My career with CIC began right here – in San Francisco, and the first meeting for field interview took place at OART, just minutes from T.I." I supposed history does have a way of going in circles.

"How is Ivan?" I asked out of serious curiosity.

"He seems to be doing fine," DG answered. "I am personally concerned about him though, because I've actually come to like him over the past two years. I hope he doesn't become aggressive and do something foolish."

"That's probably something we will spend some time discussing," I advised. "I'm assuming that Gaylord and his bunch are planning on approaching Ivan from an ideological point of view, hoping to capitalize on his life in America; making comparisons with lifestyle in Russia, and his mother and father's apparent admiration and contentment with the years they spent right here in the City by the Bay." I went on. "There's a good possibility you won't be directly involved in the recruitment. I would advise you monitor the interviews though, because there may be a few questions – there always are."

"I know Don. On the way here from the Airport, Gaylord told me I won't be allowed in the other site while the recruitment is going on. They want me to stay here at this location and listen over some commo system they have installed. I guess they'll have you and I talking to each other during that time, if needed." Then he went on - "Ivan has given me every reason to believe that he would be willing to make a move to a different lifestyle – but he's pretty close to his mom. I think he'll want to bring her into the picture. If that doesn't work out, he'll probably refuse flat out."

"That's a good point. Let's try to work that into the approach plan."

"That is the way it works, DG. Keeping you away from Ivan during this proceeding is no reflection on you, it's just that they want to avoid any face-to-face. At this point, I'm not yet sure of the final disposition they have in mind for Ivan, or if there's any future for you in this project. There is however a bright future for you in the business. Even Gaylord hinted he wants you with the 'company'."

"Not for me," DG stated emphatically, "I'm going to be DOD all the way."

"I've got an idea," I began changing the subject. "I know of a great steak house over on Powell Street. Assuming it's still there; let's go for something to eat. Its buffet style, but you get your T-bone perfectly grilled every time. Besides, I've not eaten all day."

"Ditto," DG grinned. "I was too hyped to eat this morning, and don't care for airline food."

I checked the yellow pages, to learn that *Tad's* was still on Powell Street. We turned off lights, and turned heat down, locked up, set alarms and walked out of the Bank at 1530.

The ever-crowded Tad's Steakhouse, located at 120 Powell Street in San Francisco had been in the same location since the 1950's. As a young soldier, it was always considered a treat to go to Tad's, order the steak up front and then walk through the fixin' line. By the time one reached his steak, it was prepared and perfect.

Following dinner, we spent the remainder of the evening walking from Tad's up Powell Street to Pine Street. We turned right and walked to Grant Avenue, then North, through Chinatown. We made a U-turn and retraced our route on the opposite side of Grant, sightseeing and picking up a few souvenirs. Somewhere near Chestnut, we turned up a side street and at the corner of Stockton, found a quiet bar, *"Club Crown"*, where we stopped for a quick drink. I ordered a long-awaited JWBOP, and DG had a Budweiser. It was like old times.

Once our drinks arrived two unidentified Caucasians entered and sat across the room from our table. The four of us were the only customers at that early hour of 2015.

DG and I engaged in casual conversation only, avoiding any conversations of Bangkok or Ivan, and by 2045 hours, business was picking up. I picked up the tab as we departed and moments behind us, the other two Caucasians departed as well. Outside, they stopped and entered a conveniently-parked 1975 4-door Chevrolet, and traveled in the opposite direction, away from us.

We walked circuitously to the bank, and the only surveillance as we arrived at the side door was the mounted overhead camera installed for bank security. Using DG's keys, we entered. We were both too excited to retire for the day, so we sat and talked for another three hours or so, absorbing a two-day supply of the scotch and beer and catching up on each others recent histories.

I learned that DG was on the promotion list, and that his wife Irene was planning on opening a small dancing school on Washington Street in Alexandria, not far from the Alexandria Public Library.

I asked DG to be prepared to provide his own personal opinions of anything he thought would help us in laying the groundwork for recruitment of this mid-level espionage agent. I explained that he has the personal experience factor here and recognition of Ivan's motivational factors requires a close, personal relationship and understanding of his behavioral patterns. DG has an advantage over all the rest of us since he has been meeting with Ivan on a one-on-one basis over the years, and has been able to dig into Ivan's brain and find out what makes him tick.

His opinions are crucial, his 'gut' feelings - vital.

When I asked DG if there was anything in Ivan's personality or actions that DG felt was distinctively outstanding, he responded by saying that the phrase "I'm practically an American" was a comment he had heard many times over the course of their relationship. DG had always thought that using that particular term was Ivan's way of convincing DG that he was cooperating with someone who held no ill feeling against Americans and the American way of life. Now, in retrospect, DG felt that Ivan may have been subconsciously reaching out.

"Ivan often told stories of his childhood in the US," DG stated frankly, "but he showed some reluctance to discuss those portions of his childhood that took place in Russia." DG continued that Ivan had often expressed his own philosophy regarding censorship. The limited freedom in Russia, particularly the lack of freedom of expression, was shameful to Ivan, and thus became one of his points of contention. Ivan despised being censored in the name of "edit", and because his own writings had routinely been "edited", he would accept no blame when someone in the international press corps would contest something he had written. Ivan only discussed those subjects when he and DG were alone and outside the confines of the Russian Embassy.

"Once my writing is censored, it is no longer my piece of work", Ivan had complained, and he had once confided that he refused to edit others reports in a political vain, saying "I don't write propaganda."

"Ivan" DG warned however "is a very proud man. No matter how much he loves the US, our freedom and our way of life, if he is insulted, he may just refuse to cooperate out of principle."

Even having said all that, DG felt that Ivan was still ideologically motivated. "Ivan's respect for Americans, their way of life, their education and their seemingly unlimited freedoms was not" DG explained, "just a mutual respect derived from being targeted against the US during his short career in espionage, but also from a business standpoint and from his having resided and experienced life, growing up in the United States. "He truly is 'almost an American.'"

DG recalled that Ivan had expressed his regrets for having missed opportunities to be an international correspondent and journalist. "Ivan once stated that he was in the diplomatic corps only because of devotion to his father and his father's devotion to Russia." He was simply following in his father's footsteps.

In describing the extent of their personal relationship, DG went on to say "Ivan once admitted to me that on his deathbed, his father confessed to him that he had lived with the pressure of a guilty conscience for spying on a country that had given him almost everything worthwhile in his life."

At one point near the end of 1975, when DG was expecting his transfer orders, Ivan had hinted that DG should always be prepared for the possibility that someone could contact him in Washington after his arrival in DC. Our office had learned from 'other agency' sources that the Russian Ambassador in Thailand was considering a rotation of agent handlers in order to provide for those agents who had realized little or no success in their espionage efforts. At a subsequent meeting with DG, Ivan announced that his own transfer was pending approval and explained that his friend "Alex" who had requested transfer out of Bangkok, had suddenly changed his mind, and was granted an extension of his current tour.

Ivan even informed DG that Ambassador Antakolsky would also be transferring in the near future, and Ivan felt Antakolsky's transfer may have had some influence on Alex's decision to remain in Bangkok. (Personally, I hoped that Frank's success with Bill Tanner had provided the basis for Alex's decision.)

When Ivan and DG had their first reunion in Washington, Ivan confided that he had fought very hard to obtain a transfer to D.C., so that he and DG could continue their relationship. The Russian government had not wanted to spend the time, effort and actual cost of transferring Ivan to Washington, when his talents were needed elsewhere; but acquiesced on receipt of Ivan's request.

As time went by, Ivan relaxed and became more willing to discuss his father with DG, and Ivan even confided that his father had acknowledged his own missed opportunities, and the resentment he held for the lack of recognition received for his life of dedication, which were a direct result of his chosen career path. He had worked hard for his rare promotions, while other members seemed to have been elevated almost magically to higher positions within the Diplomatic Corps and the MSS/KGB.

In Ivan's opinion, an occasional award or letter of recognition for his work and the self satisfaction of having worked diligently for his country, were his father's only salvation. In the end, his father had finally been awarded those last two medals in Ivan's cabinet – and a third, posthumous presentation that his father of course never saw.

Seduction was out of the question as a motivational factor for his recruitment, as Ivan had always seemed happy to avoid personal relationship for the sake of his career and his family. Ivan did not appear greedy, and seemed to live within his almost moderate means. He had once mentioned an encounter with a call girl, but had never discussed the details of that encounter. DG felt that if Ivan ever became Involved with a woman, it would have been with the utmost caution and discretion.

Ideological basis for recruitment was selected. We would discuss world peace; a joint effort to bring about an end to the cold war. It appeared that Ivan would be susceptible to discussion of a utopian world, where everyone lives in harmony. If this method failed, they would try monetary support/ lifestyle change; and if that failed, they would then try to convince him that he could defect, and enjoy a combination of all the above.......

As I pondered my involvement, it was hard to believe this phase of my professional life was finally reaching successful fruition. Recruitment would be the culmination of the entire Ivan Project.... 10 years in the making. The single item of which both DG and I had no knowledge would be the ruse under which Ivan would be persuaded to come to San Francisco. That was the 'other agency's bailiwick.

That night as I slept soundly, my clown friend visited me again. *He was sitting on a rail, grinning. As I walked past him, he whispered "PSSssst! Over here!" he motioned. I tried to ignore his beckon, but as I began walking away, he called again "Ivan's over there!" pointing in the direction I was walking, "Be careful, he's not as gentle as he looks. If you pressure him, he'll resist."*

"Oh, yeah?" I asked. "And how would you happen to kno...."

He had disappeared. The clown was nowhere to be seen. On a small piece of yellow paper, lying in the gravel where the clown had been perched, were two small shiny objects. I walked over and looked down.

461

Beneath two Russian medals - one bearing the likeness of Lenin, and the other a silver clustered medallion - was a note. I picked it up and recognized immediately Ivan's handwriting. "In honor of my devoted father and for my beloved fatherland, I will make this decision based only on my ability to contribute to Peace in the world." It was signed, "Ivan".

I awoke abruptly in strange surroundings. A dull orange glow from outside shown through two vertically-barred, rectangular windows. For a few seconds I lay still, trying in vain to clear my mind. It wasn't working. I rolled to my right, and fell from my bed to the hardwood floor. My senses seemed to be awakening. The faint smell of fresh, cotton sheets and the taste of Scotch began to stir other senses. The unfamiliar surroundings were beginning to make sense, and as my eyes began to adjust, I realized only that I was not at home. Then, my brain kicked into high gear, moving forward at meteoric speed, it brought me back to the present and to the Federal Reserve Bank building.

I picked up my watch from the end table, and realized the glow had faded from the dial. Turning on the light, I could now see that it was merely 0235 hours, Sunday Morning. I felt as though I'd slept through the night.

Sitting back on my bed I allowed the clown to reenter my memory lobes. *"What was he trying to tell me?"* I asked. *"Is Ivan not ready for this transition?"* I shook the thoughts from my mind and lay back down on the bed.

Recruitment, like the seduction process, is susceptible to the influences of timing. If one moves in too fast, he is considered premature; and on the other hand, if one moves in too slowly, the 'glow' of the moment has faded – perhaps forever.

"That floor was hard!" I said aloud.

I slept in peace for the remainder of the night, and awakened at 0600 hours. I showered, dressed, and within minutes after making coffee, I heard DG stirring in his room, so I began heating some Danish, boiling eggs and pouring orange juice over pebbles. By the time he walked into the nook, our continental was ready.

Over breakfast, we talked more about Ivan, and the training he had given DG. Ivan had been very thorough, and had focused his training on communication. In preparation for DG's reassignment to the US, Ivan was concerned for DG's own safety, and spent hours teaching him the value and intricacies of surveillance detection and counter-surveillance.

They had spent weekends together playing their music, and DG had arranged for a recording of *'valse bluet'* and a flip side of *'Dance of the flamingo',* which they recorded together at a local Bangkok studio.

"It took a lot of practice." DG said, "But the more we played together, the better it sounded." DG handed me a cassette of the recording, entitled DG Miles and Friends. Ivan's name was abbreviated in the credits, but DG explained that the copy he gave to Ivan had Ivan's name in full. The design on the cassettes consisted of a photo-collage of two long-stemmed roses. The stem of each rose resembled a flute. One of the roses was a black rose hybrid with red edged petals; and the second was a white rose with the same red-tipped petals. In the background, behind the roses was a distant feathered painting of the Golden Gate. The meaning was clear.

"When I gave it to Ivan," DG described, "He was really touched."

CHAPTER 25:
THE BEGINNING OF THE END.
DECEPTION

Ivan's new digital clock/calendar indicated it was Thursday March 25, 1976; and was precisely 1545 hours. He sat alone at his new desk in Washington D.C. Looking around, Ivan felt proud. The DG project was unexpectedly successful. Approval for DG's long-range utilization had been timely, as DG had received an alert to be transferred soon after the exercises last year. Ivan had come a long way over these few months. *"What great reporting,"* he thought to himself. *"No!"* he corrected his thoughts, *"What great debriefing!"*

His mind carried him back over the past year. His mother had packed her memories, her personal treasures and belongings and returned to Bangkok in time for Ivan to include her in his own travel plans to return to the US. As his full-fledged dependent, he would likely take care of her until she is no longer around. It was his duty. Besides, she'd always loved living in America.

His mind drifted even further back into an early morning in 1948. One day earlier, Ivan's parents had been notified that they would be returning to Russia. His mother had cried most of the night. The next morning, Ivan did not attend school. Instead he had strolled with his mother through Golden Gate Park. Teary-eyed, she talked of her love for San Francisco, the close relationships she had developed with her American neighbors, and how she hoped that one day, in a peaceful world, they would return to this place to spend their final days. In the distance, they could hear bagpipe music playing, and they followed the sound until it guided them to the top of a knoll. Standing there, a lone piper, dressed in traditional tartan kilt and the attire of the Scottish highlands, stood in the drifting fog and presented to the world his mournful call, as the haunting melody of *"Amazing Grace"* flowed across the park. It had been a most unforgettable moment in Ivan's life.

Ivan would be seeing DG this weekend, regarding the training he had given in the use of Dead Drops. A few days earlier, Ivan had inserted a piece of sheet music on which he had integrated several lines of secret writing (SW), into a small tubular container and placed it carefully inside the hollow center of a molded red brick. The brick was then surreptitiously placed inside a red brick flower planter behind a bus stop bench in Alexandria. Afterward, Ivan had walked seven blocks to the waterfront and executed his signal for DG. Hopefully, DG would observe the signal today, service the dead drop and leave another signal for Ivan. Ivan's surveillance team would be secretly filming DG's retrieval and signal; and Ivan could then use the film as a training aid for DG. *"DG is a good student, and will make a good spy some day"*. He thought.

Ivan sat in his mahogany desk and looked around his new office. Framing the travel poster of the Golden Gate Bridge Ivan had brought from Bangkok, was his new combination Bar and Bookshelves. The left side held his collected works on espionage, and the right side was utilized for holding the assortment of foreign liquors Ivan had accumulated. Between two bottles of Hennessey Cognac, Ivan had carefully placed the last two medals his father had received. In the center, directly beneath the 'bridge' poster was a sink, a built-in hotplate, and beneath the counter was a built-in refrigerator/ice-maker.

As he was thinking of having a shot of *Ohranj*, Ivan was startled by the telephone call.

"Romanyev." Ivan answered firmly.

"Mr. Romanyev," the unfamiliar voice at the other end started. "This is George Strübel from Bangkok."

"Strübel!" Ivan responded. "I'm sorry sir; I just don't recognize the name."

"Aren't you Ivan Romanyev from Bangkok?" the stranger queried. "… from the Russian Embassy? The card here says you are a musician, and a well-known authority on the subject of Russian classical music."

"Yes, that would be me." Ivan answered. "..But I've not used that card in years. Is there some way I can redirect your call." Ivan had noticed that the incoming call had originated from the Embassy Hotel in Arlington.

The stranger began. "It was just a shot in the dark. You see, I recognized your name from some articles you had written for the *Foreign Press* while I was in Bangkok. When I found your card in the Book & Music store, I called the Russian Embassy. They told me you had transferred back to Washington. Now, I'm passing through Washington, and called to see if I could catch you here."

Ivan immediately recalled that he had forgotten to retrieve the "bait" business cards from the Bangkok Music stores. Always cautious, Ivan continued. "Well, you see, I'm not involved in the music side any more, and as a matter of fact. I'm so very extremely busy I don't really have much spare time."

"Oh, I understand Sir," Strübel replied. "I'm a journalist, and only in town for a few more days. I was just recently transferred back to San Francisco from Bangkok, and thought we could talk over our mutual experiences. I'm truly so sorry to have interrupted your schedule."

Now, Ivan was beginning to feel some guilt for having cut Strübel off so shortly.

"Perhaps," he said considerately, "it wouldn't hurt. I do have some open time for lunch tomorrow. Could it be possible to meet somewhere close to my office?" Ivan was testing to see if the 'stranger' was familiar with Washington.

"I'm sorry," Strübel replied. "I'm not at all acquainted with the DC area. You see, my office set me up here at the Embassy Hotel in Arlington, and I'm not familiar with the transportation system. They pick me up and take me around, and then back to the airport, so I'm really at a loss. I'm so sorry for having bothered you."

"It's really not that inconvenient," Ivan was becoming more than a little curious. "I often go to an Ethiopian Restaurant not far from where you are. Perhaps I could pick you up if you are free and if you don't mind eating with your hands….."

"Actually, that would be very nice of you. Are you certain it's no bother?" Strübel asked.

"Not at all." Ivan said casually, "shall we say 1100 hours – in your hotel Lobby?"

"That would be absolutely wonderful." Came the reply.

"I'll be at your hotel at 1100 sharp. See you then."

As he hung up, Ivan immediately began thumbing through his rolodex searching for the name 'Strübel', and then checked his list of known US agency cover names. There were no matches, regardless of spelling. He checked the combined list of Foreign Embassy Staff records he had received from DG. Again, there were no matches – not even near matches. As an afterthought, Ivan checked his office computer listing of foreign journalists. Bingo! One 'George W. Strübel' was listed as an employee, journalist for the San Francisco-based 'Foreign Travelers' magazine, published weekly and printed by various press agencies, and airline information magazine publishers. Seconds later, a photograph of George W. Strübel automatically appeared within the narrative. Apparently, Strübel had worked for *Foreign Travelers* for over 15 years, and had reached the position of Senior Editor/Writer. Ivan executed 'print-screen', took out a new, empty file folder and wrote the name "GEORGE S" on the label. He placed the printed page in the folder and filed it under "S" in the second drawer of his safe.

The next morning, driving into Virginia, Ivan drove his favorite route - I-395 southward; and then took the Pentagon/Crystal City exit. He drove to Rotary Road and turned onto Army-Navy Drive.

Ivan had always enjoyed driving the larger, comfortable cars in America, but would never have considered driving such monstrosities in Bangkok. On those occasions when he was obliged to attend an official function or visit another embassy in Bangkok, he would allow one of their drivers to chauffer him in one of the black Mitsubishi Debonair staff cars. But for day-to-day activities, he had preferred driving his own medium-sized Toyopet. Now, back in the US, he could drive almost anything.

The Pentagon complex was on his right, and Ivan was thinking he could always park in one of the open, South Pentagon free-parking lots and walk through the underpass back to the Embassy Hotel. But then they would have to walk back through the tunnel to drive up the hill to the *Taste of Ethiopia*. A better choice would be to use the hotel parking lot, where his diplomatic plates would draw less attention.

He eased the midnight-blue Ford Galaxy 500 down into the underground hotel parking entrance, and the attendant directed him to park in one of the VIP slots near the elevator. After parking, he showed his diplomatic badge as the attendant approached, and was directed into the elevator. He was familiar with this hotel, and had used the lounge often when making initial contacts with some of his American potential sources. Ivan frowned at himself for his lack of success.

"I feel like Alex Topov every time I strike out," He complained to

himself. The thought of his friend Alex triggered a deluge of related thoughts, causing Ivan to wonder how Topov's operation was going with the American tennis player. He wished him the best.

The elevator arrived at the Ground floor at precisely 1040 hours, and Ivan walked into the lobby area. Glancing around, he saw no-one sitting alone. Removing a gratis *Post* from the newspaper stand Ivan sat in a chair facing the elevators. "If Strübel is a typical American," he thought, "he'll be here about three minutes early."

He glanced around this familiar site, and recalled each of the attempts he had made to befriend American soldiers and Pentagon employees over the past few months. Ivan had worked incessantly to make friends, and although there were times when he thought his new contacts were approachable, within a few weeks, they broke away and avoided his calls. Ivan was aware of the US security system, their counterintelligence programs, and their policy to report foreign contact attempts; and attributed his continuing failures to the federal mandatory training schedules involving Foreign Intelligence Service subversion methodology. Ivan made a mental note to drive to nearby Alexandria this afternoon and check for DG's signal that he had serviced the dead drop.

1055, and no sign of Strübel. Ivan checked his notebook again. "*1100 hours, Embassy Hotel, Arlington – Strübel.*" He had written.

Then, at precisely 1057, meeting Ivan's expectations Strübel exited elevator #2. He was about 10 years older than the photo. Plump, balding and white-haired, the gentleman, wearing a gray, striped suit, black leather shoes, and carrying a thin brown briefcase, looked over the lobby. As he briskly walked in Ivan's direction, Ivan made a quick assessment of the man. *"Strübel appears to be a legitimate businessman - well dressed in approximately $500 attire".* Ivan further observed *"The two hundred dollar briefcase is too thin to be carrying any equipment."* And, he wondered if Strübel had recognized him from a photo as well.

"Mr. Romanyev?" He asked as he approached Ivan.

"Yes", Ivan stood. "That would be me." He smiled. They shook hands. The stranger's handshake was warm and firm and dry.

"My name is Strübel, George Strübel," he introduced himself, smiling.

His approach was so disarming, so polite.

"Call me 'Ivan', please."

"How much free time do you have?" George asked.

"My entire afternoon is free," Ivan answered. "Actually, I pretty much establish my own schedule, and can almost do as I please."

"Wow!" George commented, "Your English is absolutely pure." I've never met a foreigner who speaks English like you."

"I'm practically an American," Ivan smiled as he fell into his routine. "I was born and raised right here in the good old U.S. of A."

"Excellent." George remarked. "That makes it easy for me. You know, sometimes when I first meet someone, I have a hard time getting used to their accent. It can make communication difficult – but in your case, I can see there's no language barrier here."

Ivan picked up his newspaper and gestured toward the elevator. "My car is down in the lot, shall we take lunch first?"

"Absolutely, I'm famished." George said. "I never get used to quick time zone changes, and when I travel I always seem to be hungry."

As they boarded the elevator Ivan casually asked "So, where are you coming in from?"

"San Francisco." George answered.

"San Francisco!" Ivan exclaimed as though surprised. "You know, that's my old stomping ground. I love that city."

"Great!" George agreed, "I love it too. And it gives us just one more thing in common."

Another car had parked very close to Ivan's Ford, so George stood aside as Ivan backed out, and then sat in the front passenger seat. Ivan exited the garage out onto Army-Navy Drive, and circled the west end of the Pentagon South lot. At the Texaco station, he turned left on Columbia Pike, and drove up the hill, past the Marine barracks and into the area which accommodated the *Taste of Ethiopia.* He parked alongside the building and they walked together into the restaurant where they were greeted by the owner, Mr. Jizatchu.

"Mr. Romanyev, and how have you been going?" Jizatchu's accent was heavy – his smile sincere.

"Been going just fine Jizatchu, how about you? And how about Adanech?" He asked of Jizatchu's wife.

"She's as usual just fine. Going back to Ethiopia next month for vacation. I don't want her leave, but she knows best. To see her family and mine too." Jizatchu had found their table and gestured for them to sit, holding a chair for Ivan.

"Wonderful! You know, you must remain close to your family, to your roots, and never forget where you came from. It's wonderful Jizatchu." He repeated. "Please give her my regards." Then, in the same breath, "I'd like you to meet my new friend from San Francisco, Mr. George Strübel."

"Mr. George. Welcome. I am Jizatchu."

George wanted to greet by Joking "Izzatchu, Jizatchu?" but decided to hold back.

"Nice to make your acquaintance Sir," George responded.

"Me, also." Jizatchu quickly snatched up the 'reserved' sign as he handed English menus to Ivan and George. He politely excused himself and left them alone.

An American couple walked in and Jizatchu greeted them.

"Welcome Mr. Sloan, Mrs. Sloan, and how have you two been going?" Ivan hadn't the slightest idea Jizatchu was speaking to Strübel's Surveillance Detection team.

Ivan turned to George. "Have you eaten Ethiopian food?"

"No," George Strübel answered, "but I'm looking forward to it. Please order what you like," he suggested, "and I'll have the same."

When the meals arrived, they were offered forks and knives to handle the food, as Jizatchu explained that the Ethiopian 'custom' of eating with fingers was a simple novelty here in the US. Both Ivan and George opted for the utensils.

"Now, what can I do for you?" Ivan wanted to get to the point.

"Actually, as I mentioned on the phone, I've read some of your writings, Ivan, regarding your experiences in foreign countries. They were also published in the Russian Diplomatic Press. I have to admit, I was a little curious at first, wandering who edited your writing; but now I must further admit that I'm so impressed with your English – there's no question but that you wrote the articles completely on your own."

"Thank You," Ivan accepted the compliment.

"What I would like," George started, "is to use some of the information from your articles, and incorporate some of your experiences into my articles." He continued, saying "I've brought some of your articles, copied from the *'Press'* and some articles I've written for my company *'Foreign travelers'* and, if you wouldn't mind, I'd very much like to send them to press in the following weeks." He paused. "And of course, with your permission, your identification would be printed in the magazine credits, and I would of course recognize any of your quotes in my articles."

"I've never done anything like this before'" Ivan admitted, "and of course I would need the permission from our diplomatic bureau in Moscow for my name to be used." Ivan said nothing about his studies at USF, and his unfulfilled desires to become an international journalist.

"We would of course reimburse you for your time and efforts," George added.

"Oh, I'm not concerned about the monies," Ivan stated truthfully. "Perhaps after lunch we could go somewhere private and discuss this unexpected offer."

"Sure," George said, "and if you agree, and everything can be worked out, my office would bring you to San Francisco for a weekend, to sign release statements, discuss the terms and discuss our intern program."

"Please," Ivan suggested, "let's slow down, and make decisions after discussing it. It will take a while for me to incorporate such activities into my own schedules. And," Ivan added, "since some of my writings are outdated, I would certainly want the opportunity to revise and update them before they are released to any press agency."

"Absolutely, that only makes sense." George agreed.

Jizatchu approached their table and poured iced water. He placed a frosted bottle of vodka, along with a small container of iced tangerine juice in front of Ivan. "Thank you, my friend," Ivan was truly grateful.

"And for you, Mr. George, what are your pleasure drinks?"

"One of those Budweisers would be fine," Came George's reply.

Following a satisfying meal of more than generous proportions, Ivan insisted on picking up the tab. They departed the *Taste of Ethiopia* at 1405. Walking back to the car, Ivan explained that he had been visiting the *'Taste'* most regularly since his return to D. C.

What George Strübel thought, but did not say was that he was already fully aware of Ivan's utilization of this restaurant from reading the surveillance files on Ivan; and that his US CI agents had also visited the restaurant during Ivan's 'personal meetings' to observe and to record Ivan's Modus Operandi first hand.

"Why don't we just go to your room," Ivan suggested, "and we can go over the details of your proposal there?"

Back at the hotel, Ivan parked in the same slot, and they entered the elevator. Ivan had not noticed the car at the end of the underground lot, and the two individuals virtually hidden in the back seat, facing them.

As they passed through the lobby area, George checked at the front desk for any messages. There were no messages, but his conversation with the front desk had tipped off the two surveillants in the car parked beneath the hotel. The two had 'coincidentally' taken up temporary residence in the room adjacent to George.

As they entered #1134, Ivan recognized the surroundings and décor from his previous visits, and noticed immediately that they had an excellent overview of the entire south and southwest sides of the Pentagon, as well as the hillside in front of the Marine Barracks.

"What's your pleasure?" George asked, opening the fridge.

"Actually," Ivan thought momentarily "a soft drink would be perfect. Perhaps the Orange Nehi."

"Good," George took out the bottle, along with a bottle of Grape Nehi. He retrieved glasses from the small kitchenette, opened the bottles and brought them to the coffee table.

A much larger briefcase, along with some loose papers and several recent but well-read copies of *Foreign Travelers* Magazine were on the coffee table. George picked up the briefcase, along with the loose papers, and placed them on the counter/divider between the kitchenette and the seating area. As he closed the snaps on the briefcase, he also pushed a small, obscured button to activate the recording device in which he had loaded a 90-minute audio tape.

Ivan had already picked up the latest issue of the magazine and was glancing through it when George sat down.

"So, let me show you what I have in mind." George said casually.

The next hour and 15 minutes was spent going over their related, respective articles and publications. George pointed out that their writing styles were not all that different, and how easy it would be to incorporate portions of Ivan's writings into his magazine.

"We can also support our writings with the thousands of current photographs maintained in our office computer libraries, and I'll make sure you have that program when you do your updating."

As Ivan listened, his suspicion of Strübel waned, and his guard began to drop. In his mind he was formulating a plan to use the opportunity to create and backstop a new cover he could use in the conduct of his own unmentionable business. *"How unique an idea!"* he thought. *"If I can begin publishing some of my writings in a US magazine, it would not only reinforce my cover within the cultural and attaché circles, but would also give me a basis for being inquisitive, asking questions, and getting to know my potential sources better. Just wait 'til Alex Topov learns about this!"*

Trying not to appear too anxious, Ivan allowed George Strübel to continue trying to convince him that it would be a good career move, and would also be beneficial to George's publication. Finally, George admitted to Ivan that he had initiated a proposal within his company to print the magazines in several foreign languages, including Russian, Japanese and Chinese, in hopes of broadening interest and marketing their products to the foreign, sister companies of the various American international airlines.

"That's probably an excellent idea," Ivan stated frankly, "and I certainly wouldn't mind being a part of your publication. But, allow me first to present your proposal to our office in Moscow. We'll see what they have to say, and I can get back to you. Are we working with a time frame here? What are our time constraints?"

The words "we'll see", "are we working" and "our time constraints" made George smile to himself. Ivan was swallowing the proposal completely. He had already introduced the gesture of a genuine, professional relationship.

"Good," George responded. "Let me give you my personal addresses and my FAX number. You can let me know what you decide. If all works out OK, we'll bring you to San Francisco and we can discuss the internship."

Smiling, Ivan agreed and they shook hands and exchanged business cards. Both wrote their private telephone numbers on the reverse and were hoping to gain from this new relationship.

Ivan drove south on State Route #1 through Crystal City, past Washington National Airport and into Alexandria on Washington Street. At King Street he turned east, driving toward the waterfront, then turned right and parked in a public lot one block south of King Street. Ivan retrieved his Hotel newspaper from the car, walked back to King Street, and turned east. At the intersection of King and Union streets he saw where DG had left his mark. The crayon mark was clear. DG had turned the corner as he made the mark on the cement telephone pole. Ivan could easily have seen it from his car. Ivan smiled to himself and paid no further attention to the mark. DG had accomplished his tasking. The instructions for next weeks meeting were included in the package. Ivan visited his favorite antique shop, where he purchased a small gold watch for his mothers collection, then walked across, into Gadsby's Tavern/Museum and restaurant. There, he ordered Vodka with Valencia Orange. He sat and read his newspaper before returning to his car. He had detected no surveillance during this return trip.

During his drive back into DC, Ivan was elated. His thoughts were progressing far above the speed limit. First, he thought, he would have to further check the validity of Strübel and his publishing firm, and then write up his proposal, incorporating his own ideas for using the writing as an additional cover for his espionage activities. He was thinking *"If our Ambassador, Kauzov and his Intelligence Chief, Vetrov are willing to affix their endorsements, I could expedite this and get an initial response back within weeks. Maybe mother would enjoy a short trip to San Francisco."*

Or was he dreaming?

Back in his office, Ivan worked exceptionally late on the draft proposal. After drinking the remaining last few sips of coffee from the lounge pot, he walked back into his office and read over the proposal one more time. It was already 15 pages, as he had included all the required details. Using previously approved cover plans as examples, Ivan wanted this one to be as complete and as thorough as possible, to avoid delays. "Answer all the interrogatives," he warned himself out loud. He decided he would go over the proposal in the morning with Vetrov before submission. Vetrov, he felt, always plays the devil's advocate well. He'll have a lot of questions.

Ivan placed his draft document in a new folder and filed it in Strübel's file, closed and spun the dial on his safe. He walked to the fridge and took a nearly frozen bottle of Ohranj from its shelf and poured himself a generous shot. Looking at his reflection in the glass cabinet door, Ivan raised his glass, and loudly said "Salud!" He downed the two-ounce shot in one healthy gulp. "Na Zdorovie." He shivered slightly as the cold drink trickled into his stomach.

As he walked from his office, Ivan spotted a note that had been slid under his door. He picked it up and read: *"I, the film is ready at the front desk. It has been developed and is ready for your review. V".*

Ivan knew this was the 35mm film from DG's training mission. He walked to his in-box at the front desk, retrieved the film and went into the briefing room where a projector was always ready for use. Ivan opened his small canister and threaded the film through the guides. He flipped the 'on' switch and the light came on as the film began to reel.

On the screen in front, Ivan watched as DG stepped off the bus which bore a lighted sign "PENTAGON-ALEXANDRIA" and walked to the adjacent bus stop bench. He paused momentarily to read the bus schedules. As though he were talking to DG, Ivan whispered *"Good move. It's always good to know which busses are serviced by this stop – just in case someone should ask at a later time."*

DG seated himself at the right end of the bench. To his immediate right was a trash can, and immediately behind both the trash can and the bench was the brick flower bed where the concealment device had been placed. DG then opened his small briefcase and took out a newspaper, which he began to read as he snacked on puffed corn from a small bag in his open briefcase. Pigeons were gathering rapidly, and DG began to share his kernels with them. DG then took the remaining snacks and scattered them on the lawn between the sidewalk and the road, and placed the empty bag on the brick wall of the flower bed. He then retrieved a small camera from the case and took some photos of the birds. DG carefully placed the camera in his briefcase, picked up the empty bag, stood and tossed it into the garbage can.

About 5 minutes later when the birds realized there were no more snacks, they began to fly away. DG had continued to read his newspaper, but now placed it back inside his briefcase and closed it. Approximately 10 minutes later, a second bus arrived, and the driver opened the door. DG picked up his briefcase and boarded the bus. As it drove away, the camera zoomed in on the sign. It read "DOWNTOWN ALEXANDRIA".

Ivan did not see the pick-up. He rewound the film and watched the activity two more times, pausing carefully here and there. He still could not see any pick-up. On this third time, he allowed the film to continue. The film depicted the surveillance team as they crossed the street and photographed the brick which was still in place. Ivan continued watching intently as the photographer's hand reached down and picked up the brick, turning it over. The message had been removed. The brick was empty.

Ivan's heart momentarily skipped two beats, as he wondered if someone had gotten to the drop before DG; then he instantly recalled that he'd already seen DG's signal. He had serviced the drop. *"Of course he accomplished the task."* Ivan sighed, laughing aloud.

As the film continued, Ivan observed DG exit the bus at the corner of King and Union Streets in Alexandria. He crossed Union and walked uphill on King Street to the designated intersection. As he turned the corner, he walked past the cement pole and the camera zoomed in. Delayed auto-focus caused the crayon mark to magically appear.

"Excellent!" Ivan thought. *"Nobody would ever notice."*

Coincidentally, DG walked to Gadsby's Tavern, entered and seated himself at a booth along the wall. Within a few minutes he was joined by his wife, Irene. *"You planned the rendezvous!"* Ivan marveled. *"Excellent, just excellent. A wonderful plan, DG."*

NOW, STILL SUNDAY - FIRST WEEKEND AT THE BANK

Back in San Francisco, DG and I walked into the kitchen closet and placed the tape on the monitoring cassette. The sound came through the office speakers, and was excellent. The recording was very professional, and DG's band had done a good job putting it together. The two selections performed by DG and Alex were also much better than I had somehow expected. Ivan had held his own.

The phone rang, and I picked it up. "Excellent sounds!" Gaylord was saying.

I hesitated momentarily, and Gaylord said again. "Those were excellent sounds. We were just testing the monitors when suddenly this music began; so we sat and listened to the whole thing. DG never gave me a copy, and I'd always wondered how it sounded. That was as professional as anything I've ever heard. I'm assuming that the flute pieces were DG and our mutual friend."

"It was," I answered, "and I agree they're pretty darned good." I replied, trying not to sound suspicious that they may have been monitoring all of our conversations as well.

Gaylord explained further that they had decided to set up and test the commo system between the safe-sites. He was about to call us and suggest we turn on the player and mikes, when the sound began to emit from their speakers as well. Rather than interrupt us, they decided to enjoy the music. Halfway through, Gaylord had recognized excerpts of DG's live performances from Bangkok - King's Palace.

I liked Gaylord, and found his candidness refreshing.

DG spoke momentarily to Gaylord, and they tested the mikes from Gaylord's location, as well as the receivers. Per Gaylord's directions, DG began the charging process of the batteries for the spare walkie-talkie/transceiver systems to be used in the event of a breakdown in the commo system or loss of power during the actual meetings.

The remainder of Sunday morning was spent walking around Market Street, and we stopped momentarily at the USO Club for a soft drink. Although the USO had been remodeled, it was still at the same location, and reminded me of the weekends I had spent there during my MP days at Fort Barry, across the bay. At 1445 hours, we caught a taxi to Club Crown for a drink. DG and I agreed that we should take advantage and enjoy this personal conversation time. Tomorrow would be the beginning of a busy week of preparation.

Tomorrow came too early.

At exactly 0900, Gaylord arrived, carrying a box of files from his office. "These are for you, Don, and we brought along copies of your old files from Okinawa, Vietnam, Taiwan, and Thailand – just in case you may have forgotten some of the important details. All the important extracts from Ivan's old man's files are here too."

There was about thirty linear inches of files in all.

I opened the box to find all the files were in chronological order. The box included early photographs of Ivan and his family in San Francisco; employment reports covering Ivan's time with the Hi-Seas Shipping and Transportation Company; records of his trips abroad and dates of his extended shore-leaves; locations and photographs whenever surveillance had been allowed. A photo album included pictures of diplomatic parties where Ivan was in attendance. Numerous photos had been extracted from press photos, and were not necessarily during surveillance targeted at any specific individual. The album however had been assembled in such a way as to give the appearance that Ivan was the main subject. Although Ivan's position in the cultural office would call for him to attend such parties and to mix with foreigners, most of the photos were of his attempts at small talk with Americans also in attendance. These photographs were convincingly judgmental to say the least.

Also Included were numerous 8mm films, and photographs taken from the entrance to the Bangkok embassy with telephoto shots of unidentified foreigners entering and leaving the embassy grounds. DG's car was also depicted, but there was no direct identification or implication of the involvement of any specific American. The photographs were cropped in such a way as to make it impossible to ascertain where the photographers were positioned or their distance from the subjects. Ivan would probably recognize DG's car.

In a separate folder, all of my reports and requests/approvals for coordination were included. Obviously omitted from any of the reports were the Case Officer/agent handler's comments regarding source's and subjects. Surprisingly, included in the file was a request to Frank for his source's assistance in planting a locator/listening device in Ivan's vehicle. Apparently it functioned as expected, and Frank had been instrumental in keeping track of Ivan's whereabouts occasionally after I departed Bangkok. I made mental notes to discuss that particular operation with Frank, should our paths cross again. They did – many times.

As I went through the files, I made note of anything pertaining to Ivan that I thought may influence his opinion and decisions. By the time I finished, it was already Wednesday afternoon, 21 July 1976.

I briefly went over my notes with DG, fine-tuning the overall approach plan. Altogether I had compiled 20 hand-written pages of notes.

Gaylord arrived at the 'Bank' at around 1800 and asked if DG and I would like to take a ride. "Of course." I answered without questioning.

DG was sitting in quiet contemplation.

"That includes you too, DG", Gaylord commented. "It's just a gimme, but I think you'll enjoy seeing our setup."

Jumping up, DG anxiously agreed to tag along.

"We want you to look over the other safe site on T. I.; but we won't be going over until after dark. Shall we all go to dinner first?" He asked.

At 1700 we locked up the 'Bank' and Gaylord drove us to the Presidio Officer's Club. We arrived at about 1730, and were escorted to a reserved, private room where we were seated and given menus.

"This place was swept this past weekend, and we believe it will be OK to discuss operational matters. Do you have any questions before we get started?"

"Of course, I'd like to know what decisions you have already made as to the approach and final pitch." I asked.

"That's a good start," Gaylord said. "So let's begin by asking what you think. You've been going over the files the past two days. What's your take?"

The approach plans.

"I believe we have no choice but to begin by approaching him with our proof of his involvement in espionage, our familiarity of his MO, and our knowledge of his targets. We have enough proof to shock him right from the start. If that doesn't get him thinking, then perhaps we can look in another, more persuasive direction."

"You've read your manuals," Gaylord replied. "That's precisely where we'll start. But keep this in mind – Ivan will already be shocked when his escort doesn't take him directly where he thinks he's going. By the time he arrives at the safe site, he'll be ready for more 'shock'. We have reinforcements on hand." He did not offer details.

He agreed that once Ivan begins to absorb the surprise of being had, a soft pedaled, ideological approach and recruitment is preferred to any decision obtained through duress or coercion; however, we should leave those options available. Gaylord provided a written outline of questions and approaches all oriented to Ivan's perceived motivation. As I looked over his list, I realized that Gaylord was definitely the Man in Charge. He had thought of more angles than I could dream. I was on his turf, and would without doubt do it his way. I was flattered they listened closely and considered each and every suggestion I made.

According to Gaylord, Ivan was due to arrive on a Northwest flight at 0730 hours, Friday. Initially, he would be staying at the *Travelodge* on Lombard. Since he was taking a two-week vacation in conjunction with this endeavor, his mother would be flying in on Tuesday afternoon. They would then be staying at the Mark Hopkins Hotel on Powell, across from Union Square Park. The park is conveniently situated over a covered parking lot, with an underground walk-through to the hotel.

We continued discussion of our approach until 1930 hours. We then departed the Presidio and drove directly out the Lombard gate, crossed onto Lombard Street and drove to Van Ness Avenue. There, we turned north, and drove to Bay Street, but instead of entering into Ft Mason, we turned right and took Bay Street along the waterfront past the piers and down to the entrance of the Bay Bridge. We followed the signs to Oakland and turned off on the exit to Treasure Island.

Exiting into Marcalla Road, we turned at a row of offices, drove to the end of the block and made two right turns, encircling homes and entering a lane between L and M streets. I assumed we were driving east, when I saw Gaylord activate a garage door remote, and we parked in a garage behind one of the homes. We walked to the house, and Gaylord opened the back door entrance into a modern kitchen. As we walked through the kitchen, we passed through a formal dining room, and beyond that, was a large living room. All blinds had been drawn. To the left of the living room was an office/den sunroom, and to the right were stairs. Beneath the stairs was the entrance to the first floor guest half-bath. The stairs lead from the front door directly up to a second floor full bath, and three bedrooms. One of the bedrooms had been converted to an interview room, and the smallest of the three bedrooms was used for housing a communications center.

Inside the commo center, were a bank of telephones, charging docks, several sets of walkie-talkies, and recorders of all shapes and sizes. The last, master bedroom was a combination, bedroom and setting room, divided by a large archway. In the corner of the MBR, behind the commo room, was a separate and private, full bath. Throughout the house, I observed several 'off the shelf'-type hidden recorders, similar to the 'trash cans' provided to our sources overseas.

"This is where Ivan will spend Friday through Monday. If the recruitment goes well, as we expect, we will give him the option of remaining in quarters similar to these for his two-week vacation, or remaining at the Mark." Gaylord stated. "Either way, we will be busy seeing to it they have an enjoyable time. My guess is he will opt for remaining at the Mark Hopkins, so that his presence and vacation in San Francisco will seem normal.

"Will you eventually move him somewhere else?" I asked.

"Oh yes, we are prepared for anything. If he goes back to DC as one of our recruited agents, we will then continue with Plan 'A'. If he decides to defect, then we have prepared other options. Plan 'B' or 'C', so to speak." He did not elaborate.

"And if he flatly refuses to cooperate?"

"We don't believe he will; however, if he does, then we will be forced to take other action. For example, we can release him to his own government here in San Francisco, and see to it they hear our side of the story of how he tried to defect, walked in with information, cooperated fully, etc, etc, etc. Regardless of our story, his future in the KGB is finished. If he doesn't come over to our side one way or the other, he and his mother will be returned to Moscow, and dealt with there."

For the first time since I met him, Gaylord looked cold. I felt a little sorry for Ivan and his Mother.

The front doorbell rang, and Gaylord announced "It must be the safe site guy." He walked to the door and looked through the peephole. "Yup, it's him he said grinning."

As he opened the door, I could not believe my eyes.

"I stocked up on Vodka and all the other important things," Said Radislovsky, my old friend from Okinawa.

He then looked at me and stared. "What the hell is this? Damn, they'll let almost anyone in here!?" He joked, handing the shopping bags to Gaylord. Rad then ran across the room to greet me. It became obvious that Gaylord had orchestrated this get-together, and neither Rad nor I were prepared for the most pleasant reunion.

I immediately introduced RAD to DG, and told DG that this 'old fart' was my idol – the one with whom I'd been working when Ivan first came to our attention. Not surprisingly, they became immediate friends.

Rad had retired from the army and accepted employment with the 'other agency' six months later. He was no longer interested in being a Case Officer, and had opted for a support-role position. The agency had sent him to various courses, including their technical assistance program, and he had served in Europe until this past year when he had been transferred to Oakland. Here, his main responsibility was managing the safe site on T. I. He and his wife Sally resided in the 'home'. Sally was now conveniently visiting their son and family in Miami.

"Have you seen the basement yet?" Rad asked.

"What's down there?"

"Let me show you." Obviously Rad was proud of something.

As we descended to the basement, I realized Rad had spent some time there. The basement was divided into two parts. On the left, directly in front of the stairs, was the domestic basement, equipped with a washer and dryer, indoor clotheslines, folding tables and a small kitchenette area. To the right, partitioned from the other half of the basement was Rad's keepsake room. The room had been designed to resemble an Army barracks, with two double-bunks, foot lockers and wall lockers. On display in one of the foot lockers were Rad's basic military issue; and in locker #2, Rad had his collection of badges, awards, medals, and unit crests identifying each respective period and location of assignment. Even the tiled floor resembled an Army barracks, and in open racks were Rad's uniforms hung in military style. Lined under the end of his bunks were two pairs of spit-shined, combat boots and a pair of low-quarter dress shoes, also highly polished.

In the corner of the room were two Army-issue field phones. "These," Rad explained, "are actually wired to the living room upstairs, and will be monitored by one of our security guys during your interview. They come down here to live in and bunk down whenever the site is in use"

I was not at all surprised. I had been wondering where Gaylord's reinforcements would be, and found it comforting they would be so close. From the back, a walk-up exit allowed direct access into the back just a few steps from the garage.

On the walls were three travel posters of European origin, and a painting of General Macarthur adorned the fourth wall. Beneath the famous painting was a small brass label bearing the quotation *"I am concerned for the security of our great Nation; not so much because of any threat from without, but because of the insidious forces working from within."*

"Obviously true," I thought.

We spent another hour or so getting reacquainted and discussing the upcoming meeting. Gaylord was very confident that Ivan would accept the pitch with very little effort on our part. He then handed me a complete copy of the photo album of Ivan's life. This was to be used for the recruitment. The photos depicted Ivan making dead drops, and signals; conducting meetings and briefing sessions with his potential and active source meetings taking place at various locations throughout the Far East, in Washington D.C., and at other locations up and down the eastern seaboard. While the activities of his potential and active sources were also photographed, many of the photos were blatantly cropped or doctored in order to conceal the identity of American persons who participated and cooperated in the reporting of Ivan's actions. At no point in any of the photographs was DG implicated. Ivan would be made aware that some of his contacts have cooperated with USI and will be dealt with separately. Only as a last resort would DG or any other American be specifically identified during this recruitment attempt.

Ivan's filmed and photographed meetings with Strübel, along with the audio recordings wherein Ivan agreed to consider Strübel's "unexpected offer" in Virginia would appear as though Ivan were wittingly cooperating with an American intelligence organization. A well-spliced film of their meeting at the airport on arrival in San Francisco, greeting, shaking hands, etc would all be made and included as part of the coercive techniques employed if needed. A second dossier had been assembled into a folder of proof of Ivan's long-time "cooperation" with USI. As a matter of fact, even recordings and documentation of this recruitment interview would look more like a debriefing session than a recruitment attempt. Ivan would never be able to escape the designation of "traitor" if the information were released to the proper media and authorities. If Ivan and his activities are exposed to the world media, his government would immediately recall him to Moscow with a full guarantee of reduced or terminated career prospects.

He would not be mistreated during our confrontation, and his life will not be threatened.

CHAPTER 26:
THE CONFRONTATION.

On Friday, as the plane descended into San Francisco International Airport, Ivan found himself anxiously daydreaming. He was in a 'what-if' mode.

If this contract goes well with Strübel, he thought *"I could retire a little early from the KGB and continue with my hobby of writing and being an international correspondent. One could lead into the next. Buddha says that 'if one does not close the door behind, the door in front will never open.'*

His thought processes continued as he thought momentarily of his American friend DG. He had come to think of him more as a brother than as a recruited asset; after all, he had never really recruited DG. It was a mutual understanding. They had helped each other. Somewhere along the line, DG must have figured things out, as his tasking became more and more secretive, and he accepted training without question. *"It was more like being co-opted than recruited"*, Ivan thought. *"DG is my friend"*. How happy DG was for him when he said he would be going on a trip with his mother to San Francisco…

Crackling with static interference, the announcement to prepare for landing emitted from the overhead speakers and passengers obediently set about securing their tables and fastening their seatbelts. When they left Washington, the description of weather conditions at San Francisco International included "fogged in, with limited visibility."

But now, most of the fog had lifted, and looking out of his window, Ivan could clearly see all but the southern end of the Golden Gate Bridge, which remained shrouded. Glancing toward the left, Ivan searched for and located the mountain top spot from where his own famous picture-poster photograph had been taken. "Beautiful," he said aloud. "Just beautiful."

Ivan handed the chit to the attendant who retrieved his wardrobe from the hallway closet and handed it to him on the way out of the plane. In the terminal, it was like coming home. "WELCOME TO SAN FRANCISCO", the sign read. As he descended to the lower-level to pick up his luggage, Ivan again observed the same famous photo of the Golden Gate Bridge; the view he had observed first hand just moments ago. He found his way to carousel 7 which had his flight number listed, and stood waiting for his luggage. *"Funny,"* He thought. *"Regardless how unique your luggage seems to be, when they come up the chute, they all look alike!"*

Finally he recognized his luggage coming toward him and he retrieved both pieces. As he turned to walk toward the exit, he observed George Strübel smiling and walking in his direction, reaching out to shake hands. They greeted as old friends would, and George took one of Ivan's pieces of luggage.

"We've put you up at the *Travelodge* on Lombard, if that's OK," Strübel announced. "Do you need to check in at your embassy right away?"

"No need," Ivan answered. "They only know I'm here on vacation – that's all they need to know. Since my mother will be arriving in a few days, they won't be expecting me to check in."

"Perfect! What's her schedule?" George asked, as if he didn't already know.

"She's coming in Tuesday morning. Is she ever excited?!" Ivan replied.

"I'll bet she is."

They walked across the overpass to the parking lot and located Strübel's new Chevy *Malibu*. They placed both bags in the trunk and Ivan hung his wardrobe on the hook over the back seat.

Half of Strübel's Surveillance Detection team was stopped at the exit, paying their parking fees when George pulled up behind them. Their car bore California Plates, framed in a metal rectangle, bearing a dealership's name in Reno. They eased away and George paid his one-hour fee. As he pulled onto the two-lane ramp toward the freeway, George passed the SD sedan. On the passenger side, the lady surveillant was looking over a San Francisco street map as though she was unfamiliar with the area. Ivan mistakenly took them for recent transplants from out of state.

Distracting Ivan from the traffic, Strübel remarked "You know, Ivan, our office is very excited about your coming aboard. It is extremely rare have any foreign Diplomat coming to work. You never know - this could lead to something big; maybe even a whole new career.

"I've not given much thought to a new career," Ivan lied humbly. "I've still a few years to go before this one is over, you know. It is a pleasant thought though."

George eased onto the freeway and drove toward 'DOWN TOWN' on highway 101. He followed the exit signs to Van Ness Avenue and to 'The Golden Gate', exiting onto Lombard Street. Minutes later, they were pulling into the *Travelodge*. The total drive had taken only 27 minutes.

George handed the room key to Ivan as they got out of the car, and helped him with his luggage inside. "I made this reservation as soon as you called me with your arrival information."

"Suppose we have dinner tonight," George suggested. "We'll have plenty of time to discuss business over the next few days. The room is already paid for, so help yourself to the amenities, and feel free to use the telephones and other services. The sky's the limit.

"Do I need receipts?" Ivan was half-joking.

"No need," Strübel replied. "We have a standing account with the *Travelodge*. We all trust each other." And then "I've made reservations at *Paprika's Fono* in Ghirardelli Square. It's an excellent Hungarian Restaurant; but if you'd rather dine somewhere else, then please… it's your choice."

"Wow!" Ivan was surprised. "The *Fono* is perfect. It was one of my father's favorite places."

"OK then, pick you up at 7 sharp?" The idea was to keep Ivan happily nostalgic and fairly busy, but not to overwhelm him.

"Great, I'll be ready."

After unpacking and hanging his clothes, Ivan took the second bag of his mother's belongings into the second bedroom and placed it on the bed. He took a quick shower, brushed his teeth, and turned on the television. The newscast was expounding forest fires in the Los Angeles area, and the probability that someone had set the forest ablaze intentionally.

Ivan turned the TV off, then picked up the telephone book and searched through it briefly. He found the name he had been looking for and dialed '9' for his outside line. *Next door, a surveillance team had already picked up their monitor and were recording as Ivan dialed the last seven digits and waited for the ring.*

The phone rang only twice, and a familiar voice answered.

"Yes. Hello? This is Yuri."

"It is I" Ivan said in Russian. "Ivan Romanyev, from Vladivostok."

494

"Ivan!" Came the excited reply. "Are you in San Francisco? How long are you staying?"

"Yes, I am. I just flew in today. We'll be here for about two weeks. I have little business to take care of that will keep me busy for a few days, then mother will be following me here for a short holiday. How are the Ulanovas?" Ivan asked, smiling to himself.

"We are all fine and here together with me too."

"What are you doing these days?" Ivan asked.

"We are running our own business now," Yuri replied. "It's like being free here. No unexpected visits from the government, no hidden taxes." He laughed. "We own our own gas station and laundry, and have a Korean employee pressing clothing."

"You know, mother is coming in on Tuesday. She will be looking forward to seeing you and your lovely Carla. By the way, how is your mother?"

Everyone is doing well. We have good doctors here and mother's stomach cancer turned out to be an ulcer. It is all gone. As for Papa – he's not doing so well. But he is happy here. By the way, Ivan, I was so shocked to hear of your father's untimely passing."

"Actually, it was not unexpected, Yuri. Father had been ill for a long time." Ivan then changed the subject "Mother will be calling you on Tuesday, and as soon as my business is done, we'll all get together for a celebration, OK? Do you still live on Union Street?"

Yes, we are in the same home. Our laundry shop is downstairs, and at the next door is our gas station – you know, where I used to work? Well, it now belongs to us."

"Wonderful – it will be like old times. So good to hear your voice, Yuri." Ivan slowly hung up the phone. He smiled to himself as he thought of those few years in Vladivostok with his friend Yuri. They had always called each other *'cousin'*, although they were not at all related. They had promised to be God Fathers to each others sons.

Ivan had not been at all surprised when Yuri showed up on his parent's doorstep in the Union District right here in San Francisco. Yuri had applied for the opportunity to migrate, located a sponsor whom he often referred to as "Uncle Vlad". After two years of attending school and working for Uncle Vlad in a restaurant, Yuri had packed his few belongings and moved into a small apartment nearby. As time passed, he corresponded regularly with his childhood girlfriend Carla, and immediately after taking the oath of citizenship, he sent for her and she joined him in his second floor flat on Union Street. They were all so young and always so excited about everything. An energized Carla talked incessantly about the possibilities of the new life now confronting them. Over the years, their families had occasionally visited each other, even when it meant traveling across the US in order to do so.

Strübel's knock came at the door at 1900 hours, and they drove in Strübel's Chevy to Paprika's Fono. The décor had not changed since Ivan had last visited the restaurant, and they were greeted and escorted immediately to their waiting table. Along the south wall, a complete mirror doubled the apparent size of the dining room. Ivan chose to sit facing the mirrored wall, to allow a full view of the other customers. When Strübel recognized Ivan's maneuver he was immediately happy he had not asked for SD during this dinner. He knew however that the 'agency' would provide some type of photo coverage for the 'album'.

Their meeting was casual, as they joked and laughed, partaking of a breathtaking dinner of goulash, and the venison special. Black bread and hors d'oeuvres' completed the meal, followed by a choice assortment of heavy desserts.

When asked of their drink preference, George asked for a double *Wild*

Turkey. Ivan asked the waiter if they stocked his favorite *'Ohranj Vodka'.*

"I believe so, sir, but let me make sure first," the waiter promised as he excused himself and walked quickly toward the bar. When he returned with their drinks, the waiter spoke to Ivan in Russian, saying "34 degrees exactly, sir. I hope that's the way you like your *Ohranj.*" Ivan was delightfully surprised. The waiter poured two ounces into the tumbler and placed the freeze-wrapped bottle on the table. He then poured George's Wild Turkey double and placed his bottle alongside Ivan's *Ohranj.* Ivan first sucked wind, preparing his throat for the cold trickle, then just before touching his lips to the glass said clearly "To our health!"

When George returned the toast, Ivan quickly inhaled half of the two-ounce shot. George in a sign of unity lifted his bourbon and followed suit.

Following dinner, George drove back to Lombard Street, but instead of going directly to the Motel, he turned left and drove east; first up the hill, and then down the 'Crookedest Street' and on to Pioneer Square and Coit Tower.

"This is one of my favorite drives." George said, as they reached the parking area at the base of the tower.

Completely in agreement, Ivan recalled "As a child, I came here often with my parents."

George parked along the north rails, overlooking the bay. They got out and stood for about fifteen minutes discussing their mutual impressions of the panorama before them. Before leaving the area, Ivan put a quarter into the slot, turned the pay-telescope toward the bay, and then down to the piers along the waterfront.

In the bright illumination of a streetlamp, he could see a clown, packing his mime props and placing them in the basket over the rear wheel of his bicycle. The clown stopped momentarily, turned and looking directly in Ivan's direction, waved as though saying "Bye-bye."

Ivan jumped back in surprise as though he were a young boy caught with his hand in the cookie jar. Realizing that the clown was a mile or two away, Ivan leaned forward and looked one more time. The clown had disappeared. Curious, Ivan scanned along the waterfront, but could not relocate the elusive clown.

The timer clicked, and the pay-telescope lens automatically closed. After a short time, they walked to the west end to take in the view toward Marin County. They returned to the car and drove back to the Motel. "I'll pick you up around 11:30 tomorrow morning if that's OK." Strübel suggested.

"That's perfect," Ivan responded. I'll have time to walk around the old neighborhood."

George departed the *Travelodge* parking lot to drive back toward his own temporary apartment. In doing so, he noticed his two Surveillance teams in position. No-one followed George Strübel.

Ivan felt wonderful. After a full meal and a half bottle of *Ohranj*, the hot hower prepared Ivan for a good night sleep.

CHAPTER 27:
THE DECISION.

♪ *I couldn't sleep at all last night* ♫ DG was singing the opening line from the 'Big Bopper's' hit song.

"Nor could I," I sang back. We joked about old times as we awaited my ride to T.I.

The large, leather, compartmented *'Overnighter'* briefcase was packed with the photos, tapes and films I would need, and placed near the door.

"Remember," I told him once more, "If anything happens that you feel we need to discuss during this interview, just push this red button. That will activate the signal, and I'll take a break and call you. That's why you're here. If you need to take a break for any other reason, use the same signal."

"I remember, but no telling what I'll do once this thing gets started. I've never done anything like this before."

"You'll do great." I assured him.

It was nearly 0700 when Rad knocked at the door. "Time to go." He announced as he entered. "You got any last questions there young fella?" He asked DG as he picked up the *Overnighter*.

"I think I'm fine." DG responded.

"You'll do great!" was Rad's enthusiastic response.

Great minds run in like channels.

We drove from the 'Bank' to the Bay Bridge, and turned toward Oakland. Even with the rush hour at full force, traffic was smooth and within 15 minutes we were at the site. We parked a block away, and walked to the front door. I noticed for the first time that none of the homes had building numbers, and all were identical in shape and size. Rad let us in with his key, and Gaylord was waiting.

"The interview area is set up in the sunroom." He announced. "And, the security guys are already in place in the basement. When Strübel pulls into the garage, he'll set off the beeper. Everything starts from there. The muscle will be out there to make sure Ivan doesn't try to break and run."

They set about inserting the new photos and films into the respective albums and canisters.

- - - -

Earlier that same morning, Ivan had walked to the nearby *"Guy's Restaurant"*, just around the corner from the *Travelodge*. He entered and sat at a booth near the front door. A fair-complexioned, smiling waiter arrived and took his order, saying "You're new around here, aren't you?"

"Not exactly," Ivan sounded casual. "I used to live not far from here."

"Welcome home, then." The waiter responded with another smile.

Ivan placed his order for the *'Healthy-king's'* breakfast, with triple everything. A steeping pot of hearty, robust black coffee was served immediately.

Within five minutes breakfast arrived, and from all appearances it was definitely fit for a king. Hearty and plentiful, the pepper-cured, lean bacon was cut thick and cooked to a medium-crisp. The biscuits were fresh-oven warm and generously buttered; and the eggs were just as he had ordered them. His potatoes were well-spiced home fries, and not the pre-packaged, oily, shredded potatoes he had learned to put aside. A side order of well-peppered pork sausage and gravy was also placed on the table.

It seemed to Ivan that the waiter was trying just a little too hard to please him. "I hope your meat is the way you like it," Smiley remarked as he gently rearranged the utensils for Ivan.

Ivan was about to say "Perfect!" when he realized that he just may have selected a restaurant which was not accustomed to serving customers of his heterosexual preference. Quickly glancing over the other patrons, Ivan realized they all seriously resembled the waiter. He hesitated momentarily, and then politely responded. "Actually, my preference would be to have the meat cooked a little more well-done." He smiled back.

The disappointed water smiled only briefly this time, and suggested "I can do it over for you if you'd like."

"Oh no," Ivan answered. "Please don't bother. It'll do for this time," still smiling.

As the waiter turned and walked back toward the kitchen, Ivan overheard him calling out: "Oh, Leroy, this one's yours."

"Oh, I just can't wait!" Ivan joked to himself.

After breakfast, Ivan took a short walk west on Lombard, then turned south and walked to Union Street. He was anxious to visit with his old friend Yuri, and realized he was only a few yards away. Ivan walked to within fifty meters from the intersection where he knew Yuri's business to be located, and after watching for several minutes noticed a car pull in to gas up. He recognized Yuri as he ran from the gas station office, talked momentarily with the driver, and then proceeded to gas up the car. He washed both the front and rear windows, returned to the pump and topped off the tank before inserting the nozzle back into the pump stand. The driver handed him some cash, and motioned for Yuri to keep the change. When the driver departed, Yuri waved with a smile and disappeared back inside the station. Ivan could tell that Yuri had found his place. He was home and he was happy. Ivan's heart was full. Tears of emotion momentarily filled his eyes as Ivan turned and walked back toward the Travelodge. *"This will be a wonderful reunion for Mom"*, he thought. Ivan saw no surveillance during his walk.

Back at the Travelodge an hour later, Ivan wondered if he should call Ströbel, and then decided not to bother. Ströbel had always been on time. He turned on the television and watched the Morning news. The weather forecast was for decreasing fog, completely lifting by 11:00 AM, and temperatures in the mid-seventies. "A good day for a nice long walk along the bay," the meteorologist had suggested.

"That sounds good to me." Ivan responded aloud. He was in a good mood.

At 1127 Ivan glanced at his watch and then looked out the window in time to see Ströbel pull into the parking lot. Habitually, Ivan glanced around the lot, searching for possible surveillance. He made note of a pair of businessmen entering the Motel office. Since they were driving a sub-compact, with luggage in the roof-rack, he dismissed them temporarily. He picked up his briefcase containing his well-prepared résumé and writing samples, and met Ströbel at the door.

They shook hands enthusiastically, and walked to Ströbel's car talking casually of the weather. Exiting to the right out of the motel, George Ströbel drove toward Van Ness Avenue, and then turned left, away from downtown San Francisco and the location of his 'office'. Observing Ivan's sudden alertness, Ströbel announced "I've got to make a stop along the way at a friend's place. I hope you don't mind."

"Of course not," Ivan relaxed.

The radio was playing *"I left my heart...",* and Ivan was habitually humming along with the tune, when they started across the Bridge. Then, without signaling, George turned off the exit to Treasure Island and made his way toward the safe site. As they approached, George noted a step-van parked adjacent to the garage, bearing the sign *Ace Landscaping and Maintenance Services.* Several green-coverall uniformed 'gardeners' were working in the immediate area. Security was in place.

On arrival, George pulled directly inside and parked. He switched off the engine, and pulled the keys from the ignition.

This action was also to Ivan's surprise, but still allowing George some benefit of doubt, he asked. "So your friend allows you to use his garage?"

George Ströbel did not answer directly, but instead said "You might as well come inside, Ivan. It's time to talk."

From out of nowhere two unidentified 'gardeners' appeared behind George's car. Ivan looked around.

"What's going on here?" he asked. "I demand you tell me what's happening!"

"Take it easy, Ivan." George suggested calmly. "We're only going to have a short discussion. Everything's under control now."

A gardener resembling *The Incredible Hulk* opened Ivan's door. The tight-fitting coverall uniform seemed to exaggerate his size and appearance. It was obvious to Ivan he had no choice. Walking from the garage to the house, Ivan looked around. In addition to the 'gardeners' on either side of him, he counted another eight. His heart was now pounding in his ears. *"They are all over the place,"* he thought. *"To cut and run now would be futile."* His mind was racing, trying to put everything in perspective; Ivan decided he wouldn't struggle at this point. He had already reached the conclusion that this was part of some conspiracy. His plans were coming apart – *"What about Mom,"* he thought.

They entered the back door as the gardeners went back to trimming hedges and raking the freshly mowed lawn around the safe site.

Ivan obeyed when asked to remove his shoes, and on request gave his jacket to Gaylord who hung it in the closet near the secured front door. He was introduced to Rad who spoke to him in Russian. Rad introduced himself only as "Richard". The fact that Rad spoke fluent Russian did not seem to relax Ivan in any way. He was introduced to Gaylord and then to me by our first names only. Looking directly into Ivan's eyes, I saw not the slightest indication that Ivan recognized me from our few near encounters in Bangkok. As I shook hands with Ivan, I noticed perspiration beading on his forehead, nose and upper lip. His hands were cold and damp. He was totally unprepared for any confrontation.

Rad, Ivan and I walked into the sun room, where a small rectangular dining table had been arranged with four chairs. At one end of the table, several photo albums and a small *Kodak Super-8* movie projector with a built-in, 12-inch viewing screen had been set up. Note pads and short pencils were placed on each side. Three more chairs were placed in the outside corners of the room. The blinds had been opened and tilted slightly upward to allow ample lighting. I counted two miniature movie cameras partially obscured from view by the drapes that had been opened to the corners of the room. Through reflective plastic curtains I could clearly see the 'gardeners' outside doing their job. I knew they could not see us, but since two of them wore ear phones resembling hearing aids, I assumed they were listening in.

Gaylord entered the room with a coffee pot, a tray carrying 4 mugs and a heap of varied, fresh donuts, which he placed in the center of the table. When Gaylord left, Rad came back in and offered Ivan a chair at the end of the table, near the projector. Ivan was slightly taken aback at the apparent level of hospitality. When Rad offered donuts, Ivan raised his hand in polite refusal; but as Rad poured coffee, Ivan accepted. He waited until I had taken a sip from my cup, then took a quick drink and sat quietly. Gaylord came back in to take his seat at the opposite end of the table, facing Ivan. Rad and I sat on opposite sides. Rad, sitting at Ivan's right started the conversation.

"I'm sure that by now you've figured out why you are here."

Ivan did not respond. He stared directly at 'Richard'. He was sizing him up. Rad may have been nearly twice Ivan's age, but his well-tanned appearance, pronounced cheekbones and piercing, black eyes gave him away. This old, half-occidental/half-Mongolian Giant was an obvious force with whom the average man would not desire altercation.

"I'm the projectionist," Rad said smiling. "I'm just here to get things started. But first, I'd like to show you the family photo album." He picked up the album bearing the Roman numeral I. The album was an expensive, combination smooth and suede calf, leather-bound holder, bearing a gold-embossed title in English. It read: **The Romanyev Family Album**. Rad opened it for Ivan to look. The first page was a full, 8X10-inch wedding photo of Ivan's parents.

Ivan glanced at the photograph, and then took a second look. It was precisely the photo in his mother's family collection album. "Where did you get this?" He demanded.

"From the archives of the *Vladivostok Press*," Rad replied. "There are many more. Here," he moved the album toward Ivan's hands.

"Help yourself. But please don't destroy it. It is yours to keep. We have more copies of all the pictures. I just wouldn't want to have to put it all together again."

Grabbing the album, Ivan began going through it. As he flipped through each of the twenty-odd pages, I watched his face undergo an almost metamorphic change. He saw photos he had never before seen, and some not seen since childhood; of himself and his father and mother. Several photos also included his Uncle 'Peter' Romanyev and Peter's family as well. His expression transformed from one of total refusal to that of shock, to gradual acceptance, to humility. Ivan had been humbled. I couldn't help but feel just a little sorry for him.

"So, now what?" he asked loudly. He was trying to sound intimidating, but his voice broke.

'Richard' turned to Gaylord and nodded.

Gaylord turned off the overhead light and closed the blinds behind Ivan. Rad turned on the small projector and moved his chair around to sit beside Ivan. Following Rad's lead, I moved to Ivan's other side, and in the semi-darkness, we quietly watched the film. Rad's face was without expression, but Ivan watched intently as the images of himself and his life with the KGB opened and passed before his eyes.

It began with a few short clips of his father's activities, of their family picnics and outings; and continued with the senior Romanyev's 4th of July weekend trip to meet with Ivan in Monterey, Carmel and Big Sur California. Ivan's turquoise and beige, 1959 Ford Convertible was shown, as Ivan drove to Monterey and gassed up before meeting up with his father. Also depicted were films of the placement of technical equipment designed to track and record his travels and conversations, but there was of course no mention that most of the recordings resulting from that venture were inaudible. Shown also were the security measures his father had taken, to include the rental of an additional car, and their ritualistic switching of the parking spaces outside their hotel window to prevent anyone else from parking in those slots.

Intermittent were shots of Ivan's frequent travels between San Francisco and Monterey, including films of his classmates, identification of the motels where he resided during his travels, and specific coverage of the hotel room in the Pacific Park Hotel in Monterey. It was obvious they had been closely followed. Ivan appeared to be frozen in shock, watching the film.

The film went on to depict a copy of Ivan's application to suspend his course of studies at San Francisco State, and notes from his 'advisor' describing their follow-on discussion and Ivan's final decision to travel the world.

Quick excerpts of Ivan's years as an Able-Bodied Seaman/Radio Operator with *Hi Seas Shipping and Transportation Company*; and narrated surveillance filming of some of his port visits were also shown. It must have occurred to Ivan that one of his shipmates was involved in keeping track of his activities. It occurred to me.

The continuing sequences included filming of Ivan walking in and out of the classrooms at SF State, photos of Ivan aboard the *USS Maritime* and various other ships on which he had served while working for the *Hi Seas Shipping and Transportation Company*. They depicted the ports of San Francisco, Manila, Singapore, Saigon, Kao Hsiung, Naha, Osaka and Pusan; along with Ivan's respective road trips to Olongapo, George Town (Pinang, in the strait of Malaca), Vung Tao, Taipei, Tokyo and Seoul. On rare occasions, Ivan was seen traveling with his seamen friends, but most of his road trips were solo. The majority of his extended visits were to countries where American soldiers were stationed or visiting for their R&R - Rest and Recuperation.

Ivan appeared completely mystified at how closely he had been followed on those shore-leave trips, and even more impressed by the quality of the photography. A few of the photos of Ivan were intentionally enlarged, but still retained unmistakable identification.

The last segments included filmed bursts of Ivan servicing dead drops, and conducting one-way and two-way passes and out-of-door training sessions with his sources. The filming was accomplished in such a way as to obscure the actual identity of the sources, but as he watched the films, Ivan nodded slightly in recognition, and his facial expressions told me that he was able to clearly recall each and every location, source and activity. This 90 minute portion of the film further depicted even more contacts, meeting sites, signals, and flashed through many of Ivan's attempts at conversation with Americans at Embassy events, local establishments, bars, coffee shops, restaurants, American clubs, hotels and other hangouts known to be used by Americans, both overseas and in the Washington D.C. area. A ten-second clip revealed Ivan sitting at a table in the Kings Palace in Bangkok. Frank and I were not in the film, and DG was not shown. Of course, I was personally acquainted with the photographers.

Finally, the film scanned a set of blurred, barely recognizable American CIC credentials, and then showed Ivan seated in the Chao Phraya Hotel Dining Room in Bangkok. As an unidentified American Army officer entered, Ivan stood and displayed what appeared to be a set of credentials, and they sat at the table engaging in conversation over their meal.

'Richard' reached over and stopped the projector as Gaylord turned the lights back on. I estimated another 30 minutes of the film had not yet been shown.

So much had been said without my having uttered a sound.

I looked at Ivan. He was looking down at the blank yellow pad on the table. When he looked up, both Rad and Gaylord had left the room. I stood.

"Before we continue, Ivan, let's take a few minutes break."

Ivan nodded in agreement, and asked where the bathroom was located. *'Incredible'* stood as Ivan walked through the living room. As Ivan entered the restroom, the Hulk positioned himself outside the door. I descended to the basement and called DG. He was anxious.

"What's happening over there?" he asked. "It's really quiet. All I can hear are a few words of narration and a few comments now and then."

"We're just showing home movies and looking over family albums. Things will pick up after a quick lunch," I promised. "You might as well take a lunch break, but don't forget to put fresh tapes in before you start again."

We had spent over two hours already, since Ivan's arrival at the garage. It would be a late lunch break.

DG changed the tapes immediately, and left the monitor on just in case something worth recording began. He placed a frozen TV dinner in the oven and set the timer for 15 minutes. He sat back down in front of the recorder to wait. DG was tapping his foot, checking the sound, tapping his foot, adjusting the output, and tapping his foot. The words 'apprehension and anxiety' could not accurately describe his exhilaration.

Ivan sat in the bathroom and looked around. There were no windows, and the only way out was the way he'd entered. He sensed *'Incredible'* standing outside. The restroom was totally silent. The soundproofing was excellent. As he looked up, Ivan saw a single camera aimed at the seat. This caused him to immediately begin staring at his stocking feet. As he stood, the lens refocused automatically. *"This is really embarrassing."* He thought. As he rinsed his hands, Ivan looked at himself in the mirror. Dark circles had formed around his eyes. He looked worn-down. Ivan splashed cold water over his face, towel-dried and finger-combed his hair. He walked out and directly back into the sunroom where he sat and began skimming again through the Romanyev family album.

I used the basement bath before returning to the sunroom. Ivan sat alone, looking over the album. Watching him was almost depressing. I would try to sound upbeat.

"We've ordered pizza," I stated. "I understand you like combination pizza and Bud."

"I'm not at all hungry." Ivan retorted. "I don't know what you people expect of me." He was trying to establish his position. "I don't even have to be here, you know."

He paused, and then turned to me and asked "What's your connection here anyway?"

"I'm just a bystander," I answered. "But we'll have plenty of time to discuss me when we've taken care of everything else." I suggested.

"I told you, I'm not hungry." Ivan responded without hesitation. "I would very much like just to get this all over with."

"So would I," I was trying to soothe the situation Ivan was creating. "But everyone else is hungry, so we might as well be patient."

Ivan knew he could not get the upper hand considering the situation here at the safe site. "I can wait." He said.

I was fully cognizant of the instability, the volatility of this situation, and also aware that it was my job to try and establish some rapport.

"So, how do you like the album?" I asked casually.

Ivan hesitated as though deep in thought. He took a deep breath and let it out. He then looked up and staring directly at me said. "It's OK," he was probably being truthful. Then after he thought a little more said "I've not seen some of these since my childhood. Did the pictures really come from Vladivostok?"

"The wedding photo did." I answered. "Most of the rest are archive shots, taken during your father's assignments."

"You must have people everywhere…" Ivan was leading me.

"We're just like you," I answered. "We try to cover every angle." I smiled.

Our conversation was turning into a game of cat and mouse. I let it ride, knowing that DG was recording every word. I knew we would get into details once lunch was over.

Just then, the doorbell rang, startling Ivan almost out of his chair. The Pizza guy was delivering Pizza, beer and soft drinks. I placed the donut tray and a fresh pot of coffee on the living room coffee table, while Gaylord paid for the delivery.

Just as the pizza guy was about to close the door, Ivan jumped up and shouted to him. "Help me please! I'm a Russian Diplomat being held against my will!"

The Pizza guy looked at Ivan and replied pitifully "I really doubt that, Ivan," and smiled as he quietly closed the door.

Ivan collapsed back down into his chair like a deflated balloon. He had been put down by a witting pizza guy.

Gaylord then brought the pizza into the sunroom.

Moments later, the red light on the camera over Ivan's head came back on. Reflection of that small red light on the window pane in front of Ivan caught his eye, and as he glanced upward he couldn't help but think of the cameras located within the Russian Embassies. Rad watched quietly.

Again, Ivan restated "I really do have diplomatic immunity, you know."

Rad responded. "And you know, Ivan, we are not your enemies here. Those of us sitting around this room are probably the very best friends you could possibly have right now, given the circumstances. You might as well join in, pop a Bud, and have a slice of pizza."

I looked at Rad - he was smiling. I looked at Ivan - he was puzzled. He knew Rad was right, and his choices were limited. But there were so many unanswered questions. He decided to present a semblance of cooperation. He opened a Bud, poured a glass full and tore off a slice of pizza. Taking a bite, he commented "Not bad. Not bad at all."

"Good." Rad observed. He turned to me and nodded. It was my turn to talk, and on that cue, Gaylord and Rad took their beers, a small pizza and departed back into the living room, almost out of earshot. Ivan finished his piece of pizza, inhaled two more large gulps of beer. He then leaned back in his chair, again folding his arms in a signal of stubborn resistance.

I opened photo album II, saying "Over the past decade, Ivan, we've come to the conclusion that somewhere along the line you had decided to follow in your father's footsteps. Now, that is admirable."

I went on. "Admirable is – shall we say – 'nice' – but it's not always the right choice, you know."

Ivan was watching the album, as I turned the pages, depicting even more examples of him making dead drops, and leaving signals; conducting meetings and briefing sessions with his potential and active sources; and of meetings taking place at various locations throughout the Far East, in Washington DC and other locations up and down the eastern seaboard. Each separate group of photos was prefaced with a title page: Boston, Philadelphia, Baltimore, Washington DC, Norfolk, Fayetteville/Wilmington, Charleston, Panama City, and Miami. Another group of photos also included vacation shots of Ivan in northern Thailand as well as in Florida. None of the photographs were taken with Ivan or DG's cameras, but were taken by the American surveillance teams following Ivan on his debriefing and training missions. Many of the photographs framed a view of the top of the surveillance car, or included a portion of the windshield visor, steering wheel or rear-view mirror. Ivan knew they were taken by someone following his every move.

Again, without explaining, I handed album II to Ivan. Unfolding his arms, he quickly began paging through the pictures, occasionally nodding his head slightly in acknowledgement. Halfway through the album, he pushed it aside and leaned back, crossing his arms again. He sighed in deep thought.

"Your contacts" I explained, "once confronted with all this proof, have been cooperating for some time, as you can see. It was nice of you to accept this reassignment to the US. For one thing, it put you on our turf. Once here, you have continued along the same path of espionage. Actually, we have no choice other than to confront you with this evidence." I then asked: "Ivan, aren't you aware of the immigration laws pertaining to the abuse of diplomatic privilege?"

Ivan's non-response was a positive answer.

"And, how about the same group of regulations pertaining to the conduct of espionage?"

Ivan unfolded his arms and continued leafing through the album. Glancing up at me, he asked "Am I under arrest here, or something?" Ivan was still trying to sound both challenging and antagonistic. This time, I didn't respond, and Ivan returned to the album. Although there were no clear photos of his source's faces, it was clear that he recognized each of his 'accomplices' and was fully aware of his predicament. He had no plausible denial.

Now, Ivan reached the photographs taken since his assignment to Washington DC and began also to recognize his more recent activities. His eyes widened and pupils expanded as he reached the pictures of his initial contact and follow-on luncheon with George Strübel. He was angry. He knew without a doubt that he had let his guard down.

I spoke. "These photographs can be used as proof of your attempts to cooperate with US Intelligence. They depict your successful undertaking with Mr. Strübel." I turned on the audio player, and Ivan overheard his own words wherein he referred to the "unexpected offer" during their very first meeting;

"And you mutually agreed during one of your subsequent telephone calls to meet with Strübel here in San Francisco. Did you report this meeting to your embassy as a contact with a known or suspect Foreign Intelligence Service official?" I asked.

"Of course not," Ivan answered; now looking directly at me. "How was I to know he was a spy?"

"That's really funny." I responded, smiling sarcastically. "You - calling George Strübel 'a spy'. It sure doesn't look that way here."

"Or," I continued. "Did you make up some story about a possible post retirement job offer?"

I was now leading him.

"Of course – that was the TRUTH!" Ivan almost yelled.

"But," I said, "If you look closely, this is nothing more than a clandestine, personal meeting!" I said, pointing to the luncheon at the *Taste of Ethiopia*, the follow-on back at the Embassy Hotel in Arlington. There were photos of Ivan and Strübel having lunch, and getting in and out of Strübel's car in the underground parking lot. "And this is the two of you greeting at San Francisco International less than 48 hours ago."

I turned the audio on again, while we listened once more to the telephone call from Ivan to Strübel to set up their meeting arrangements in San Francisco, and then photographs of their drive to the *Travelodge*. "If I go on," I told Ivan, I can also include your dinner at the *'Fono'*, and your casual drive to Coit Tower."

"We have two more albums to go through here," I said, reaching for photo Album III.

"There's no need," Ivan held up a hand. "I've seen and heard enough."

There was an extended pregnant pause.

"What options do I have?" He asked pointedly. Then he repeated himself emphatically as though his mind was vacillating. "I DO have Diplomatic Immunity. Are you trying to arrest me?"

This time I answered that question. "No. You are not being arrested, and you are not being held against your will. We are more professional than that. You will see."

"Then I am free to go?"

"Certainly!" I was bluffing, and I knew *'Incredible'* would back me up. "But, I definitely wouldn't advise it. You see, Ivan," I paused. "If we let you go, exactly where will you go? How will you get there? What will you do?" I continued. "What about your mother and the vacation you have planned with her? Our intention is to see to it that you have an enjoyable time together - for your vacation, and for the rest of your lives."

Ivan was quiet. I glanced at Rad in the living room, to see him give me the thumbs up. It was time to call it a day. We had already decided that too much pressure would be counterproductive this first day. It was time for Ivan to think.

"What do you say we call it a day? We can relax, have dinner, and pick up tomorrow where we left off. A new day, perhaps a new vision." I closed the photo album.

Ivan slowly nodded his head, as 'Richard' came back into the room.

"I am expected to stay here?" Ivan asked, glancing around as though the temporary quarters were inadequate.

"All your belongings are up in the master room." Rad replied. Handing a small note to Ivan, Rad continued "Make yourself at home and please - call your mother and give her this phone number. If she should call you back, her call will pass through the 'switch' at *Travelodge*, and will be directed immediately to the telephone here in the living room and to the extension up in the master. No-one will answer this line except you. There's no need for her to change her plans. You are still booked at the 'Mark', beginning Tuesday afternoon." Rad went on. "If you feel the need to call your embassy, then we must make other arrangements and take different precautions."

"There's no need." Ivan relented. He was not surprised that he had already been moved in.

-

Later, after a long evening of discussion with DG, I began a restless, sleepless night in the 'Bank'. Following the first day at the safe site, I was unexpectedly exhausted, but still could not fall asleep. I could hear DG moving around in his room as well. At 0130 hours, I knocked on his door.

"Need a sedative?" I asked.

DG grinned as he walked into the den area. "I thought you'd never ask." He poured a double of chilled *Ohranj* while I prepared my JWBOP. We drank silently. And sleep eventually came.

Meanwhile.

In the Master suite, Ivan discovered that he was surprisingly comfortable. Security was awake and alert, and with each movement outside his room, he was greeted politely with "Good evening Mr. Romanyev."

He walked down stairs and went to the refrigerator where he retrieved a *Hungry-Man* TV Dinner. He selected a small beer, popped the lid, took two long drinks, sat and waited the ring of the microwave.

He pondered his situation, asking himself *"Now just how did I let this all happen?"* Walking through the events that brought him to Washington, Ivan clearly recalled that at one point after DG returned to the US, consideration was being given to passing the project to someone already assigned to Washington. Ivan was asked to provide a letter of introduction to DG for another agent handler. Ivan refused, saying that their cooperation was based on a personal relationship, and that such personal loyalties could not be transferred to a stranger. Had he acquiesced, someone else would likely be sitting in the hot seat now.

Without warning, *Incredible* entered the kitchen. Interrupting Ivan's thought processes he asked "Is there anything I can help you with Mr. Romanyev?"

Politely refusing the offer, Ivan responded, saying "There's no need. And there's no reason to bother anyone."

"It's absolutely no bother – and if there's anything else you need – even just conversation, please feel free to call on me. I'm bunking down in the basement." He smiled.

"Thank You," Ivan answered. "Perhaps tomorrow."

"Anytime, anytime at all." *Incredible* walked back into the shadows of the living room.

Ivan inhaled the last two swallows of beer and tossed the can toward an opened garbage container near the rear door. He missed and stood to pick up the can. He glanced at the doorknob while looking through the glass panes.

Without hesitation, he grabbed the doorknob and tried to turn it. The door was solid, as though it were cemented in place.

"The panes are also shatterproof." Incredible's voice echoed as he walked casually back into the kitchen.

Ivan whirled around, half in panic, to see the hulk towering over him. "I couldn't resist," he said embarrassed. "I should have known."

Hulk's broad grin displayed a perfect set of slightly oversized teeth. "And the door is solid steel." He rapped on the door panel, allowing Ivan to recognize the metallic sound.

Perspiration had suddenly reappeared on Ivan's brow. Again, *Incredible* disappeared back into the darkened living room.

"I was just curious," Ivan called after him. "I wouldn't have tried to leave." Now he was even more embarrassed. That was a stupid lie.

Immersed in thought, Ivan sat.

Moments later, the ring of the Microwave startled Ivan. He retrieved the meal and placed it on a tray. Opening the refrigerator door, Ivan spotted the chilled bottle of *'Ohranj'* on the bottom shelf. Placing the *Ohranj* and a small glass on the tray Ivan carried dinner back upstairs, placing it on the pullout shelf of the desk. Carrying the ice-cold bottle, he wandered around the second floor, going from window to window, looking over the hillside. In the bright moonlight, and with lights extinguished in the suite, he could see the Bay to the south, and the Golden Gate standing majestically off in the distance toward the west. Ivan watched the red flashing lights on both towers, and said to himself "No fog so far tonight." But fog could be seen creeping in beneath the towers, and bridge traffic was steadily moving back and forth, barely visible and partially engulfed in the mist.

Beneath his window, Ivan could see the neatly maintained neighborhood. He glanced around the room, appreciating the décor.

"How could I have been so stupid", he asked himself. *"That guy,"* he was thinking of the Hulk-like figure, *"really moves quickly. Or maybe he was just standing back in the shadows watching.... waiting..."* He smiled to himself. *"He was 'Hulking around.' "*

The *'Ohranj'* was beginning to freeze his hand, so he placed it on the night stand coaster. He couldn't help but notice that the coaster was an advertisement for the King's Palace in Bangkok. He checked dresser drawers, and found his clothing folded and placed therein. His suits were hanging uniformly in the closet, and his mother's suitcase had been placed on the shelf. He was impressed with the extent of detail to which the US Government took care of things.

He sat at the desk, pondering the day's discussions. This would not be an easy decision for him. He had come to San Francisco with the mindset of making a rather routine decision regarding the establishment of a cover for continuing his espionage activity. He had also considered laying the groundwork for a new career once he left the KGB. Now, he has learned the Americans have known about him for years and have different ideas.

This guy Don seems some how to have developed a more extensive knowledge of his activity than most of the others, and has apparently been following him for an extended period. Ivan could not believe the photos and films they'd taken of his parents and of their trips together over the years. He wished he had copies of all the movies and photos the Americans had taken. It crossed his mind to ask for copies.

Ivan was thinking of the training he'd been given as a new counterintelligence operative. He had memorized his planned reaction if he were ever confronted with exposure.

"Blackmail me?" He would ask, laughing. *"Who are you kidding? Just make copies of all the pictures for me – in color; and send them on to my embassy – to my government. You can't blackmail me!"*

"It just doesn't work that way. These Americans are offering me something I actually want. I need only to decide which way to go; to make sure mother is being taken care of and that we are protected." He admitted to himself.

He returned to sit on the bed. He glanced at the *'Ohranj'*, picked up the bottle and spun the lid off with his thumb. He watched as it sailed across the room and hit flatly against the window pane, landing on the sill behind the curtain. He carried the bottle to the desk, where he sat and tried to eat. His appetite was easily satisfied and at 0130 hours, Ivan tilted the bottle and drank several swallows directly. Throwing the remainder of the dinner in the small cinch-bag garbage can, he then walked over, retrieved the lid, and screwed it back on the *Ohranj*. He placed the remaining few ounces of the *Ohranj* in the door rack shelf of the small fridge which was located in the bottom portion of the night stand. Almost immediately Ivan began to feel relaxation dominating his body, and after a hurried shower, he returned and fell asleep face down.

Day two at the safe site.

Sunday began as a dreary day. By 0900 the early dense fog that had settled in during the early morning hours seemed to be trapped in over the bay and Treasure Island was completely shrouded. Visibility was at a bare minimum.

When Ivan arose, he found clothing laid out for him. The garbage bag had been removed, and a new one replaced in the container. He rinsed and shaved, combed his hair, dressed in the clothing that had been placed beside him, and descended the stairs. He shuddered as he envisioned *'Hulk'*, moving around him silently as he slept.

When I entered the safe site, Ivan was sitting on the living room sofa, talking with Rad and *Incredible*. To my surprise, all three were speaking Russian. They had consumed some fresh pastry and were drinking coffee – together.

Fresh coffee and donuts were also waiting in the sun room as Ivan and I entered and took up our respective positions. The red lights went on.

"Did you sleep well?" I asked casually. "And how about your Mom - did you get through?"

"She's due in Tuesday on schedule." Ivan responded without precisely answering. His voice was casual – almost cooperative. No more perspiration.

I offered coffee and Ivan accepted readily. As I poured his coffee, Ivan studied me closely. I understood his reluctance to accept me. He knew nothing of my association with DG, of my involvement in observing and to some extent controlling his activities over the past 10 years. He had no reason to respect or disrespect me.

"So, are we continuing the blackmailing issue?" He probed.

"Blackmail is not really the issue." I answered, resuming my position at the corner of the table. "There is no reason to introduce such uncivilized methodology into our relationship. We've already gone beyond that point." I paused. "I'm sure you gave your *'decision'* plenty of thought last night… I will admit though that we are prepared to show that when confronted with photos and films, identification of your DD sites, your signals, personal meetings, tasking, the fabricated reports, etc, you expressed a strong willingness to cooperate…" I left the rest unsaid.

After another few moments of hesitation, Ivan spoke slowly. "I've done some studying in my lifetime, and I fully understand the categories under which defection is allowed." Ivan continued, trying to read my facial expression, "You know I could provide intelligence information; I would be good propaganda; and I could lecture at any of many institutions in the US – to include your intelligence schools..."

"Are you offering your services?" I interrupted.

"Of course there would be provisions – or maybe requests on my part, were I to cooperate."

"For example..."

He paused. "My mother is of primary concern to me. Her safety, her livelihood and well-being are my responsibility. Could she remain with me?" He then explained, "I fear that something terribly adverse could happen to her as a result of my decision if she was forced to return to Russia on her own." he continued, "The KGB would not hesitate to utilize her to pressure me in some way."

Ivan was thinking consequences, and in that statement he had clearly outlined his thought processes. I liked the direction he was moving, and allowed him to ponder.

"Would I be able under any conditions to return and retrieve any of my personal belongings from my office - from our apartment in Arlington?" He was bargaining; considering his courses of action, and at this point, I knew he'd given his situation enough thought to see things our way. Gaylord was right, it wouldn't take long.

Pencil in hand, Ivan looked down at the notepad on the table. He seemed transfixed at the single word *"Decision"* he had scribbled on the pad the day before. It seemed to hypnotize him.

"What about my friends – what would they think of me?"

I had yet to answer any of these questions, so I interrupted him again.

"What could it matter?" I asked. "You needn't be concerned about the thoughts or opinions of your KGB friends. Chances are you will never again experience face to face contact with any one of them. Should that happen, what would they do? Would they complain? You know, if the word were to get out of your decision Ivan, the rest of the world would admire you. The opinions of a few KGB agents who insist on prolonging the cold war and spying on the free world are not necessarily of prime concern. Soon enough, our world will have shrunk, our gates will have opened, travel restrictions will be lifted and you will have personally sacrificed and contributed to world peace. You must think of what that would mean - to you – and to your mother. What are her ambitions and desires?"

Ivan continued now to look down, contemplating. I glanced at the yellow, notepad in front of him on the table. *"Decision"* remained his only written remark. I immediately recalled the handwritten statement made by Ivan in my last dream involving my clown friend.

Without prompting, I found myself reciting the statement as though it were a famous passage from an equally notorious writing. "A great philosopher" I started, "once said. *'In honor of my devoted father and for my beloved fatherland, I will make this decision based only on my ability to contribute to Peace in the world.' ."*

Startled, he stared at me for a moment, and then demanded. "Where did you get that?"

"I'm not exactly sure," I lied, fearing I had awakened the proverbial sleeping giant. "I believe I recall it from my childhood. I suppose - I've always felt that way myself."

"It's mine!" He responded. "It's from my diary – that very remark is a quote from a personal writing of mine."

Now, I was surprised. I wanted to argue *'No, it's mine, I dreamed it!'*, but recognizing his suggestion, I opted to promise "We do not have, nor have we ever seen your diary. Where ever you've left it, I'm sure it is still in place and intact." Pausing momentarily, I then suggested "I presume though, this statement is also <u>your</u> philosophy?"

Again, it was time for a lunch break, and as I was about to descend to the basement and call DG, the red light started flashing.

"Perfect timing." I announced over the phone.

"Sorry." DG came back. I just have to use the restroom.

"Go ahead and take time for lunch too," I suggested. We'll be ready to start again by 1400 hours."

After an extended lunch hour, and fast food lunch, at 1400 hours we sat back down in the interview room. The recording light glowed.

Ivan said nothing. He sat there staring at me. After a full minute he cleared his throat and said. "Let us say I would choose to defect? To ask for political asylum. What would be the end result of such a request?" Then, as a last and final charge at the windmill, Ivan stated weakly "I really do have Diplomatic Immunity, you know!" I knew he was trying to influence my answer.

As I hesitated, Ivan spoke slowly, asking "And if I decide not to cooperate?"

Again I did not respond immediately, allowing Ivan to think over the question he had just asked. At the very least, He had to know that if he returned to Russia, he would be placed into exile; he and what remains of his family would be embarrassed. He would lose all dignity and respect - even from those who could have admired him under other circumstances.

Finally I responded, saying "I am prepared to describe your activities throughout your entire career, Ivan. The American media, and especially the Washington bureau of TASS news agency, would be appalled at how much information we have been able to put together on your life story. Beginning with Ivan Romanyev, born the son of a known KGB operative; to his initial and occasionally successful attempts to meet with American soldiers throughout Asia; to his recognized attempts to impersonate an American counterintelligence officer in Thailand; to his continuing participation in espionage activities right here in the Washington area... as you now know, they are all well documented."

Although not part of my 'Plan A', I explained that I was prepared to threaten exposure of Ivan's recruited American assets as agents for a foreign country, expose Ivan in the same scenario and have him cast out of the US. He would be designated Persona non-grata, and barred from ever returning. I suggested that when he returns to Russia, the KGB would likely arrange for his mother to be identified as his support operative – his accomplice.

"But we both know, Ivan, it doesn't have to happen that way. As I have said before, this is not a blackmail situation. We seek your cooperation, and we are the ones who can disavow knowledge."

I knew Ivan would not take this lightly, realizing the extent to which he would be dealt with by his comrades. To be designated PNG in the United States would not only be unacceptable, but would be the most dreadful decision Ivan could make; and would likely permanently dissociate him from his mother. I was counting on his personal relationship with DG, as well as any thoughts he might have on how his mother might react to such an accusation. I was also counting on his common sense.

To Ivan, knowledge of the fact that he had been unsuccessful in his espionage endeavors was probably already devastating.

Ivan's facial expression was that of full realization. He had been exposed. His plausible deniability was non existent. He could not avoid the truth. His decision would determine the extent to which he would be punished or rewarded for his actions. I knew he would not ask again what might happen if he refused. He already knew the answers. I had said enough.

As I looked directly at Ivan, I saw true emotion. A glimmer of tears welled in his eyes.

I wondered *"Were his tears of joy, sorrow, anxiety or relief?"*

I decided *"All of the above."*

CHAPTER 28:
THE FINAL DECISION.

Ivan had made up his mind. "Now I can be an American with little or no effort, and no feelings of guilt. Somehow I don't feel as though I am betraying my country; but rather that if the world is ever to realize openness, realize peace, then I will have been instrumental; I will have contributed in bringing us together. I only wish my father had been given this opportunity. I'm sure he would have made the same decision, 20 years ago."

"I too wish that were so, Ivan." I responded. "You never know, perhaps your father would still be here today."

He paused momentarily, then looked at me and said "Our family always loved America. I'm practically an American you know."

He continued. "You know, I have an old friend right here in San Francisco, and I've already called him since my arrival."

"Yes, I know," I responded. "And if you are not allowed to meet with Yuri and Carla, they could accidentally spill the beans by calling your embassy, looking for you."

Ivan's eyes opened widely when I mentioned "Yuri and Carla". He suddenly realized that we already knew of his friends. Of course we did.

"Allowing you to meet with the Ulanova family is already in the plans; and will be conducted under controlled conditions and scrutiny."

Ivan was visibly relieved. "I don't know how to say 'thank you'."

I spoke. "If you agree to remain here in the US, you will be tried in absentia in Moscow. You may be sentenced as well, but you will be living free here in America. There are conditions, of course."

Ivan must make this final decision on his own - without consulting his mother, his government, his old friend Yuri or anyone else. He understood clearly the price that must be paid.

"Now, what must WE do?" he asked.

I was relieved to hear him say 'we'. That statement was his submission to a degree of collaboration.

"We will be in escort of your visit with Yuri and Carla; but sadly, you must agree that this will be your last contact with them. If you were to confide your decision or your plans to them, it would present a terrible burden on them if they were ever to be contacted by representatives of your government. The less the Ulanovas know, the safer it will be for them.

Ivan nodded slowly in agreement.

Gaylord had entered the sunroom and was sitting in the other corner chair. "Does your mother have any health problems?"

"Like both her parents, she suffers from emphysema." Ivan spoke to Gaylord. "But she has been taking good medication for the pat few years. She's showing improvement daily."

"Is there anything else?"

"She is also beginning to show signs of rheumatism or arthritis." Ivan explained.

"You probably should call her and instruct her to bring her health records if they are already in her possession. At the very least, she should bring a list of any prescription medication she is taking. You need explain only that because she is traveling, it's good to be able to duplicate any medicines she is taking in case of loss or other emergency."

"What could happen?" Ivan asked.

Realizing Ivan's apprehension, Gaylord responded "It is routine. Health is an important part of her well-being. With very limited information, we can duplicate her health records under an assumed name; and even arrange for her complete physical checkup while you're here on vacation as well. It will all be done in such a way as to protect her true identity – and yours."

Now was not the time to hesitate. Gaylord encouraged him, saying "Go ahead Ivan, call your mother. Casually talk to her about your retirement plans, just a few years down the road. When you mention the new job as a writer/correspondent, it will open more doors."

"How do I do that?" Ivan had asked. "How, without tipping anyone off?"

Ivan was hesitant to make that first move. It is sometimes simple to make such a decision, but the first step requires some insistence, some urging.

Gaylord asked "Your mother is staying at your apartment in Arlington, is she not? Do you have any reason to believe your telephone or apartment is being wiretapped?"

"Not yet," Ivan responded. "They only do that when they are suspicious of someone. They would have no reason to be suspicious of me at this point. I don't think they are even trying to follow me while I'm here, but sometimes they do that just for practice. If I do not return to Washington on schedule following my two-week vacation, enquiries will begin within a few days."

"Okay, you'll call from here," Gaylord decided. "Make conversation by asking your mother if she's ready for the trip. Engage in small talk, and then casually mention that this new position of correspondent for a magazine will eventually require you to travel occasionally after you retire in a few years. Then ask her how she would feel about eventually moving back to San Francisco where the magazine maintains its head office." Gaylord warned. "Say no more. As for the medications, just give your mother a reminder to bring her medications. Say nothing that would tip off anyone. You do not want someone listening to your conversation to think that relocation could be imminent."

Surprisingly, Ivan was taking notes. They talked for awhile fine-tuning a simple dialogue for Ivan to use.

Rad became involved in the conversation. "Don't worry Ivan; we'll be there with you. You won't make any mistakes." He assured. "We won't let you."

"You know," Ivan said, "These past few years, the KGB has been extremely active in hunting down defectors at any cost. Some times they spend years searching for them. Their goal is to embarrass the defectors, and to try almost anything to bring them back to Russia for punishment and for propaganda purposes. If that is not possible, the alternative is to alienate them from any connections they may have left behind." He paused. "...or to assassinate."

As Ivan nervously stood, we all stood and shook hands with him. His handshake had become warm, and although still nervous, he was no longer perspiring quite so much. He had made his decision. Now he would begin to finalize the situation. In his eyes, I saw submission, acceptance, relief and finality.

He walked to the telephone stand and picked up the phone, dialed 9 for an outside number, and then direct-dialed his apartment telephone number in Arlington.

"Hello, Mum," he started. His every word, every innuendo was being recorded and filmed.

Before leaving the TI safe site, Gaylord opened a fresh bottle of Hennessy V.S.O.P. The five of us, including *Incredible* and his partner tipped a round in anticipation of Ivan's new beginning. The long-awaited 'special occasion' had arrived. The only one missing was DG.

Ivan's personal belongings were repacked and waiting. After dark, he was returned to the Travelodge, and on Tuesday, after checking in at the Mark, Ivan rented a car and drove toward the airport where he would meet his mother. Although he knew he would be under our constant watch, he felt at ease; he felt safe..

His mind had been going full speed since this encounter began; but now, he could finally begin to relax, as his lifelong dream was beginning somehow, almost magically, to unfold.

He found himself quoting himself in thought. *"Now I can be an American with little or no effort, and no feelings of guilt. Somehow I don't feel as though I am betraying my country; but rather that if the world is ever to realize peace, I will have been instrumental in bringing us together."*

"I've made the right choice." He said firmly and aloud.

"Mum, over here," Ivan called loudly to his mother as she passed through the gate.

As they awaited the arrival of her luggage, Ivan observed his mother. Since his father had died, Ivan had not seen his mother happier than she seemed at this very moment. She even seemed younger. She did not yet know what was in store. As the carousel began to rotate, Ivan put his arm around his mother's shoulders.

Once back on the freeway going into downtown San Francisco, Ivan started the chant: "♪ *California Here I come, right back where I started from…♫*" they sang on their way to the Mark Hopkins. Enroute, Ivan talked of his retirement, and the chances of working for the California office for the next few decades. Not once did Ivan mention the fact that they would likely never return to San Francisco once this vacation was over. There was no mention of his changing status.

CHAPTER 29:
THE DISPOSITION.

And so, their vacation began. Quiet and peaceful. Over the next two weeks, I had said 'good-bye' to DG, who returned to his new duty station at Fort Benning Georgia. I continued to support the 'other agency' for an extended period.

Ivan was allowed to focus on his vacation while our surveillance activity ran 24-hours a day. He and his mother made several calls to non-official friends in the San Francisco area, all of whom were associated and acquainted with Ivan's parents; and both he and his mother were allowed to visit Yuri and the Ulanova family on two occasions. He received one call from an acquaintance, Mr. Leonid Shevchenko, of the Russian Trade Mission in Washington. Ivan was friendly, talked of his mother's friends, and casually informed Shevchenko that he would be returning to Washington on schedule.

"They're checking up on me," he thought. We thought so too.

Ivan was 100 percent cooperative, even to the extent of wearing a miniature transmitter whenever he visited friends or was not within eyesight. Ivan was escorted to the safe site every two or three days regularly as directed, where he was briefed on the progress of his relocation. During his entire stay in San Francisco, US counter-surveillance teams did not detect any hostile surveillance.

Near the end of the two week period, Gaylord informed Ivan that the majority of his personal belongings had been removed from his furnished apartment where his rent was paid through the end of his lease - for 6 months. He would not see those personal items for approximately nine months, as they would be transferred, stored, repacked and reshipped under various ownership documentation several times.

Following the two-week vacation in San Francisco, Ivan ceased contact with all his previous friends in the San Francisco area. It was 100 percent likely Ivan's acquaintances would eventually be contacted by the Russians regarding Ivan's disappearance. With absolutely no contact from Ivan, there was less possibility of Ivan ever being located.

His mother would be briefed to the extent required.

Gaylord was designated Ivan's Case Officer for the debriefing which began in San Francisco.

Within 72 hours following his expected return to Washington, the Russian embassy filed an enquiry with the State Department regarding Ivan's possible disappearance. Two days later, the same type enquiry was filed for his 'missing' mother. The Department waited three days to respond to each enquiry and then responded negatively, with no information available. With assistance from US officials, the Russian Embassy began their own investigation, and learned Ivan had turned in his rental car on schedule, and had scheduled a taxi pickup the next day to take himself and his mother to the airport. The next day, a couple believed to be Ivan Romanyev and his mother were picked up by Yellow Cab from the Mark Hopkins and taken to San Francisco International where they were dropped off at the Northwest Airlines Departure gate. The taxi driver was contacted and confirmed the photograph shown appeared to be that of Ivan and his mother.

On board, the First-Class purser recalled an individual resembling

Ivan from the photograph shown; and stated that he was traveling with an older, non-descript woman believed to be his mother. Records showed they arrived in Washington, and picked up their luggage. Russian embassy staff members had waited for the arrival of four more flights, and neither Ivan nor his mother was seen. The Russian Embassy will continue their efforts in the Washington DC area.

Ivan's apartment was sealed by the Russian Embassy. Their investigation showed that to the best of their knowledge, no-one had entered the apartment, and Ivan's belongings remained in place. Apparently they were totally unaware of the earlier visit by USI. The apartment remained unoccupied and was not leased for the next two years.

Sometime during the month of August 1976, Ivan's father's cremated remains, along with his few memorable collections, musical instruments and items of personal value were surreptitiously taken from the Russian Embassy office; the theft was reported to the city police, but no specific information of the action, to include date or time of the theft could be determined. It was believed that an unidentified member of the janitorial staff had somehow managed to move the items past the security cameras in a trash cart - undetected. Also reported missing were his Father's medals.

A few days later, the Russian Embassy filed another complaint with the state department, adding a few more missing items to their list of those taken from their offices.

In October, Ivan's books and other personal items from his office showed up in a Post Office box of the Chicago FBI. Fearing an attempt by the Russians to locate a defector, the FBI contacted the "other agency" through secure communications, and by describing the items they were able to ascertain the identity of the rightful owner. The Bureau also learned that one of the "other agency's" sources had removed items from the Russian offices. The TV camera in Ivan's office had somehow been deactivated during the theft, and there was no photo-record of the incident. Following a complete 'sweep' of the items, the FBI was eventually allowed to courier a special package indirectly to their SF office using a circuitous route. The package was retrieved by agents from the "other agency".

When the items were returned to Ivan, he commented only "my family is now complete."

Debriefings of Ivan occurred at various secret, unspecified locations, and covered a period of 5 months. Ivan was able to provide extensive information regarding his and other Russian Agent handler's activities, and included:

1. The identity of operatives and their cover names, along with the identity of many recruited agents and sources at various locations throughout the world.

2. Requirements and tasking aimed at US and other free world targets. Most of the information provided by Ivan pertained to those activities specifically aimed at the disposition and plans of US military forces, their methods of operation and the technological expertise of their operatives.

3. Information on the training and testing of KGB operatives in the US and KGB facilities identification.

4. Russian knowledge of US MO, personnel, locations.

5. Ivan was able to provide lists of wanted Russian defectors and their suspected locations.

Ivan constantly displayed concern as to what could happen to his own sources, specifically DG, and at one point during his debriefings stated "I have more concern for DG Miles, more respect for his opinion and feelings than I do for that of my own countrymen. Will he ever know what happened to me?"

The canned response to Ivan was: "DG will be treated and handled in accordance with US regulations regarding espionage."

During the entire six-month transition period, time was taken to provide both Ivan and his mother with backstopped identification, and following his final debriefing, they were taken to their new home at a location in Midwestern United States. Surveillance and surveillance detection methods were employed throughout their transition and moves, and for 90 days thereafter. As a matter of routine, Ivan is periodically contacted by the US Marshals Service to insure his safety.

On the six month anniversary of the initial call from Gaylord, I began studying Japanese language at the Presidio of Monterey, California. Among my classmates was my old pal Frank, who had just returned from Bangkok.

Neither Ivan nor his mother have any desire or intention of returning to Russia.

Nine months into his entry into the witness protection program, Ivan and his mother's household goods were delivered to their new home in the Midwest, where he was employed at a major network station as a foreign correspondent and consultant. He travels to Europe and Asia frequently, and reports regularly. In addition to his salary, Ivan is paid a $60,000 per year stipend for his continued cooperation.

Beard and longer, gray, curly hair, together with a minimum amount of surgery has transformed Ivan into a pure, blue-blooded American.

In case you were wondering:

In 1979, Ivan married a local Schoolteacher, and immediately transformed her into a wife and mother. Their two children eventually attended colleges at US institutions located at opposite ends of the US map, and have since embarked on careers of their own.

With no knowledge of his KGB background, it is merely coincidental that the interests of both his children are in foreign affairs and international journalism. As part of their programs of study, both children studied the Russian Language. Of course, there may have been some influence in their choice of language.

Over the years, Ivan has contributed to numerous historical documentary and "opinion" manuscripts regarding the Soviet Intelligence apparatus, their espionage activities targeted at US and other personalities and activities in the west. Information from his various writings on espionage, sabotage and subversion activities during the cold war have been incorporated into the curriculum of the various intelligence and security training facilities of the US Government.

Throughout debriefing efforts of the late 1970's, he provided the identification of operatives and exposed operations in the Eastern bloc, resulting in the identification and termination of numerous espionage endeavors. Since the mid 1980's, Ivan's knowledge began to wane and the US President issued directives changing intelligence collection focus away from the Russians. The value of Ivan's knowledge of Russian KGB operations targeted against the West had begun to erode.

Following the establishment of the Commonwealth of Independent States however, Ivan was energized into writing a series of opinion articles on KGB activities of the CIS, and of evaluating the collection potential of the current Russian regime.

In 2004, Ivan purchased a small vacation condo near Tampa, where he spends his winter months. His plans include full retirement at that location on an unspecified date.

As a member and performer with the local Jazz Musician's Club in his new hometown, he attends weekly meetings and occasionally performs with one of the local night club groups.

His fresh start with new friends, a new family and environment, have provided Ivan with a renewed sense of life. These days, his memories allow him to reminisce of his childhood, to recall his dreams and daydreams of years gone by. His old friends and acquaintances have taken on the air of another life, another time and another place – in an all too different world.

Although he expresses no regrets, Ivan will sometimes experience mild pangs of guilt for having made these life-altering decisions. His feelings are normal, after all – he is human.

"If only they knew," He has said to himself of his friends, in an effort to rationalize the sacrifices of turning far away from his fatherland. *"Would they not have made the same decisions?"* The answer, of course is "Yes."

Each and every aspect of his life is now fulfilled.

In early morning hours, on any given winter day, Ivan may drive South from Tampa on route 41, through Gibsonton, Apollo Beach, and Ruskin, in the direction of Bradenton. There, he occasionally walks the beach with his wife, his ageing mother, and his other best friend, a Golden retriever named "Alex", who relentlessly chases tennis balls.

END

CREDITS AND ACKNOWLEDGEMENTS:

I truly believe in the philosophy of Chinese Author SUN TZU, and endeavor to apply that philosophy to my own writings.

Chinese Author Sun Tzu was born in the year 544 BCE (traditional), depending on your source of information, and died at age 52. During his lifetime, Sun Tzu served as a military commander and authored numerous books on military strategy – the most legendary being *The Art of War*, wherein he constantly expresses the basic philosophy "Know your Enemy".

In the conduct of war, whether it be cold war or actual warfare, knowing your enemy is a basic and mandatory law. He who does not apply that uncontaminated philosophy is bound to suffer the consequences.

The following are attributed to Sun Tzu:

1. All warfare is based on deception. There is no place where espionage is not used. Offer your bait to the enemy to lure him.

2. Appraise war in terms of the fundamental factors. The first of these factors is moral influence.

3. Nothing is more difficult than the art of maneuvering for advantageous positions.

4. Keep your friends close, and your enemies closer.

5. Be extremely subtle, even to the point of formlessness. Be extremely mysterious, even to the point of soundlessness. Thereby you can be the director of the opponent's fate.

6. Military operations involve deception. Even though you are competent, appear to be incompetent. Though effective, appear to be ineffective.

7. Victorious warriors win first and then go to war, while defeated warriors go to war first and then seek to win.

FALLING OFF THE FACE
OF THE EARTH

1. POLITICAL ASYLUM

Definition: The protection, by a sovereign state, of a person who is or will be persecuted in his own country for his political opinions or activity

Asylum in the United States is described as:

The United States honors the right of asylum of individuals as specified by international and federal law. A specified number of legally defined refugees, who either apply for refugee status overseas, as well as those those applying for asylum after arriving in the U.S., are admitted annually. Application however does not gaurantee automatic acceptance into any program.

As noted, more refugees have found homes in the U.S. than any other nation and more than two million refugees have arrived in the U.S. since 1980. During much of the 1990s, the United States accepted over 100,000 refugees per year, though this figure has recently decreased to around 50,000 per year in the first decade of the 21st century, due to greater security concerns. Still, of the top ten countries accepting resettled refugees in 2006, the United States accepted more than twice as many as the next nine countries combined. As for asylum seekers, the latest statistics show that 86,400 persons sought sanctuary in the United States in 2001.

2. THE WITNESS PROTECTION PROGRAM.

In the United States, the Witness Protection Program, also known as the Witness Security Program, or WitSec, was officially established under Title V of the Organized Crime Control Act of 1970, which in turn sets out the manner in which the United States Attorney General may provide for the relocation and protection of witnesses or sourcees of the federal or state government in an official proceeding concerning organized crime, espionage, or other serious crimes against the government. See 18 U.S.C.A 3521 et. seq.

Under the provisions of this program, the Federal Government has also granted individual states the ability to provide similar services, and frequently coordinates with state authorities in the selection of a final location. The WITSEC program was initiated in the late 1960s by Gerald Shur when he was in the Organized Crime and Racketeering Section of the United States Department of Justice. Most sources are protected by the United States Marshals Service, while protection of incarcerated witnesses is the duty of the Federal Bureau of Prisons.

The Witness Protection Program was designed to create total anonymity for certain subjects and sources and help them blend into a new life, in a location where they most likely will not be recognized. The U S is now more than 300 million, and within the continental US there are thousands of cities in which to hide protected witness. Following the acceptance of a witness into the program, the Marshals Service is tasked with creating a new identity and finding a new city for the witness, his family and any endangered associates. This requires the coordination of multiple government agencies, good timing and total secrecy.

The United States Attorney General makes the final determination as to who qualifies for protection. The subject receives pre-admittance briefings by Federal Agents or US Marshals Service personnel and once he agrees in writing to enter the program, he and his family are removed from their current location and taken to a temporary, secure holding area where they will undergo indoctrination and complete physical examinations. If they are able, they will also be subjected to a battery of mild psychological interviews. Follow-on counseling and advice by cleared psychologists, psychiatrists or social workers will be arranged if a need has been substantiated

Then sources and their family are relocated to an interim and more secure location selected by the Marshals Service - usually a in a different state. Here, sources and their families typically receive their new identities, with authentic documentation such as Social Security cards and driver's licenses. Adequate housing, medical care, job training and follow-on employment opportunities are also provided. As far as choosing a new name, criminal witnesses can have their pick. However, they are advised to keep their current initials or same first name. Name changes are routinely accomplished by the court system, but the records are sealed.

As for defectors or political transplants, they will enter the program under completely new identities, bearing little or no resemblance to their previous profiles. Their identities and backgrounds are furnished by the respective federal agency handling the case. Backstopping of their backgrounds may be essential to their personal security.

Entering the Witness Security Program is not like winning the lottery. There is no forgiveness of loans or other obligations. In most cases, before entering the program, sources must first pay any existing debts and satisfy any outstanding criminal or civil obligations. They also must provide appropriate child custody documents proving that involved children are actually theirs. Sources are not to travel back to their hometowns, fatherlands, or contact unprotected family members, friends or former associates. In order to do everything possible to preclude the possibility that the witness could be followed, the witness is made to adhere to an extremely convoluted and indirect transportation path, before finally reaching the distant location where they will live under new identities. Often, the transit involves a long chain of seemingly random air flights, with times and locations which are intended to prevent potential third-party surveillance or detection by hostile persons or entities. These convoluted movement patterns may include changes of direction and use of a large number of support personnel, to limit the possibility of surveillance or being traced. On rare occasions, sources may be required to use interim identification during portions of the final move.

Since their past transgressions are not completely ignored, in the case of <u>criminal</u> wittnesses, the US Marshals Service is obligated to notify local law enforcement in the new community of the presence of the witness and of his background. The Marshals Service may also mandate random drug or alcohol testing and set other conditions to ensure the success of the program.

Defectors and persons who have successfully saught political asylum, are not treated as criminals, and their backgrounds remain confidential. They are coached into a new background which is backstopped in accordance with their respective names. In return, the Marshals Service will:

Obtain at least one reasonable job opportunity for the witness and eligible members of the family.

Provide assistance in finding appropriate housing and arranging for financing if needed.

Depending on the source's financial situation, the US government may provide subsistence payments on average of $60,000 per year to defray expenses related to the move. The source's previously accumulated debts are generally paid by the US Government during the transition.

For criminals, 24-hour protection is provided by the US Marshals while they are in a high-threat mode, during pre-trial proceedings, court appearances, and while they are preparing statements to be released in conjunction with their agreements with the appropriate federal agencies. Marshals will provide protection during the transport of these subjects to their new location, and during their processing time.

Defectors/Political Asylum subjects are provided 24-hour security surveillance by the agency handling their respective cases, and this protection may continue indefinitely into the future, depending on their individual status.

Since 9-11, Witness security is open to more than just sources testifying against Mafia members. In recent years, federal agencies such as the Department of Homeland Security, CIA, FBI and certain military agencies, have stepped up their efforts to locate sources who will testify against terrorist organizations and foreign intelligence activities that are directed against the United States. This has increased the complexity of hiding sources, as many of those who can testify against a specific foreign entity likely reside within US borders. Foreign-born sources require additional documents from the Immigration and Customs Enforcement division of the Department of Homeland Security.

Sources who are illegal aliens cannot be relocated until the immigration requirements are satisfied and the necessary documents are provided to the OEO or Marshals Service. Additionally, everyone involved in managing the program must adjust to cultural and language differences. Appropriately, education is provided.

Since the beginning of the program, more than 7,000 sources and over 9,000 family members have been inserted into the program. They have been protected, relocated and provided with new identities.

The United States Marshals Service, a division of the US Department of Justice, provides for the security, health and safety of government sources and their immediate family members whose lives are in danger.

Portions of this explanation have been edited for obvious security classification reasons.

Att: Wikipedia and AP

- -

GLOSSARY

A.

AFRTS – Armed Forces Radio and Television Service

A.C.E – Aggressive Counter-espionage

B.

Backstopping – methods used to make a cover story appear authentic. (also applies to political asylum/witness protection participants.)

Bio-data – personal/biographical information

Benjo – Japanese – for bathroom or toilet.

Black – term used for 'covert' and sometimes for 'clandestine'.

Brevity code – term used for an open method of encoding a secret message. i.e. "The date is <u>March 21</u>." could mean "Our meeting will take place in room <u>321</u>" at a prearranged location.

Ban Me Thuot (Coffee) – From Ban-me-thuot Viet Nam – personally, author believes it to be one of the world's tastiest, and unique, full-bodied coffees.

C.

C.O.L.E. – Coverage of Local Establishments.

(Pronounced Chao Phraya), also called 'Menam'. It is the principal river of Thailand, flowing into the Gulf of Siam. Many attractions of Thailand bear the name.

Charolais – a large light-colored breed of beef – named after the region of origin in France.

CIOP – an operational proposal

CIOC – an operational concept

Commit – surveillance term, meaning take control, to move or conduct surveillance (in a specific direction).

CYA – Cover Your A _ _ .

D.

Dangle – term used for a person who is introduced (dangled) in front of the opposition in order to attract their interest.

Dien Bien Phu - (Battle) French/Indochina Battle – 1954

D.A.S.R. – Army special roster – removes designated personnel from normal personnel channels, and handles all matters in a secure manner.

Dead drop – concealed location for depositing materials surreptitiously, for sending or receiving to/from an agent.

E.

'Eyes only' term for distribution of documents, marked 'eyes only' indicates distribution beyond listed addresses is not authorized.

F.

Flash items – a term used for items carried which can reinforce the individual's cover. i.e. an International Driver's License in cover name; cover business cards, etc.

FTX – Field training exercise.

H.

Hooch – GI slang for barracks, room, personal space, etc.

Hoogen – Japanese – a dialect.

HUMINT – Human Intelligence.

Hibachi – Japanese for an open cooking/heating stove.

Headliner – main attraction.

I.

ICP – Initial Contact Point (for personal meetings).

J.

Jyou-yang, jyou-yang – Chinese polite term meaning "I'm flattered to meet you."

J.W. BOP - Johnny Walker Black On the Pebbles (Crushed Ice) – author-coined.

K.

Keyed/Keying – turning the key to activate the STU in secure mode.

Klicks – slang for kilometers.

Kinpatsu – Japanese word for 'Goldilocks'.

Klong – Thai for 'canal'

L.

L.N. – local national

Legal Traveler – someone who travels legally between countries (such as a businessman) to conduct legitimate business.

M.

MAC – Military Assistance Command

Miso – A tasty, salty soy paste used for flavoring (Japanese).

M. I. – Military Intelligence

M.O.S. – Military Occupation Specialty – A numerical code for a military job position.

Motor Stables – beloved military detail – maintenance of assigned vehicles.

MO – (Lat) Modus Operandi / Method(s) of Operation

Murphy's Law – a guarantee that if something can go wrong, it will.

N.

NOFORN – a caveat placed on classified information, meaning 'NO FOREIGN DISSEMINATION'

Nakunarimashita – Japanese for 'passed on'.

O.

O.F.C.O. – Offensive Counterintelligence Operations – See ACE.

O.I. – Operational Interest.

OPCON – Operational Control

OPSEC – Operational Security.

OWVL – One way voice link – term for a sound/voice link, encrypted and transmitted to a single user – one time only, and for one-way communication only. (Abbr. descr.)

One-way pass. Secretly passing material in one direction.

P.

PNG – (lat) Persona-non-grata. A person who is not welcome. A foreign diplomat who is no longer acceptable to the government of the country to which he is assigned.

Pirated – unauthorized, non-patented copy. Illegally copied.

Plausible Denial – An alibi or other means by which someone could deny involvement in illegal activity.

P.O.V. – Privately owned vehicle.

Phong Co-van – Advisor's Office

Phung-huang – The Phoenix Program – originated in November 1966, when MACV-J2 and the VM National Police formed CT-4. Phoenix program mission was to identify and neutralize the Viet Cong Infrastructure (VCI) in Military Region IV (basically the province of Gia-Dinh, Saigon and Cho-lon Metro areas). The program was incorporated by Prime Minister Tran Van Khiem on Dec 20, 1967. (Ironically, the Phoenix is a mythical animal which appears during times of peace and prosperity.)

Positive Intelligence – as opposed to counter-intelligence.

Pu-ying – Thai language for 'girlfriend'.

Passage material – fabricated, edited or fragmentary material cleared for passing to the opposition as an attractive piece.

Q. 'Quakers' – Author-coined nickname for members of "The Other Agency".

R.

Rolling pickup – surveillance term. To pick up a passenger while the vehicle is rolling.

Rabbit – slang. For someone who acts as a moving target for surveillance training.

Runner – nickname for a company delivery boy. A "gopher".

RFI – Request for Information

S.

S.A.E.D.A. – program for detecting subversion attempts.

Sakana – Japanese for 'fish'.

S. D. – Surveillance Detection

S.L.D.R. – a Lead Development Record (Report)

SOS – a favorite GI mess hall breakfast "Shit on a shingle" (Chipped beef and gravy)

S.T.U. – a Secure Telephone Unit.

Soiree – French – party or get-together.

Samlar – Thai for three wheeled 'Taxi'; also 'tuc-tuc'.

'Sanitized' – term used for information which has been edited of classified information, rendering it of little value.

Soi – Thai for 'Alley' or 'lane'.

Spotter – term for one who searches (spots/trolls) for potential sources.

Safe house/Safe site – a secure location used in the conduct of espionage. Safe house keeper – one who maintains the site.

SMERSH – Abbrev. The Counter-intelligence School in Moscow.

T.

'The Other Agency' – Author–coined. Author's Pet name for the agency in the field that controls US intelligence operations.

Tradecraft/tradescraft – Special skills of the trade. i.e. authentic-appearing documentation is created by the 'tradecraft' section.

Tech sweep – an inspection designed to detect electronic or other technical surveillance.

Tet – Vietnamese for "New Year".

Tofu – Japanese – for bean curd.

Toyopet – Japanese name for automobiles originally manufactured by Toyota Motors.

Two-fer (tufor) - GI slang "two for the price of one".

Turn-around (operation) – a 'double' operation.

Two-way pass – surreptitiously exchanging items between two parties simultaneously.

U.

USARPAC – US Army, Pacific

USI – US Intelligence

Umbrella Operation – term used when several separate, but related operations fall under the purview of one approved concept.

W.

Walk-in – a source who voluntarily walks into a foreign diplomatic office.

Watakushi-no - (Japanese) = "My" or "Mine"

Wasabi - Green, spicy, horseradish-like Japanese flavoring paste.

Z. Zabuton – Japanese – cushion for sitting on the floor.

NOTES

Notes:

During the Holocaust, concentration camp prisoners received tattoos only at one location, the Auschwitz camp complex, which consisted of Auschwitz I (Main Camp), Auschwitz II (Auschwitz-Birkenau), and Auschwitz III (Monowitz and the sub camps). Incoming prisoners were assigned a camp serial number which was sewn to their prison uniforms. Only those prisoners selected for work were issued serial numbers; those prisoners sent directly to the gas chambers were not registered and received no tattoos.

Initially, the SS authorities marked prisoners who were in the infirmary or who were to be executed with their camp serial number across the chest with indelible ink. As prisoners were executed or died in other ways, their clothing bearing the camp serial number was removed. Given the mortality rate at the camp and practice of removing clothing, there was no way to identify the bodies after the clothing was removed. Hence, the SS authorities introduced the practice of tattooing in order to identify the bodies of registered prisoners who had died.

Originally, a special metal stamp, holding interchangeable numbers made up of needles approximately one centimeter long was used. This allowed the whole serial number to be punched at one blow onto the prisoner's left upper chest. Ink was then rubbed into the bleeding wound.

When the metal stamp method proved impractical, a single-needle device was introduced, and used to pierce the outlines of the serial-number digits onto the skin. The site of the tattoo was changed to the outer side of the left forearm. However, prisoners from several transports in 1943 had their numbers tattooed on their left upper forearms. Tattooing was generally performed during registration when each prisoner was assigned a camp serial number. Since prisoners sent directly to the gas chambers were never issued numbers, they were never tattooed.

Tattooing was introduced at Auschwitz in the autumn of 1941. As thousands of **Soviet prisoners of war** (POWs) arrived at the camp, and thousands rapidly died there, the SS authorities began to tattoo the prisoners for identification purposes. At Auschwitz II (Birkenau), the SS staff introduced the practice of tattooing in March 1942 to keep up with the identification of large numbers of prisoners who arrived, sickened, and died quickly. By this time, the majority of registered prisoners in the Auschwitz complex were Jews.

In the spring of 1943, SS authorities throughout the entire Auschwitz complex adopted the practice of tattooing almost all previously registered and newly arrived prisoners, including female prisoners. Exceptions to this practice were prisoners of German nationality and "reeducation prisoners," who were held in a separate compound. "Reeducation prisoners," or "labor-education prisoners," were non-Jewish persons of virtually all European nationalities (but at Auschwitz primarily Germans, Czechs, Poles, and Soviet civilians) who had run afoul of the harsh labor discipline imposed on civilian laborers in areas under German control.

The first series of prisoner numbers was introduced in May 1940, well before the practice of tattooing began. This first series was given to male prisoners and remained in use until January 1945, ending with the number 202,499. Until mid-May 1944, male Jewish prisoners were given numbers from this series. A new series of registration numbers was introduced in October 1941 and remained in use until 1944. Approximately 12,000 Soviet POWs were given numbers from this series (some of the POWs murdered at Auschwitz were never registered and did not receive numbers). A third series of numbers was introduced in March 1942 with the arrival of the first female prisoners. Approximately 90,000 female prisoners were identified with a series of numbers created for female prisoners in March 1942 until May 1944. Each new series of numbers introduced at Auschwitz began with "1." Some Jewish prisoners (but not all) had a triangle tattooed beneath their serial number.

In order to avoid the assignment of excessively high numbers from the general series to the large number of Hungarian Jews arriving in 1944, the SS authorities introduced new sequences of numbers in mid-May 1944. This series, prefaced by the letter A, began with "1" and ended at "20,000." Once the number 20,000 was reached, a new series beginning with "B" series was introduced. Some 15,000 men received "B" series tattoos. For an unknown reason, the "A" series for women did not stop at 20,000 and continued to 30,000.

A separate series of numbers was introduced in January 1942 for "reeducation" prisoners who had not received numbers from the general series. Numbers from this new series were assigned retroactively to "reeducation" prisoners who had died or been released, while their superseded general-series serial numbers were reassigned to new "general" arrivals. This was the only instance in the history of Auschwitz of numbers being "recycled." Approximately 9,000 prisoners were registered in the "reeducation" series. Beginning in 1943, female "reeducation" prisoners were given serial numbers from their own new series, which also began with "1."

There were approximately 2,000 serial numbers in this series. Beginning in February 1943, SS authorities issue two separate series' of number to Roma (Gypsy) prisoners registered at Auschwitz: one for the men and one for the women. Through August 1944, 10,094 numbers were assigned from the former series and 10,888 from the latter. Gypsy prisoners were given the letter Z ("Zigeuner" is German for Gypsy) in addition to a serial number.

Camp authorities assigned more than 400,000 prisoner serial numbers (not counting another approximately 3,000 numbers given to police Camp authorities interned at Auschwitz due to overcrowding in jails who were not included in the daily count of prisoners).

\- \-

Note: Born in Ho-Pei, China in 1905, PC Lee first learned piano at a Christian church at age 7. He graduated from a Chinese university, with majors in education, and music.

In 1935, he went to the U.S. to further his studies in music at Yale University, graduating with a Doctorate. He was forced to stay in the U.S. because of the civil war in China. In order to promote chorus, Lee often traveled to Taiwan to speak on this subject, and he was once the conductor of the Taipei Philharmonic Chorus.

Dr. Lee authored the music to the Taiwan National Anthem (*San-min Ju-yi*). In addition to his countless efforts in chorus, he also authored and produced many great pieces, such as "We're In Each Other" and "The Bamboo Flute".

Dr. Lee and I corresponded at least annually through Christmas 1975; and in 1979, Dr Lee passed away at the age of 73.

Also noteworthy is that the Chinese Nationalist Anthem can be sung in simultaneous harmony with the American National Anthem.

Note: The Big Red One.

The 1st Infantry Division is an organization of approximately 20,000 soldiers organized to conduct sustained combat operations anywhere in the world. A division contains all of the types of units necessary on the battlefield: infantry, artillery, armor, engineers, aviation, intelligence, logistical and medical support and many others. The 1st Infantry Division was organized as the "First Division" on June 8, 1917, on the docks of Hoboken, NJ, just prior to sailing for France in World War I.

It has been on continuous active duty ever since and has been "first" many times: first overseas and in combat in World Wars I and II; first ashore at Omaha Beach in Normandy, France, in 1944; one of the first two combat divisions deployed to Vietnam in 1965. Called the "Big Red One" for the red numeral 1 that has been its shoulder patch since 1918, today's 1st Infantry Division is headquartered at Fort Riley, KS. Several of its constituent brigades including thousands of soldiers are serving in Iraq and Afghanistan. The important history of the Big Red One is one compelling example of courageous service to country provided by generations of Americans in all units and services.

Note: The Tet Offensive.

Tết is the Vietnamese name for the Lunar New Year.

The Tet Offensive began early on 30 January with greater severity than anyone had expected. When the communists attacked, much of the Viet Nam Air Force was on leave to be with families during the lunar new year. An immediate recall was issued, and within 72 hours, 90 percent of the Viet Nam Air Force was on duty.

Tan Son Nhut Air Base, under the command of Air Force Colonel Farley Peebles, began receiving enemy rounds at approximately 0200 on 30 January. The chapel on the base received one of the early direct hits. By 31 January, millions of Americans were eagerly glued to their television sets, watching as the Viet Nam war entered their living rooms

Had it not been for the quick reactions of the US Air Force (USAF) 377th Security Police Squadron in the early hours of the attack, the entire base would have been in danger of falling. Four USAF Security Policemen and two other Combat Security Police received Silver Star medals for valor when they lost their lives at Bunker 051. The outnumbered Security Police, assisted by US Army Helicopter and ground units, killed nearly 1000 enemy combatants in the first few hours, and the base was secured by American, Army of the Republic of Viet Nam (ARVN) and VNAF forces by 12 Noon on 31 January 1968.

Over the next three weeks, the VNAF flew more than 1,300 strike sorties, bombing and strafing enemy positions throughout South Vietnam. Transport aircraft from Tan Son Nhut's 33rd Wing dropped 15,000 flares in 12 nights, compared with a normal monthly average of 10,000. Observation aircraft also from Tan Son Nhut completed almost 700 reconnaissance sorties, with VNAF pilots flying O-1 Bird Dogs and U-17 Skywagons.

The VNAF effectively contributed to the defense of their nation during the Tet Offensive. Taking the offense, supported by ARVN ground units, they achieved a high level of strike performance. Tan Son Nhut Air Base was the target of major communist attacks during the 1968 Tet Offensive.

Unfortunately, many reports were being ignored, simply be-cause they were so numerous and so conflicting that with-out verification our analysts were not able to determine which reports were accurate. As it turned out, most of reports contained a bulk of unevaluated, unverifiable information and those pertaining to actual troop movements toward and into Saigon could probably have stood a little more analyses. Again, hindsight is 20/20, and varied reports were voluminous.

- -

Political events of Taiwan leading up to my assignment: (ccr: Taiwan Copywriter: THE BROOKINGS INSTITUTION)

In the Cairo Declaration, a communiqué issued jointly by President Roosevelt, Prime Minister Churchill, and President Chiang Kai-shek on December 1, 1943, it declared that the "purpose" of the "three Great Allies" was to affirm that all the territories Japan had stolen from the Chinese, such as Manchuria, Formosa and the Pescadore Islands, shall be returned to the Republic of China." The following

Potsdam Proclamation of July 26, 1945, was signed by the President of the United States and the Prime Minister of the United Kingdom, was concurred to by the President of China and subsequently adhered to by the Soviet Union. It was agreed that the terms of the Cairo Declaration were to be carried out.

The Cairo Declaration was the starting point for planning by the United States Government for the initial postwar treatment of Formosa (Taiwan). A primary question arose in this connection. It was: What would be the legal status of the Island between the time of a formal Japanese surrender and a formalized, Japanese release of Taiwan to China under a treaty of peace? That is, would the island's sovereignty continue to rest in the hands of the Japanese during this period?

Many argued that the Cairo Declaration was neither a formal treaty nor an executive agreement, but merely a "communique."

The United States government officially went on record elaborating on the lack of legal binding power of the Cairo Declaration, thus voiding the basis of both the Chinese Nationalist KMT party's and Beijing's mythical "One China Principle" claims.

Thus, the National Archives and Records Administration had not filed this declaration under treaties since the declaration was a "communique" and it did not have Treaty Status or an Executive Agreement Series number. For over a half century, the Cairo Declaration was used by both the Communist government and the Taiwan Kuomintang (KMT) ruling party as one of the key historic documents to bolster their own "One China" claim. The KMT had cited the Cairo Declaration as legal basis for ROC's claim on Taiwan. Conversely, and Interestingly enough, the PRC government also cited the Cairo Declaration to augment its claim that Taiwan was part of China and this principle became the foundation for the Communist Chinese government's policy on Taiwan for the next 50 years.

Late in 1949, however, the island suddenly acquired world-wide importance and came within the sphere of active interest to the United

States. This all happened after two decades of fighting a bloody civil war. Chinese Communists, led by People's Republic of China (PRC) founder Mao Tse-tung, captured the final pieces of mainland China, and drove Chiang Kai-shek and his Nationalist forces onto Taiwan. This followed the precedent of the defeated Ming dynasty of three centuries earlier. As a result of this and other far-reaching developments in the Far East, the fortunes and the future status of the island became inextricably enmeshed with the problems of the United States in relation to China as a whole, as well as to Korea, to Japan, to the Far East in general, and to global power relationships.

During the late 1940s the US suspended direct, "offensive" military aid to Taiwan while both the U.S. and the United Nations refused to consider diplomatic recognition of the PRC. Then, on June 25th 1950. The Korean War began when Communist forces in North Korea crossed into South Korea.

Two days later, on June 27, U.S. President Harry Truman agreed to protect Taiwan against any possible attack from mainland China and sent the Seventh Fleet to patrol the waters between Taiwan and China.

1951 Economic and military aid from the United States resumed with the establishment of the Military Assistance and Advisory Group in Taiwan. From this time until the mid-1960s the U.S. provided $1.5 billion in aid to the Republic of China (ROC) on Taiwan with the hope of changing the island into an industrialized nation. Taiwan accepted the offer and began a giant land reform project that redistributed the country's farmland and helped turn the economy around.

1954 Sept. 3, Mainland China punctuated its promise to "liberate" Taiwan. The first of several attacks were launched on Quemoy and Matsu, the two largest island groups along the mainland coast held by the ROC. So-called "propaganda rounds" were fired back and forth with Taiwan for the next 15 years. Dec. 2, Sensing the possibility of a conflict in the waters between China and Taiwan, U.S. President Dwight Eisenhower signed a Mutual Defense Treaty with the ROC promising protection from mainland aggression. This treaty would remain in effect even beyond the US recognition of mainland China nearly three decades later.

1960-1968 Taiwan experienced steady economic growth. During the 1960s the economy had an average growth rate of 10%, and dependence on economic and technical aid from the U.S waned. The US continued military aid to TW in accordance with previous treaties designed with the security of Taiwan in mind.

In July 1971,, The U.S. formally announces its "two China" policy, supporting admission of the People's Republic of China into the U.N. while preserving Taiwan's membership in the General Assembly. This highlighted America's inevitable shift towards improved relations with Communist China throughout the 1960's early 1970's.

Sept. 15, U.S. Secretary of State Henry Kissinger secretly visited China. Less than six weeks after the trip, on Oct. 25 Taiwan was "expelled" from the United Nations and the seat was given to the People's Republic of China.

1972. US President Richard Nixon made an historic visit to China and issued the Shanghai Communiqué as an official statement further severing United State's diplomatic ties with Taiwan (ROC).

The actions of the US and the UN caused a domino effect around the world with several major countries switching their diplomatic recognition from Taiwan's capital city, Taipei, to Beijing during the 1970s.

From the time of my assignment, and over the next two administrations, both US Presidents Ford and Carter continued their military support of Taiwan as a 'show of force and support' to help prevent any attempts by mainland China to take over Taiwan.

Also noteworthy: Later, *during the Reagan Administration, US military support to TW was limited to the sales of a few obsolete*

F-type fighter planes, and obsolete weapons technology – strangely, at the same period, Reagan deleted most of the COCOM restrictions thus allowing the sale of more advanced weaponry and technology to our new friends, the Russians.

Note: Secretary Laird's tenure had seen the establishment of the Defense Investigative Service, the Defense Mapping Agency, the Office of Net Assessment, and the Defense Security Assistance Agency (established with the sole purpose of administering all DoD military assistance (MAG) programs). Later, in 1972 Congress passed legislation creating a second deputy secretary of defense position, a proposal Laird strongly supported (even though he never filled the position).

Laird had paid special attention to two important interdepartmental bodies: the Washington Special Action Group (WSAG), composed of senior Defense, State, and CIA officials, which gathered information necessary for presidential decisions on the crisis use and deployment of U.S. military forces; and the Defense Program Review Committee (DPRC), which brought together representatives from many agencies, including the Defense Department, the State Department, the Council of Economic Advisers, and the Office of Management and Budget, to analyze defense budget issues as a basis for advising the president, placing, as Laird commented, "national security needs in proper relationship to non-defense requirements.")

Note: Dick Cheney's political career had begun a year earlier in 1969 when as an intern for Congressman William Steiger during the Nixon Administration, he joined the staff of Donald Rumsfeld, who was then Director of the Office of Economic Opportunity from (1969–70). Cheney held the position as: White House Staff Assistant and as Assistant Director of the Cost of Living.

(It was Cheney who suggested in a memo to Rumsfeld that the White House should use the Justice Department in a variety of legally questionable ways to exact retribution for an article published by The New York Times investigative reporter Seymour Hersh).

Of course, the other dignitary considered influential to the subject was **Donald Rumsfeld** himself. (Rumsfeld had resigned from Congress in 1969 - his fourth term - to serve the Nixon administration as Director of the United States Office of Economic Opportunity, Director of the Economic Stabilization Program, Counselor to the President, and as a member of the President's Cabinet (1969–1972);

Note: The Phoenix Program, initially intended to identify and neutralize Hanoi's Fifth Column (Those political and administrative entities through which the Vietcong tried to control the South Vietnamese) within South Vietnam. Phoenix was basically designed to reach out to the enemy, determine his intentions and influence his conduct. Instead, it became a controversial paramilitary campaign of arrest, interrogation and torture that the 'other agency' had helped run. Interrogation Centers were organized under the Phoenix Program in 1967, and it was estimated that between 1968 and 1971, Phoenix had killed more than twenty thousand Vietcong suspects.

Note: The Chokchai Steakhouse Restaurant, founded in 1971, was located on the top floor of the Chokchai building on Sukhumvit road (then the tallest building in Bangkok). It was renowned for delicious beef steak and an excellent 360 degree view of Bangkok. The Chokchai menu also bragged of its succulent pork chops, chicken and varied fish steak filets; not to mention its unforgettable sweet cream for those who prefer rich, rich desserts, and for its milk ice cream, for those of us who prefer the low-cal versions.

Best Selling Steak: The Chokchai Steak House served 3 grades of beef steak. 1) The Chokchai Premium (Charolais) Steak is from a cow that is never more than three years old. Preparation includes a 30 day dry-aging process, giving it a special quality equal to any Steak served anywhere in the world – to include the famous Kobe steak from Japan; 2) The Chokchai Dry Aged (American Brahma) Steak, that goes through the dry aging process for 15 days; and 3) The Regular Beef Steak

Note: Wat Arun. .

Perhaps a better known symbol of Bangkok than the Grand Palace, the most recognized photo on many a "visit Thailand" poster is Wat Arun, "the Temple of the Dawn." Unfortunately, being a cover model has its drawbacks, and the temple is probably a little too popular for its own good; but still, such an outstanding monument is well worth a visit. Construction of the towering prang with its four smaller siblings (photo on the left) was started by Ramah II in the early part of the 19th century, and completed by his successor Ramah III. The temple in which the prang sits is actually much older dating from the Ayuthaya period. During King Taksin's reign, just before the founding of Bangkok (then Khrongthip), it served as part of his palace

Note: The Thai media. Noteworthy, Thailand has a well-developed media sector, especially by Southeast Asian standards. Compared to other countries in the region, the Thai media is considered relatively free, although the government has historically exercised considerable control over all broadcast media.

It should also be noted that iTV Thailand was operated by Shin Corp, under license from the Prime Minister's Office. (In 2007, it became the TITV under the Department of Public Relations, and in 2008 the Thai Public Broadcasting Service absorbed the rights, but it still retains the title of TITV.)

Note: The Battle of Dien Bien Phu.

Dien Bien Phu - the battle that changed Vietnam's history

Opinion: Many believe the Battle of Dien Bien Phu to be one of the greatest battles of the 20th century as well as a defining moment in the history of Southeast Asia. Try if you will, though, and you'll probably still not find reference to that battle in most history texts. I personally think that the world is remiss for such an omission. I feel that the importance of Dien Bien Phu could be comparable to that of Pearl Harbor

After World War II, France reestablished its government in Indochina, and by 1946, communist leader Ho Chi Minh, heading a Vietnamese independence movement, was fighting French troops for control of northern Vietnam. The 'Viet Minh', insurgents used guerrilla tactics that the French found difficult to repel.

By the end of 1953 as both sides were preparing for peace talks in the Indochinese War, the French military commanders picked Dien Bien Phu, a village in northwestern Vietnam near the Laotian and Chinese borders, as the place to pick a fight with the Viet Minh.

"It was an attempt to interdict the enemy's rear area, to stop the flow of supplies and reinforcements, to establish a redoubt (a stronghold) in the enemy's rear and disrupt his lines," said Douglas Johnson, research professor at the U.S. Army War College's Strategic Studies Institute. "The enemy could then be lured into a killing ground. There was definitely some of that (type) thinking involved."

Hoping to draw Ho Chi Minh's guerrillas into a classic battle, the French began to build up their garrison at Dien Bien Phu. The stronghold was located at the bottom of a bowl-shaped river valley, about 10 miles long. Most French troops and supplies entered Dien Bien Phu from the air -- either landing at the fort's airstrip or dropping in via parachute.

Dien Bien Phu's main garrison was also to be supported by a series of firebases -- strong points on nearby hills that could bring down fire on an attacker. (Rumor has it that the strong points were given women's names, supposedly after the mistresses of the French commander, Gen. Christian de Castries). The French assumed any assaults on their heavily fortified positions would fail or be broken up by their artillery.

The size of the French garrison at Dien Bien Phu swelled to somewhere between 13,000 and 16,000 troops by March 1954. About 70 percent of that force was made up of members of the French

Foreign Legion, soldiers from French colonies in North Africa, and loyal Vietnamese.

Viet Minh guerrillas and troops from the People's Army of Vietnam surrounded Dien Bien Phu during the buildup within the French garrison. Their assault on March 13 proved almost immediately how vulnerable and flawed the French defenses and assumptions were.

Dien Bien Phu's outlying firebases were overrun within days of the initial assault. And the main part of the garrison was amazed to find itself coming under heavy, withering artillery fire from the surrounding hills. In a major logistical feat, the Viet Minh had dragged scores of artillery pieces up steeply forested hillsides that the French had written off as impassable.

The French artillery commander, distraught at his inability to return fire on the well-defended and well-camouflaged Viet Minh batteries, went into his dugout and committed suicide.

The heavy Viet Minh bombardment also closed Dien Bien Phu's airstrip. French attempts to resupply and reinforce the garrison by parachute were frustratingly unsuccessful - as pilots attempting to fly over the region found themselves facing a barrage from anti-aircraft artillery. It was during the resupply effort that two civilian pilots, James McGovern and Wallace Buford, became the first Americans killed in Vietnam combat.

The supply planes were forced to fly higher, and their parachute drops became less accurate. Much of what was intended for the French forces -- including food, ammunition and in one case, essential intelligence information landed instead in Viet Minh territory. Meanwhile, the Viet Minh steadily reduced the French-held area -- using what their commander, Gen. VO Nguyen Giap, called "a tactic of combined nibbling and full-scale attack."

Closed off from the outside world, under constant fire, and flooded by monsoon rains, conditions inside Dien Bien Phu became inhuman, as casualties piled up inside the garrison's hospital.

Dien Bien Phu fell to the Viet Minh on May 7. At least 2,200 members of the French forces died during the siege -- with thousands more taken prisoner. Of the 50,000 or so Vietnamese who besieged the garrison, there were about 23,000 casualties (including an estimated 8,000 killed).

The fall of Dien Bien Phu shocked France, brought an end to French Indochina, and convincingly changed history.

Following the French withdrawal, Vietnam was officially divided into a communist North and non-communist South -- setting the stage for U.S. involvement.

In 1963, as Washington was deepening its commitment in Vietnam, Soviet Premier Nikita Khrushchev made a telling remark to a U.S. official. "If you want to, go ahead and fight in the jungles of Viet Nam. The French fought there for seven years and stil had to quit in the end. Perhaps the Americans wll be able to stick it out for a little longer, but eventually they will have to quit too."

*Note: Credit: **Man With the Golden Gun**, Roger Moore's second outing as James Bond whisks our hero off to Hong Kong, Macau, Thailand, and then the South China Sea in search of a solar energy weapon. His opponent is Scaramanga (Christopher Lee), who rules the roost on a well-fortified island. Scaramanga's aide-de-camp is Nick Nack, played by future Fantasy Island co-star Herve Villechaize. Britt Ekland plays the bikinied Mary Goodnight, whose clumsy efforts to help Bond thwart Scaramanga are almost as destructive as the elusive solar device. The Man With the Golden Gun was adapted by Richard Maibaum and Tom Mankiewicz from Ian Fleming's last James Bond novel, published posthumously in "rough draft".*

(If you watch the video today, try using slow motion as Roger Moore enters the Chokchai building and cautiously, yet hurriedly moves

*into the showroom. He casually takes a seat in the sports car –
then without warning starts the car, accelerates and crashes out
onto the street. The camera will pass my agent's signal point on the
glass window overlooking the showroom – yup. There it is: a dark,
horizontal crayon mark, approximately 6 – 8 inches long. Go ahead
– take a look. It's there.)*

\- -

Note: Commonwealth of Independent States, (CIS), governmental
organization founded on December 8, 1991, composed of former
Soviet republics as a partial successor to the Union of Soviet Socialist
Republics (USSR). The commonwealth originally consisted of
three members—Belarus, Ukraine, and Russia. Two weeks after
establishment of the commonwealth, eight other former Soviet
republics - Armenia, Azerbaijan, Kazakhstan, Kyrgyzstan, Moldova,
Tajikistan, Turkmenistan, and Uzbekistan—were also admitted
as founding members, subject to the approval of their respective
parliaments. Although Azerbaijan initially failed to ratify the
founding documents, the country formally became a member when
the documents were ratified by its legislature in 1993. Estonia, Latvia,
and Lithuania had become independent republics earlier in 1991 and
declined to join the commonwealth. Georgia joined in 1993.

Att. Columbia Univ Library

**Note: Chiang Kai Shek. *(OP) The Columbia Encyclopedia, Sixth
Edition – Chiang Kai-shek.***

Chiang Kai-shek, 1887-1975, Chinese Nationalist leader. He was also
called Chiang Chung-cheng. After completing military training with
the Japanese Army, he returned to China in 1911 and took part in
the revolution against the Manchus. Chiang was active (1913-16) in
attempts to overthrow the government of Yüan Shih-kai . When Sun
Yat-sen established the Guangzhou government (1917), Chiang served
as his military aide. In 1923 he was sent by Sun to the USSR to study
military organization and to seek aid for the Guangzhou regime. On

his return he was appointed commandant of the newly established (1924) Whampoa Military Academy; he grew more prominent in the Kuomintang (KMT) after the death (1925) of Sun Yat-sen.

In 1926 Chiang launched the Northern Expedition , leading the victorious Nationalist army into Hankou, Shanghai, and Nanjing. Chiang followed Sun Yat-sen's policy of cooperation with the Chinese Communists and acceptance of Russian aid until 1927, when he dramatically reversed himself and initiated the long civil war between the Kuomintang and the Communists. By the end of 1927, Chiang controlled the Kuomintang, and in 1928 he became head of the Nationalist government at Nanjing and generalissimo of all Chinese Nationalist forces. Thereafter, under various titles and offices, he exercised virtually uninterrupted power as leader of the Nationalist government. In 1936 Gen. Chang Hsüeh-liang seized him at Xi'an, to force him to terminate the civil war against the Communists in order to establish a united front against the encroaching Japanese. Despite the resultant truce, Chiang's release, and the 1937 outbreak of the Second Sino-Japanese War, the agreement between Nationalists and Communists soon broke down. By 1940 Chiang's best troops were being used against the Communists in the northwest. After the Japanese took Nanjing and Hankou, Chiang moved his capital to Chongqing.

As the Sino-Japanese War merged with World War II, Chiang's international prestige increased. He attended the Cairo Conference (1943) with Franklin Delano Roosevelt and Winston Churchill. He and his third wife, Soong Mei-ling, were the international symbols of China at war, but Chiang was bitterly criticized by Allied officers, notably Joseph W. Stilwell, and argument raged over his internal policies and his conduct of the war.

After the war ended Chiang failed to achieve a settlement with the Communists, and civil war continued. In 1948 Chiang became the first president elected under a new, liberalized constitution. He soon resigned, however, and his moderate vice president, Gen. Li Tsung-jên , attempted to negotiate a truce with the Communists. The talks failed, and in 1949 Chiang resumed leadership of the Kuomintang to oppose the Communists, who were sweeping into Southern China in strong military force and reducing the territories held by the Nationalists.

By 1950 Chiang and the Nationalist government had been driven from the mainland to the island of Taiwan (Formosa) and U.S. aid had been cut off. On Taiwan, Chiang took firm command and established a virtual dictatorship. He reorganized his military forces (U.S. aid resumed with the start of the Korean war) and then instituted limited democratic political reforms. Chiang continued to promise conquest of the Chinese mainland and at times landed Nationalist guerrillas on the China coast, often to the embarrassment of the United States. His international position was weakened considerably in 1971 when the United Nations expelled his regime and accepted the Communists as the sole legitimate government of China. He remained president until his death in 1975.

Bibliography: Chiang Kai-shek's writings have appeared in English as China's Destiny (1947) and Soviet Russia in China (1957). See also P. P. Y. Loh, The Early Chiang Kai-Shek (1971); and biographies by W. Morwood (1980) and S. Dolan (1988**). Ccr: The Columbia Encyclopedia, Sixth Edition. Copyright 2008 Columbia University Press.**

Note: Samlar. Thai language word for three-wheeled taxi, a scooter-motorized, three-wheeled taxi. Now referred to as 'Tuc-tuc', taken from Hindi, they remain popular modes of hired transportation in India and throughout Southeast Asia as well

Note: The Royal Bangkok Sports Club was charted and established by Siam King Chulalongkorn on 6 September 1901. Horse racing began at the Club in January 1903, and over the years until 1910 when King Chulalongkorn died, the club expanded. Drainage of the rice paddy grounds instigated the preparation for expansion, and the introduction of other sports to include Cricket, Golf, Tennis, Rugby, Squash and Polo began

A riding club was set up and the Swimming pools were added to the facilities, and the club gained international recognition before WWII. But the club was occupied by Japanese forces in 1941, and the revenue-producing horse races were suspended. The Thai government retained chairmanship of the club through 1946, and the end of the war provided for international charter. In 1947, horse racing was resumed. The Ladies Golf subcommittee was formed and RBSC applied for a government loan. In 1948 reconstruction and restoration of the facilities began.

Difference between Double Agent and Dual Agent.

a. The most common double agent is created when an Agent from one side is identified and recruited by the opposition. He is then targeted at his original base, with the opposition fully in control – hopefully.

b. A Dual agent is when two friendly countries, both of whom have access to the same agent, have recruited that agent to conduct espionage against their mutual target. Generally, only one side is fully witting of his dual role, and maintains priority control of his espionage activities - hopefully.

A defector's odds of successful political asylum. It is said that only one percent of defectors are successful. Most foreign persons seeking political asylum are of no value to the US Government, and only one in ten are even given consideration. Of ten of those, three will be interviewed, and of the three, only one is generally selected.

More from Sun Tzu: (From other than 'The Art of War'):

War is based on deception.

To fight and conquer in all your battles is not supreme excellence; supreme excellence consists in breaking the enemy's resistance without fighting.

If you are near the enemy, make him believe you are far from him. If you are far from the enemy, make him believe you are near.

If you know the enemy and know yourself, you need not fear the result of a hundred battles. If you know yourself but not the enemy, for every victory gained you will also suffer a defeat. If you know neither the enemy nor yourself, you will succumb in every battle.

Supreme excellence consists in breaking the enemy's resistance without fighting.

1372538R00313

Printed in Germany
by Amazon Distribution
GmbH, Leipzig